THE ⎵ ⏝
BEATRICE ALRIGHT

BROOKE HARRIS

Storm
PUBLISHING

This is a work of fiction. Names, characters, businesses, places, events and incidents are either the products of the author's imagination or used in a fictitious manner. Any resemblance to actual persons, living or dead, or actual events is purely coincidental.

Copyright © Brooke Harris, 2025

The moral right of the author has been asserted.

All rights reserved. No part of this book may be reproduced or used in any manner without the prior written permission of the copyright owner. This prohibition includes, but is not limited to, any reproduction or use for the purpose of training artificial intelligence technologies or systems.

To request permissions, contact the publisher at rights@stormpublishing.co

Ebook ISBN: 978-1-80508-747-2
Paperback ISBN: 978-1-80508-748-9

Cover design: Rose Cooper
Cover images: Shutterstock

Published by Storm Publishing.
For further information, visit:
www.stormpublishing.co

ALSO BY BROOKE HARRIS

Memories of You
The Promise of Forever
When You're Gone
The Forever Gift

To Aisling, for talking about my books even more than me x

ONE

I pause outside the main hospital entrance. Icy wind claws at my cheeks and I cup my hands, bring them to my mouth and blow hard. Eccles Street is beautifully still, as if the usual hustle of Dublin city is on mute. Moonlight shines through a blanket of cloud, casting shadows at my feet. Inside my head is blissfully silent too. And I know to enjoy it. The sweet spot of calm when one day winds to an end before another begins never lasts long.

An approaching siren slices through the air in the distance. I glance overhead as clouds part. The sun will be up soon. I take a deep breath and step forward. The huge, glass automatic doors part and a grey-haired man in chequered pyjamas shuffles out. He slips a cigarette between his lips and bobs his head up and down as he asks, 'Do you have a lighter, love?'

'I don't smoke, sorry,' I say. 'But I think they sell matches in the tuck shop. It's open after nine.' I glance at my watch and realise that's more than an hour away. 'Or they might be able to help at the nurses' station.'

Without a word, he turns and shuffles back inside, struggling to keep his slippers on.

A lady in a black bomber jacket and with car keys in her hand races towards me from the car park.

'Are you a nurse?' she asks, breathless. 'Where should I go?'

I cup my ear to hear her better as the siren grows louder.

'It's my grandfather. He had a fall. They asked me to hurry. Room 114, they said. Or 124. I can't remember.'

'Mr Cullen,' I say, thinking of the jolly ninety-six-year-old who loves to dance, even an IV line and oxygen tank not slowing him down. My heart pinches, knowing that, if someone called his granddaughter at this hour, his time is limited.

She nods and her keys rattle in her shaking hand. 'Yes. Yes. Tom Cullen. Do you know where he is?'

I smile, happy to help at a time I can only imagine must be so difficult for her. 'Room 124. Reception is just through here, on the right.' I point over my shoulder at the glass door behind us. 'You have to check in there first.' I look at her teary eyes and shaking hands, and realise she's not taking in a word I'm saying. 'I can show you, if it helps.'

She nods and we jump aside together as the ambulance comes skidding into the bay. Blue scrubs and white coats hurry out of the doors to meet the paramedics and the patient and I know the chaos of another day at St Helen's Hospital has begun.

Inside, I leave Mr Cullen's granddaughter in the capable hands of Órlaith at reception. Grab a coffee from the vending machine in the hall and glance at my watch. If I pick my feet up, I won't be late. I hurry inside, taking large strides; my mind is already on the ward and the day ahead when I feel someone grab my arm. A young woman, I guess about my age, in her late twenties or early thirties. She lets go as suddenly as she clutched on and apologises as she wipes her hands against her jeans.

She looks my uniform up and down – a navy, knee-length skirt and matching short-sleeve top, that I layer over a once-white, but edging towards cream, long-sleeve. 'How bad is it in here?'

The chunky bangles around her wrist chime as she continues to rub her palms against her thighs until they must burn.

'How bad is what?'

My mouth gapes, and I don't mean to stare but she's a dead ringer for Ginger Spice back in the day. Her head-to-toe light-blue denim and dyed, pomegranate-red hair is ultra-cool.

'The germs.' She whispers as if the word itself is dirty.

Her eyes are locked on mine and her back is poker straight as she keeps one foot jutted forward, as if she's ready to make a run for it at any moment.

'Just be honest,' she begs. 'Is this place crawling?'

'I hope not. I'm the one who cleans it.' I smile, proudly.

She visibly deflates. 'You're not staff?'

'I am. Just not medical.'

'Sorry. I'm sorry. It's just... your uniform.' She points.

I scrunch my nose. 'Confuses a lot of people, don't worry.' I tilt my head towards a nearby automatic hand sanitiser and she races towards it like a greyhound desperate for water. I'm about to take my coffee upstairs and clock in when she bursts into tears and tells me she wants to visit her boyfriend but she had such bad OCD she can't bring herself to take another step.

'I'm not family, so they won't tell me anything over the phone,' she says, sobbing, and I try to pass her a tissue but she shakes her head. I shove the tissue back into my pocket and guide her towards a waiting area, taking care not to touch her. She doesn't take a seat. But she does give me her mobile number and her boyfriend's name.

I promise to investigate and message her later with news. I skid onto the ward fifteen minutes late and of course bump into Elaine as I round the corner.

'You're late,' she says, in the *I'm-the-ward-manager-and-your-boss* tone that she rarely uses.

I open my mouth to explain but before I have a chance she says, 'Oh, Bea. C'mon. Third time this week.'

'I know. I know, but—'

She cuts me off. 'Look, someone's been sick on ward seven. Bile. It's making the other patients feel unwell. So, unless you want a chain effect...'

'Okay,' I say, turning towards the storage closet, and I know now is not the best time to mention that we're running low on antibacterial floor wash.

'And for God's sake wash your hands.' Elaine points at the name and number scribbled across the back of my hand in blue pen before she turns, taking the clipboard from under her arm that I hadn't noticed before to start writing as she walks away.

By the end of the day, my feet burn. I haven't sat once. Not even on my break. I ate a banana and a packet of Tayto in the closet while I quickly counted supplies and filled out the order sheet. I spent the rest of the hour searching for OCD girl's boyfriend. I felt awful when I had to message her that I couldn't find him. She messaged me back to say she had the wrong hospital and she was making her way to St Mary's instead. The only other message on my phone is from my boyfriend, Declan.

> Hey. Caught in work. Overnighter. Sorry. Can't pick Ellie up from crèche.

I curse Declan under my breath. He hasn't picked our four-year-old daughter up from crèche in weeks. And his excuses are endless. *Layover in Boston/New York/wherever. Bad weather can't fly. Birds on runway.*

I can't actually complain. Declan was a pilot when we met. Truth be told, if it wasn't for bad weather and flight delays, he never would have noticed me, panicking over lost luggage in JFK Airport. I was a skittish student, abroad alone for the first time. He was a handsome stranger in uniform, coming off duty. We hit it off straight away. I spent my summer working as a waitress in Al's Diner in Brooklyn and my evenings in Declan's arms. I can say without hesitation that I had the time of my life. Three months later, my student visa was up and it was time to go home. Part of me worried that would be the end of things for me and Declan. But two days before I moved back to Dublin, I discovered I was pregnant. And the rest is history. I moved into Declan's flat in Blackrock as Ellie grew in my belly. College went out the window. Declan's work kept him away a lot and I couldn't juggle lectures and a newborn. I can't lie, it was hard and lonely at first. But soon, Ellie and I found our feet. Together. I got a job in St Helen's Hospital as a cleaner. It just about covers the cost of Ellie in crèche. But, with Declan taking care of the rent and the rest of the bills, it works. Although, my best friend, Cora, never has a good word to say about Declan.

'He's so old, it's kinda gross,' she complains about our twenty-one-year age gap.

I was twenty-five when Declan and I met, and he was forty-six. I'm almost thirty now, and Cora still won't let it go.

'I just think he takes advantage of you, that's all. You had to make all the sacrifices. You had to drop out of college. You had to move into his flat. You have Ellie all the time, while he's off seeing the world.'

'It's hardly like he's on holiday,' I reminded her, always. 'And besides, he takes care of us. If anything, I'm lucky.'

'Yeah, well, I still think you should have stayed living with me. And I still think you should go back to college. They're crying out for doctors and you were so good at it.'

I know Cora means well, but going backwards is not for me. I am happy. So happy, I'm almost certain Declan is going to pop the question soon. He's been acting nervous or awkward lately, and I saw a jewellery website left open on his laptop a few weeks ago. I don't tell Cora though. She and her boyfriend, Finton, have been together forever, but I have a feeling marriage is nowhere on his radar yet. With engagement rings on my brain, I message Declan back.

> No worries. I'll collect Ellie. Hope you take off soon 😊 I love you xx

Declan doesn't reply, but he thumbs-up my message, and I hope that means they're about to take off. Maybe he'll be home tonight after all.

TWO

When my shift finally ends there's a blister forming on my heel, and the distinctive smell of vomit and bleach sticks to my hair. I wait until I'm outside to slip off the offending shoe and give my foot a moment to breathe. There's a hole in my tights and the chipped crimson nail polish on my big toe pokes out at me. *Great!* Sighing, I twist my foot at my ankle to draw an invisible circle in the air. My bone cracks and it's both satisfactory and disturbing. I toss my black leather work shoe into my bag and swap it for the comfy runner that I pull out.

'Whoah!' I say, bending wobblily to pop my runner on the ground so I can wriggle into it without having to undo or retie the slack laces. The laces used to be white, but now they're a creamy-yellowish-beige and I can't remember the last time I actually tied or untied them. They're certainly a well-loved runner, and most likely a million seasons out of fashion, if they were ever in. They are also the only pair of shoes, aside from my work shoes, that I own.

I press a hand against the wall to steady myself as I switch my foot in the air to slide the other shoe off. As I slip this runner on and straighten up too enthusiastically, I feel my nail snag the back of my tights. I wince, knowingly. When I gain my balance, I roll onto my tiptoe and twist my head over my shoulder to check the damage.

'Oh no. No. No,' I say, aloud but not talking to anyone except myself.

There's an unmissable ladder running from my heel all the way up to the back of my knee. I'll have to stop off in Tesco on the way home. I'm so tired I could sleep standing up, but I'll need another pair of tights before my shift tomorrow. I bought the cheapest ones I could find last week. *Barely There Black*, it said on the box. They weren't kidding. Although, in the interest of honest advertising, the box should have said, *Barely There Dark Grey Things That Are So Flimsy You'll Never Get Away Without Shaving Your Legs Underneath*. Thankfully the hospital wards are roasting, even in mid-December, and I don't need anything heavier. Or more expensive. I've got thirty-two euro to last me and Ellie until payday at the end of the week.

I make my way carefully down the concrete steps outside the main doors of St Helen's. Someone has had the good sense to scatter salt all around, and the large grains crunch under my feet as they offer me grip. It's not long after five p.m. and it's already dark. Although today was the type of day where it never really seemed to get bright. Thick clouds hung overhead all day and teased the idea of rain but never followed through and there's a breeze now that Mrs Morgan on St Paul's ward told me earlier is a Nasty East Wind that could slice you in two. Mrs Brennan argued that it is in fact the North Wind with its blade-like abilities. She then asked Mrs Morgan what she knew about the weather anyway with her nose stuck in a book instead of frittering away the afternoon flicking through the news channels the way she did. Bickering escalated pretty quickly from there and I intervened with cookies and hot chocolate. Thankfully, by the time I was leaving my favourite patients had settled their argument and were enjoying a game of chess in the day room. I've no doubt I'll hear a long story in the morning about who won, who cheated, and how they're never playing with each other ever again. Until the next day, of course.

'Wherever the wind *is* from it's bloody cold,' I say, again aloud but still not talking to anyone in particular.

A pair of doctors walk past me. A man and a woman. They're not much older than me, I think. Mid-thirties, maybe. And I wonder if they're a couple. Maybe they met at work. Or even earlier, in college, I muse. Their voices are loud and bulky as they chat about Christmas shopping and picking up a turkey and I decide that *Yes!* they are most definitely together. In the five years Declan and I have been a couple, we've never spent Christmas together. He's always in the air on the day.

'The money for flying on the twenty-fifth is too good to turn down,' he tells me every year.

I don't mind. Christmas was never my cup of tea. I bounced around from foster home to foster home as a kid and I always felt like an outsider at strangers' tables no matter how hard they tried to make me feel welcome. But this year is Ellie's first Christmas truly understanding the magic of Santa and I decide that she, Declan and I really need to spend the day together and start making some family memories. We need to be the happy people at the dinner table with colourful paper hats on our heads and bellies stuffed to the brim with turkey and ham. I make a mental note to talk to Declan about it when he gets home.

The couple smile at me and say something about the weather before getting into a large, expensive jeep. A sudden wave of jealousy washes over me and it's even colder and nastier than the East, or North, or wherever-the-feck-it's-from wind and I hate myself for it. It was my choice to have Ellie. And my choice to drop out of medical school. My choice to move in with Declan and shape a family. And it was the best decision I ever made. Ellie is the best part of my life. And, besides, I still get to work in a hospital, meeting lovely patients every day. It may not be how I planned things, but I wouldn't change it for the world. The couple's car purrs to life and I pull my coat a little tighter around me as they drive by. I tug the strap of my bag that insists on falling down my arm back onto my shoulder, lower my head so my face isn't into the wind and walk.

If I hurry I'll catch the five-thirty bus, otherwise I'll be waiting until six and traffic will be horrendous heading out of town by then. Today is 8 December. Also known as Annual Stay The Hell Out Of Town Day because every man, women and child of the country has descended on Grafton Street to officially mark the start of Christmas shopping. Or something like that. It's the same every year. They come to shop, mingle and of course take in the sights Dublin has to offer in the festive season. The city really is very beautiful in the festive period, if you have the time to enjoy it. Huge, fluffy green garlands stretch from one side of the streets to the other, lit up and sparkling after dark. And there's a humongous, real tree, decorated from top to bottom, right outside the gates of St Stephen's Green Park. Órlaith, the receptionist in work, said it's a giving tree. You can take a card from one of the branches and inside is the name of a boy or a girl and their age. Then you buy an appropriate gift for a child in need, and lots of local businesses are drop-off points. It's a lovely idea but I wish Órlaith never told me about it. Every time I walk by and I can't afford to take a card, my heart hurts.

Unfortunately, Christmas spirit seems to be passing me by. It has been for a few years, but I try not to dwell on that now. Every family has their share of troubles and I'm no special case. Most days I can remember that just fine, but at Christmas time I have to try harder.

I shove the sleeve of my coat up my arm just enough to glance at my watch. I've ten minutes to catch the bus, but the footpath is frosty. The further away from the hospital doors I walk, the more slippery the path becomes. There's no salt scattered down here.

Nonetheless I hurry. I'm feeling the pressure of making it across town in awful traffic to pick my daughter up from crèche on time. I've already been late twice this week as I raced against a sea of enthusiastic carol singers. Alannah, the crèche manager, didn't hesitate to inform me that Ellie cried her eyes out both times at 'being the last child standing'.

Alannah is a terrible liar. Ellie almost never cries. Not even when she falls, or argues with her friends, or when I get unreasonably cross because I'm tired, or stressed out, or when Declan wants the noise in the apartment kept down but Ellie wants to sing the newest song she's learned in crèche. On the rare occasion tears actually fall, her porcelain skin goes all red and splodgy for ages afterwards. Cora gave me some fancy vitamins for her and said she might be a little low in iron. Ellie is always clear-skinned and smiling when I pick her up from crèche, no matter what time.

I pull my coat tighter around me and hurry more, determined not to be late today.

'I'm coming, Ellie.'

My legs fly into the air so suddenly that I don't have time to screech before the thump of my back hitting the ground forces a huge puff of air out of me. I stare, wide-eyed, at the cloud of my own warm breath that hovers above my face.

'Mind, it's slippery,' a husky voice says.

Sprawled on the icy footpath in the shape of a corkscrew, arms above my head either side and legs twisted around each other, I begin to laugh. It's an embarrassed giggle, really, as the ice finds its way through my coat and my uniform to nibble at my back and I realise how ridiculous I must look. And how lucky I am that I'm not actually hurt. Well, except for my pride.

'I've noticed,' I say, sitting up and glancing around to find the owner of the pearls of wisdom.

I spot a man sitting on a nearby bench. He's alone and somewhat melancholy looking. I didn't notice him before as I tried to rush by.

'Are you all right? Nothing hurt?' he asks.

'Yes. Fine, thank you.' I blush as I drag myself to my feet and dust myself off.

'Good. That's good,' he says.

I take in the sight of the concerned man speaking to me. A nearby streetlamp bathes him in hues of orange, highlighting the lines and folds that time has gradually etched into his face. His wrinkled brow and hunched shoulders match his husky voice and I realise he's quite elderly. He's decidedly dapper in a tweed trench coat in striking grey, black and red checks. A scarf hides the collar of his coat. It's large and colourful. The type that someone has lovingly hand-knitted – his wife perhaps, I think. He's not wearing a hat. He's so well wrapped up for the elements, much better than me, that his bare head comes as a surprise. He's mostly bald, but strands of silver sit above his ears and I imagine run around the back. A bunch of supermarket flowers is resting across his knees. They're a jumble of colours and shapes and the Tesco sticker is big and bold on the front of the cellophane wrapper. But the most striking thing about the man, who watches me with equal curiosity, is his bright blue eyes hiding a spark of laughter that I suspect he's too gentlemanly to let out.

'It's okay,' I say. 'You can laugh if you want to. I mean, I'm already mortified, you might as well go for it.'

'I wasn't going to laugh,' he says, his brows arched. 'Although now that I know you're not hurt I am going to tell you that was as funny as hell. Probably the funniest thing I've seen all day, and I saw Mr Simmons in room 84B piss his pants this morning at breakfast.'

'You're a patient,' I say, suddenly very concerned that he shouldn't be out here and especially not alone.

The man begins to laugh, at last. 'No, sorry. That was mean. I'm only joking. I don't know a Mr Simmons. I was just trying to make you feel a little better.'

'Oh,' I say, still not sure if he's a patient or not, and I wonder if I should call someone.

'You're a nurse?' the man says. 'Or, doctor?'

'Eh. Neither,' I say, rubbing my shoulder, which is sorer than I first realised.

'But your uniform.' He points.

'Cleaner. I mop up vomit. Wipe bottoms. That sort of thing.'

'Ah, so you're the poor sod who'd have the pleasure of changing Mr Simmons' pissy pants?'

I laugh. 'Yes. If Mr Simmons, his pee or his pants were real. Then yes. I'd change them.'

'Bet you're glad I made him up then, eh?'

I smile.

'Are you going to sit down?' the man asks, shuffling from the middle to the end of the bench.

I glance at my watch and sigh. I've only minutes left to catch the bus, and my shoulder is really starting to ache.

'You should. You look awful.'

His honesty surprises me.

'Sit,' he says again, rather sternly.

'Okay,' I say, walking carefully to the bench, overly aware that I could slip again at any second.

'There you are,' the man says, as I fill the space beside him. 'I bet that's much better. Was a nasty fall, that.'

I nod, wishing he would stop talking about it. 'So, you're really not a patient...'

'Just visiting.'

'Visiting Mr Simmons?' I wink.

He laughs. I like his laugh. It's a croaky chuckle that sounds like rice rattling in a tin can and I can't help but laugh along with him.

'I'm Malcolm, by the way,' he says, extending his hand.

I shake it, and wince as my shoulder twinges. 'Bea.'

'Bea.' He pursues his lips, disapprovingly. 'Short for something, or did your parents simply choose to name you after a winged insect?'

'Beatrice.' I giggle, unoffended. 'But I'm just Bea.'

'Okay, well, I'm not Mal. I'm Malcolm.'

'It was very nice to meet you, Mal-Colm,' I say, as I stand up.

'You're not leaving, are you?'

I glance at my watch. Five fifteen. I shrug. ''Fraid so. I've a bus to catch.'

Malcolm looks me up and down and nods.

'Goodbye,' I say, treading carefully as I walk away with the icy wind viciously nipping at the tip of my nose. I've barely taken a couple of steps when I glance over my shoulder and ask, 'Are you getting the bus? Maybe we can walk together.'

'I know what you're trying to do,' Malcolm says. 'But I don't need help. Beside, I'm not as clumsy as you. I've decent shoes on. See.' He points towards the chunky boots on his feet that look sturdy enough to scale Everest. 'Good night, Bea. And by the way, I quite like bees. Without them, humans would cease to exist in a matter of months.'

I know. I read something on Wikipedia about bees preventing famine of something like that.

I smile. 'Good night, Malcolm.'

It takes longer than usual to reach the bus stop. I'm cautious about ending upon my back again. There are three of us waiting. A guy without gloves, sporadically blowing into his hands and rubbing them together. And a woman shifting from one foot to the other to stop her toes from cramping, while announcing every couple of minutes, 'Christ, it's cold.'

The bus arrives shortly with windows so fogged up they almost look frosted. I let the guy and the woman on first. It's packed and they go straight upstairs. The doors close behind me and the bus begins to move, tossing me forward, and I shuffle along the aisle until I spy a seat down the back next to a woman with a duffle coat and a barrage of Penneys shopping bags.

'Mind if I sit here?' I ask, pointing to her bags taking up the seat beside her.

She groans, rolls her eyes and gathers her bags onto her lap.

'Thank you,' I say, as the moving bus shoves me into the seat.

She doesn't reply as she uses the sleeve of her coat to wipe a circle in the condensation so she can stare out the window. My fingers tremble as they adjust from the cold outside to the heat of the bus. I almost drop my phone taking it out of my bag to call the crèche.

'Hello, Little Apples, Alannah speaking.'

'Alannah. It's Bea, I'm so sorry but—'

'Take your time. Ellie is finishing a painting,' Alannah says in that clipped tone that I know means, 'Have fifteen quid ready when you get here, *you're late.*'

I hang up and am about to slide my phone into my pocket when instead I pause and call reception at the hospital.

'Hello, St Helen's. '

'Hi, Órlaith.'

'Oh, Bea. Hi,' my favourite receptionist says. 'Everything okay? Didn't I see you leave?'

'Yeah. I'm on the bus now. Listen, Órlaith,' I say, shuffling closer to the edge of the seat as bags challenge me for space. 'There's an elderly man sitting on a bench not far from the main doors. I don't think he's a patient but it's so cold and icy. I fell already.'

'Oh, you didn't. You're not hurt, are you?'

'No. No. I'm fine. But the path isn't salted down there and, well...'

'Oh, Bea, what are we going to do with you? You really are a worrier, aren't you?'

'He says he's fine. But if he fell, he could be there for a while and no one would even know.'

'Okay. Okay,' Órlaith says, and I can tell she's smiling. 'I'll have one of the porters walk down, have a little look around, make sure everything is okay.'

'Thanks.'

'Now, go home and run yourself a warm bath. Sounds like you need it.'

I close my eyes. The wet patch on my coat and uniform nips at my back and I fantasise about a hot bubble bath. 'Good night, Órlaith,' I say.

'Na'night, love.'

THREE

I slide through the doors of the crèche at one minute to six. The relief that I made it is so great, I can hardly feel that my heel is completely skinned and has started to bleed.

'Evening,' I say, wanting to bend in the middle to catch my breath.

Alannah looks up from behind the reception desk, which is painted in rainbow colours that are chipped on one side, and checks her watch.

Smiling, she says, 'Hi, Bea. How was your day?'

'Oh... you... know,' I puff out, tilting to the right slightly as I yield to a stitch. 'Same old, same old.'

'I'll fetch Ellie for you now. Have a seat.'

I sit down in the waiting area next to a water cooler that is always empty and make small talk with the handful of other parents waiting too. A dapper father in a suit arrives at two minutes past six. He pushes his long, warm coat off his hip to fetch his wallet.

'Sorry about this,' he says, pulling his card out. The other woman on reception, whose name I can never remember, tilts the card machine towards him and he taps his card casually.

'Hammered in work,' he goes on, shaking his head. 'I'll probably be late all week, I hope that's okay.'

'It's no problem,' she says, smiling brightly as she twirls a strand of bleached-blond hair around her finger. 'It's what we're here for.'

'Mammy,' Ellie squeals, running towards me.

I stand up and lift my little girl into my arms.

'What's this?' I tuck her golden curls behind her ear to reveal a graze and bump above her left eyebrow.

'Josh hurted me,' Ellie says, scrunching her face disapprovingly.

'Well, that's not quite true, is it?' Alannah is quick to cut in.

'Oh.'

'You know kids, Ellie and Josh had a little disagreement over some building block.'

'Josh taked the lellow one,' Ellie explains, her chest heaving now as she refuses to give in to tears. 'But lellow is my favourite.'

'But we must share,' Alannah says. 'I don't know how many times I've told her this, Bea. She really needs to learn to share.'

I kiss the bump on Ellie's head and place her down. I take her hand in mine as I look at Alannah. 'Did Ellie have the yellow block first?'

'Technically, yes.'

'Technically.' My eyes widen.

'Ellie takes the yellow blocks all the time. The other children are left with blue or green or red.'

'Right,' I say, not quite able to believe how serious Alannah is about building blocks. 'And are the yellow blocks particularly special? I mean, is there something wrong with the red ones, for example?'

Alannah inhales sharply. 'No. Of course not. But Ellie must learn to share. It's okay that she likes yellow, but so do other children. You are going to have to talk to her, Bea. This cannot go on.'

Ellie tugs my hand. 'Can we go now, Mammy?'

'I'll talk to her,' I say, desperate to put an end to this ridiculous conversation.

'That's all I ask,' Alannah says, with a patronising smile. 'That's all I ask.'

Outside, I hear the father in a suit tell his little boy that, 'You cannot hit other children, Josh. I don't care what colour blocks they have.'

I sigh, hoping the children and, most importantly, Alannah, will have forgotten all about building blocks by tomorrow.

Ellie and I get the bus to the flat. The bump above her eye is going down, although I suspect it will leave a nasty bruise, and she sings the same line of a Taylor Swift song over and over with the same adorably mispronounced lyrics.

'Shh, chickpea,' I tell her when her voice becomes too screechy for the shared space of a busy bus and even the guy talking loudly into his mobile phone starts to glare. My mind is on the bottle of wine in the fridge that one of the patients gave Elaine. She passed it on to me because she doesn't drink white.

'It's snowing,' Ellie announces excitedly as the bus skids slightly at our stop and we hop off.

'It's snowing. It's snowing.' She throws her arms in the air and tries to catch the measly few flakes attempting to fall but melting before they hit the ground.

'Be careful,' I warn her, remembering my fall earlier. Ellie ignores me, too excited by falling sleet that makes Christmas suddenly feel imminent instead of almost two weeks away. I grip her hand tightly and she skips alongside me as we navigate the slippery footpath towards our apartment block. My breath catches when, from the roadside, I notice the light in the kitchen is on. I never leave lights on. The snow begins to fall more heavily and I pick up the pace.

Ellie is a chatterbox in the lift, and down the corridor, and I think my head might explode by the time I open our apartment door. Inside, Ellie kicks off her shoes and runs straight for the couch, hoping to catch the bedtime story on CBeebies. I hear the telly come to life. And then I hear Declan. His voice is carrying from our bedroom and I can tell he's on the phone.

'I'm doing it tonight. I know, I know, I should have done it ages ago.'

My heart races and I really, really wish I didn't have a hole in my tights the night Declan chooses to propose. I need a shower to wash the smell of Mrs Quinn in room 108's vomit from my hair and I still need to have a conversation with Ellie about sharing, but bubbles of excitement are fizzing inside me.

I take off my shoes, leave them beside Ellie's and go to kiss her on the head.

'I'm going to change my clothes,' I tell her. 'You stay watching your show, okay?'

'Okay, Mammy.'

I tiptoe to our bedroom and slowly open the door.

'You're home,' I say when I find Declan sitting on the edge of our bed. He's not in his uniform, as he usually is when he returns from a flight. Instead, he's barefoot in jeans and a navy knitted jumper that brings out the bright blue in his beautiful eyes.

'I am.'

'That was a quick flight,' I tease playfully, glancing at my watch. 'New York to Dublin in two hours.'

I'm giggling, knowing he was most definitely not in New York today. I assume he used a delay as a decoy to keep me out of the apartment while he got ready.

'Long day?' he asks.

I flop onto the bed beside him and rest my head on his shoulder. He feels tense and a little nervous.

'The longest.'

'Are you tired?'

'Nope,' I lie.

'Good. Good.' There's a wobble in his voice, and I want to reach out and tell him not to be nervous, but I have a feeling he has this rehearsed, and I don't want to mess it up, so I sit quietly and smile.

There is a long silence, and oddly it feels awkward as my stomach begins to somersault. I think I might be nervous too, despite knowing my answer will be a huge resounding YES!

'Bea.'

He's so serious. I'm slightly dizzy with excitement and I wish I'd remembered to eat before I left work. I wonder if he has a meal prepared. Or a takeaway. There's always food in the movies, and champagne. I just know Declan will outdo any movie I've ever seen.

There's another awkward pause and I listen for Ellie in the sitting room. CBeebies is blaring and I know we have time. The bedtime story won't come on for another fifteen minutes. *In fifteen minutes, I will be an engaged woman.*

'Bea,' he repeats, taking my hand. 'We have to talk.'

My pulse is racing, and I swear my heart feels like a little bird with fluttering wings that might fly out of my chest with anticipation.

'We do?'

His brows pinch. 'Yes. We do.'

'I'm ready when you are.'

'Ooookay.' Declan draws in a huge breath that seems to fill his chest until it seems as if it might burst. 'Bea. I'm married.'

'Yes!' I throw my arms in the air and lean in to kiss him, but instantly pull back.

'What?' he says, pulling back too.

'What?' I echo, wondering what the hell I just heard him say.

'Bea, I'm married.'

And there it is. Repeated, I hear it clearly. Declan didn't say, 'Bea, will you marry me?' He said, 'Bea, I already am.'

I've never fainted in my life, but for a brief moment I think I might.

'WHAT?' My arms are down and I'm on my feet. 'Did you just say *you're married*?'

Declan isn't looking at me any more. His eyes are on my feet. Where my toe pokes out through my tights.

'Did you?' I snap. 'Did you seriously just say you are already married?'

'Bea, calm down. Please? Ellie will hear you.'

'Did you?' I stomp my toe-poking foot. 'Did you say it, Declan?'

He gets to his feet and places his hands on my shoulders. I shrug him off as his touch burns me.

'It's complicated.'

My eyes sting and I bend in the middle as if I've been gut-punched. It hurts as if I have been.

'This can't be happening,' I gasp. 'This can't actually be happening. When? How long? Have you always been married? Jesus, Declan. What the hell. Who the hell are you? Actually don't answer that. I don't even want to know. Married. My God, married.'

My thoughts are spilling past my lips before they have time to fully take shape in my head.

'We have an understanding. My wife and I,' he says calmly, as if he hasn't just turned my whole world upside down.

'Oh. Oh. An understanding. Well, that's all right then.' My words are clipped and reflect the anger that swells inside me like tiny bombs exploding.

'What I mean is, she understands how lonely travelling so much can be.'

'So, she knows about me?'

He winces and steps closer to me. I step back.

'She knows I don't do well alone.'

'So, there are others?' I ask, a little sick trying to squirm up the back of my throat.

We repeat the process of him stepping forward and me stepping back. We're standing in the middle of our bedroom now. It's not a particularly large room, but all the furniture feels unusually far away. As if I'm stranded on an island, and I can see familiar landmarks but they are too far to swim to.

'Are there others?' I repeat, eyeing up the door as if it's one of those landmarks that feels almost impossible to reach.

'There were. Before.'

I tap my chest with my fingertip. 'Before me.'

'Before Ellie.'

A noise comes out of me, something guttural and full of hurt, as I hear our beautiful daughter's name pass his lips. Our precious little girl, who is sitting on the sofa watching her favourite show. I thought I would tuck her into bed tonight engaged to her father, and we would be one big, happy family. I dreamed of it.

'What are you saying, Declan?'

Declan takes a deep breath and this time, when he moves forward, I don't step back. I look him in the eye and wait for an answer I'm afraid might ruin my life.

'I'm saying she found out about Ellie.'

My mouth rounds into the shape of an 'oh' but no sound comes out.

'She can handle the affairs, but a child is different,' he says, as if somehow his wife is being difficult.

'Ellie is four,' I tell him, as if he doesn't know our daughter's age. 'You hid your daughter's existence for four years. Who the hell does that?'

'Listen, baby.' He places his hands on me and I don't budge. I can't muster the strength to move. Not even to shake him off. 'None of this is your fault. Or Ellie's.'

My eyes widen until they burn, and from nowhere a bolt of

energy rushes through me and I push him away. He stumbles, and falls onto the bed. He looks up at me, open-mouthed as if he's hurt. I want to scream. I almost do, but I remember my little girl in the next room just in time. I can't scare her.

And so, I keep my voice low when I ask, 'Why are you telling me this? Why now?'

'Elsa is devastated,' he says, getting to his feet again.

'Elsa!' I repeat his wife's name. 'Your wife seriously has the same name as Ellie's favourite Disney character. I can't believe this. I actually can't. How many times have you watched that damn movie? And all the time you must have been thinking about *her*. This is too much. My God, it's too much.'

Declan presses his fingers between his eyes the way he always does when he feels a headache coming on.

'She always wanted a daughter,' he says. 'But we have three boys.'

'You have other kids?!' I throw my arms in the air as if I am a wounded solider surrendering. 'Of course you do. Oh, this just gets better and better.'

I can't breathe. For a moment it is as if his words have wrapped round my neck like a noose and they are choking me. It's a while before I draw in air again and realise that he's staring at me, pitifully. As if he's expecting me to ask something about them. How old they are, perhaps. Do they look like him? Or, worse still, do they look like Ellie? The sudden discovery that my daughter has three brothers is monumental and I can't function. I need to sit. I need to feel his arms around me. Holding me, hugging me, comforting me. I ache to feel his lips on mine as he whispers that everything will be all right. I need him to love me, the way just moments ago I believed he did. I need him to rewind the past ten minutes and take it all back. I need the life we were supposed to have. But instead, I cannot bear the sight of him.

'Are you leaving her?' I ask, my voice cracking like radio static.

He doesn't reply.

'Is she leaving you?'

He shakes his head.

Finally, the realisation of what's really happening slices through me like a sharp blade. 'You're leaving me. Us.'

'They're my family,' he says, softly. 'Elsa and the boys. They're everything, Bea.'

Tears spill down my cheeks, but I'm not crying. I'm too broken to cry. 'And what about us? What are we? Ellie is your daughter.'

'It was a mistake.'

I clutch my chest, wounded deeper than ever.

'She is not a mistake,' I hiss. 'She is the best of us.'

He's still shaking his head and it turns my stomach. 'It was just supposed to be a little fun. You were so young and beautiful. And, like I said, Elsa was okay with me having a little fun while I was away from home. But then you got pregnant. And, well, to be quite honest, Bea, I didn't sign up for that.'

'And you think I did? I was in college, for God's sake. I gave everything up for you.'

'No,' he says, firmly. 'You gave everything up for Ellie.'

I swallow hard. I can't argue with that.

'You're a great mother, Bea. And if things were different with Elsa and me, we could have a great life. We could, I promise. But I can't leave her. I love her. I love my boys.'

'So, what happens now?' I ask, as tears wet the collar of my uniform. 'Does she want to meet Ellie?'

'No. God no.' He jumps back, clearly horrified by the idea.

I nod. I get it. This must all be as shocking for his wife as it is for me.

'Okay,' I say, trying desperately to gather my thoughts. 'Just the kids, then.'

'What?'

'Ellie and your sons. They need to meet, don't they? They're siblings.'

'Half-siblings,' he snaps, coldly. 'And no. They won't be meeting. The boys don't know about her. They won't ever know about her.'

'I... I...'

'Elsa and I have agreed to put this behind us. For the boys' sake. We have a perfect family. I will not let anything destroy that.'

'You have a perfect lie.'

He shrugs. 'I'm sorry, Bea. It was never meant to get this far. You're a great girl and I didn't mean to mess things up for you.'

'And Ellie – how are you going to explain this to your daughter?'

'I'm not.'

My mouth gapes. 'You're going to keep lying to her too, are you? Well, no.' I stomp my foot and realise my toes have gone numb from the cold. 'Your wife might be happy for you to live this pretend, *perfect* life.' I add air quotes, that instantly annoying him. 'But I'm not. I have to tell Ellie that she has brothers. I want her to meet them. Have a relationship with them. I never had a family. I don't want that for Ellie.'

He's shaking his head again. 'Absolutely not. I told you, the boys can't ever know about this. About any of this. And that includes Ellie. I'm sorry.'

I throw my head back, as if I'm gulping for air. I think I am. 'You're sorry. Well then, if you're sorry that's all fine, isn't it.'

'Bea, please. I get how hard this is. It's hard for me too.'

I force myself to look at him. 'You can't take her family away from her. I won't let you.'

'Can you hear yourself?' He sighs as if he's exhausted by this conversation. "You didn't know they existed until I told you, so don't give me nonsense about family. They're not your family, Bea. They are mine.'

'And they are Ellie's too.'

'No,' he snaps, becoming angry. 'You are Ellie's family.'

'And you,' I snap back

'Just you!' He points an accusatory finger at me. 'It's just you and Ellie now. Forget me. It's best that way.'

'You're her father. She can't just forget you. It doesn't work like that.'

His finger begins to wag. 'It does now.'

'Declan, stop it. Stop talking like this. I know you. I know you wouldn't just walk out of her life like that. Even if you leave me, you're still her blood.'

Declan lets his pointed hand flop by his side as his stiff shoulders round, and I almost reach out to him, but I stop myself just in time.

'She's given me twenty-four hours, Bea,' he says, so softly I have to strain to hear him. 'Elsa has given me one day to tidy this mess up and come home. If I don't, she'll take the boys and go.'

I study him. I can see he's torn but it doesn't offer me any comfort.

'So you see, I have no choice.'

'There's always a choice.'

'I've let the landlord know,' he goes on. 'The rent is paid until the eighteenth of this month. I've told him that I won't be renewing the lease after that.'

My chest tightens as I do the maths in my head. 'That's in less than two weeks.'

'You can stay until then, of course.'

'And then what? That's a week before Christmas.'

'You'll have to figure that out for yourself.'

I finally realise why our room feels larger and emptier than usual. Declan's stuff is missing. There's a large suitcase near the bed that I didn't notice before now, obviously packed with his stuff. All that remains is an empty bottle of his favourite Versace aftershave on the bedside table, and the tiepin I bought him for his birthday is next to it. I saved for a whole year to have enough for the slender gold clip.

'You're leaving tonight?' I say, pointing at his case.

'I'm on standby for a flight, yes.'

'Where are you going?'

'Home.'

'But this is home. This is your home,' I say, finally starting to cry, as the reality that our apartment was never somewhere his heart belonged sets in.

'I live in London. Well, just outside it.'

'London?' I say, as if it's the other side of the world, not a fifty-minute flight away. 'Jesus Christ, Declan. You don't even live in the same bloody country as me.' I try to imagine him in a big red-brick house in the suburbs, tubing around the city at the weekends with a beautiful wife on his arm, pointing at Big Ben and saying, 'Oh, is that the time, darling? We should get some tea and crumpets.' But the image doesn't fit. His strong Northside-Dublin accent and refusal to use public transport fits here, with me and Ellie.

'No. No. No!' I say, accepting how untrue my life is. Declan is only in the apartment for three or four nights a month and never two nights in a row. Suddenly, I feel painfully stupid.

He fetches his case, and says, 'I really am sorry, Bea.'

I follow him into the sitting room, where he bends over the back of the sofa to kiss Ellie's head. She giggles, but she doesn't take her eyes off the telly.

'Goodbye, beautiful girl,' he whispers, choking up.

'Bye-bye, Daddy,' Ellie chirps, so used to a quick kiss from her father before he dashes off to the airport not to be home again for days.

My heart almost stops beating knowing that, some day, she will realise he is not coming home again.

'Declan?' I say, as he reaches for the front door.

He turns back to look at me, and neither of us have words. He is not the man I thought he was, and now, with my life in tatters, I am not the woman I thought I would become. I follow him into the hall and call after him again. I don't know why. Maybe I'm expecting him to turn round and tell me it's all a big horrible mistake and he loves me and Ellie, and he'll fix everything.

'Declan,' I try one more time, loud and scratchy.

I hear our neighbour's yappy dogs bark, before her door swings open and she glares at me in her dressing gown and slippers.

'What's all this?' she says. 'Who's shouting?'

'Sorry, Mrs...' I search my brain for her name but, as always, I just can't remember. Ellie and I call her the dog lady, because she is never without dogs on leashes despite the sign downstairs that clearly states *no pets*.

'No one's shouting, Mrs Johnson,' Declan says.

'Another trip.' She smiles at his case. 'Some job you have. Who wouldn't love to travel the world.'

'Ah, it's not as glamorous as it seems. It can be a lonely business.' He sighs.

It's exactly what he said to me when we first met, and I felt so sad imagining him all alone in one hotel room after another that I fell into bed with him. I doubt he would want to share a bed with Mrs Johnson, her dogs or her flannel slippers, but he just can't shake off the charm, even as he abandons his daughter.

'Go back inside, Mrs Johnson,' I say, and it comes out like a direct order.

'Excuse me,' she snaps back.

'Bea is right, Mrs Johnson. It's freezing out here, and you

don't want to get sick for Christmas,' Declan says as if he's terribly concerned for her health.

She giggles like a smitten schoolgirl. 'You're right. Absolutely. My Chi-Chi and Co-Co need me well.' She rubs the two small balls of gleaming white fur at her feet and closes the door.

Declan turns away without another word and continues walking.

'I hate you,' I shout, half expecting Mrs Johnson's door to fly open again. 'I fucking hate you.'

Finally, he stops and turns back. 'No, you don't,' he says with a confidence that makes me want to throw something. 'But I hope you do. I hope when you wake up tomorrow you hate my guts. It will make this all easier.'

'I already do. I hate you,' I repeat, louder than ever. 'I hate you, I hate you, I hat—'

I cut myself off quickly as I feel small hands wrap round my legs. I look down to find a head of golden curls snuggled against my hip. When I look back, Declan has turned the corner and is gone. I hear the upbeat theme tune of CBeebies ending for the day coming from our apartment, and Ellie breaks away from me and says, 'I'm hungry.'

I look into my little girl's big, beautiful eyes and I wonder how anyone could ever possibly leave her.

FOUR

'Oh, Bea, no. You can't be serious.'

I called Cora as soon as I could. It took ages to get Ellie settled tonight. I did my best to keep it together, but I suspect she could sense something. I saw a TikTok with some kids' psychologist recently, that said young children pick up on the things we don't say. I wonder if she can tell how full of hate and hurt I am right now. God, I hope not. My voice cracked as I read *Winnie the Pooh and Friends* for the umpteenth time and tickled her arm for what felt like infinity. When she finally dropped off, I cried in the loo for over an hour.

'I knew he was bad news. From the bloody start,' Cora says, as I sit on the edge of the bath and hold my phone shakily to my ear. 'I said it, didn't I?'

'Yeah.' I sigh, thinking about all the times Cora raised red flags and I took offence.

'*He's too old for you. He's never home. He's so guarded with his money; do you even know what he earns? Does he ever give you money for things for Ellie? Kids aren't cheap, Bea.*'

'He's given me ten days,' I say, as if Declan is a judge passing sentence on me for crimes I didn't commit.

'Ten days for what?'

I shrug as if she can see me. 'To get out of the apartment. He's not renewing the lease.'

Cora takes a deep breath and I can tell she doesn't know what to say. 'Oh, Bea,' is all she can manage.

'Well, I suppose it makes sense,' I say. 'We're broken up. We're not going to be living together any more. He doesn't need this place.'

'But you do,' Cora tells me. 'And Ellie. It's her home. It's all she knows.'

'Not any more.'

'He can't do that. He's Ellie's dad. He has to provide for her.'

'It's already done. He's not renewing the lease.'

Cora tsks and is quiet for a moment, as if she's thinking and fuming at the same time. 'Right, well, you'll have to take him to court. It's the only way. If he's too much of a shit to face up to his responsibilities morally, you'll have to tie his hands legally. Ellie needs a home. And so do you.'

'No. No way,' I jump in, instantly scared. 'Declan would run circles around me in court. He'd hire the best of the best. He wouldn't spare a penny. He could even file for custody of Ellie.' The thought of it sends a shiver down my spine. 'No way. No legal stuff. I'll figure this out on my own.'

'You'll figure it all out in two weeks?' Cora asks, and I can sense her concern.

'Yes,' I snap, equal parts defensive and panicking.

'Okay, well, start with the landlord. Yeah? Give him a call. Get him to transfer the lease to you before it runs out. Happens all the time with breakups. And it would be the least disruptive thing for Ellie. You spend most of your time there just the two of you anyway, so...'

'It's expensive,' I tell her.

'I know. Rents are crazy, aren't they? God, we're paying over two grand a month for our place and it's only one bedroom. I can't even imagine what something as fancy as your apartment costs.'

'Neither can I,' I admit.

I hear Cora swallow. 'Erm, don't you know?'

'Not really. Declan never said.'

'Jesus, Bea.'

'I know. I know,' I say, accepting now how messed up everything is. 'But he was living here before we met so I couldn't just ask, you know.'

'Was he? I mean, he lied about so much. How do you know he didn't just rent that place as soon as he knew you were pregnant and he was going to play pretend for the next four years?'

'Erm.' My brain hurts almost as much as my heart. 'I don't, I guess.'

'It doesn't matter,' Cora says, softly. 'None of that matters now. It's over, Bea. You can move on and get on with the rest of your life.'

'Where will I go?' I say, choking back panic.

Cora can't possibly know that, after I pay for crèche, I only have five hundred euro a month in my bank account. It's been just fine before now. I budget carefully for groceries, new clothes for an ever-growing little girl, and the odd medication if needed. Thankfully, Ellie rarely picks up the sore throats or chesty coughs doing the rounds at crèche. There's usually a few euro left over at the end of the month that I use to treat us to a trip to the cinema or bowling. Declan took care of the rest. Electricity. Heating. Takeaways. Wine. If you asked me about our setup six months ago, I would have smiled with smug confidence and said, 'It works.' Hell, if you asked me six hours ago.

'You can try a flatshare, Bea. Don't worry, there's always people looking to split rent,' Cora tells me. 'I know living with strangers is a bit of a worry with a kiddo, but you could interview anyone before they moved in. And if they're nice, they might even babysit for a night or two and we could actually, *finally* get out for some drinks.'

'A flatshare,' I say, thinking. My mind is racing as I try to think of a way to make it work. If I cut back on food, maybe I could afford my share of rent. I could let out both rooms and Ellie and I could share the sofa. She loves to sleep snuggled up. And she gets good meals in crèche during the week. I'd only need stuff for the weekends. As for me, I could make do with an apple or a yoghurt and some bread. A loaf would last me a week. I'm starting to believe I might actually be able to do this.

'Bea?' Cora says after a while and I realise I've been quietly thinking for ages.

'Um.'

'You'll be okay. I just know it.'

Her confidence in me should fill me with hope, but I'm so full of worry that I don't have any more space.

'I better go,' I say, my bum gone numb from the edge of the bath digging into me.

'Okay. Give Ellie a cuddle for me, won't you?'

'Of course.'

'And I'm serious about that night out, Bea. You need to let your hair down now more than ever. And maybe Finton will babysit.'

Finton will absolutely not babysit. We both know this. But I say, 'Sure, Cora. After Christmas, yeah?'

'No. No way. We can't wait that long. We have to celebrate your new single life sooner. While all the decorations are up. Maybe that new bar on Baggot Street. It does nibbles and stuff. Everyone in work says it's lovely, and not too pricy.'

I can only imagine that not too pricy for all the medics Cora works with translates to much, much too pricy for me.

I sigh, shattered, because, as much as I would love to go for nibbles and drinks with my best friend the way most people our age do, I know it will never happen.

'I better go,' I say, again. 'Ellie is crying.'

Ellie is not crying. She's sleeping soundly. But I am. I am crying and I'm not sure I'll ever be able to stop.

FIVE

The following morning, I take Ellie to crèche as usual. She holds my hand tightly, watches out for traffic the way I've taught her and skips contently alongside me all the way.

'Baltic out there, isn't it?' Alannah says as soon as we arrive.

'Freezing,' I reply as I set about peeling off Ellie's coat and hat and gloves and placing them in the small box with her name on it under the reception desk.

I kiss the tip of her nose that's red from the cold and encourage her to run along and play with her friends.

'She might be a little cranky today,' I warn Alannah once Ellie is out of earshot. 'It was late when she got to sleep last night.'

'Oh. Okay. Not to worry. I just remind them all that Santa is watching and they need to be on their best behaviour. It usually does the trick.'

My heart pangs at the mention of Santa. Ellie wrote her letter weeks ago and we posted it in the glittery cardboard box outside our local Tesco. Ellie asked for a Barbie house and some Crayola. I have neither yet.

'I'll see you later,' I tell Alannah, then pull out my phone and start walking towards work. St Helen's is at the far side of the city, but I need to save the bus fare. Besides, it's dry and crisp outside and I could use the fresh air as I work up the courage to message Declan.

> Hello

He doesn't reply, but I can see he's online and soon two blue ticks appear below my message and I know he's read it.

> Can you pass me on the landlord's contact details please?

This time, his reply is instant.

Why?

> So I still have somewhere to live.

> I'm going to rent the place myself.

> BTW Ellie has asked for Barbie stuff and some crayons for Christmas.

> Are you still buying them for her?

A cheaper flat would be better.

Somewhere nearer work.

I will send you money for Ellie's gifts.

> I don't think where I live from now on is any of your business.

> You dumped me. Remember?

My phone pings with a notification from Revolut. The money is already in my account. Down to the exact penny. He must have checked the prices online while we were messaging.

I wait for him to send on the landlord's number or email

but, when they don't come by the time I've reached work, I send another message.

> Thank you for the money.

> Can you please forward the landlord details asap as I am anxious to get this sorted out.

Adam Shaw 082 65729921 👍

Please don't mention me.

I told Adam I was living alone so…

I don't ask him why he concealed Ellie and me. It doesn't really matter now; it was all just part of his big elaborate lie.

> I won't mention you.

Thank you.

And just so you know, I won't be keeping this phone.

> Are you changing your number?

No.

This is a second phone.

I don't need it any more.

I'm sure you get what I mean.

I'm sorry.

> Oh

I really am sorry Bea!

> How will I reach you?

Like I said, forget me.

> But I don't know where you live? Or anything about your life in London. What if I need to get in touch about Ellie? What if she is sick or something? You'd want to know right?

I'm sorry Bea.

Good luck with the apartment.

Goodbye.

I send several messages after that, in various tones. From pleading with him to forward some contact details – his address, his other number, even what area of London he's in – to much more aggressive and angry messages calling him out on his horrendous behaviour. There are a lot of swear words and angry emojis in those messages. But none of them deliver and I can only guess he has switched his phone off. The sinking feeling that comes with knowing he won't switch it on again almost drowns me.

I'm not late but Elaine is glaring at me with narrow eyes and folded arms as soon as I reach the ward.

'What?' I shrug.

'Did you ask Órlaith to check on a patient yesterday?'

'Eh...' I try to rewind my mind to the day just past, but all I can think about is Declan's back as he walked out the door.

'She said you rang and asked her to send security outside to check on an old man.'

'Oh. Yes. I did,' I say, remembering the man with scarcely any hair and no hat. 'I was worried about him.'

'Just not worried enough to check he was all right before you walked off.'

'He said he wasn't a patient.'

Elaine rolls her eyes.

'I checked on him. I asked Órlaith to send security to double-check. But it's not my job to—'

'Oh, Bea, really. I thought you'd have more compassion.'

'I do,' I say, as a mix of anger and upset swirls inside me. 'I was in a hurry to get to the crèche to pick my daughter up and I had to go. Is he all right? Did something happen?'

Elaine puffs out. 'Did you know Mr Flynn went walkabout last night?'

I search my brain for a Mr Flynn but an image won't come.

'Room 115. Tall man. Kidney stones and dementia.'

Panic flashes inside me like a bolt of lightning. I've worked on the geriatric ward for three years, and I've been warned over and over that all eyes must be kept on senile patients. I try to remember if Malcolm was tall. He was sitting but his legs didn't seem particularly long. And he seemed fully lucid to me. If he was at all confused, I wouldn't have left him.

'Did you find him?' I ask, worried.

'Mr Flynn. Yes, we found him. Turns out he was locked in Mrs Ward's bathroom.'

'Oh. That's good.'

'We didn't find your friend in the car park though. Turns out, this time, he really wasn't a patient. But for heaven's sake, Bea. If you are ever unsure again. Do. Not. Walk. Away.'

I nod. Accepting the scolding and regretting asking Órlaith for help.

'Now, let's forget about all this and get to work, yeah?' Elaine says, unfolding her stiff arms and smiling.

The day passes in a decidedly average way. I wash floors, change bed linen, clean bathrooms and unblock stubborn shower drains. At some point between it all I text the landlord.

> Hello. My name is Beatrice Alright and I am interested in renting your apartment. I work at St Helen's Hospital and I have a 4yr old daughter. I am very tidy and have no pets. Please could you let me know how much it would cost monthly? Thank you!

His reply is almost instant.

> Hello Beatrice. Which apartment are you interested in?

I blush, and realise that he owns more than one apartment in the city. I imagine he's rather wealthy and there's a pang of envy in my gut for this stranger.

> Number 17 Burken Cross please.

> No. 17 is available from Dec 18th. I will need a reference and a direct debit set up. I have a lot of interest so whoever sends me the deposit and one month's rent in advance first gets it. Rent is 3000 per month. Bills extra. Let me know if you would like to proceed and I will send you my bank details. Regards, Adam

I almost drop my phone. I have never had six thousand euro in my bank account. Ever. It would take me years to save up that much. Even if I rent both bedrooms, a section of the hall and the bloody balcony I still can't come up with funds like that. Declan was right, I was wasting my time texting Adam. I text him again with my fingers shaking as the harsh reality of my predicament grips me.

> I can't afford it, I'm afraid. But thank you.

> No worries. Best of luck finding something in your budget.

His final message is kind and encouraging but it fills me

with overwhelming stress. I suspect it will be near impossible to find something I can afford. Panic sets in and I find myself sitting on the floor of the cleaning closet for at least half an hour, simply rocking back and forth with my knees tucked against my chest. Thankfully, almost no one comes in here except me, so it's the perfect place to hide while the panic subsides. I'm glad when I find I've no appetite, and I think of the money I will save not buying lunch. I spend the other half an hour of my break searching the internet for flats anywhere and everywhere in a remotely commutable distance from work. I send several enquiring emails and finish my shift.

When I return to the closet at the end of work to fetch my bag and my phone, I am met by countless helpful and friendly emails. But one after another confirms that their properties are too expensive. Even flats in areas of town I'd be afraid to live are more than I can afford. I move on to enquiring about sharing with others. The ads almost all insist that pets are not welcome, but none of them say anything about kids. There's a couple of places that I could just about afford, if I stopped getting the bus and walked everywhere, but as soon as I mention Ellie they ghost me.

I don't notice I'm crying as I leave work, but when I face into the wind and start walking a voice calls after me, asking, 'Bad day?'

I stop and turn to find Malcolm sitting on the same bench as yesterday. His head is once again hatless, but he's wrapped in another colourful scarf. A grass green, like a summer's day. It's bright and cheery against the otherwise grey world. The grey car park, the grey hospital, the grey sky. My grey life.

'Yes. Pretty bad.' I sniffle.

He reaches into his pocket and pulls out a tissue. I don't move.

'I haven't blown my nose in it, if that's what you're thinking.'

I wasn't.

'It's clean,' he says. 'And you look like you need it more than I do.'

I shuffle towards him, wondering if this winter frost will ever thaw.

'Still in those silly things?' he says, pointing at my runners that the grip is long worn down on. 'In my day people dressed for the weather. Not any more, though. Young people are a slave to fashion.'

I glance at my worn-out runners and wonder how anyone could possibly consider them a thing of fashion.

'I don't have different ones,' I find myself confessing out of nowhere as I take his tissue and dab under my eyes. I crumple it up and shove it in my pocket.

I wait for him to blush, or feel uncomfortable the way most people do when they realise someone else's misfortune. Or, worse still, I wait for him to pity me. But he doesn't.

He pats the empty space of the bench beside him and says, 'Sit,' the same way you might command a dog, perhaps.

I check my watch. I don't really have time to pause. But I think about the money I saved skipping lunch. I could treat myself to a trip on the Luas. I'd be at the crèche in half the time.

'Thank you, Malcolm,' I say.

'You don't need to thank me. This bench doesn't belong to me. It's public property. You can sit if you want to.'

I sit in the empty space beside him and bop my knees up and down to keep warm.

'That's unpleasant,' he says, shortly.

'Excuse me?'

'If I wanted to bounce around like a fella at sea in a storm, I'd set sail. But I don't. I want to sit here on my bench. Nice and still.'

I notice my nervous twitching and steady myself. I'm blushing when I say, 'I thought it wasn't your bench.'

He chuckles. But it's quickly followed by a chesty cough that shakes the bench more than I ever could. It takes some time but, finally, his coughing fit subsides and we sit as we are. Two strangers, on a wooden bench, under an old oak tree that guards the hospital like a huge, strong security guard. Lost in silent thought, tears once again trickle down my cheek and I'm about to excuse myself when he says, 'Do you want to tell me why you're crying?'

I wipe around my eyes with the tissue again, embarrassed. 'Oh, you really don't want to know. Trust me.'

'I can't trust you. I don't know you,' he says, matter-of-factly. 'Likewise, you can't possibly know what I do and don't want to discuss. You don't know me.'

His blunt honesty shocks me. My tears stop and I find myself smiling, curious about this old man.

'You're right. I don't know you. So, how about you tell me something about yourself.'

'No thank you.' He folds his arms firmly.

'Really?' I pull my head back until I have three chins. 'You're seriously not going to share a single detail about yourself.'

'No thank you.'

I huff out. This man is infuriating, and yet I'm reluctant to get up and walk away.

'What's your favourite colour?' I ask.

He takes a deep breath, but doesn't open his mouth.

'Is it green?' I point to his scarf.

He makes a face.

'Okay, fine. Not green. Red, then?' I redirect my pointing to the red strip in his chequered coat.

He rolls his eyes.

'Blue?'

Nothing.

'Black?'

He moves, but only to tighten his folded arms.

'Yellow? Purple? Silver? Bloody magenta? Seriously, you're not going to share your favourite?'

He doesn't reply.

I puff out and get to my feet. 'Okay, well, thank you for sharing your non-bench with me. I best be off.'

I could swear I see disappointment flash across his face as I stand up.

'Oh, and for the record,' I say, taking care to get my balance, 'I think your favourite colour *is* green. Like your scarf. And like your eyes.'

He smiles and I know I'm right.

'Goodbye, Bea,' he says. 'I will see you tomorrow.'

I'm startled for a moment as I realise that he plans to sit on this same bench again tomorrow as my shift ends. I'm riddled with curiosity about why, but I know it's pointless asking. If I can't get his favourite colour out of him, I doubt he'll tell me anything as private as what he is doing out there every evening. And even more curiously, I find I'm already looking forward to seeing him again when he does.

'Goodbye, Malcolm.'

SIX

Cora comes by to babysit. She takes Ellie to the cinema and out for pizza after and I use the time to shop for Ellie's Santa presents. I buy a small pack of crayons and a colouring book full of unicorns and fairies that I know she will love. Smyths on Jervis Street have a Barbie dream house on sale for half price. The guy working there tells me the sounds and lights don't work.

'Dunno what's wrong with it. We've tired lots of different batteries but nothing.' He shrugs.

'But everything else is perfect?' I ask, looking again at the price tag that feels too good to be true. 'There's no missing parts, or anything?'

'Ah no, nothing like that. All the bits and pieces are fine. And it comes with a free Barbie.' He points to a small selection of blond dolls in hot-pink boxes. 'But your kid probably won't be too happy if the thing has no sound. Like, the doorbell is supposed to ding and it plays a song when you press the radio, that sort of thing.'

I can only imagine Ellie's face when she wakes up on Christmas morning and finds Santa has left her a multicoloured house that's just about as tall as she is. I cannot wait. And for a moment, I almost forget that wishing for Christmas means wishing us closer to leaving the flat. I try not to let my head go there.

When the staff guy says, 'Oh and I'm sorry but we've no box, so I can give you an extra ten per cent off, if that's any good?' I have to fight the urge to hug him.

'That's perfect. Thank you so much.'

I pay, and can't believe I have enough left over to buy a small turkey and ham and some Christmas crackers. Getting on and off the bus with a giant doll's house is ridiculously difficult and people stare. One woman even scolds me. 'Couldn't you wait until you got home to assemble that thing, like a normal person? You're taking up all the space.'

I *am* taking up an inordinate amount of space. I place it on my knee, but it juts out into the aisle and another woman with a buggy can't pass by. I try shoving it the other way but the man beside me complains that it's crushing him. And yet, I cannot stop smiling. It will all be worth it on Christmas morning.

I make it back to the apartment just in time to hide it in the wardrobe before Cora and Ellie return. I hear them in the hallway singing some song, obviously from the movie, and when I open the door Ellie greets me with sticky green lips and a luminous green tongue.

'She wanted a slushie.' Cora makes a face. 'I hope that's okay.'

'Thank you.'

'Those fizzy apple yokes are quite nice,' she says, staring at the nearly empty slushie that Ellie is sipping.

I smile. I've never bought Ellie one before. Declan has, of course.

I step aside so Cora and Ellie can come in. Ellie kicks off her shoes and goes straight for the couch, hoping for some TV before bed.

'And this is for us,' Cora tells me, rattling the plastic bag dangling from her hands. I hear a wine bottle clink and I smell Chinese food.

'Oh Cora, I...' I choke back emotion.

My best friend smiles. 'Tell you what, why don't you plate this up and open the wine. I'll get that little munchkin of yours to bed, yeah?'

My stomach rumbles loudly and I realise I haven't eaten yet today, and something tells me Cora knows it. I look for the bottle opener as Cora takes Ellie by the hand and promises to read *Winnie the Pooh*.

'Of course I can do the voices,' I hear her say over the sound of brushing teeth in the bathroom.

Although Ellie is asleep in record time, by the time Cora returns I've devoured half the takeaway and I've knocked back a glass of wine.

'Sorry. Oops, sorry. I was starving.'

Cora doesn't tell me she knows, but her face says it all.

'It's okay. I had pizza with Ellie. The chow mein was for you.'

'But there's two?'

'Thought you could put the leftovers away for tomorrow, maybe? Ellie couldn't decide between pizza or Chinese earlier, so this way she can have both.'

I throw my arms round her and hold her tighter than I have in years.

'I love you, you know.'

Cora knows. And I know just how much she cares about me, but, ever awkward with affection, she wriggles free and says, 'Well, if you love me that much, you'll pour me a glass of wine.'

I pour a large glass for her and top up my own, and, already feeling a little tipsy, I lead us towards the sofa in the open-plan living room. I turn on the telly, for some background noise, and I pour my heart out to my best friend.

'Oh, Jesus, Bea. I had no idea it was that bad. Why did you put up with him for so long?'

'Because I never thought of it as putting up with him. I was happy. I loved him. I never considered that he was the one with the good job, and the security, and that if he left me I would be screwed. Because I never thought he would leave me.'

'Are you going to confront the wife? You should. I would. I'll go with you, if you like.'

I have no doubt Cora would. She would go round to their house and beat their front door down if I let her.

'I don't know where he lives. London somewhere. I am an idiot.'

Cora hugs me then. She doesn't bristle like a stray cat the way she usually does. She just holds me and lets me cry and tells me she will do everything she can to help.

SEVEN

Ellie wakes during the night and I make it in to her room just as she throws up everywhere. Seeing a fizzy apple slushie for a second time at four a.m. makes my own stomach heave. I hold my breath as best I can, strip the bed and run a bath. Ellie thinks bathing in the middle of the night is the best thing ever and she's wide awake and splashing. Kneeling at the edge of the bath on a damp mat, my eyes are burning and I can scarcely keep them open. Ellie shoves a rubber shark towards me, making a nom, nom, nom noise. I don't budge. She drops the shark and it makes a small splash.

'Mammy, aren't you scared?' she says, with her big, round eyes that her father gave her staring inquisitively at me.

I fetch the large, fluffy towel from the rack and scoop her up. She giggles and snuggles into me as I dry her.

'C'mon, chickpea, you can sleep in my bed tonight.'

Ellie seems so small and delicate tucked up on Declan's side of the bed. She's asleep within minutes. My eyes still burn, but they are wide and staring at the ceiling now as sleep eludes me.

I get up and put the pukey bed linen in the washing

machine and wash the floor in Ellie's room. I climb back into bed beside Ellie and replay her words in my mind.

'Mammy, aren't you scared?'

Silently, as I watch my beautiful little girl sleep, I answer her question in my head. 'Yes. So very scared.'

In the morning, Ellie and I walk to crèche and I'm hoping the fresh air will do me good. But I am like a zombie by the time I reach work. My shift drags and I consider napping in the supply closet on my break, but when I check my phone I've a missed call from Alannah and, instantly, I know what it's about.

'It's spreading like wildfire,' Alannah says when I call. 'They all have it. Time of year. The little ones are always sick just before Santa comes. You'll have to come get her. And keep her home. Not just until the puking stops, but until she's been well for at least three days. I can't tell you how many of them come back in here while they're still dying. I'm sick of ringing parents to come get sick kids. We're thinking about putting a fining system in place.'

Alannah would charge parents for the air their kids breathe if she thought she could, but nonetheless I agree to keep Ellie at home until she is better.

Elaine makes no effort to hide how put out she is when I explain.

'Sick just before Christmas is coincidental, isn't it? I mean, if I had a euro for everyone who called in sick and then suddenly had their Christmas shopping done, then I'd be a very rich woman.'

'I really am sorry,' I say, panicking about the wages I will lose while I miss work.

'Is there no one else who could watch her?'

'It's just Ellie and me.'

I hope she doesn't mention Declan. I got drunk at the last

work party and made a big song and dance about how my boyfriend was a pilot. I was mortified for weeks afterwards, but I only did it to get under Elaine's skin. She'd been sticking me with the worst shifts for weeks because she knew how badly I needed them. For once, her inability to listen serves me well. She has forgotten I ever mentioned Declan, as she says, 'Well, go on then. Go pick Ellie up. But ring me as soon as she's better. I need you back here as soon as possible.'

Outside, I'm surprised to find Malcolm in the usual spot, where the arms of the old oak tree stretch and yawn behind him. I wasn't expecting to see him, since I'm leaving work so early, and I wonder how long he sits out here every day. Hours, perhaps? And I am more curious than ever about why. Once again, he is without a hat while the rest of him is well wrapped up for the weather. Today, his scarf is brown and burnt orange, like the leaves of the oak tree in autumn. He sits with his eyes closed, his head bowed and his gloved hands clasped on his lap. For a moment I envy his serenity. He's so calm, he's like a statue. A non-breathing statue. Before I have time to think, I find myself running towards him.

'Malcolm. Malcolm. Malcolm,' I call out, getting louder each time. 'Oh God, Malcolm.'

Speed and an icy footpath is, as ever a menacing combination, and I find myself landing on my coccyx just as I reach him. He jolts and his eyes shoot open.

'What are you doing down there?'

My butt burns, but not nearly as much as my face.

'Slipped.'

'Shoes.' He points.

'Shoes,' I repeat. 'Are you all right?'

His eyes widen. 'Am I all right? I'm not the one on the ground.'

'Yes. But—' I cut myself off.

'Oh.' He scoffs. 'You thought I was dead, did you?'

'Ha-ha. No. God no,' I lie, my heart still racing a little from the fear of it. How would I ever explain something like that to Elaine?

'You know old people sleep. And sometimes, we even wake up again.'

I don't know what to say to that, so I simply admit, 'Speaking of sleep. I didn't get much myself last night.' As if tiredness can explain a multitude. Falling over. Twice. Summer shoes in winter. Teary eyes. Assuming that all the elderly people I befriend will pass away. The latter is a downside to working on a ward for the old and frail, and I won't lie, it causes plenty of the tears too.

'Are you going to nap there?' he asks, with a wide grin that exaggerates the lines and folds around his mouth, but nonetheless suits him.

'Maybe. I'm getting used to it down here.'

He pats the bench beside him and my heart sinks when I must shake my head. 'Afraid I can't today.'

'Oh.'

'In a rush.'

'Ah. That's the thing with young people, isn't it? Always so busy hurrying from one place to the next because you think you have all the time in the world. But, really, you're just chasing your life away. I should know.'

I'd love to ask him what he means. It's the nearest he's come to telling me anything about himself, but I glance at my watch and I have mere minutes to catch the next bus.

'You're not going to start running again, are you?' he asks, and he seems both disappointed and concerned that I might actually break my neck. I'm slightly concerned that he might be right.

'I'm late.'

'Thought as much. Right, then. You'll be needing these.' He leans forward and pulls out a pair of fire-engine-red wellington boots from behind his back. 'They were my wife's. For the garden. I reckon you're about the same size.'

'Oh.'

I think he wants me to take them. It makes a range of emotions swell in my near-empty stomach. Confusion. Awkwardness. Some sort of sweet gratitude.

'They're not going to fit me,' he says. His grin falters slightly and I wonder if this is making him feel as weird as it's making me.

'I... I...'

'Take them. Don't put them on, if you'd rather not. But at least I've done my bit trying to keep you upright.'

He shoves the wellies towards me. They look brand new. There's not a scuff mark anywhere and I think I catch a glimpse of a price tag stuck inside.

'She didn't have athlete's foot or anything like that,' he says, rather seriously, as if he's concerned that foot fungus is the cause of my reluctance.

'Oh. Erm, right, okay. Thank you.'

I take the bright wellies and, just as I thought, when I look inside there is a small price sticker on the insole.

'Thank you very much, Malcolm. This is kind.'

'This is sensible,' he says, with a firm nod.

'Yes. That too.'

'Are you going inside?' I ask, as I slip off my runners and pull on the wellies, which, surprisingly, are a good fit.

'Not today.'

There are a million questions I want to ask this curious old man. *Why don't you wear a hat? Do you ever go inside? Why do you come here? How long do you stay? Why on earth did you buy brand-new wellies for someone who works here?*

But all that I have time to say is, 'Will I see you again?'

'I should think so. Tomorrow.'

'Oh, not tomorrow.' I sigh. My feet feel rather warm and cosy in the wellies. 'My little girl is sick, so...'

A flash of worry pans across his face as he turns to look at the hospital.

'Oh, no. Nothing serious. Just a tummy bug. She's not a patient. I just work here.' I run my hand over my uniform as if to silently say, 'See.'

He nods, accepting my explanation.

'Okay. Well. I better go.'

I start running, and I almost chuckle out loud when I can pick up decent speed without slipping.

EIGHT

Ellie gets sick twice on the bus. The guy sitting beside us makes a face that tells me I really need to do something about the small puking human sitting on my knees, as if I can just press a button and deactivate vomit mode.

I apologise and tell him it's going around and it's highly contagious. He moves and I sit Ellie into his free seat and slowly the feeling returns to my legs. I clean up as best I can with a bunch of baby wipes and throw them into a plastic bag. By the time we reach our bus stop, Ellie is sleeping on my shoulder and normal colour is returning to her face. I scoop her up, along with my bag of vomity wipes and my regular bag, and waddle down the bus aisle, struggling to keep hold of everything. Wellies are no longer the best footwear for the situation, and slow me down as I feel the eyes of the other passengers on me, delighted my sick child and I are getting off.

Back at the flat, Ellie manages to keep down some toast and apple juice. Within half an hour she is a ball of energy again and asking if we can play Twister. I just about have enough energy to pop *Frozen* on the telly and boil a kettle to make some instant noodles for my dinner. Ellie is asleep before Elsa strikes

Anna with her magic and I flop onto the couch beside her, blow on my noodles and text Cora.

> So I can't send her to crèche for at least three days.

So stupid. If she's better, she's better. Can you pretend she wasn't sick. Say it was something she ate?

> Like fizzy apple slushie?

😂😂

> Can't. All the kids have it so the rule is the same for everyone. Work are pissed with me too. As if I can control my kid getting sick.

Wish I could watch her but I'm slammed at work. You wouldn't believe the amount of falls people have putting up Christmas lights. I have broken legs and arms coming out my ears.

I laugh out loud for a moment as I imagine my best friend with various broken limbs attached to her head.

Maybe you should text Declan. Let him know Ellie is sick. Ask the 🥒 for help?

> Can't. He turned off his phone.

What? Why? He can't keep it off for ever.

> It's his second phone. The one he had so he could hide me and Ellie from his wife. Turns out we were only ever second-phone level of affair.

ASSHOLE!!!

> Totally. Anyway I gotta go. Need to get Ellie into bed. And I'm shattered too. Talk tomorrow xx

Yeah okay. I'm here if you need me. Night night xx

Ellie shares my bed again and her small, warm body snuggles into me and keeps me cosy. But I can't sleep. The thought of missing three days of wages, especially so close to Christmas, is stressing me out so much I can feel a couple of hives appear on my ankle. I lie awake and scour rental websites yet again, crossing my fingers that by some miracle a remotely affordable apartment will appear. To my surprise a lady in Finglas emails me back and says she has a small two-bed town house, rent is just about in reach and she loves kids. I make a plan to view the house tomorrow evening and set my phone down. I wrap my arms round Ellie and am asleep within seconds.

What feels likes a blink later, I am bounced awake by a four-year-old jumping on the end of my bed.

'Ellie. No,' I croak, my eyes sticky with sleep and struggling to open. 'Stop it. Get down.' All the horrible injuries Cora has told me about from children bouncing on the bed race through my mind. Broken collarbones. Dislocated knees. Concussions. Aside from how painful they sound, I just couldn't afford A&E.

'Ellie, get down,' I try again, fully awake now and with my voice loud and firm.

Ellie hops off the bed and folds her arms, making a pouting face. I drag my hands round my face and ward off a sulk or tantrum with the suggestion of Coco Pops for breakfast. Thankfully there's some left and the milk is still in date too.

Ellie hops off her chair as soon as the last spoonful enters her mouth. 'Let's go. Let's go,' she says, emulating our usual, slightly frantic morning routine to get out the door to crèche and work on time.

'Not today, chickpea, you're sick, remember?'

Ellie holds her tummy as if she's checking if anything is going to happen. Then she shakes her head, smiles and says, 'All better.'

Orangey-grey light shines through the curtains from the streetlamp outside the window and I can tell the sun still isn't up. I glance at Ellie, who is bursting with so much energy I can see her battling the urge to jump on the bed again. Thankfully, whatever bug she had is out of her system. If we hurry, we could easily make it on time. But Alannah's words are ringing in my ears. 'I'm sick of ringing parents... fining system... home for three days.'

I'm not sure which is worse. Three days without wages or the wrath of Alannah and a potential fine. And that's when I have an idea. A probably terrible, most definitely a bit risky, almost certainly stupid idea. But if the past few day have taught me anything, it's that Ellie and I are alone in this life and we have to figure things out and find solutions where we can. So, I tell Ellie to get dressed and I rummage down the bottom of my wardrobe to find the colouring book and colouring pencils I bought for Christmas. The plastic Smyths bag rustles and I pull it out and stuff it into my handbag. Then I dress in my uniform and stick a packet of pop tarts in the toaster. Ellie and I put on our coats, the toaster pings, and with a strawberry pop tart each we leave the apartment.

Ellie attempts to turn left at the end of our road, as we usually do for crèche, but I hold her hand a little tighter and say, 'Not today. Today we are going this way.'

I hadn't taken into consideration how far a walk to the hospital is for little legs, and after a while Ellie complains that her feet hurt. I carry her for as long as I am able and then, refreshed, she walks again for a while. We repeat the pattern of carrying and walking until we finally reach the main doors of St Helen's.

Ellie's eyes widen with delight. 'Is this your work?'

'Yup,' I say proudly as if I run the hospital, rather than clean a handful of upstairs wards.

'It's very nice,' she tells me, then she covers her ears as an ambulance comes into the bay with its siren blaring. 'And noisy.'

'C'mon. Let's get inside,' I say, squeezing her hand.

Órlaith is chatting to someone at reception and doesn't notice us pass. I guide us into the tuck shop and, with some coins that I was saving for the vending machine for lunch, I buy a lollipop and a carton of Ribena. And then I lead us into the lift and up to the fourth floor where I work.

When the lift dings and the doors open, I peek my head out. The corridor is silent and the storage closet is in view. I grip Ellie's hand so tightly she winces and yelps.

'Sorry. Oops, sorry,' I say, loosening my grip immediately. 'But we've gotta hurry. In here. Quick, quick, in here.'

I guide us into the closet unnoticed and flick on the light.

Ellie scrunches her nose. 'Ew. It smells funny in here.'

I rarely notice the smell of bleach and surface polish any more, but I agree it is a bit stinky. I move some mops and buckets and put my back into shifting the industrial floor polisher aside to make some room in the middle of the squashed closet. I take off my cardigan and place it on the floor and encourage Ellie to sit down on it. She eyes me, unsure, but drops onto her bum and crosses her legs as she looks up at me.

'I have a surprise,' I tell her, and before I get another word out I can see her face light up with anticipation.

'We're not going to crèche today.'

Her face falls.

'Wait. Wait. We're doing something even better.'

I reach into my bag and pull out the colouring book and bright pencils.

Ellie squeals with joy and I quickly place my finger over my lips and whisper, 'Shh.'

I pass her the book and pencils and she flicks through the pages, stopping when she comes to the outline of a fairy riding a unicorn and begging to be coloured in. Next, I give her the lollipop and Ribena.

'You know how you love to play hide-and-seek?'

She scrunches her face, not so sure she does.

'Well, this is the bestest, most fun game of hide-and-seek. You get to stay in here and colour your pictures and enjoy your treats.'

She nods, liking the sound of this game.

'But you must, must, must not come out, okay? That's how you play. You have to stay hiding and then you win.'

No one ever checks the storage room except me. I am certain no one will find Ellie in here.

'Okay, Mammy,' she says, then she scoots over and makes room for me in the space between her and the sweeping brushes.

'Oh, chickpea, I can't play.' I sigh, and my heart sinks when I watch her little face fall. 'I have to go to work now. But you're going to have so, so much fun colouring in.'

Her bottom lip drops and quivers.

'But I'm going to come back lots and lots and check that you're still winning, okay? And remember—'

'—keep hiding. That's how you win,' she finishes for me with a grin.

'Yes. Yes. You clever girl.'

I kiss the top of her head and promise I will be back soon. Ellie takes a yellow pencil from the box and begins colouring with a happy, smiling face. I take a deep breath, close the door behind me and, with my heart practically beating out of my chest, I clock in for my shift.

NINE

I check on Ellie regularly. The first couple of times, I find her colouring happily and sucking on her lollipop. After that, she's curled up napping on my cardigan and I'm guilty of being pleased that the walk to hospital tuckered her out. It's lunchtime before I know it. I sneak some snacks from the catering trolley – a couple of rice puddings and two apples. Then, I pour two small glasses of water from the cooler next to the nurses' station and tiptoe towards the storage closet.

'I like picnics,' Ellie chirps as she dribbles rice pudding down her chin.

I sit cross-legged beside her. Despite the cramped space, it's the most I've enjoyed my lunch break in a long time. I would love to take her outside for some fresh air, but the stress at the thought of sneaking her back in makes me chicken out. Instead, I give her my phone and tell her she can watch *Bluey* with the volume down. Her face lights up with delight at this unexpected screen time, and I know she'll sit happily for another hour at least.

'This is so funner than crèche,' she tells me as she stares at the screen.

I kiss her head and remind her of the rules of our game of hide-and-seek.

'I'm winning.'

'You are winning, chickpea. You're the best hider.'

'I'm winning,' she says again, but her attention is less on me and more on the colourful animals and low music coming from my phone.

I back out the door, and bump into Elaine just as I'm closing it. I yelp as if I've seen a ghost.

Elaine is most obviously unimpressed. 'Everything all right?'

'Sorry. I didn't see you there.'

'It's patients' quiet time,' she reminds me as she places a finger over her lips.

'Yes, sorry.' I lower my voice to a whisper. 'I was just looking for the, eh... the mop.'

'And you didn't find it?' she asks, pointing at my empty hands.

I wince, wishing I could stop talking, but I'm on edge and words keep tumbling out no matter how much my brain aches for them not to.

'Left it on the ward. I don't know where my head is at today.'

'Probably on your daughter.'

A shiver runs down my spine. '

Oh... Ell... ie,' I say, as if I have to search my brain to find my own child's name.

'Yes.' She looks at me with a pinched expression, telling me that she's worried I've lost my mind. 'She was unwell yesterday. You left early to attend to her.'

'Oh. Eh. Yes. Tummy bug. All good now.'

'Kids.' She sighs. 'They like to keep us on our toes. I'm glad it was nothing.'

'Yes. Yeah. Me too. Kids.'

I roll my eyes for effect.

'Don't suppose we have any wipes?' she goes on, eying up the door behind me.

The handle digs into my spine, and I realise I have my back pressed firmly against the door, guarding it. My heart begins to race as she watches me, and I can tell she's waiting for me to step aside so she can open the door and check.

'I spilled coffee all over my desk earlier and it's still sticky. That's what I get for trying morning yoga before work. I just can't do without my sleep.'

'We don't have any,' I blurt.

She crooks her head.

'Wipes. We don't have any. I forgot to order them.'

Her eyes narrow but I cut across her before she has time to say anything.

'I hear you about the sleep thing. Ellie kept me up when she was sick and I just totally forgot to order. I'm sorry. I'll get on it now, though.'

She nods, accepting my excuse, and is just about to walk away when she suddenly becomes very still and says, 'Do you hear that?'

I hear the gentle hum of Bluey and his animal friends talking behind the door. I pretend to listen intently for a moment before I say, 'No. What?'

'Squeaky voices?'

'Really?' I make a face and act curious. 'I don't hear anything.'

She listens again, and shrugs. 'Never mind. It's gone now.'

'The wind,' I rush in to say.

'Yeah. Maybe. It's a bit draughty up here, certainly.' She pulls herself upright and, with a single clap of her hands, she says, 'Right. Best get back to it. Can you see to the floor in room 128. I think Mr Purcell wet the floor again. He says he didn't, of course, but—'

'I'll see to it.'

She smiles and takes her time walking away and I know she can just about still hear the faint hum of music.

I wash and polish the floor in room 128 until it sparkles.

'He peed there, you know,' Mr Canterbury says, proudly pointing at Mr Purcell in the bed next to him.

Mr Purcell jolts upright to protest his innocence. 'I did not, you lying old codger. It was you!'

'Now. Now. What does it matter?' I jump in, waving my arms as if we're in a war zone. 'It's all cleaned up now.'

'It matters to me,' Mr Purcell says, in a tone that hints that if he wasn't lying in bed he would stomp his foot like a tantrum-throwing toddler. 'This fella is driving me cracked. I want to move beds.'

'I can have a word with the ward manager,' I suggest, knowing Elaine will never agree to swapping patients around.

'My son is coming in later,' Mr Purcell goes on. 'He's a solicitor.'

'You can't sue me for peeing on the floor,' Mr Canterbury grumbles, his elderly voice crackling like an open fire on a winter's day.

'So you admit it.' Mr Purcell laughs, as delighted with himself as if he's solved a serious crime. 'It was you.'

I leave them to argue it out, and make my way to the storage closet once again to check on Ellie.

'Hey there, chickpea,' I say, as I push the bucket and mop inside. 'Are you having fun watching *Blue—*' I drop the handle of the mop and it topples the bucket over, sending soapy water all over the floor and soaking my cardigan. 'Ellie,' I call out, ignoring the water that pools around my ankles when I don't see my daughter sitting in the spot where I left her. 'Ellie. Ellie. Ellie, where are you?'

I charge into the pokey room and push sweeping brushes aside and move anything that is movable.

'Chickpea, we're finished playing now. No more hiding, okay? Come on out.'

My heart is thumping so hard it's almost painful as panic rises inside me.

'Ellie. Oh God, please, Ellie, where are you?'

When she doesn't answer, I run into the hall shouting her name.

'Ellie. Ellie. Ellie.'

I race through the corridors of various wards. I don't care if it's patients' quiet time. I am like a foghorn repeating my daughter's name over and over and over.

I'm such an idiot, I tell myself as I race down flights of stairs and search the next floor. *Why couldn't I just take the day off work like Alannah told me to? Why did I think I could hide a four-year-old in a closet all day? I'm an idiot. Idiot. Idiot. Idiot.*

I'm sweating when I reach reception and I can't tell if I'm crying or if it's beads of perspiration racing down my cheeks.

'Órlaith,' I shout, across the whole reception area where people are patiently queuing to speak to her.

She looks up when she hears me and, seeing my face, she stands up and asks, 'What? What is it?'

'Ellie. Have you seen Ellie?'

'Your daughter?' she asks, as I realise Ellie and Órlaith have never met. Órlaith wouldn't know if she saw her or not.

'She's here somewhere,' I just about manage to say, before my voice breaks. 'She's run off. She's all alone. Oh God, Órlaith. She's only four.'

'Hang on. Hang on,' Órlaith tells me as if I might run off before she reaches me.

She steps out from behind her desk. No one in the queue seems to argue. All eyes are on me. Each stranger looks at me with pity. As if they understand my fear.

'Where could she be?' I pant, bending in the middle as

Órlaith reaches me. 'She's not upstairs. I looked everywhere. Where would she go?'

Órlaith can't possibly have answers for my questions, but yet she is calm and I can see on her face that she is formulating a plan. My stomach turns with distress and if there was anything more than a couple of mouthfuls of rice pudding inside it, I think I would be sick.

'Let's call security. They'll look around. And they can check the cameras.'

I nod. I hadn't thought about the security cameras.

'I mean, how far could she get?' Órlaith says, so calmly it's almost soothing. 'She only has little legs.'

I think about how tired Ellie's legs were on the walk to the hospital this morning and I hope she is still much too tired to wander far. Suddenly I am cursing the long nap she took earlier.

Frank, an elderly security guard with a thick grey moustache and round, black-rimmed glasses, jots down a description of Ellie. And Flint, his young colleague who looks like he should definitely still be in school, hurries away to check the security tapes.

Órlaith offers to fetch me tea or coffee from the vending machine but I can't stomach a sip.

'Excuse me,' a voice with a hint of an American twang says behind us.

Órlaith raises her hand as if she's double-jobbing as security. 'Now is not a good time, sir.'

'But—'

'It's patients' quiet time,' she snaps. 'Visiting hours resume at three.'

'Oh, it's not that, it's—'

'Mammy,' Ellie calls out with delight. 'Hello, Mammy.'

I look up and see a smartly dressed man with a warm winter coat and brown hair, with my daughter on his hip.

'That's my mammy,' Ellie tells him.

'See. I told you we'd find her,' he says as he sets Ellie down. She runs to me.

I scoop my little girl into my arms and nuzzle my face into her hair that smells cool like the frosty air outside.

'Oh, Ellie. You scared me. Where did you go?'

'I needed to do a wee-wee,' she says, with a simple shrug.

'Oh.'

'I didn't wet my pants or nothing,' she continues proudly.

I look up at the man, who is still standing next to us, waiting either to be thanked or dismissed or both.

'Where did you find her?' I ask, still shaking.

'The car park.'

I inhale sharply. 'Oh, Ellie, no. What did we say about cars?'

'They're dangerous,' Ellie parrots.

'I don't think she meant to cause any trouble,' Mr stranger with an unusual accent says. Dublin, but with a hint of somewhere in America sticking to some of his words.

'Well, thank you,' I finally say. 'Thank you very much. I'm so grateful you brought her back inside. I was worried sick.'

'Ellie told me you work here, so we knew we'd find you.'

'Oh, did she?'

I cringe, realising my many warnings about not talking to strangers have clearly fallen on deaf ears.

'Don't be too hard on her,' he says, 'I think she got just as much of a fright.'

I wasn't planning to be hard on Ellie. Every second of this mess is my fault. I never should have left a four-year-old alone in a damn broom cupboard all day; but something about this stranger telling me how to parent my daughter rubs me the wrong way.

'Well, as I said, thank you very much for your help, Mr...?'

'Shayne,' Ellie says, introducing him with a gummy smile.

Ellie and Shayne seem better acquainted than I would like.

'Thank you, Shayne,' I try again and I wait for him to acknowledge my gratitude and leave.

'You know, you should really have a word with the crèche. Anything could have happened to Ellie out there.' He throws his thumb over his shoulder, towards the car park.

'Oh, we don't have a crèche on-site,' Órlaith says and I can almost see the cogs in her brain turning. Now that the panic is over, I have no doubt she is wondering what Ellie is doing here in the first place.

'Oh.' He half smiles, befuddled. 'But Ellie said you worked here.'

I want to tell him he already said that, but instead I unzip an uncomfortable smile and say, 'I didn't just leave my child running around a car park while I was working, if that's what you're implying.'

'I wasn't.' He folds his arms. 'But, since you mention it, I did find her alone in the car park. And you were working.'

'Who says I was working? I didn't.'

He's staring at my uniform. Órlaith's eyes are on me too and I will her to keep her mouth shut. Thankfully, it's Ellie who speaks.

'I'm hungry.'

'I'm glad you found your mom,' Shayne tells her, then he turns towards me and adds, 'And it was nice to meet you...'

I know he's waiting for my name but I don't give it. I simply widen my smile and wait for him to walk away. He pulls one side of his long, warm coat over the other, bows his head and walks through the automatic glass doors and into the cold outside.

'What is Ellie doing here?' Órlaith asks, finally twigging that this whole situation isn't right.

'Long story,' I say, on the verge of tears.

'Well, you better get her the hell out of here before Elaine sees her.'

'My shift doesn't end for another couple of hours.'

Órlaith rolls her eyes and exhales heavily. 'You owe me big-time,' she says, glancing at Ellie and then at the reception desk.

'You won't know she's here,' I say. 'She has some colouring. I'll bring it down.'

Órlaith waves her hand and lets me know there's no need for a colouring book. She's got this.

'Come on, honey,' she says, reaching for Ellie's hand. 'Do you like lollipops?'

This time Ellie checks with me if it's all right to take the hand of a stranger. 'Go on,' I encourage. 'It's okay.' And then I mouth a silent *thank you* to Órlaith.

Órlaith winks, takes Ellie's hand in hers and leads her towards the tuck shop before it closes.

TEN

I wait until the end of my shift before I return to the storage closet, collect my cardigan and tidy up. I remove all evidence that Ellie was here before I leave. Downstairs, I find Ellie behind the reception desk. She's perched on a leather chair like a tiny Alice in Wonderland on an oversized throne. She's smiling contently, and I'm relieved that getting lost earlier doesn't seem to have traumatised her like it has me.

'Thank you sooooo much,' I tell Órlaith as I reach the desk.

'No, Mammy,' Ellie says, seeing me. 'I don't want to go home. I busy.'

'Oh, I see. Very, very busy,' I tell her as she swings the large swivel chair from side to side with a kick of her legs. 'But your shift is over, Miss receptionist. It's time to go.'

'More tomorrow?' she asks, and I think her question is directed towards Órlaith and not me.

'More any time you like,' Órlaith says, then she lifts Ellie out of the chair and sets her down. Ellie runs towards me and wraps her arms around my leg.

'Is everything okay?' Órlaith asks, lowering her voice. 'What happened today?'

'Everything is fine. Just the crèche being difficult.'

'Right. Right. I know.'

Órlaith does not know. She's single and still lives with her parents despite being nearly forty.

'I have a dog. A maltipoo,' she goes on. 'And it's such a worry leaving him home all day while I'm in work.'

I don't remind her that her mother is home with her dogs all day. Or that, although dogs and young children sometimes wet the floor or chew toys, that's about where the similarities end.

Ellie covers her mouth with her hand but it doesn't hide her loud tittering. 'She said poo. Did you hear her, Mammy? She said poo.'

'Shh.'

Another thing dogs don't do is mortify you with the things they repeat. Thankfully, Órlaith laughs.

'I'll see you soon, Ellie,' she says, pulling some *Toy Story* stickers off a long roll.

Ellie takes them, delighted, and says, 'Tomorrow.'

Órlaith glances at me and I can tell she knows that things are most definitely not all right.

'C'mon, Ellie. We have to let Órlaith get back to work now.'

'You know, I had a lovely time with Ellie today, Bea,' Órlaith says. 'So, if you ever need help—'

'Oh gosh. Yes. Erm. Thanks.'

'Well,' she finishes up, reading my embarrassment. 'Safe home. Forecast says it's supposed to snow, so hopefully it doesn't play havoc with the traffic.'

'I like snow,' Ellie says, then bursts into the chorus of 'Let It Go' from *Frozen*.

'Shh,' I tell her again, then I wrap her up for the weather, take her hand and walk outside.

Ellie shrieks with delight when she discovers snow has already started to fall and a soft, fluffy blanket covers the ground already. I put on my red wellies, scoop her into my arms and

THE SECRET LIFE OF BEATRICE ALRIGHT

start walking. The snow is crisp and easy to walk on. I charge like a racehorse. It's two buses and Luas across town to the new flat, and I told the landlady I'd meet her at six p.m. She's been texting me frantically since three thirty to make sure I'm still coming.

I'm practising in my head what I'll say to try to negotiate the rent down when a deep voice cuts through my thoughts.

I look over Ellie's shoulder and find Malcolm sitting in the usual spot. Snowflakes land on his head and catch in eyebrows and I find myself once again wishing that he would wear a hat.

'Hello, Bea,' he says, then he points at my wellies and says, 'Much better.'

'Yes. Much better,' I echo.

'Who do we have here?' he asks.

Ellie lifts her head off my shoulder to chirp, 'I'm Ellie. I'm four.'

'My daughter,' I add.

'Hello, Ellie-I'm-Four,' Malcolm says.

Ellie laughs and brushes my hair aside so she can whisper loudly in my ear: 'He's silly.'

'I'm not silly. I'm Malcolm.'

Ellie laughs again. The sound of her innocent chuckles warms me from the inside out and I realise it's been a few days since I heard her giggle. I guess I've been so busy worrying about the apartment and work, I forgot to take the time to make her laugh.

'Ellie,' Malcolm repeats, shaking his head and puffing out warm air that creates a small cloud in front of his face. 'Hmm.'

'Is something wrong?' I ask.

He scrunches his nose.

'No. Not wrong. Just...' He shrugs and today's scarf, a silver and maroon cable knit, bobs on his shoulders. 'Didn't you think to call her Lily or Rose or Daisy?'

'Do you like those names?' I ask, confused.

'No. I don't care for children named after flowers, or cities or colours. But I also don't think parents should call children after insects. But if they do, well then, surely that child would grow up and keep with tradition. Bea and Lily. Or Bea and Rose... you see.'

'Well, it's Bea and Ellie,' I say, sounding irritated but I'm not.

I love Ellie's name. It's the perfect fit for my little girl and no one could ever make me doubt how well we fit together. Ellie is the best part of me. And Declan too, although I try not to think about that now.

I check my watch and say, 'It was nice seeing you again, Malcolm.'

'A busy Bea,' he says with a wink.

'Afraid so.'

'Well, don't let this old man keep you.'

'Tomorrow?' I ask.

'Tomorrow.'

My stomach somersaults as I walk away. I have absolutely no idea how I'll make tomorrow work. I can't send Ellie to crèche for another two days and after today I can't bring her to work again, that's for sure. Despite the cold, a bead of stressed-out perspiration trickles down my spine.

'I need to do a wee-wee,' Ellie says, out of nowhere.

I squeeze my eyes shut and don't bother asking if she can hold it. I find myself secretly missing the days of nappies when I could take her anywhere without regular pitstops. I check my watch again. We'll most definitely miss the bus if we go back inside.

'I'm bursting. I'm bursting,' she insists, dramatically.

We've no choice but to hurry back inside, and into the busy toilets at reception. Ellie is hopping from one foot to the other by the time a stall is free. After, I roll up her sleeves and let her wash her own hands while I take out my phone to text the landlady of the flat.

> Could we meet at 6.30 instead please? So sorry. Got delayed at work.

> Have a viewing at 6.15. First come first served. Unless you want to pay a deposit now to secure?

I don't waste time thinking about it. I need this flat. It doesn't matter if it's like the Ritz or a cattle barn. It's all I can afford.

> Perfect! Thank you.

> Revolut is fine. I'll let the other person know it's gone as soon as I get your deposit.

Ellie is happily making bubbles between her hands with the soap as I open my banking app. I got paid recently but I'm still two euro short of the 500-euro first month's rent. I take a deep breath and send 490 euro and cross my fingers that she's not a stickler over a tenner. I keep the remaining eight euro for bus fare.

I slide my phone into my pocket.

'C'mon, chickpea,' I say, trying to sound cheery and not exhausted and hungry. 'Let's go see our new flat.'

'Yay,' Ellie cheers, having absolutely no idea what she is delighted about.

Outside, we run into Malcolm again, who looks surprised to see us.

'Still here,' he says.

'This little one needed the bathroom,' I say, placing my hand on Ellie's head.

'When you've got to go, you've got to go.' He smiles. 'Trust me. I understand.'

'And now we're very late,' I say.

'You should invest in an alarm clock. It might help you rush less if your time management improved.'

'Children don't pee to the clock, Malcolm,' I tell him.

'Well,' he says, with a firm nod. 'Maybe they should. I always make sure to use the facilities before I leave the house. Serves me well.'

'Do you ever go inside?' I ask, shifting from slight irritation to concern once again for the hours he seems to spend sitting out here in the cold. 'There are bathrooms inside. And a coffee shop. The coffee isn't great, to be honest. But it's warm—' I cut myself off before adding anything about a scone or biscuits, in case money is as tight for him as it is for me.

'I don't drink coffee,' he says. 'Terrible stuff.'

I don't mention tea, feeling it may be redundant. They could sell unicorns and rainbows in the tuck shop and I still doubt Malcolm would set foot through the doors. Instead, I ask, 'Are you waiting for someone out here? Do they give you a lift home?'

'I can walk just fine, thank you very much.'

A strong breeze whips by and ruffles the fine silver hairs splayed across his head and they flap like a flag. Ellie laughs. I tell her to shush. But Malcolm bobs his head, making his hair flap faster. Ellie laughs and laughs, and finally I can't hold it in either. I decide that maybe this is why he doesn't wear a hat – because he doesn't want to hide his dancing hair.

Malcolm tires quickly. And when he is still again, Ellie stops laughing and, very seriously, she tells him, 'We are going to see our new flat now.'

'Oh, how very nice. Does it have a nice big bedroom? With lots of room for all your toys,' he says, kindly, and my heart pangs. Any size room will be just fine, I think.

'I didn't seed it yet,' Ellie tells him.

'Oh, a viewing.' He smiles, understanding. 'Somewhere nearer work?'

It takes me a moment to realise he's shifted his focus from Ellie to me.

'Erm, something like that.'

'Do you want to come?' Ellie chirps.

'Oh, Ellie. I'm sure Malcolm is busy,' I tell her, noting that I really, *really* need to have the stranger danger conversation with her again.

'I'm not busy,' he says.

'Oh.'

Ellie throws her arms above her head. 'Yay.'

I wait for him to tell Ellie he is only joking and wish us on our way, but Malcolm is button-lipped as he looks at me like a lost puppy waiting to be picked up and brought home.

'It's all the way across town,' I say, trying to put him off and then immediately feeling bad because he's clearly lonely – why else would he be out here all by himself every evening?

'We go on the bus,' Ellie says, as if public transport is a big, exciting adventure.

'I like the bus,' Malcolm says.

Ellie's grin widens from ear to ear. 'Me too. And the Luas. I like the Luas lots and lots.'

'I've never been on the Luas,' Malcolm says, and I can't tell if he's serious or not.

I feel tugging on my coat and look at Ellie as she pulls me down so she can whisper in my ear. 'Can old peoples go on the Luas, Mammy?'

I nod, hoping Malcolm didn't hear her.

Ellie pulls her lips away from my ear and announces loudly, 'You're allowed on the Luas, Malco.'

'Malco,' he echoes, as if a child's mispronunciation brings him joy. 'And I can ride for free.'

'Can I go for free?' Ellie asks.

'No.' I swallow, wishing. 'Half price.'

'Half price,' she tells Malcolm, as if I am surplus to this strange conversation about transport fares and eligibility.

'Right, well. We better be going.' My clipped tone slices through the air, icier than the weather, as I give Malcolm another opportunity to bow out.

He stands up, surprisingly sprightly, and bends to fetch something under the bench. He stands up again, exceptionally unsprightly, and I notice two tennis rackets in his hands. With a degree of difficulty, he attaches one to the sole of each of his boots and secures them with what seem to be large rubber bands. He stands once again, and I except Ellie to laugh at his ridiculous appearance, because I'm trying hard not to. But she doesn't. She takes his hands and says, 'Ready?'

'Ready.'

I'm lost for words as my small child holds hands contently with a new friend – a friend with a wispy grey combover blowing in the wind, and two tennis rackets beneath his shoes that leave waffle footprints behind him with every step.

At the Luas stop a group of teenagers snigger at Malcolm's footwear. He straightens his curvy spine as best he can and holds his head high.

'Joke will be on them when they fall,' he tells Ellie.

She agrees, although she's not entirely sure to what.

I fetch return tickets and we hop onboard. A woman about my age gets up and gives Malcolm and Ellie her seat. I stand next to them, dizzy and hungry as I grip the silver pole. We take one bus and then another and every so often someone titters at Malcolm's footwear. He is wholly unfazed. And, slowly, I find myself admiring his tenacity that keeps him so sturdy on his feet in the snow.

'We're here,' I announce as we reach the address of the new flat at six twenty-nine p.m.

'Nice. Very nice,' Malcolm says, looking up and down the

road, which is lined with a mix of terrace yellow brick houses, Weetabix-like apartments and tall, leafless trees that I imagine in summer are green and vibrant and beautiful.

Bubbles of excitement fizz inside me as I imagine Ellie and me living on this inviting road. I double-check the address on my phone, and press the buzzer for number seventeen.

It takes a moment, but soon there is a crackle and a deep voice says, 'Hello.'

Surprised to hear a man's voice, I clear my throat before I reply. 'Hello. I'm looking for—' I cut myself off, realising that I don't actually know who I'm looking for. I saved the landlady's number in my phone as Ms New Flat and, in my desperation to secure a viewing, I forgot to get her name. I try again. 'Hi. I'm Bea Alright. I'm here about the flatshare.'

'That flatshare?'

'Erm yes. The room. The lady on the phone said to come at six thirty.'

'Love, I think you have the wrong flat. There's no room for rent here.'

'Oh. Gosh. Sorry.'

'No problem. Bye now.'

There's a crackle and a sound like hanging up and then the voice is gone.

My face stings as Ellie and Malcolm stare at me. 'I could have sworn...' I check my messages again and then I cross-reference the building name and number. 'Number seventeen, Yellow Oak Block,' I mumble.

'This is Yellow Oak Block,' Malcolm confirms, pointing to the plaque clearly displayed on the wall. 'Maybe you pressed the wrong button.'

I perk up. 'Maybe.'

'I don't know why they can't label things like this correctly,' he says, pointing to the small square of flat buzzers stacked on the wall like piano keys.

I try buzzer after buzzer and the answer is always the same. *Wrong flat.* Finally, I try the first buzzer again. The man who answers is less patient this time. At last, he says, 'Look, love, the only ones here are my partner and my dog. We have no interest in renting out a room to anyone. Sounds to me like someone is having you on.'

'I paid a deposit,' I say, desperately.

'Well, then, I'd say someone has scammed you because this is *my* flat and it is not for rent.'

My intake of breath is sharp and almost painful.

'Go home, love.'

The buzzer goes dead once more and I know not to ring it again. I call the landlady's number and the automated *'this number is not in service'* reply almost doubles me over. I think of my near-empty bank account as I look around the street. I would so happily pay every penny I have for Ellie and me to live here. I think about crèche and work tomorrow. I think about Declan and the lease on the apartment where I was once so happy. I think about my empty stomach that rumbles. Finally, I look at my little girl and think about how I am possibly going to keep her safe with no money and no roof over our heads.

The inside of my head is so noisy and busy, I have to hold it with my hands because it feels as if traffic might burst through my skull at any second. I don't know how long I've been standing on the footpath with my head in my hands before I feel Malcolm's hand press firmly on my shoulder.

'The little one needs feeding.'

I lower my hands and glance at Ellie. There are tears in her eyes and she's staring back at me with the concerned expression of an adult.

'I'm hungry,' she mumbles, and I wonder how many times she has told me this information and I was too lost in blind panic to see or hear her. Suddenly, I am wildly grateful that Malcolm is here, holding her hand. Keeping her safe, when I seem to have lost the ability to. My movements are slow and convalescent-like. I wrangle with my brain to speak. To say something reassuring for Ellie's sake.

The words *let's go home* circle my head like a hamster on a wheel. But when I try to open my mouth nothing but a throaty gasp comes out. Home? Soon that word won't exist for us. And the fear is crippling me. Finally, my eyes focus and fall on Malcolm's back as he leads Ellie away. They're moving at a snail's pace, and I could easily catch them with a couple of fast strides. But nonetheless, a wave of protectiveness surges inside me and kick-starts me.

'Hey,' I call out. 'What are you doing?'

Malcolm continues to walk as Ellie looks over her shoulder and smiles.

I hurry after them, taking Ellie's hand in seconds.

'Eh, what the hell do you think you're doing?' I say, jutting my head to scowl at Malcolm. 'You can't just walk off with her like that. Are you mad?'

He shrugs. 'We're hungry.'

'So hungry,' Ellie says, slipping her hand out of my grasp to rub her belly.

'Yes. Me too,' I say, taking her hand back quickly. 'But, Ellie. You know you can't just walk off with strangers like that. What have we talked about?'

Ellie's brows pinch and her nose scrunches. 'But this is Malco.'

'Malcolm,' I correct. Her mispronunciation is much less adorable now than earlier. 'And I know his name, chickpea. But it doesn't mean we really know him. Do you underst—'

'Sit!' Malcolm cuts me off and points to a street bench not dissimilar to the one at the hospital. All it's missing is an overhanging oak tree.

'Excuse me?'

'Sit,' he repeats as if I was asking what he said and not why the hell he said it.

'I really don't think—'

'She's hungry.' He smiles at Ellie.

'So hungry,' she says, exaggerating.

'So are you and so am I,' he goes on. 'This is as good a spot as any for a bite.'

Ellie climbs onto the bench, with an effort that mirrors scaling Everest. Ankle first, then knee, then belly, followed by her other ankle, other knee, more belly. She pushes up on her hands like a gym bunny about to break into fifty push-ups, and finally she pulls herself into a sitting position, swinging her legs back and forth with satisfaction. When I turn away to look at Malcolm I spot his hunched frame shuffling into the brightly lit Spar behind us. I puff out, knowing we need to wait for him, and sit beside Ellie. I launch into a lecture about stranger danger.

'But he's Malco,' Ellie reiterates, as if she's known Malcolm for an even greater time than her four years on this planet. She reinforces her point by gesturing, stretching her small hands, still chubby at the wrist with baby fat, out by her sides, and bobbing them up and down as if she's pleading with me to just accept their close bond. I close my eyes for a fleeting moment and wish that life was really as simple as my small child thinks it is. My eyes shoot open again when I feel the bench bounce as Ellie hops down. She runs up to Malcolm as he is returning through the shop door with a plastic bag dangling from his hand. Ellie takes his other hand and they walk very slowly towards me. I scoot down and make room for another bum on the bench. I put my hands on Ellie's waist and hoist her up, tucking her in beside my hip. Malcolm lowers himself wearily beside her. Then he opens the plastic bag and rummages, head deep, around inside. He pulls out a roll, wrapped in paper and with steam dancing in the dark evening air. He leans forward and passes it to me.

'I hope you like chicken. It's all they had left.'

'I like chicken,' I say, my voice catching and coming out husky. It's a combination of the chilly December air and a wave of gratitude. He also passes me a Diet Coke before diving his head back into the bag to pick out the same for Ellie.

'Coke,' she shrieks with delight, taking the can, then remembers she's not allowed fizzy anything from a can and shoots me a pleading gaze.

'Just this once.' I wink. I am in no way ready to spoil her fun with the usual rules about sugar and teeth.

Lastly, Malcolm pulls out a steaming roll for himself and a can of Coke and we sit, without a word between us as we savage our makeshift dinner. Ellie fills up a few bites before the end of her roll and, although I'm stuffed, I finish it off for her, not sure when I'll eat something quite so delicious again.

After, Malcolm folds the bag with extreme precision and manages to make an exact square from its plastic form. He shifts on the bench, making it creak beneath us all, to slide it into his pocket.

'Had to pay a euro for this thing,' he grumbles, with a roll of his eyes. 'A euro. They must think people are made of money.'

I'm about to launch into a rant about the cost-of-living crisis and how out of touch the government are when a car pulls up beside us so suddenly the brakes screech and make us all jump. Malcolm clutches his chest and I find myself quietly checking that he's all right. The window of the car rolls down, and before anyone else has time to utter a word Ellie shouts, 'Shayne!'

I squint and look into the car. I can't quite believe my eyes when I see the guy from the hospital reception sitting behind the wheel. He's less dapper now, and looks almost frazzled. Instinctively, I pull Ellie close to me and grit my teeth as I ask, 'Are you following us?'

'What?' I can hear his offence. 'That's a weird question.'

'Is it?'

'Yes!' He takes his hands off the wheel to fold his arms.

'Ouch, Mammy. You're squashing me,' Ellie says, and I realise I'm holding her too tightly. I loosen my grip but I don't let go fully.

'I think it's a completely reasonable question actually,' I go on, my heart beating quickly. 'You had my daughter earlier. And now, here you are again.'

He turns off his engine, and I brace myself in case he gets out of the car.

'I think you mean: I found your daughter earlier and returned her after *you* lost her. Which you didn't seem all that bothered about, actually.'

'Of course I was bothered,' I snap. 'And I said thank you, didn't I?'

'You didn't say it like you meant it.'

'Well, I meant it. Thank you. Now, can you please answer my question. Why are you following us?' My words are clipped and confident but inside I am trembling. If this Shayne guy turns out to be a psychopathic serial killer, I'm not sure I could save a child and an old man at the same time.

Shayne leans forward to stare past me at the bench. 'Hello, Grandad,' he says.

Malcolm huffs. 'Spying on me again, are you?'

'It's not spying.' Shayne rolls his eyes. 'It's just a tracker on your phone so I know where to find you.'

'Techy nonsense.' Malcolm waves his hand dismissively.

'Well, building apps is my job.'

'Damn phones,' Malcolm goes on, patting his pocket, where I guess he keeps his phone.

'I wouldn't be able to find you without it. And when you're not where you're supposed to be when I come to pick you up, I'm very glad you have it.'

So, Shayne picks Malcolm up every day at the hospital, I decide, joining the dots in my head. I'm glad he has someone come to fetch him. But it still doesn't explain why he's going there every day.

'Your grandfather,' I say, staring at Shayne as I look for a resemblance.

'Yes. Hi. I'm Shayne Fairbanks,' Shayne says, opening the door of the car to step out.

I'm no longer nervous, but I am embarrassed. I wish I hadn't been so noticeably on guard just now. I notice Shayne and Malcolm's eyes are similar, and their chins. Shayne certainly has more hair; a floppy mop of brown curls bobs on his head, ruffled by the wind.

'You two know each other?' Malcolm says, drawing an invisible line in the air to join Shayne to me.

'Not exactly,' Shayne says. 'We met briefly. At the hospital. I was looking for you actually. You weren't answering your phone and I was worried.'

He slides his phone out of his coat pocket and turns his screen towards Malcolm to share that he has made seventeen attempts to call his grandfather today, all of which have gone unanswered.

'That thing,' Malcolm grunts, scrunching his face to read the screen. 'Can't get a minute's peace any more. Everyone going around with mobile phones in their pockets. In my day a man could go for a walk to clear his head and no one pestered him until he came home.'

'You've been gone since lunchtime,' Shayne says. 'And you forgot your hat.'

He pulls a colourful hat from his other pocket. It's a perfect hand-knitted match for Malcolm's scarf and I find myself wondering if Shayne has a loving grandmother at home who is wonderful with a pair of knitting needles.

Malcolm shakes his head.

'But it's cold, Grandad...' Shayne trails off and I pick up a sense of something between them. An unresolved argument or something.

'It really is very cold,' I tell Malcolm.

'Gosh, really, and here I was hoping to do some sunbathing this evening.' Malcolm chuckles, amusing himself much more than either Shayne or me.

'Okay, suit yourself, but will you at least get in the car? I have the heated seat on, so you should warm up soon.'

'Who says I'm cold?' Malcolm says.

'I'm cold,' Ellie joins in, her teeth chattering like a prop in a play.

'I'm getting the Luas and the bus,' Malcolm goes on.

I shove my hand into my pocket and feel around for the loose coins that I know will be enough for a Luas or a bus. But not both. Ellie and I have a long walk ahead and if Malcolm joins us, at his pace it will take hours.

Shayne sighs. 'I'm here now. The car is warm. Please, Grandad, can we just go? I will give your friend and her daughter a lift to anywhere they want to go. How does that sound?'

'That's the problem with you young people. Always so busy. Busy Bea is just as bad. So busy buzzing from one place to the next, she doesn't even take the time to check we're in the right place in the first place.'

Shayne seems confused and looks at me as if he is expecting me to explain. I bend and scoop Ellie into my arms. All the feelings of worry and distress bubble to the surface again, and if I'm going to start crying again I would really rather it wasn't in front of these people.

'Get in the car, Malcolm,' I say. 'Take the damn lift.'

'I will, if you will,' he says.

I breathe in until I am light-headed. After what he just said about the whole flat hell scam, I can barely look at him. But

Ellie is flagging and she really should be in bed in an hour, not dragging her little feet across Dublin. I swallow my pride and say, 'If you're still offering, a lift would be great, Shayne. Thank you.'

'Of course. But I don't have a car seat, I'm afraid. Will she be ok?' he asks, glancing at Ellie who is tugging on my arm and complaining about being tired and cold.

'Erm... it's just a short ride. She'll be fine,' I say, crossing my fingers behind my back as I add another parenting faux pas to my ever-growing list.

'Can I get your name? If I'm going to be your Uber, that is. I mean, I doubt Busy Bee is your official title, and you didn't share your name at the hospital, so I'm guessing it's something terrible like Prudence or Gertrude or something even worse.'

'Gertrude is my mother's name,' I say, and wait for him to squirm.

'Mine too,' he says, calling my bluff.

I let the joke hang in the air just long enough to make him uncomfortable before I say, 'Bea. My name is Bea.'

His face lights up and he says, 'Now, *that* really is a lovely name. It reminds me of summer.'

ELEVEN

We reach the apartment faster than I expect. Travelling by car instead of two buses and a Luas cuts travel time by more than half. Regardless, both Malcolm and Ellie are sound asleep. Ellie's head is flopped on my shoulder and she is drooling. And Malcolm's head is flopped back against the head rest and he is drooling.

'The circle of life,' Shayne jokes as he finds a parking spot almost directly outside the main doors to the apartment block.

I thank him sincerely, unhook my seat belt and get out. By the time I walk round the back of the car to fetch Ellie, Shayne is at her door, opening it for me. He shoves his hands into his pockets and shuffles his feet awkwardly. I have a horrible feeling that he is going to say something I don't want to hear. Like ask me for money for fuel. Or even worse, ask me on a date. I bend into the car and take my time getting Ellie out, giving him time to work up the courage to spit whatever it is out. When he doesn't say anything, I finally say, 'Well, good night. And thank you again for the lift. I really do appreciate it.'

'And I appreciate you taking care of him,' he blurts.

I know he's talking about Malcolm. But he's also talking

about Malcolm in the same way I talk about Ellie. He's thanking me the way I thanked Órlaith earlier for watching Ellie.

'I'm not so sure who was taking care of who tonight,' I say, honestly, thinking of the yummy sandwiches Malcolm bought. Or how he took Ellie's hand and reassured her when my brain turned to mush over the flat scam. That reminds me, I really need to text that landlady and demand my money back. It wouldn't get me a flat, but at least I'll have a deposit to start looking again. ...

'Look, I don't know what he told you about why he was at the hospital—'

'He didn't tell me anything,' I say, quickly, picking up on the same undertone that was present between Malcolm and Shayne earlier when I thought they were arguing.

'Oh. Erm. Okay.'

I can tell he's instantly sorry he brought it up and I try to deflect. 'It's none of my business. Honestly.'

Shayne runs a hand through his hair and it must get caught in some curly knots at the back, because he makes a face before pulling his hand down.

'It's just. It's complicated,' he says.

Ellie stirs on my shoulder and I'm glad of the excuse to leave. 'I better get her to bed,' I say.

'Yeah. Of course.' He seems disappointed. 'It was really nice meeting you, Bea.'

'Yeah. You too. Take care of him, won't you,' I say with a sting of sadness as I glance into the car at a sleeping Malcolm. His mouth is gaping and his breathing sucks his bottom lip in and puffs it back out with a quiver. I suspect I won't be seeing him on the hospital bench any more, now that Shayne has found him, and I find myself oddly discontented. As if I resent Shayne for taking Malcolm away. I know it's a ridiculous feeling. Especially when just hours ago I was lecturing Ellie about talking to strangers. But something about this old man feels familiar. Maybe he just stirs a familiar feeling in me. The feeling of wishing for a family. Wishing for parents and grandparents. Wishing for a circle of people around me, who would be there for me at the best of times and the worst of times. Wonderful times like Ellie's birth, or her first steps. As cherished as those memories are, they are tinged with sadness because they are my memories only. I was, as ever, alone for the majority of Ellie's milestones. Declan was in the air for her birth – somewhere over Ohio, he would later explain. And her first birthday. He was in LA. He was there when she cut her first tooth, but it was a coincidence. He was on a layover between flights. I guess now he was on a layover from his wife. From his family. I'm not foolish enough to think that having loving parents, or even a somewhat cantankerous grandfather, would make Declan's betrayal any easier. I still really, really wish I had family around me. People to love me, and hug me, and tell me it will be all right even if they are only lying and saying it simply because it's what I need to hear.

I'm a terrible judge of ages. When I was in junior cycle in secondary school, I used to think my English teacher was at least sixty. She wore cardigans and runners in the late noughties, while everyone else was layering tops and struggling to walk in chunky high heels. A few years after I finished school she got married and had a load of kids, so she must have been half as old as I thought. Still, I take a stab at guessing Shayne's age. He has fine lines around his sea-grey eyes, but nothing deep. And although there is the odd fleck of grey hidden in his hair, his scraggy beard is grey-free. I assume he's about my age. Certainly, no older than his mid-thirties. Thirty-four, I decide. As my imagination places a solid age stamp on him, my gut aches and I realise I'm jealous. Shayne Fairbanks is thirty-four years old and he still has his grandfather in his life. I haven't even had parents since I was eleven. Grumpy or not, Shayne doesn't know how lucky he is to have Malcolm.

'You take care of him,' I find myself saying again, with a wagging finger pointed towards the car.

'I try to.'

My finger stills and I lower my hand. *Try harder*, I want to say, thinking of the snowflakes that stick to Malcolm's bare head in the cold. Instead, I say, 'Get him to wear a hat.'

'I can't. I knitted this for him.' Shayne pulls the colourful woolly hat from his pocket again to show me.

'You knitted it?'

'You sound surprised,' he says.

And he sounds offended.

Nonetheless, I am honest. 'I am. You don't seem like a knitter.'

'Don't I?' He taps his chest. 'Why not?'

I don't tell him that I invented an imaginary wife for Malcolm who lovingly knitted his scarf and hat while sitting by an open fire in their lovely home. I don't tell him because I know it's not normal to create imaginary families for people. But it's a bad habit. When I see people sitting alone on the bus, or in the hospital waiting room, or even ordering a coffee, I like to create friends and family for them. Just as I used to create a family for me in my mind. I'm very good at it. Straight after my parents' crash I invented a little sister. She looked just like my mam, because I looked just like my dad. Our neighbour, whose name I can't remember but I know she had a lot of cats, came to tell me that my parents were gone. She said people would come and get me soon and I would have a new family. I spent my first night in foster care that night. Three days later I went to my parents' funeral. I was terrified. But at least I wasn't alone. I brought my imaginary sister with me. I bounced around several foster homes after that, keeping little sis with me always. Right up until my eighteenth birthday, when the state was no longer paying for me and the family I had been with for three years let me go. I got a job in retail, started medical school and shared a flat with Cora and some of the other girls from college. College life was wild. I balanced hours on the wards with a stupid amount of study. Any hours that were left over, I was working to make rent. I rarely slept and survived on a diet of black coffee and rich tea biscuits and, although I was tired, I was never exhausted. And still, through it all, I kept my imaginary sister. She wasn't as present as during those years in foster care, but she was there. Like a security blanket in the back of my mind. But I realise now that I haven't thought about her in a long time. Not since the day I found out I was pregnant with Ellie. Not since the day I was going to have a family again.

'You okay?' I hear Shayne ask, and I wonder how long I've been zoned out.

'Scarf,' I blurt.

'Sorry?'

Ellie grows heavy in my arms and I readjust my grip. My back cracks, and I exhale, feeling more comfortable now.

'Did you knit the scarf too? All the scarves? They've very nice.'

Shayne unzips a smile. 'No. Grandad knits those himself.'

'You're joking.'

'Nope. Grandad taught me to knit when I was a kid. I wasn't sporty like all the other boys in my school.'

'So, he thought he'd toughen you up with knitting skills,' I tease.

'Something like that. Yeah.'

'Well, I think it's brilliant.'

'You do?'

'Sure. The world needs more male knitters.'

'Erm. Sure,' he says.

'I'm joking.' I smile. 'It doesn't really matter if you're male or female when it comes to knitting, does it? Although, I don't knit, so maybe...'

He laughs, and I'm glad.

'No. It really doesn't matter. And, erm, could we keep this knitting thing between us?'

'Sure.' I nod.

Although I know as soon as I go inside I am going to call Cora and tell her about my horrible day. The day I hid my daughter in a cupboard. Lost her. Got scammed out of my last penny. Ate a particularly delicious sandwich with an old man on a roadside bench, and finally got chauffeured across the city by a male knitter. We'll laugh for a while. And then I'll probably cry. Actually, I will definitely cry. I decide I need to stop thinking about it right now, because I'm already starting to feel tears swell.

'Well, you take care of that grandfather of yours, won't you?'

'You said that already,' he reminds me.

'I did?'

'You did. Twice. And I will. I promise. I'll stick a hat to his head, if I have to.'

I laugh. It's a genuine hearty giggle and it's the first time since Declan walked out that anything has made me feel light enough, even for a moment, to giggle.

It starts to snow again, heavier than before, and Shayne looks at Ellie sleeping on my shoulder.

'You gotta get her inside.'

'I do,' I say, but suddenly I don't want to go.

I want to hear more about his knitting and what type of glue he might use to secure a woollen hat to a bare head.

'Goodbye, Bea.'

'Bye, Shayne. Maybe I'll see you around,' I say, although I doubt it.

He smiles in a way that says he doubts it too. I watch as he walks back to the car, starts the engine and drives off, taking care as the roads grow slippery under falling snow.

'Goodbye, Malcolm,' I whisper, then I pull Ellie close to me and hold her so tightly she wriggles in her sleep.

I am more grateful than ever for the perfect little girl in my arms. I can cope with anything as long as I have my Ellie, I tell myself. Then I go inside, put her to bed and change out of my uniform into my favourite fluffy pyjamas with a cute tiger on the front of the top and a matching tiger print on the bottoms. Then I remember that Declan bought me these pyjamas for my birthday a couple of months ago, and I think about taking them off. But I'm too comfortable and too tired. I settle for calling him all sorts of names under my breath and plodding in my bare feet into the kitchen. I fetch a wine glass, open the fridge and pour Pinot Grigio from the bottle that has been open for more than a week. It's bitter, and doesn't even taste like wine any more, but even so I take the glass to the couch, curl up with a blanket and take out my phone to call Cora.

As usual I am distracted by a barrage of notifications from the crèche app. I exhale wearily and click into each one. Something about an outbreak of head lice and advising on the best, no doubt very expensive, shampoo to use to get rid of them. There's something long and rambling about lost hats and gloves. And, finally, there is a reminder that tomorrow is Christmas jumper day. The children should wear their brightest and favourite jumper, apparently.

We are kindly asking for a donation of €5 from each child, which will be passed on to charity. Happy Christmas.

The message is signed off by Alannah and her name is followed by *xoxo* as if she's the star of *Gossip Girl*.

I breathe a sigh of relief that there is actually a bright side to being unable to send Ellie to crèche tomorrow: I don't have to worry about Christmas jumper day for another year. The round neck of my pyjamas suddenly feels tight and I tug it away from my neck. I can't imagine what next week will look like without a new flat lined up. It's beyond impossible to imagine how Ellie's and my life will look this time next year. I have to imagine it will be better. I have to.

I'm barely a half glass in when the wine hits and in a fit of temper I message the scamming landlady.

> I want my money back!!!

I wait a moment, and when there is no reply I knock back the remainder of my glass of wine and type again.

> I know you scammed me. I want my money back!!!!

I add an extra exclamation mark for firm effect.

> Hello????
>
> Answer me????
>
> You stole my money!!!
>
> I'm going to the police!!!

It takes my winey brain several messages to realise that there is only a single grey tick appearing after the message sends.

'She blocked me,' I say with a gasp, as if anyone can hear me. 'She bloody blocked me. Of course she did.'

Feeling smaller and stupider than ever, I call Cora. The phone rings for a few seconds before she picks up.

'Hello,' she says, sounding slightly out of breath.

'Hey.'

'Hi.'

'Can you talk?' I ask.

There's some giggling and I think Cora is covering the phone with her hand as she says something incoherent to someone in the background.

'Hey. Hey. Yeah. Sorry. You okay?'

'I—'

There's more giggling and Cora playfully says, 'Stop it. stop it. It's Bea. I gotta take this.'

I hear a grumble of frustration, at which Cora covers the phone again, but I can still hear her promise she'll be quick.

'If it's a bad time—'

'No, no, it's fine.'

She's definitely out of breath and it sounds like she's been running. Cora does not run. Even brisk walking bothers her. I cringe when I realise that I'm disturbing her and Finton having sex. I am beyond glad I didn't video call her.

'I can go,' I say quickly. 'Sorry. Forget I called.'

'Bea. Stop. It's fine. Finton is going out now anyway. I can talk. You sound off. What's wrong?'

I know Finton is not going out. I can only imagine him sitting beside Cora on the couch or in bed or splayed across the kitchen table, rolling his eyes and cursing me. But I know that, even if I hang up now, Cora will call me back. And so, I let it all out. There are times where I am crying so hard I'm an incoherent mess and yet Cora seems to hear and understand everything.

'Right. That's it,' she says. 'We're going to the guards about this scamming bitch.'

I agree, although since I don't actually know her name, where she lives or even if she really is a she, I doubt there is much they can do.

'And you and Ellie are coming to stay here.'

I don't have time to thank her before she's jumping in to reassure me, as if I might decline the offer. She could suggest Ellie and I sleep in the shed at the base of the garden and I wouldn't decline.

'It'll be just like when we were in college again. God, those days were the best, weren't they?'

My mind floods with memories. Five students crammed into a two-bedroomed apartment overlooking the canal, within walking distance of Trinity College. Dishes stacked in the sink. Empty vodka bottles lined up next to the bin, waiting until they took over almost the entire floor space before someone caved and took them to the recycling bank. Hair straighteners left next to random sockets. Half-eaten takeaways littering the coffee table. Make-up stains on the carpet that we covered up with a rug. Five girls who I thought were the family I had long hoped for. But, over the years in college, I slowly remembered what I knew all along. *People leave.* First it was Jessica. She didn't pass her second-year exams and she moved home to Galway to work on her parents' farm. We all texted for a while, but she reconnected with her school friends and things fizzled. Lorna was next to go. She met a guy studying bio-something-or-other and they took a year out to travel Australia. I saw her back on campus the following year. She had several new piercings, a smattering of tattoos and a new-found love of pottery. She transferred into a different degree and we lost touch. Andi left soon after that. She never actually gave us a reason. She simply stopped coming to lectures. One day, Cora and I came home to find her stuff gone and key left on the table. We tried texting and calling but she never replied or picked up. There was a rumour that she had an affair with one of our married professors. I remember hoping it wasn't true, because what kind of self-respecting girl would do that? I think of Andi now, more than I ever have before. I guess because we're more similar than we ever were before. I wonder what she is doing now. I wonder if she is okay? *God, I hope so.* For both our sakes.

I cry harder than ever as I remember a time my life was better than it ever had been before. I was a somebody. I had great friends. I was on the path to a wonderful career and stability for the first time since I was eleven years old. And then along came Declan. Declan with his beautiful face and sexy uniform. Declan with his charm and charisma. I was never looking for a fast pass to the perfect life. But then came Ellie with *her* beautiful face and Declan's eyes and it felt as if the perfect life just sort of landed in my path. A voice inside my head taps at my brain like a tiny woodpecker. This is all your fault, you know. *Tap, tap, tap.* You let this happen. *Tap, tap, tap.* You left college to look after Ellie. You let Declan pay the rent and the bills because you took the first job you could get and you couldn't match his big salary. You believed him when he said he wished he could be home more but his work made him so busy. You are the problem, Bea. *You.* Ellie deserves so much better.

I don't say goodbye to Cora. The wine and exhaustion finally get the better of me and I fall asleep on the couch with the phone mashed against my face.

TWELVE

My head bangs and for a moment I blame the wine, before I realise the noise is outside my brain and coming from my front door.

'Bea! It's Cora. You there?'

I rub my eyes and sit up. The knocking on the door has stopped but my head is still banging.

'Bea!'

'I'm here. I'm here,' I say in a throaty gargle.

'Let me in. It's freezing out here. Don't they ever turn on the heat in this bloody place?'

The door to Ellie's bedroom is ajar and I can make out her small body curled up and sleeping under the duvet. I check my watch. It's barely seven a.m. and still dark outside, as streetlamps shine through the curtains and bathe the living area in an orange hue. Despite the warm glow, the apartment is freezing. My morning breath dances in the air in front of me and I grab a blanket from the couch and drape it over my shoulders like a cape.

'Bea!' Cora calls again, loudly.

'Sorry. Sorry. Coming.'

I swing open the door and find Cora holding three takeaway cups tucked in a paper tray and a brown paper bag in her other hand. I'm stepping aside to let her in when the door across the hall opens and the sound of dogs barking fills the corridor. Cora jumps, but thankfully no coffee spills.

'Good morning,' Mrs Johnson says, struggling to keep hold of her boisterous dogs' leashes. The dogs yap and try to get close to Cora. Her expression is hilarious, sitting somewhere between *I'm a cat person* and *I haven't had any coffee yet.*

'Desperately cold, isn't it?' Mrs Johnson says, as she locks her door.

'Very,' I say, sounding as if I am shocked by chilly conditions in December.

'Is the heating broken out here?'

'Not sure,' I say.

'It's freezing,' Cora reiterates.

'Must be broken again,' Mrs Johnson says. 'We had awful trouble with it a few years back too. Before you moved in. Declan was living with that blond girl at the time. Do you know her? Pretty, slim girl. I wasn't sure if she was his daughter or his girlfriend,' she adds, and I think she's actually asking me if I know Declan's ex.

'Ellie is Declan's only daughter,' I say, my voice cracking. A week ago, I would have said Ellie was his only child.

'Right. Right. Lovely girl.'

'Yes. You said.'

Her dogs bark again, playfighting with each other, and Cora pushes closer to me.

'Anyway, could you ask Declan to call the landlord? He got the heating sorted out last time so quickly, it's probably best if he takes care of it again.'

I nod. 'Sure.'

Cora looks at me wide-eyed and I stare back. I'm confident she won't say anything but my stomach still flips.

'Great. Thank you,' she says, growing distracted as she tries to pull her dogs apart. They bark and bark and I can't wait to close the door.

'See you later,' I say.

Finally, Cora steps inside and I close the door behind us with a sigh. I can still hear the dogs, the whole way down the corridor.

'She doesn't know?' Cora says, placing the cups and bag on the kitchen countertop just inside the door.

'No. I didn't get a chance to go across the hall, knock on her door and say, *Hey, guess what? Turns out Declan is already married. And I'm just his bit on the side. Who knew.*'

'Oh, Bea, I'm sorry,' she says, taking the cups out of the tray with care not to slosh coffee through the small hole in the lid. 'I didn't mean... I just meant, I'm sure it's hard.'

The hardest part is that I don't actually have anyone to tell. Aside from Cora, the only other confidant in my life was Declan.

'It's fine. I'm sure she'll figure it out when the apartment is empty soon,' I say.

'Yeah. I guess she will.'

There's a moment where we both look around the apartment. Cora has joked more than once that I'm the posh friend. Declan's and my apartment is more than twice the size of Cora and Finton's. It's in a quiet residential area overlooking the Phoenix Park, but still within walking distance of the city. Cora and Finton are in the suburbs and regularly get caught in morning traffic on their way to work. Declan and I enjoyed date nights in exclusive restaurants, while Cora and Finton favour takeaway and Netflix while they save for a bigger place.

'I'll miss it here,' I say at last.

Cora looks at me with heartbreak-heavy eyes. She knows I'm not talking about the four walls, or the great location. I will miss the life I was supposed to have. The life I so desperately wanted to give my daughter.

Ellie appears at her bedroom door and her crazy bed hair makes Cora laugh immediately.

'Someone had a good sleep,' she says, hurrying over to scoop Ellie into her arms.

Ellie squeals with delight, surprised to see Cora. She drops her head onto her shoulder and they share a cuddle.

'I brought you some brekkie,' Cora says. 'How does hot chocolate and a cookie sound?'

'How does sugar and more sugar sound?' I say.

Cora looks concerned for a moment before she realises I'm teasing. 'Eh, you can't talk. I thought you were going to turn into a pop tart when we were in college. It was literally all you ate for three years.'

'The strawberry ones are still my favourite.'

'Mine too.'

Cora places Ellie on a stool at the breakfast bar and passes her one of the cups and a cookie.

'Be careful, it might be hot,' I jump in.

Cora jams her hands on her hips. 'Well, she needs something to heat her up. Is the heating broken in here too? It's Baltic.'

'I haven't turned it on in a while,' I say. 'Declan usually takes care of the bills and since, well...'

I trail off, not quite sure what point I'm trying to make, but Cora continues to look at me as if she's looking for an explanation as to why Ellie and I have practically been living in a freezer since Declan left.

'I know he'll pay the bill when it comes in. But it's killing me that I need him to, you know?

'But it's December. It's bloody freezing,' she says.

'I know!' It's my turn to jam my hands on my hips. 'But I don't want his damn money, okay. I can look after myself. I hate that I ever let him pay for anything. I hate that I can't afford this place on my own. That I have to move because without him I have bloody nothing. I hate that I let myself get into this position.'

Ellie looks up at me with a mouthful of cookie and round eyes that look as if they might start to cry at any moment.

'Mammy?'

I pull her close to me and kiss the top of her head. 'I'm sorry, chickpea. I didn't mean to shout. I'm just tired.'

Her little body stiffens and she doesn't seem convinced.

'You finish your cookie, okay? Everything is okay.'

When I pull away from her Cora passes me the coffee and croissant that's been waiting on the countertop. She smiles with a look that tells me she naively believes everything will be okay.

'I love that coffee shop downstairs,' she says, as casually as if we've just been talking about the weather or fashion and not my life completely falling apart.

She runs her finger along the café logo on the paper bag. 'Such a nice little place. And it opens at six. How brilliant is that? Nowhere opens before work. I mean, shift workers are people too. Right? We need morning coffee too. Right? God, if I lived here, I would be in there every day.' She takes a mouthful of her coffee. 'Mmm. Heaven.'

I've only been in the café below the apartment block a handful of times, with Declan and Ellie. The coffee is expensive and the cookies are outright extortion. Ellie knows it's somewhere we go when her daddy is home, but not somewhere we go on our own. I wonder if some day, when she's all grown up, she'll look back and realise why.

I sip on the coffee. Cora is right, it is incredibly good.

'Everything will be all right, you know,' Cora says, after a few minutes of everyone being lost in their own thoughts.

'Yeah.' I say, but I know I'm not convincing her and I'm certainly not fooling myself.

'I've taken the day off.'

I make a face. 'You didn't have to do that.'

She shrugs casually. 'Swapped shifts. It's no big deal, one of the girls owed me a favour anyway. We're going to get you packed up and ready to go. You'll feel better when you've made a fresh start.'

'I'm not sure your couch counts as a fresh start?'

Cora sets her coffee down, folds her arms and looks at me like a school principal about to give a troubled but brilliant pupil a stern talking-to. 'You're leaving this apartment behind you and you are starting over. It's as fresh as it gets. And it's my couch now, but that's just a start. You've got this, Bea. I know you do.'

The coffee swirls in my otherwise empty stomach. Maybe Cora is right. I just need to sleep on her couch until my next payday. Then I should have enough to start looking for a flat-share again. I just have to make it through Christmas.

'Right,' she says, with a commanding clap of her hands that makes Ellie jump. 'Where are your black sacks? Let's get packing.'

I don't have black sacks but there are some Tesco plastic bags under the sink. Cora turns on her Spotify and Ellie requests Taylor Swift on full volume. Then, before the sun is up, we dance around my apartment as if we haven't a care in the world.

'My poor neighbours,' I shout. Certain that, although 'Bad Blood' is one of my favourite songs, no one wants to wake up to it blaring through their ceiling.

'Give them something to remember you by.' Cora laughs, twerking and encouraging Ellie to copy her.

I hope when Ellie is older she forgets the coffee shop downstairs and, instead, remembers this moment. The day we danced our cares away.

THIRTEEN

The snow is relentless. The guy on the radio said it's the coldest December in fifty years and it's all anyone at work can talk about.

'There's inches out there,' Mrs Morgan on St Paul's ward says as she stands by the window overlooking the car park.

The heating is blasting in the hospital, but she's wrapped in a fleece dressing gown and fluffy, boot-like slippers as if just looking outside chills her to the bone.

'You should say there's centipedes out there,' Mrs Brennan croaks from her bed across the ward. Her health is deteriorating quickly, and I am worried she might not see the year out, but she still manages to wag her finger towards the window to argue with Mrs Morgan. 'All the young people say, centipedes. Don't they, Bea?' She looks at me with a smile that warms my heart and I wish so much I could reverse time and know her as a young, healthy person. I can only imagine the fun we would have.

I sweep the floor, taking care to get the brush in under the beds where dust likes to gather. My back cracks audibly and I can see them both look at me with concern. I snap upright, to ease their worries, and softly say, 'I think you might mean centimetres.'

Mrs Morgan begins to laugh, folding in the middle.

'Stop it,' Mrs Brennan grumbles, mustering sudden energy from somewhere to pull herself up in the bed. 'Stop laughing at me.'

Mrs Morgan laughs louder. A deep, rattly laugh that highlights that she's been a heavy smoker for most of her life.

'Oh, say what you like,' Mrs Brennan says, lying back down and turning her back like a sulky toddler.

'Ah, don't be like that,' Mrs Morgan says, cutting out her giggling and straightening up, obviously worried she has offended her frenemy. 'Inches or centimetres. It doesn't change the fact that there's plenty of it out there. It'll be a white Christmas for certain.'

'My last Christmas,' Mrs Brennan says, turning back.

Mrs Morgan jams her hands on her hips, ready to scold Mrs Brennan again. 'None of us know how long we have, but you owe me at least ten games of chess, and with the snail's pace you play at you'll be at it for ever.'

There is a moment of shared silence, while we all wish it was that simple. It's not long before my two favourite patients return to chatting. They move on from discussing the weather to talk about politics. I leave them to it, and make my way to the storage room to fetch the *mind the wet floor* sign before I start washing.

The storage room is as chaotic as ever and it takes some time to find the plastic safety sign. When I finally spot it and take it off a low shelf, something beside it rolls onto the floor. I look down and discover a yellow colouring pencil rolling around my feet. Recognising it as Ellie's, I pick it up. I know she'll be delighted when I give it to her later. I'm about to slide the pencil into my uniform pocket when my phone vibrates and startles me. I take a breath and slide my phone out. I exhale with relief when I find Cora's name on the screen and not the crèche.

'Hello,' I chirp.

'Oh, you sound happy.'

'Thought you were the crèche. You've no idea how happy I am that you're not.'

'Right. Okay. Getcha,' she says, sounding equally happy but not actually getting me at all.

'What's up?' I ask.

'Nothing important. I'm just excited for later. For yours and Ellie's first night at our flat.'

'Me too.'

Although I am more relieved than excited, but I love how excited she is.

'Finton is working late so I thought maybe we could grab a takeaway and some wine and make it a girls' night. Whatcha think?'

I wasn't prepared to finance a takeaway and alcohol. But Cora is giving me a roof over my head; the least I can do is indulge her girls' night.

'Sure,' I say, sounding even more chipper than before.

'Oh. Great.'

She picks up on my extreme enthusiasm and I try to tone it down a bit.

'Is Indian okay? I can pick some up on my way home from work. There's a lovely place round the corner from here. What will you and Ellie have? I always go for the butter masala. It's unreal.'

'Sounds good,' I say, although I have absolutely no idea. Declan didn't like Indian food and I couldn't splash out on takeaways when Ellie and I were alone.

'Oh super, nice and simple if we're all the same,' she goes on. 'And red or white wine?'

'White please.'

'White it is.'

There's a pause, and I know I have to fill it with, 'Let me know what I owe you and I'll give it to you when I get there.'

'It's cool,' she says, breezily. 'Just send it to me whenever.'

I swallow. I can't imagine what it must be like to have the financial security to pay out and not have to worry about the exact moment you will get the money back.

'Anyway,' she says in a singsong tone. 'I better get back to work. I'll see you later, roomie.'

'Yeah. Later.'

She hangs up but I hear my name. The tone is clipped and I know when I turn round I will find Elaine behind me.

'Mrs Brennan has been sick,' she says.

My heart sinks. Mrs Brennan hasn't eaten much in weeks. I finally saw her nibble some toast earlier. I'm so disappointed it hasn't stayed down.

'I was just on my way to wash the floors,' I say, to reassure her that I'll have the ward spotless as soon as possible.

'With that?' Elaine points to the colouring pencil in my hand.

'Oh. Eh. No.'

'Are some of the patients colouring?' she says, arching her brows. 'That's good. I've heard colouring can be very therapeutic.'

'Yes. I think so,' I say, although I've never heard that. I make a mental note to bring Ellie's pencils and colouring books to work. Maybe Mrs Brennan and Mrs Morgan might like to give it a go.

Elaine smiles and says, 'Well, don't let me keep you.'

I smile and try not to look like I would rather stick the colouring pencil through my eye than clean up yet more vomit from a ward floor.

FOURTEEN

At the crèche, I can't find Ellie's gloves. I ask other parents to check their children's boxes, but no one finds them.

'We're on our fifth pair so far this winter,' one of the other mams tell me with an eye-roll. 'This place just eats your belongings.'

'Yes. For sure.' I say, remembering that time that Ellie lost a shoe. Declan sent me money for a new pair immediately and Ellie and I stopped by the shops on the way home. My chest tightens. Replacing Ellie's clothes as she loses them or grows out of them is an issue I have never considered before.

I ask Alannah to keep an eye out for them, but she's not entirely convincing when she says, 'Yeah, sure, of course.'

Outside, I tell Ellie to put her hands in her pockets to keep warm but she takes them out regularly to pick up snow and squeal with delight, despite the snow nipping at her fingers and turning them red. When we finally get on the bus, she falls asleep on my shoulder in less than five minutes. It's almost an hour's ride to Cora's stop and I use the time to search for flat-shares on my phone. I'm trying hard not to fall asleep myself by the time we finally reach Cora's stop.

I rack my brain for the code for the doors to the apartment block, and try a few combinations before I remember. We take the lift to the fifth floor and Ellie sings 'Shake It Off' at the top of her lungs. She seems to only know that single line, and repeats it over and over. I apologise to the man who gets off on the third floor.

'A big Taylor Swift fan,' I explain.

He nods. 'Have a good evening.'

'Yeah. You too.'

When the doors open and spit us out on the top floor, Ellie is overflowing with energy after her bus nap and I wonder how I am ever going to get her to settle down to sleep tonight. She juts her head forward and makes an exaggerated sniffing sound. I can smell the Indian food from the hallway too. It smells incredible and my mouth practically waters. The flat door is ajar and I realise Cora is only home seconds ahead of us. I knock but there's no answer. So, I peek my head round the door.

'Oh, you're home,' I hear Cora say.

At first I think she's talking to me, but then I hear a man's voice reply and quickly realise Finton is home early.

'Thank God you got food,' he says. 'I'm bloody starving. Is it Indian?'

The voices turn lower and mumbling.

'Hey,' I call out loudly. 'Okay to come in?' I say even louder, feeling almost intruder-like.

Cora comes skidding into the small, open-plan living area that I have never realised before is incredibly white. White walls, white tiles, white kitchen cupboards and a white sofa. Colour is introduced in the form of oversized cushions on the couch and matching ones on the kitchen chairs. Even the kettle and toaster match this neon-cushion theme that can best be described as *Love Island* meets a dental hospital.

'You're here,' Cora shrieks, throwing her arms above her head in delight.

Ellie copies her, then runs past me to fling her raised arms round Cora's waist. Cora bends and picks her up.

Finton comes through the bedroom door soon after. He's changed out of his work clothes, which I know will have been a smart suit and block-coloured tie, into a navy tracksuit that makes him looks like he's still a kid in college.

'Hi, Finton,' I say, smiling.

'Hey, Bea. Great to see you guys.'

'Thank you so much for letting us stay,' I start, fumbling over my words as I try to show my gratitude and hide my embarrassment that I'm in this needy situation.

He swats his hand. 'Don't mention it. Cora's told me everything.'

I blush.

'What a dick.'

'Who's a dick?' Ellie asks, whipping her head round.

'Oh, shit, sorry. Didn't mean to swear,' he says, then covers his mouth with his hand when he realises he did it again.

'Right. I'm going to get out of here before I assassinate a unicorn or a fairy or something,' he says, and I'm glad Ellie doesn't know what that means. 'My girlfriend would let me starve, so I'm going to the chipper.' He dots a kiss on the top of Cora's head as he passes and asks her if she needs anything while he's out.

He takes his coat from the rack next to me and leaves, closing the door behind him.

'I'm starving,' Cora announces, pointing to the paper bag of food resting on the kitchen counter. 'Why don't you use my room to change, and I'll get some sheets on the couch for you guys. Then we can eat.'

'Sure,' I say, beyond grateful, then I turn to Ellie and say, 'C'mon. Let's get your hands washed.'

I'm walking towards the bathroom when Cora calls me.

'Bea,'

I turn round. 'Mm-hmm.'

'Everything is going to be all right, you know.'

I smile. Cora keeps saying that, and I wonder if it's me or her she is trying to convince. 'Yeah,' I say. 'I think so.'

FIFTEEN

'So, what do you think? It's the best Indian, isn't it?' Cora asks, as I fork the last bite of chicken butter masala from my plate into my mouth.

'Mmm,' I say, chewing. 'So good.'

'It's yucky,' Ellie complains.

She has pushed the food around her plate for fifteen minutes and I can see even Cora's boundless patience wavering.

'Looks like puke,' Ellie goes on.

'Ellie.' I snap her name, warning her to mind her manners.

'It's okay,' Cora tells her. 'If you don't like it, you can just leave it. I have some popcorn in the cupboard. How about that instead?'

Ellie agrees to the compromise. Cora puts some cartoons on Netflix and settles her on the couch with a small bowl of microwave popcorn. She places the remainder of the popcorn in a larger bowl on the oval, whitewashed kitchen table between us and tells me to help myself. She opens the wine and conversation flows effortlessly. For all of about five minutes, until Ellie is too hot. Too bored. Too stuffed. Too anything except calm and sleepy the way she would normally be at this hour of the evening. I find myself apologising.

'She had a nap on the bus,' I say.

Cora nods. 'Bus naps are the best, to be fair. I'm sure she'll tire herself out eventually.'

Cora is right and Ellie finally grows sleepy, but not until it's bedtime for Cora and me too.

'I'm so sorry about tonight,' I say, looking at the bottle of wine that is still more than half full. 'I know you really wanted a girly night.'

'Pfft, there'll be plenty of girly nights,' Cora says with a wave of her hand. 'She's probably just excited to be in a new place. That's all.'

'Yeah.' I agree, and I will make sure Ellie doesn't fall asleep on the bus on the way home ever again. I'll play an hour of I-Spy with her every evening if I have to.

'Well, good night,' Cora says, yawning. 'Help yourself to some orange juice or toast or whatever in the morning, if you're up before me. And I got some Coco Pops for Ellie. I know they're her favourite.'

My eyes tear up. I'm so grateful I have a friend like Cora. 'It's cos they make the milk—'

'—go chocolatey,' she cuts in, singing the theme tune from the TV ad.

'Thank you,' I mouth, too teary to push words out.

'No problem. Na'night.'

Cora retreats to her bedroom and closes the door behind her. It's strange when Ellie and I are alone. Ellie has napped on Cora's couch plenty of times, usually when Cora and I lose track of time chatting over tea or wine. But Ellie isn't just napping now. The couch is her bed. My bed. A space where we can rest but we don't truly belong. My blue and red striped Tesco shopping bags, stuffed under the coffee table, stand out garishly against the Alaskan chic décor. Overthinking and over-tired, I duck my head into the first bag and rummage around until I find my toothbrush. Then I wash up quickly and try to get comfy on the couch beside Ellie. The cosy two-seater is too compact for an adult to stretch out completely and my ankles and feet hang over the edge. I lie on my side, lining myself up the couch edge, in a balancing act of not falling off or rolling in and squashing Ellie. Then I cover us both with the blanket, and I'm asleep the second my eyes close.

My eyes fly open again when I hear 'Ouch, fuck,' grunted from somewhere.

I lean up and peek over the back of the couch, my eyes taking a moment to adjust to the darkness.

Finton is standing between the couch and the kitchen area in his boxers. He's hopping on one foot and his other foot is in his hand.

'Bloody Lego,' he hisses.

He puts both feet on the ground and kicks something. I hear the clip-clop of a Lego brick scurry across the tiled floor.

I lie back down and pretend to be asleep. I thought I'd cleared up all the Lego earlier. I'll look for the brick in the morning and apologise to Finton. Standing on a Lego brick is the worst, but I'm sure he'll see the funny side in the morning.

SIXTEEN

In the morning, I fold the blankets and leave them neatly on the couch. I try my best to stuff the Tesco bags fully under the coffee table and out of view. I can't find the offending Lego block and I hope it's lost under the couch or behind a floor lamp, never to be stepped on again. Ellie and I both have some orange juice and Coco Pops and then I clean up. I hear Cora and Finton getting up, but we leave the flat before they leave their room. On the bus, I talk to Ellie about keeping the flat tidy.

'We're guests,' I tell her.

'Do we have to have that yucky dinner again?' she asks.

'No. No more takeaways,' I say, remembering I still owe Cora money for it.

At the bus stop, I spot a Tesco Express and decide to pick up some ingredients to make spaghetti Bolognese later. It was Cora's favourite when we were in college and Ellie loves it too. I hope Finton likes it. The recipe needs wine but they only have full-size bottles and it's very expensive, so I decide it'll will be fine without it.

Then I drop Ellie to crèche and head to work. Each time I

pass the empty bench in the car park, I find myself disappointed and relieved in equal measure that Malcolm isn't there. I'm disappointed that we won't get to share a chat. But relieved that whatever issue was keeping him here seems to be resolved.

A new routine quickly develops. Pop into Tesco and pick up whatever is on special offer to make dinner for four. Drop Ellie to crèche, trek across the city in morning traffic, spend a day cleaning floors and grubby bathrooms, break my neck to get back across the city in time for Ellie. Sing songs, watch *Bluey* on my phone or play I-Spy on the bus to make sure Ellie doesn't fall asleep. Lie on a couch that is much too small for two and scroll through flat listings on my phone until I fall sleep.

After ten nights on Cora's couch, my back is screaming. I try shifting but every movement seems to disturb Ellie. Her chubby little arms are tight round my neck and one leg is draped over my tummy as I lie next to her. She was restless and found it hard to fall asleep tonight, and even now she's jumpy and jerky and I wonder what she's dreaming. She was unusually quiet when I picked her up from crèche earlier and I hope Alannah wasn't sticking her nose in, as per usual.

'Where's your daddy?' I imagine her asking my confused little girl. Or, 'Did your mammy really not know your daddy was already married?' Or, worse still, 'Are you going to live on your mammy's friend couch for ever?' I try to push the thoughts of things Alannah couldn't possibly know out of my racing mind. I'm confident that the news of my breakup and moving flat has given parents at the crèche plenty to gossip about, but I doubt any of them have any idea of what the reality of it is really like.

My arm under Ellie goes dead and I try to slide it out without disturbing her. Most nights, I move from the couch to a space on the floor between it and the coffee table where I lay down blankets for myself. It's cold, but at least I can stretch out.

Cora gave me the extra blankets when I lied and said Ellie and I were chilly. Ellie has got used to rolling to the edge of the couch in the morning and peering down to find me when it's breakfast time.

'Wake up, Mammy,' she says every morning with her round blue eyes, so like her father's, wide and locked on mine. 'I'm hungry.'

Ellie and I finish breakfast most mornings before Cora and Finton come into the kitchen. It works best for everyone this way. Sometimes I leave pancakes or French toast for them. And I replace the orange juice regularly. And yet, most evenings I still feel Finton's narrowed eyes on me and Ellie when he comes through the door after work and finds that we are home first. We try to be as invisible as possible. I turn off CBeebies and we go for a walk for as long as Ellie's little legs can keep going. Finton is always watching TV when we return, but as soon as he sees us he turns it off and goes to his room.

Cora is always quick to cover for him. 'He's just tired. Long day, you know the drill.' Or, 'He has a headache.' Or, 'He's work to catch up with on the laptop.'

Finton must be the most overworked, headache-prone, exhausted adult I've ever known.

'Keep watching, don't let us disturb you,' I've tried to say countless times, but his reply is always the same.

'It's fine.' Said in a tone that indicates it is very much not fine. 'You need to put her to bed anyway.'

Finton regularly refers to Ellie as 'her', as if he forgets her name or just refuses to take the time to learn it. He doesn't particularly like children. And he doesn't make an exception for my child. He's told Cora countless times he never wants to have any of his own.

'Finton's right,' Cora says. 'We work so hard we don't really have time for kids. It wouldn't be fair on them.'

Cora does work hard. She's a radiographer at a private

hospital and she volunteers at a homeless shelter once a week. But she still finds time to read Ellie stories, or join us in the park for a game of tag. And every now and then, when she's noticed Ellie take a growth spurt, she'll buy her new pyjamas or a pair of shoes. 'They were on sale and I couldn't resist,' she says.

It's harder than usual to shuffle away from Ellie tonight and by the time I stand up I'm hopping on one leg because I'm so bursting for the loo. I'm only gone five minutes when Ellie starts calling out.

'Mammy. Mammy. Where are you, Mammy!'

I race back. 'Shh. Shh,' I say, scooping my daughter into my arms and stroking her hair. 'Shh. Shh. I'm here. I'm here.'

Ellie wraps her arms round me and nuzzles her face into the crook of my neck. 'I got scared,' she whispers and I can feel her little heart racing in her chest.

'It's okay. I'm not going anywhere,' I promise. 'I'm never going anywhere.'

Ellie settles quickly and soon she's contentedly sleeping in my arms, but it's too late. I hear someone get out of bed and walk across the creaky bedroom floor to flick on the bedroom light.

Oh no.

I lie Ellie on the couch and cover her ears with my hands, wishing the walls of the tiny flat weren't so paper-thin.

'It's two a.m.,' Finton grumbles.

There's some mumbling. I know Cora is whispering. And I know she's choosing her words carefully. My stomach somersaults. It's the third time this week that they've had an argument in the middle of the night.

'I will not keep my voice down,' Finton whines.

There's some shushing and more mumbles.

'I don't care if she hears me,' he continues. 'It's my bloody flat.'

'Finton, please?' Cora says, raising her voice to cut him off. 'Things are already hard enough for her.'

'Well, she should have thought about that before she got herself knocked up by a married man.'

'She didn't know Declan was married,' Cora snaps, her voice growing louder.

'Sure,' Finton snaps back. 'They never do.'

Gentle snores vibrate from Ellie's floppy body and I'm so grateful that she's finally in a deep sleep. I keep my hands firmly on her ears and wait for Finton and Cora to go back to bed the way they usually do.

But Finton keeps talking. He's calmer now. Not as loud, but he's still mad. His voice is jumping around and I guess he's pacing.

'Ten days, Cora. Those two have been here for ten bloody days,' he says. 'You told me it would be a couple of nights.'

'I know. I know,' Cora says.

I can hear the flop of bare feet against the timber floor as one of them takes exaggerated strides. 'Am I ever getting my damn couch back?' Finton grumbles. 'I couldn't even watch the match tonight cos the kid was asleep.'

'They have nowhere else to go.'

'And how is that our problem?'

'She's my best friend, Finton.'

The pacing stops and Finton calmly says, 'Exactly. *Your* best friend. Yours, Cora. Not mine. And don't get me started on the kid.'

'What do you want me to do?'

Finton groans deeply. 'Look. I get this is tricky for you, but when I asked you to move in I thought I was asking to live with my girlfriend. Not my girlfriend, her best friend and her best friend's kid. It's a one-bedroomed flat. It's a little cramped, you know. She needs to find her own place. Stand on her own two feet for once.'

'I'll talk to her, okay?'
'Okay.' His tone softens. 'Good. Thank you.'
'She just needs a bit more time—'
'Oh, for fuck's sake,' Finton grunts. 'I'm going back to sleep.'

SEVENTEEN

I watch Ellie sleep for a long time. I can't remember the last time she slept so soundly. The irony hurts as I glance at the bags of our stuff under the coffee table. I packed everything up during the night. I couldn't sleep anyway. As ever, our stuff fits into a couple of Tesco plastic bags. The big ones with *bag-for-life* written across the bottom. Although, the writing on one of the bags is fading now, and says *bag-for-if*. My heart aches as I read the words that so accurately sum up Ellie and me. Bag for if. If your boyfriend is a liar. If your father is a cheat. If you've nowhere to go and no one to turn to. If you're scared. If only it was all so different. *If!*

I wipe the tear that trickles down the side of my nose, paste on a wide smile and wake Ellie.

'C'mon, sweetheart,' I whisper, kissing her cheeks. 'It's a beautiful day.'

My daughter turns away from me and tucks her knees close to her chest as she snuggles her favourite teddy. Sir Loves-a-lot is missing one eye and the patch just below his ear on the same side is hugged threadbare. But Ellie loves him nonetheless. I do too. Because on the days when it's hardest and I worry that I can't keep going, Ellie asks me if I want to hug Sir Loves-a-lot. The three of us snuggle together and in that moment, just for a moment, everything feels okay.

'My tummy hurts,' Ellie whispers, with her eyes still closed, and when she wrinkles her nose her puffy round cheeks scrunch.

'You're hungry,' I explain. 'I'm starving too.'

Cora and Finton were in the middle of their dinner last night when Ellie and I got in. When Cora asked us to join them Finton nearly choked on his broccoli. So, Ellie and I had dinner on the couch instead. We shared a couple of packets of crisps and a rice cake bar that I picked up in the vending machine in work, and Ellie happily munched away while watching *Paw Patrol*.

'Coco Pops,' Ellie suggests, sitting up and opening her eyes. She's suddenly so full of energy and smiles and I've no doubt she's thinking about the chocolatey milk that she loves to drink when she gets to the bottom of the bowl.

'Not this morning,' I say, glancing at my watch.

It's 6.23. Cora's alarm will go off in seven minutes for her early shift and I'd really like to be gone by then.

'But I so hungry.' Ellie rubs her stomach for effect.

'I know,' I say. 'Okay, arms up.'

Ellie knows the drill, and she raises her arms above her head and I tug her pyjama top off and pull on her favourite pink unicorn t-shirt and matching jumper. I do the same with her leggings, then stuff her warm pyjamas into one of the Tesco bags. I guide her arms into her coat and zip it up before I add her hat and gloves.

'Quickly,' I puff out, as I straighten the cushions on the couch and leave the blanket folded on the coffee table.

'I'm so hungry,' Ellie says again, and she adjusts her hat that she doesn't bother to complain is scratchy the way she normally does.

'We're going out for breakfast this morning,' I tell her, trying to sound excited.

'Out?'

'Mm-hmm.' I pick up the plastic bags, taking them both in one hand. I reach my other hand out and Ellie curls her chubby fingers round mine.

'Right,' I say, tilting my head towards the door. 'Let's go.'

I take one last look around Cora and Finton's flat. Content that there is no trace that Ellie and I were ever there, I open the front door just as Cora's alarm goes off. The chilly contrast in the corridor takes my breath away. There's floor-to-ceiling glass at each end of the long corridor and a stairwell almost directly in front of us. A draught seems to sneak in the windows and climb the stairs to accumulate into a tiny, freezing cyclone on this very spot, trying to claw at the skin on my face and force me back into the flat.

I wait for Ellie to complain about the cold, or her empty stomach or her uncomfortable hat, but she squeezes my hand and chirps, 'Let's go out.'

'Let's,' I say.

I have no idea where to go. Or if anywhere local will be open this early. We might need to ride around on the bus for a while to keep warm. Luckily, Ellie loves the bus.

EIGHTEEN

'Thank you,' Ellie says, smiling at the bus driver as we get off.

He raises his hand to his forehead and salutes his young passenger. 'Have a good day, little lady.'

'I will,' Ellie says with certainty as she skips down the steps.

'Thanks,' I say without making eye contact with the driver, hoping he doesn't notice that we're getting off the bus at the same stop we started at over an hour ago. I reach for my daughter's hand. 'Ellie, be careful, don't fall.'

We're swept into a sea of commuters and the buzz is refreshing. It's still dark outside – a typical December morning – but there are lots of people about. It seemed to happen suddenly and all at once. An hour ago Ellie and I were almost completely alone as we walked the cobblestone streets of Temple Bar. Now, there are people all over. Men in suits and long winter coats with mobile phones stuck to their ear. And women in heels regretting their choice of footwear as they tried not to get a stiletto caught between the cobbles. There's construction workers in high-visibility jackets and lots of people whose clothes don't hint at what they do all day. There aren't any other kids though. It's still too early for crèche drop-off.

The city is coming to life and a sprinkling of shutters are rising. I spot an open café on the corner – opposite the main gates of Trinity College.

'Here we are,' I say as I curl my fingers a fraction tighter round Ellie's, and, stride with pseudoconfidence towards the door.

Heat warms my face as soon as we step inside, and the tips of my bare fingers tingle, adapting. Inside is cosier than I was expecting, with mismatched furniture pushed too close together. Ellie pulls her hat and gloves off and breaks away from me to choose the long, narrow table just inside the window. It's much too high for a four-year-old.

'Here,' she announces, reaching for a backless stool with two hands.

The legs squeak as she drags them across the rustic pine floor. I take her hat and gloves and help her climb up.

'Careful,' I warn, unzipping her jacket. 'No messing if you're sitting up this high. You're a big girl now.'

I push the stool forward and tuck Ellie in to the table before I take a seat next to her. There are laminated menus dotted on the table, and Ellie reaches for one as if she can read. She's instantly disappointed when there are no pictures.

The menu is more elaborate than I was expecting. *Poached eggs and avocado. Overnight protein oats. Smoked salmon on sourdough bread.* Foods that come with a high price tag and are certain to make my four-year-old poke her tongue out.

'Morning,' a chirpy young waitress says, appearing at our table with a small pad and pen in her hands.

'Hello.' Ellie smiles, swinging her legs back and forth and worrying me that she's going to fall off the high stool.

'Is there a separate kids' menu?' I ask.

The waitress shrugs. 'No, sorry. Just what's there.'

'Erm... eh, can I get a small black coffee and—'

'Ribena,' Ellie pipes up.

'A small black coffee and Ribena please,' I repeat.

'Sure,' the waitress says, writing it down. 'And for food?'

'Coco Pops,' Ellie says.

The waitress giggles. 'No Coco Pops,' she says, smiling at Ellie. 'But I can ask the chef to hold the sauces or anything like that?' she says, shifting her gaze to me.

'Oh. Eh. Would the eggs be cheaper without avocado?'

'No. Sorry. The price would be the same, but most kids like the plain poached egg option.'

I glance at the menu again. It's almost fifteen euro for eggs and avocado.

'I like eggs,' Ellie tells the waitress.

'So plain poached eggs, is it?'

'Mm-hmm.' I wince.

'Cool.' The waitress writes it down. 'Anything else?'

'No thanks.'

'So that's poached eggs, hold the avocado. Ribena and small black coffee.'

'Erm, actually, no coffee after all,' I say, trying to add the prices in my head. 'I'm not really hungry.'

'You said you're starving, Mammy,' Ellie says.

'No. No. I'm fine.'

'You did. You did. At Cora's house. And on the bus. And then your tummy went gurglely-wurglely on the bus. 'Member?'

I blush.

'Do you have a loyalty card?' the waitress asks. 'Every tenth coffee is free so...'

'No. I don't.'

My face stings and I wonder if it's as hot and red as it feels.

'Okay. No worries,' she says. 'Just Ribena and eggs.'

'Yes. Thank you.'

She leaves our table and I breathe a sigh of relief.

'Is your tummy not rumbly no more?' Ellie asks, steadying her little legs so she can lean closer to me.

'Not any more, sweetheart.'

I'm grateful for the radio playing in the background, loud enough to hide my stomach grumbling.

Ellie sings along to Ed Sheeran and Taylor Swift, making up her own words, and soon the food arrives.

'Yummy.' Ellie smiles and the smell of her snow-white eggs with gooey golden centres on lightly toasted bread makes my mouth water.

The waitress places a takeaway cup with steam swirling out the top in front of me and for a moment I panic that she misunderstood. I really can't afford a coffee.

'Someone ordered a black coffee and left without it,' she says, pulling her shoulders towards her ears.

'Oh. Eh.' I cringe, and tears of embarrassment swell in the corners of my eyes. 'Thanks, but I'm okay. I really need to cut down on my caffeine.'

She looks at me knowingly and says, 'It's already been paid for. And it's just going to go to waste if...'

I don't have a reply. The steam is tantalising and I can almost taste the rich, aromatic beans. I force myself to meet her pitying gaze.

'Look,' she says, and I think she feels almost as awkward as I do. 'I'll leave it here. And, sure, just put it in the bin if you don't want it. Yeah?'

'Okay. Thanks,' I mouth, not quite able to push the words out in case my tears start to fall.

Ellie gobbles her breakfast in record time. And the coffee fills me with warmth.

I pay at the counter and I take the change.

'Have a good day,' the waitress calls after us and I wonder if she knows how much I would love to leave that change as a tip, if only I could.

With a full tummy, Ellie skips all the way to the crèche.

'Mor-ning,' Alannah chirps as she greets us at the door of the crèche. Her Christmas jumper with a brick chimney and a pair of Santa legs stuck upside down makes Ellie laugh.

'Oh, you like it,' Alannah says, pressing a button on her sleeve that makes the chimney light up. Ellie squeals with joy and claps. 'It's Christmas jumper day next Friday,' Alannah continues.

'What? No? I thought that was last week?' I squeak.

'It was supposed to be. But so many of the kids had that horrible vomiting bug and missed it. So we rescheduled. Cos it's a fundraiser, we really want the numbers up, you know?'

'Oh, I know.'

Alannah crouches to come down to my daughter's height. 'I can't wait to see yours, Ellie. I bet it's something special.'

I swallow a lump as Alannah stands back up to smile at me. I can practically see the euro signs in her dark brown eyes.

'Well, in you go,' Alannah says, placing her hand on Ellie's back, encouraging her forward. 'The boys and girls are making a Santa jigsaw. You should go help them. I'll be in in a minute. I just want a quick word with your mammy.'

Ellie looks back at me and I smile. 'Go on, chickpea. I'll see you later.'

Ellie hugs my leg, before giving me a quick wave and running off to join her friends behind the glass wall that has been hand-painted for Christmas. Reindeer and holly and stars stare at me in festive reds and golds.

'Getting the shopping done early,' Alannah says, pointing to the Tesco bags in my hands.

'Something like that,' I say, cringing and praying she doesn't ask what I bought.

'Good idea. Gosh, I went into town last night trying to pick up a few bits for my family Secret Santa. Ugh, never again. Place was thronged. Couldn't wait to get out of there.'

'Town is very busy, so I best get going, or I'll be late.'

'Um,' Alannah says, making a face as she tilts her head to one side in a way that tells me I don't want to hear whatever she's going to say next.

'Yes?' I say, nonetheless.

'Speaking of being late,' she goes on, and all I can think about is how the bag in my left hand is slipping; it feels as if the handle is going to snap from the weight of all Ellie's teddies. 'I hate to be the bearer of bad news, but we've had to put our late fee up.'

'Oh.'

'I know. I know. But nothing crazy. Just a tenner an hour.'

My eyes bulge. 'That's almost double.'

She shrugs. 'Blame management. So, instead of fifteen euro, it'll be twenty-five an hour. Or part thereof.'

'Part of? So, if I'm ten minutes late, it'll be twenty-five quid?' I can feel my palms begin to sweat.

'Management.' She shrugs again, wincing as if it pains her to share this information.

'But the buses are a joke. They're always a few minutes late. Last week I waited thirty minutes and then it passed by me full.'

'I know, traffic is awful, isn't it? But it is what it is. At least this way, staff are compensated. You'll be glad to hear it all goes straight to them.' She shrugs once more and the tic makes me want to scream. 'And at this time of year every penny counts, you know yourself.'

You know yourself. It's a generic phrase. But I doubt Alannah knows just how much every penny counts for Ellie and me. Or I certainly hope not, at least.

'I better go,' I say, swallowing.

'Of course. Of course. Have a good day. See you at six.'

'See you at six,' I say, panicking that 6.01 will cost me twenty-five euro that I don't have.

NINETEEN

The snow is at least five inches thick, or as Mrs Brennan would say twelve centimetres, and it plays havoc with traffic. I'm late for work and, in spite of the cold snap outside, I am sweating when the bus pulls up at the hospital stop.

'Watch it,' someone shouts at me, as one of my Tesco bags hits him in the leg when he descends the bus steps ahead of me.

'It's just teddies,' I snap back.

'Yeah, well, next time keep your shopping to yourself, right?'

'It was an accident. Jesus. Sorry.'

'Now, now, where's our Christmas spirit,' a lady with even more bags than me says, appearing behind us as the bus pulls away.

The man's face softens. 'Look, I'm sorry. Just feeling the pressure of all the bits and pieces that need to be bought at this time of year. Need to win the damn lotto.'

'It's okay. Me too,' I say.

The three of us part and go our separate ways, but I think about Christmas the whole walk into the hospital. I left Cora's flat in such a kerfuffle this morning that Christmas was the last thing on my mind. But the big day is next week and, as of right now, Ellie and I might be spending it on the street.

I take Malcolm's wellies off at the main doors and slip into my worn work shoes. Upstairs, Elaine is waiting for me.

'And what time do you call this?' she asks, pressing her finger against the face of her watch as if I can see it from where I'm standing.

I sigh. 'The weather.'

'Yes. Yes. I suppose none of us can control that. It took me an hour longer than usual to come in this morning. The M50 was at a standstill.'

'I don't drive,' I say. 'Had to wait on the bus.'

'Right. Right. Well, can you get an earlier one tomorrow, then?'

I grimace. 'I would. But I have to drop my daughter to crèche and they only open at eight.'

Elaine turns, but I still catch her rolling her eyes.

'Okay, fair enough, but I'll have to adjust your wages if you're going to be late all this week. I'm sorry, but it's only fair to those who *are* making it in on time.'

The tips of my shoulders are burning from the weight of the plastic bags in my hands and I wait for Elaine to say something about them. Ask me if I was late because I'd been running around Christmas shopping, that way everyone else does. But instead, she says, 'Nice wellies.'

I glance into the bag in my left arm. The handle is digging into my palm now and stinging, the bright red wellington boots are sitting on top and hiding a multitude of teddies bellow.

'Sensible choice in this weather,' she continues. 'I might get myself a pair.'

I smile, relieved by the shift to small talk.

'Right, well, dump your stuff and get going. Could you start with the men's toilets please? They're not pretty, I'm afraid.'

Normally my stomach would heave a little at the thought of

it, but I'm so relieved Elaine didn't notice my entire life was wrapped up in Tesco plastic that I hurry towards the storage room with new-found energy. I dump the bags in the back and pull out the mop and bucket.

The day is long and full of bodily excretions. One of the other cleaners asks me if I'd like to join her and the new girl in the café across the street for lunch.

'They do the nicest acai bowls,' she tells me.

'I'd love to,' I say, wringing out my mop that smells like feet, underarms and bleach all at the same time. 'But I already have plans. Thanks so much though.'

'Maybe next time,' she says.

I try hard to smile. 'Yeah. Definitely.'

'She never comes,' I hear her whisper to the new girl as they walk away.

'Then why do you keep asking her?'

'Dunno. Just thought maybe some day I'd find out why she's so weird?'

'Is she weird?'

'God yeah.'

They continue talking, no doubt about my personality, as they fade out of earshot. I sneak an unopened rice pudding and some apple juice off a tray a patient has finished eating from and make my way into the storage room to have my lunch. I've just taken my phone out to scroll through flat listings as usual when it begins to ring, and Cora's name pops up on the screen. I take a deep breath and answer.

'Hey,' I say, trying hard to sound casual.

'Heya. Where did you go this morning? I was on the early shift. I thought we could have brekkie together.'

'Oh, erm, yeah, sorry. Ellie was up and singing her head off, so I thought we'd hit the road early.'

'You know I love Ellie's singing,' she says.

Ellie has a voice like a strangled crow, but Cora always smiles when she sings. Finton is a different story, and the moment of pause between us tells me that we're both thinking about that.

'I didn't want to wake Finton,' I go on. 'I know he's on a later shift today.'

'Yeah, yeah, he is. God, what time did ye guys leave? Was anywhere even open?'

'We got brekkie,' I say, proudly.

'Oh. Okay. Cool.' She sounds as if she doesn't believe me and I fight the urge to elaborate about Ellie's eggs. 'Well, anyway, it's my turn to cook tonight so I was wondering what Ellie would like. I won't make curry, don't worry.'

I laugh. 'Actually, we won't be home for dinner.'

'Oh.'

'Yeah. Erm. I found a place.'

'What?' Her voice rises an octave. 'When?'

'Just…' I stutter. 'Erm, literally just now. But it's ready and available immediately.'

'Really? Somewhere came up this close to Christmas?'

She sounds disappointed.

'Yep. So I have to pounce.'

'Yeah, yeah. Of course.'

I can tell now she is definitely disappointed, and I'm not sure why. I thought she would be thrilled to get her space with Finton back.

'Erm, okay, I'm delighted, Bea. Is it a good location for work? Send me the address, yeah? Just in case you're moving in with a bunch of serial killers or something and I have to come and hit them over the head with a Christmas stocking.'

'A Christmas stocking?'

'Well, I'd fill it with rocks first, obviously.'

I laugh. 'Duh, obviously.'

I hear Cora inhale, and seriously she says, 'I'm happy for

you, Bea. See, what did I tell you? I said everything would be all right, didn't I?'

I wince and hope I can push words out before I choke up. 'You were right.'

'Okay, cool,' she says quickly, and I know this is the part of the call where she has to hang up soon and go back to work. 'But send me on the address, because I would love to come around and meet your new roomies. I'll bring cake. And I promise to leave all Christmas stocking and rocks at home.'

'Yeah. Course.' I swallow hard. 'I'll send everything on later. Okay.'

'Cool. Cool. Gotta go. Someone's here for chest X-ray. Byeeeee.'

'Bye.'

I slide my phone back into my pocket and drop my face into my hands. I take some deep breaths, enough for the smell of bleach to make me light-headed, and look up again.

'Welcome home, Beatrice Alright,' I say out loud as I look around the storage room.

The idea hit me while I was on the phone with Cora. I hid Ellie in this storage room for a day. Sure, I lost her, but that's because she was awake. Sleeping kids don't go walkabout. And she and I only need somewhere to sleep. By day, she's in crèche and I'm in work. So by night we can be in here. Who will ever find out? It feels slightly genius and slightly insane at the same time. But it's a solution and the absolute best answer I can come up with right now.

I glance around at Ellie's and my new home, then I sit down and lean back against an industrial-sized drum of antibacterial floor wash to enjoy rice pudding, and I'm sorry I didn't nick some jelly too.

TWENTY

Elaine asks me to stay late to make up the lost hour's work this morning.

'Two patients on St John's ward have gone home, and their mattresses need scrubbing before we re-dress the beds.'

I think of the grubby, plastic-covered mattresses that must be as old as I am. I don't mind washing them; the trouble is that I never feel I can get them fully clean. Even with the strongest antibacterial spay we have.

'Is it Mr Carter and Mr Flynn?' I ask.

Elaine's eyes narrow.

'Gone home,' I clarify. 'It's just Mr Carter has a new grandson, and he was so hoping to meet him this Christmas.'

Elaine's lips curl into a smile so subtle that if I blinked, I'd have missed it.

'Yes, Mr Carter is gone home. But, really, Bea, patients' family life isn't our business.' Her words are matronly but her tone is soft and her smile is widening. It's a rare glimpse of her softer side and I can tell she is as happy for Mr Carter as I am.

'So, you'll stay, then?' she continues.

'I would if I could,' I say. 'But I have to pick my daughter up—'

'Yes. Yes. At crèche,' she cuts in.

'I could come back,' I add quickly and overly enthusiastically.

'I didn't think you had anyone to watch her?'

'Oh. I don't. But I could bring her here. She's a great kid, and as quiet as a mouse if she has a colouring book.'

Elaine raises her hand to hush me. 'No, no. Goodness, the wards are no place for a child. It's fine, Bea. Go home.'

I swallow a lump of air that seems to stretch and burn on the way down. Suddenly, sneaking Ellie onto the ward this evening doesn't seem like such a good plan. And yet, it remains my only plan. I just have to make sure Elaine doesn't find out.

As I wrap up for the day, Mrs Morgan sings Christmas carols at the top of her lungs. Mrs Brennan tries to join in but just singing the chorus tires her out. Elaine places a portable radio next to the window and puts Christmas FM on for them instead. I work as hard and fast as I can and I manage to free up time to wash the vacated mattresses before leaving to collect Ellie.

It's finally stopped snowing, but I change into my red wellington boots all the same. The blanket of glistening, white, cloud-like snow that covered the ground so beautifully this morning has been disturbed by people, going about daily life, trying to get from one place to the next. The car park and the road have been cleared to make way for traffic. Mounds of mucky, slushy snow are piled high to the sides and everything and everywhere seems grubby. There's a man sitting on the bench under the oak tree. For a moment my heart soars, but this man is wearing a woolly hat and petting the huge, black dog sitting at his feet. As I get closer, I take in his face. He's about my age and it's obvious it the dog who needs the sit-down and not him.

'Hello,' he says as I pass.

'Hello.'

I pause for a moment but we don't exchange more words. He doesn't tell me to be careful because the footpath is slippery. He doesn't comment on my footwear, or ask me if I'd like to sit down. He doesn't really notice me at all. I wasn't expecting him to, of course. But, still, I found myself longing to sit under the branches of the tired, old tree and chat.

Snowploughs have tidied the city and traffic moves freely. I'm on time for crèche, and relieved to save twenty-five quid. But my relief soon plummets when Ellie and I get back to the hospital and Elaine's car is still in the car park.

'Let's go for a walk,' I tell Ellie.

She shakes her head. 'I'm hungry.'

I use the twenty-five euro I've saved to buy us both a McDonald's and I splurge and add a coffee to the order. After, I swear out loud; Elaine's car is still in the car park.

Ellie's face is a picture, with round eyes and lips pulled into an 'o' shape, upon hearing my bad language.

'Sorry, chickpea,' I say, covering my mouth with my hand. 'We mustn't say that word.'

'But you did,' she tells me with a cheeky smirk.

'I know. I'm very bold.'

I suggest a walk and Ellie protests with a stomp of her foot.

'It'll be fun,' I lie, feeling every bit as fed up as my four-year-old. 'We can go see the Christmas lights.

It is surprisingly fun. Grafton Street is beautiful after dark, as we walk up and down the pedestrianised shopping street with our necks craned back to take in the sparkling garlands that stretch from one side of the street to the other. Ellie counts them all. Other children walk alongside their parents doing exactly the same. I wonder if they are out on a winter's evening for a pleasure stroll, or if they are out, like us, because they have nowhere else to go.

After an hour, Ellie is fed up and we are both cold. I scoop her into my arms and carry her for as long as my tired back will allow as we make our way back to the hospital. Thankfully, Elaine's car is finally gone.

I place my finger over my lips and tell Ellie to be quiet as we go inside. The usually busy reception area is painfully quiet and without any people it appears larger than usual too. I take a deep breath, hold Ellie tight in my arms and keep my head down as I rush past reception. I don't recognise the woman on the desk and I rehearse something about forgetting my bag in my head in case she stops me, but she doesn't look up from her computer.

I hurry into the lift and my insides are making a fuss as we hop out on the fourth floor and duck into the storage room in one fast-paced charge.

'Here we are, chickpea,' I say, stopping short of adding *Home Sweet Home*.

I wait for Ellie to mention the distinctive smell of hospital cleaning products, or to complain about the cramped space, that, although there is room for her little body to lie out flat on the floor, there really isn't room for me to do the same. But she doesn't say a word. She cuddles me tight and I slide to the floor, rocking gently back and forth until she is asleep in my arms. Every day won't be like this, I tell myself. Although, away from Finton's pointed glares and Cora's walking on eggshells between him and us, I already feel better.

I wait until Ellie is soundly asleep before I lie her on the ground and scurry around to find what we need. I take blankets off an empty, freshly made bed and I fill us two large glasses of water from the water cooler in the hall. I even sneak a couple of chocolates from the box of Milk Tray on Mrs Morgan's bedside locker. She's always trying to feed me chocolate, but although I'm sure she won't mind, the sneaky act, while she lies sleeping, still makes my stomach flip.

Back in the storage room, I make a comfortable space for Ellie. I fold blankets for under and over her and I lift her into her makeshift bed. Then I find a spot for myself next to the sweeping brushes. I sit with my back to the wall, tuck my knees against my chest and cover myself with a blanket. Minutes turn to hours, but I can't sleep. There's a hum of something electrical coming from the hall and it buzzes like a bee in summer. I smile. The thought reminds me of Malcolm.

I eat the chocolate and then, wide awake, I once again sneak into the hall. The wards are eerie at night as the sound of fluorescent lights overhead battle for space to be heard over snoring. It's harder than I thought to walk around unnoticed, as nurses patrol the wards, appearing sporadically to check on patients. I duck in and out of the toilets, or hide behind a trolley. But, inspired by my Milk Tray heist, I nab some tinsel from the hall – a sparkly, green strip – and I manage to pick up a red strip round the corner. There's an artificial tree at the end of the corridor and I slide a handful of decorations off and stuff them into my pocket. I turn round to retreat to the storage room with my haul, then stop in my tracks and jump.

'Elaine!' I squeak when I see her standing in front of me with her arms folded.

'What are you doing here?' she asks.

'Forgot my keys,' I say without pausing.

She tilts her head. 'But you said you don't drive.'

'House keys,' I go on, as a slight wobble creeps into my voice.

'Where's your daughter?'

'Oh, erm.' Heat creeps up my neck. 'Not with me.'

Her lips twist to one side and her expression says, *I can see that*. The air is thick with tension as I cut through it, saying, 'Well, I better get going.'

Elaine's eyes drop to the green and red, glittery tinsel in my hand. Her folded arms pull a fraction closer to her chest.

'For Mrs Brennan,' I say. 'She's been so poorly lately, I thought I could decorate her bedside locker to cheer her up.' The lie leaves an instant bad taste in my mouth. The tinsel is not for Mrs Brennan, but the way Elaine's expression softens tells me she doesn't know that.

'Okay, well, bye then,' I say, walking away brimful of guilt for using a poor old lady's health as a cover-up for my stealing.

'Bea?' Elaine calls after me.

I stop in my tracks and inhale sharply before I turn round. 'Yeah?'

Elaine's arms hang by her sides now and she's looking at me with the concerned expression of a parent, or a caring teacher. 'Is everything all right?'

'Hmm?'

'It's just, you don't seem yourself lately and if there's anything—'

'Everything is fine,' I say much too quickly and eagerly.

Her face is saying a million things all at once and yet I'm not entirely sure what any of those things are. We've never really spoken outside of discussing which cleaner brand to switch to to save on the budget, or checking the roster, or buying new bed pans. I've never actually thought of Elaine as a person outside of work. She has existed to me only as my boss. A woman who tells me where to go and what to do for eight hours a day. I never imagined her with a life, or a family or friends outside of work. But the way she is looking at me now tells me she has thought those things about me. Has she thought about my daughter, and the man I wanted to marry, the life I believed I had and would have? Can she tell it's all gone? Does she know everything is all gone?

'Okay. If you're sure,' she says.

'Mm-hmm,' I say, choking up.

I'm not sure how I feel about this side of Elaine. If she wants to be a concerned colleague, now, with my small child stashed and sleeping in the storage closet, is the worst possible time.

TWENTY-ONE

Ellie is ecstatic when she finds a Christmas jumper ready and waiting for her. It didn't take me all that long to pull it together last night. I found a lovely woolly white jumper in the lost and found box. I knew it would be too big, but I tell myself that oversized is all the rage, even for four-year-olds. I borrowed a suture needle and some thread, although I made sure to bin it after so some poor sod doesn't end up with tinsel stitched above his eyebrow, and I turned up the sleeves and tacked red tinsel all round the cuffs. I stitched the green tinsel across the front in my best attempt to create a Christmas tree. It wasn't exactly clear what it was until I attached the decorations I took from the actual tree. I doubt I'm going to win a prize for my artistry any time soon, but Ellie's shriek of joy and huge hug and kiss, morning breath and all, is the best prize I could ask for.

'Right, chickpea,' I say, peeling her chubby arms from round my neck. 'You need to brush those teeth.'

I wait until everyone is distracted by breakfast before I sneak us into the patients' bathroom and freshen up. After, we dress quickly. I help Ellie into her new jumper and we're both delighted with the results. It can't be comfortable, with so much wool and tinsel, but Ellie never once complains, although she does occasionally scratch her neck. I slip into my uniform in record time and set about hiding the evidence that Ellie and I spent the night. I fold the blankets and stuff them next to our bags behind the floor polisher. That thing is so big and heavy, no one ever moves it unless they absolutely have to. And, really, the only person who absolutely has to is me. Then it's time to sneak out of the hospital before breakfast finishes up.

Ellie sings lines of various Christmas songs, mashed together to create one unique and slightly pitchy tune, and people on the bus are charmed by her excitement. The guy sitting beside us is sipping something cinnamon, and a lady behind us is chatting on her mobile about her shopping list.

'And fresh herbs, don't forget the fresh herbs. Your mother will complain about the stuffing if we use the dried stuff.'

Christmas spirit is thick in the air and there's a sense of happiness that encapsulates everyone. As if the air is made of carols and glitter, and for a little while it's all so lovely to get lost in the sense of it all as I stare out the window and watch the city pass by. Ellie is still singing as we reach crèche.

'Look, look, 'lanna,' Ellie calls out as she charges through the door ahead of me, peeling off her coat and hat and leaving them on the ground. 'Do you like my jumper?'

Alannah looks momentarily horrified, before she pastes on a smile and with a clap of her hands says, 'Wonderful, Ellie. It's very lovely.'

I pick up Ellie's things and stuff them into her box as usual. There is an unmissable, foldaway table next to the storage unit. On top is a rectangular box which looks like a shoe box covered in colourful wrapping paper. Someone has written €5 *Christmas Jumper Day* across the front in thick black marker and there is a plastic Santa proudly standing next to it. It seems to have a motion sensor, because every time one of the other parents drops their donation into the box Santa springs to life, jiggling on the spot and announcing, '*Ho, Ho, Ho, Merry Christmas.*'

Ellie's face fills with joy each time and I am painfully aware of Alannah's eyes on us. I reach into my pocket and pull out a clenched hand, then I walk over to the table and drop my hand into the box full of fivers and coins. I leave a fist full of air behind and whisper, 'Sorry, Santa.'

I jump when he loudly replies, '*Ho, Ho, Ho, Merry Christmas.*'

Alannah laughs and encourages Ellie to run along and play with her friends, and they all happily show each other their jumpers. The other kids' jumpers boast shiny unicorns in Santa hats. Or well-known cartoon characters dressed for the occasion. Unsurprisingly, Ellie's is the only hand-made creation. Surprisingly, however, the other kids seem to love her jumper, and they giggle when Ellie tickles their noses with the tinsel.

'You didn't have to go to so much trouble,' Alannah tells me, staring Ellie's way.

'Weren't we supposed to make our own?' I say, cringing on the inside. 'I thought it was a make-and-do thing.'

'Erm, not really. But I love it. Maybe we'll introduce that idea next year.'

'Do. Do,' I say. 'It was a lot of fun.'

I'm not lying. I enjoyed making Ellie's jumper, and the concentration tired me out and I finally slept afterwards.

I leave as Alannah strikes up a conversation with one of the staff members about whether or not it's too late to suggests parents make a jumper.

'We could run a competition; wouldn't that be fun?' I hear her say as I hurry out the door and start running so I don't miss the bus. I have just enough time to make it back to the hospital and walk inside as if I am arriving for the first time today.

TWENTY-TWO

Routine takes shape quickly. I use opportunities throughout the day to sneak some food and board games into the storage room. Ellie's favourites are strawberry jelly, cornflakes and apple juice. And she loves snakes and ladders, checkers and Connect 4. A lot of the red Connect 4 discs are missing. Ellie is always yellow and she always wins. We try to sneak into the storage room at the earliest opportunity, but sometimes Elaine stays late and we have to lap the grounds or take a walk into town to kill time. Ellie rarely complains; she's too busy asking how many more sleeps until Santa.

Cora calls regularly.

'So, how's the new place? Is Ellie settling in? You still need to send me on your address. Come here for drinks. Or, I'll come to you.'

The chitchat is effortless and I never lie.

'Oh, you know. New place is a bit cramped but we're making it work. Commute is good. But work is busy. I feel like I live here.'

'I hear ya. I hear ya.'

There are plenty of missed calls too. I've started letting

Cora's number go to voicemail more and more often, especially as Christmas edges closer. I can't have another conversation about joining her and her parents for the big day.

'Please. Just have a think about it. That's all I'm saying,' her most recent voice message begins. 'Finton is going to his parents so...' There's a pause before she goes on. 'Mam and Dad haven't seen you in ages and you know how much they love Ellie. They'd be so happy to have her bubbly little face brightening up all our Christmases. And it would get my mam off my back about when I'm going to settle down and pop a kid.' She giggles awkwardly. 'Anyway, pleeeeeeease. What do I have to do to convince you? Seriously, Bea. Call me back!'

My reply to Cora's badgering is always consistent.

'Ellie and I need this Christmas alone. We need to stand on our own feet. It's a lovely offer, and please tell your mam and dad I was asking for them.'

Of course, it couldn't be further from the truth. The last thing I want for Ellie is a Christmas alone with me, hiding out in a tiny room with no windows. But four-year-olds talk. I've no doubt that, after a couple of games of I-Spy with Cora's parents, Ellie would be full of stories about our closet life. It's hard enough trying to throw Alannah off the scent – not that she cares, she's just curious. But Cora and her family have known me since day one of college. They can read me like a book. I wouldn't be able to hide something this huge from them. Not in person. I try to push thoughts of Cora's mam's amazing roast spuds and gravy from my mind and resign myself to a Christmas dinner of pot noodle and a bar of chocolate for dessert.

I wait until Christmas Eve to collect Ellie's Barbie house from Cora's flat. I've left it until the last minute for a variety of reasons. It's going to be almost impossible to hide a three-storey, luminous pink doll's house in such a small space without Ellie spotting it. But more to the point, I waited for a day Finton was home and Cora was not. I haven't seen my best friend since I left her flat. I don't realise until I'm on the bus on my lunch break, on the way to the flat, that I've actively been avoiding her. It's not because I don't want to see her. It's because I can't. It's one thing to tell her in a message that my life is fine. It's another thing entirely to lie to her face.

Finton greets me at the door of the flat. 'Oh, hi, Bea,' he says, clearly shocked by my unexpected arrival. 'Cora's not here, I'm afraid.'

'Yeah, I know,' I say.

He makes a face that asks, *Then why the hell are you here?*

I answer his unasked question. 'I just stopped by to pick up Ellie's doll's house?'

He stares blankly.

'The Barbie one?'

There's still nothing from him and I don't understand. It's a huge pink box. It's kind of hard to miss. Cora hid it in the bottom of their wardrobe, but surely he's come across it by now.

'It's Ellie's Santa present,' I go on.

His brows pinch before he says, 'Oh, shit. That thing.'

Relief washes over me and I wait for him to ask me in.

'Shit, Bea. I thought Cora bought that for Dotty.'

'Dotty?'

'My niece,' he explains. 'She's four. Barbie mad.'

'Yes. All four-year-olds are. Blame Margot Robbie.'

He laughs as if I'm hilarious. But I know for a fact he doesn't find me funny.

'Listen, I hate to rush, but I'm on my lunch break and I really need to get back. I've been late a few times too many recently and my boss is going mad.'

'Right, right,' he says, and his voice is strained as he claps his hands and presses them down on his head. 'Look, Bea. I gave that thing to my sister. For Dotty, you know. I really thought—'

'You gave it away?'

It's a startled question but it comes out like a snappy statement.

'Yeah,' he says, lowering his hands to let them fall limp by his sides. 'Like I said, I thought Cora bought it for Dotty. You know how much she loves kids.'

'Can you get it back? I mean, your niece hasn't opened it or anything. Just swap it for something else.'

'Can't. My sis is gone to Mayo for Christmas. Left yesterday.'

'Fuck!'

My head is spinning and I want to cry. I think I might already be, but I can't tell.

'I'm sorry. I didn't know. I'll pay you for it. How much was it?'

I look at my watch and shake my head. 'It's Christmas Eve,' I tell him as if he doesn't already know. 'Everywhere closes early.'

'Maybe you could pick one up after Christmas, they might even be cheaper in the sale. Kids get some much stuff for Christmas anyway, she probably won't even notice.'

'There is no other stuff,' I say, as tears stream down my cheeks. I cannot bear to think of Ellie's face tomorrow morning when she wakes up thinking Santa forgot her.

'I know,' he says, in a sudden lightbulb moment. 'Cora got something for her. It's here somewhere, hang on.'

He hurries into the flat, leaving me standing at the door. Time ticks by in painful slow motion until he returns with a colourful forest-green bag that proudly declaims *Happy Christmas, Princess* across the front in a swirly gold font.

I look inside. There are jammies, a Barbie in a rectangular pink box complete with a dog and bowl and a tiny bone, a giant lollipop and a rainbow-coloured skipping rope.

I breathe out, making myself almost light-headed. 'Thank you, Cora,' I say, choking back tears, as if she can hear me.

'It's good?' he asks like a schoolboy looking for praise from a teacher.

'It's life-saving,' I say, and it's only a slight exaggeration.

'Oh, here,' he adds, shoving his hand into the back pocket of his jeans to pull out his wallet. 'For the Barbie house. How much was it?'

I'm about to tell him when he shoves four fifty-euro notes at me. I'm not quite sure what to say as I fumble and take the money.

He smiles, as if he's delighted with himself, as he says, 'Anyway, I really am sorry about the mix-up. I hope you guys have a great Christmas. I'll tell Cora you called, yeah?'

I should probably wish him a happy Christmas too. He is the love of my best friend's life, after all. But all I can manage as I stand outside the flat that he hasn't invited me to step foot into is, 'Okay. Bye.'

I walk away clutching the bag of small gifts that will be much easier to hide in the storage room than an oversized doll's house. I promise myself that, if I have to sing Christmas carols until I lose my voice, I am going to make sure Ellie has a wonderful Christmas.

TWENTY-THREE

Although there are no windows in the storage room, I wake up on Christmas morning to find it's snowing again. It's not quite seven a.m. and Ellie is still asleep, but TikTok is already full of videos of people exclaiming, *Happy White Christmas*. There's a short clip of an overweight fifty-something man lapping his garden in just a pair of white boxers, singing 'Jingle Bells' off-key at the top of his lungs. Next is a couple in matching ski suits make snow angels outside their huge, red-brick house. Kids have snowball fights. Someone in a Santa hat walks their sausage dog that they've dressed up as a reindeer, complete with antlers that jiggle when the dog runs. I scroll through a few more videos, before playing a couple of games of Tetris while I wait for Ellie to wake.

Finally, there is some tossing and turning, before her eyes open. It takes a moment for her to wake fully, but when she does she jumps up, throws her arms above her head and asks, 'Did he come? Did he come?'

I produce the green bag from behind my back and Ellie squeals with joy. I place my finger over my lips quickly and say, 'Shh. Shh. Remember, we have to be quiet in here.'

Ellie nods, although I know she's not listening as she reaches her hands out to take the bag. She peeks inside, almost ducking her whole head in, and when she pulls out each small gift her face is so full of joy it almost melts me like a puddle on the ground.

She tries on the jammies, which are a size too big, and I'm delighted that she'll get this year and next out of them. Then we open the box and take Barbie and her puppy out and I tell her that lollipops are okay for breakfast on Christmas. Ellie plays with her new doll contently while she sucks on her lollipop, but after a while she grows restless of the confined space with just a small yellow bulb above our heads for light. I make up games, and she plays on my phone for a while, but when I check my watch, after what feels like hours upon hours, it's only nine a.m. I know I can't keep Ellie cooped up in the storage room all day, so I suggest a walk.

'How about we bring your new skipping rope outside, eh?'

The wards are unusually quiet. Any patient who was well enough to go home for Christmas has, and only the very ill and sleeping remain. It's easier than usual to sneak about, and I take the opportunity to do some laundry. I bring a bag of our dirty clothes into the patients' bathroom. It's hard to get more than a few squirts from the wonky soap dispensers, but I prioritise socks and underwear and scrub everything else as best I can. I use the shower head to rinse with warm water, and I squeeze item after item, all while keeping an eye on Ellie. I have posted her by the door like a little security guard and every so often I say, 'Well, any sign of Santa? Or his reindeers? Keep looking. Tell me if anyone is coming.' After, I drape our dripping clothes around the storage room, confident that no one will be in there today, and finally we go outside to enjoy the freshly falling snow for ourselves.

Ellie tilts her head towards the sky, opens her mouth and catches as many snowflakes as she can on her tongue.

'One, two, teeee,' she says, with her tongue out. 'Four, fiwve, six, Malco,' she shouts.

I look across the car park, surprised, but sure enough I see the back of his bald, snowy head as he sits on the bench.

'Malco, Malco, Malco,' Ellie calls out, racing towards the bench.

'Ellie. Cars,' I scold, instinctively.

Thankfully the car park is almost empty and no one is driving in or out as she trudges through the snow that is nearly up to her knees. I catch up with her almost instantly and we reach the bench together.

'Well, hello,' I say, and my surprise to see him comes out in my voice.

'Hello,' he replies solidly as he looks at me and then Ellie.

'What are you doing here?' I ask.

'Sitting down.'

I giggle sheepishly. 'Well, yes, I can see that, but it's Christmas Day.'

'Do people not sit on Christmas Day? Are we supposed to stand for twenty-four hours?' he deadpans.

I sigh and try again. 'I mean, it's Christmas, shouldn't you be with family? Where is Shayne?'

'He is with *his* family. His father and that new wife of his.'

I note that this must make Malcolm Shayne's maternal grandfather.

'And your daughter, Shayne's mother,' I say, hoping I've got the family tree correct. 'Are you spending the day with her?'

Malcolm's eyes narrow and I think I may have pried a little too hard.

'Not this year,' he says, after a long pause.

I'm instantly curious. *Is she busy?* But who is so busy they would leave their elderly father alone on a car park bench on Christmas Day? Perhaps she lives abroad, I think. But again, surely she'd have arranged for her father to travel to her. I'm searching my brain for other possibilities when Malcolm says, 'I haven't spoken to her in years.'

I look at Ellie. She is rolling snow into balls at my feet, and I can't imagine a time when she won't be the most important person in my world. I can't possibly comprehend what it must be like for a parent and child not to speak.

'She works here. Like you.'

'Oh,' I say, my heart heavy as I realise that his daughter must be what brings him to this bench so often.

There's a flash of something on his face, curiosity, I think, and I know what he is going to ask.

'What are you doing here?'

Although I guessed his question correctly, my brain doesn't have time to compute a reasonable answer. I'm not wearing my uniform, so I can't say I was working.

'We didn't really have anywhere else to go,' I say, truthfully.

My honesty seems to confuse him even more. 'No family,' he says, and it's not a question.

I shake my head.

'No friends?' he goes on, and this time I can tell he's asking.

'I have a good friend, but…' I inhale and cold air stings my lungs. 'Ah, it's complicated.'

'Life is,' he says.

'No one should be alone on Christmas Day,' I say.

'Who's alone?' He draws an imaginary circle round Ellie and me and him. 'Can you cook?'

I pull my head back until I have three chins at the strange, sudden shift in the conversation.

'Cook?'

'Yes. The art of making raw things safe to eat. Can you cook, Bea?'

I yelp suddenly as an icy snowball flies into my welly and instantly starts to melt. I look at Ellie, who is grinning, delighted with her throw. I balance on one foot as I take off my boot and shake the offending, freezing ball out. Malcolm's deep chuckle fills the air, but it is quickly silenced by a small snowball hitting him in the knee.

'Ellie,' I gasp, quickly pulling my welly back on.

There is a brief moment where I'm lost for words before I begin to apologise. But I don't get time to say anything before Malcolm's laughter grows louder.

'Gotcha.' Ellie giggles.

'You got me,' Malcolm says, rubbing his knee, for what I hope is dramatic effect rather than Ellie having actually hurt him.

'That's enough now,' I warn, catching Ellie bending down to gather more snow from the corner of my eye.

Deflated, she stands up and dries her hands on her front, turning her minty-green coat teal in wet patches.

'So can you?' Malcolm asks, pulling my attention away from Ellie's coat.

'Cook?' I ask, wondering if the wet patches will dry out and leave a stain. 'I can cook.'

'Are you any good?'

'I think so,' I say. 'I mean, I'm no Gordon Ramsay or anything but—'

'Good,' he says, getting to his feet. It takes some time for him to rise fully upright and Ellie finds the process fascinating and hilarious. 'I'm starving.'

'Me too,' Ellie concurs.

I'm very hungry too but I don't say anything. I'm not entirely sure what's happening here.

'My house isn't far,' Malcolm says, pointing as if I will find his home at the end of his finger. 'I've nothing in, mind you. So we'll have to do a shop first.'

'Excuse me?'

I'm so confused.

'We're going shopping,' Ellie pipes up as if she's helping to explain.

'You can cook. I can't. Seem the logical solution is you come to my house and cook dinner?' Malcolm says, and I swear his explanation is less helpful than Ellie's. I stare blankly.

'Look,' he goes on. 'I'm hungry. The kid is hungry. And I've a big kitchen. You said yourself you'd nowhere to go, so it all just makes sense, doesn't it?'

'You want me to come to your house and cook you Christmas dinner.'

'Yes,' he says, concisely.

That's ridiculous, I think. *It's bonkers, awkward, weird, totally unexpected and simply batshit crazy.*

'Okay,' I say, 'let's do it.'

The words that come out of my mouth are a direct contradiction to the thoughts swirling in my head. And yet, I think, I'm excited. The idea of a warm home and a big dinner are tantalising. More than that, I can tell how delighted Malcolm is by the prospect of sharing his table with Ellie and me.

'The shops will all be closed,' I say, and I watch his face fall. 'But there's a petrol station round the corner. I doubt we'll get a turkey or ham, but I'm sure we'll find something we can make work.'

'Yay,' Ellie cries excitedly, although I can tell she has no idea what is happening.

TWENTY-FOUR

I was wrong. The petrol station is selling off small turkeys for half price and the guy behind the counter throws in a free ham.

'No one is going to want these after today,' he says.

We buy potatoes, vegetables and chocolate cake for dessert. Malcolm insists on paying for everything. So, when his back is turned, I pick up a Christmas card and leave the exact amount of cash on the counter.

Malcolm wasn't exaggerating when he said his house wasn't far. It's less than a ten-minute walk to his front door. And I know which house is his before he says a word. It's a large, red-brick, Georgian house, identical to its neighbours that line both sides of the road. But while the other houses have been upgraded over the years with new, cream or grey windows, and had their large front gardens landscaped and tall, wrought-iron electric gates fitted, Malcolm's house has a personality all of its own – standing out from the crowd, proudly and uniquely. The front grass is long enough to poke up through the layers of snow like tiny green spikes. The gate must be as old as Malcolm himself and it's in need of a lick of paint. There's a glass porch and inside is a free-standing coat rack that is home to several long chequered coats. There are pairs and pairs of wellington boots scattered inside the porch too. I count them and get eight in total. And finally, there are some flower pots without flowers. Instead, some tennis rackets sit in the pots as if they have sprouted from racket seeds and grown into small racket trees. Rackets that I know Malcolm plucks at will and attaches to the bottom of his wellingtons.

'This way,' he says, with a plastic bag dragging from each hand. I worry that they were too heavy and offer to carry them, but he scowls at me and says, 'My arms work just fine.'

I don't bring the bags up again. Not even when we have to stop for a moment on the corner for him to catch his breath. There is a narrow path in the snow, leading from the gate to the door, and I wonder if Shayne hand-dug it. We have to walk single file to fit. Malcolm goes first, then Ellie and then me. The porch door slides back with a creak and Malcolm kicks his shoes off. Ellie and I do the same. The front door creaks even louder as it opens. Inside smells of an open fire and burnt toast.

'Ew,' Ellie says, holding her nose.

I glare at her with wide eyes, but she doesn't take her hand down and I don't want to scold her and draw Malcolm's attention.

The hallway is long and narrow and full of colour. Lilac walls. A multicoloured carpet with a dominant maroon tint and a pattern that reminds me of ocean waves. The stairs are a creamy-yellow, but I can tell they were once white and have darkened over the years.

'Can I watch telly now?' Ellie asks, already taking herself through an open doorway that I can see leads to a sitting room.

'You can,' Malcolm tells her as he follows her.

I poke my head round the door and into a room with the exact same décor as the hall. I watch as he turns on a large, cube-shaped television in the corner that reminds me of the one my parents had when I was Ellie's age. There doesn't appear to be a remote control, and Malcolm brings the thing to life by pressing buttons on the front. Ellie lowers herself to sit on the floor, cross-legged, in front of the big black box as a Disney classic comes on the screen.

'*Lady and the Tramp*,' I say. 'I love this one.'

Ellie has stopped listening and is fully engrossed in the image of two dogs sharing meatballs at a restaurant-style table. Something rattles and I shift my gaze to Malcolm, to find him tossing some coal from a dusty black bucket onto a barely burning open fire. He tucks in a large safety guard that encapsulates the whole fireplace and says, 'There. That should heat up soon.'

'Don't touch,' I warn Ellie, who's never seen a real fire in her life before. 'It's very hot.'

Malcolm leaves the room without another word and for a moment I'm not sure if I should follow him or not.

Soon he calls out, 'Dinner won't cook itself.'

I take my cue and find the kitchen at the end of the hallway. The kitchen is blue. Very blue. The walls are the colour of the sky on a summer's day. The cupboards are a slightly darker shade, edging towards turquoise, and the floor tiles are a vibrant mix of both colours. It's how I imagine being lost at sea might feel. There is a small, brown table in front of a large window overlooking a garden that I can tell under the snow is completely overgrown. Various sized and shaped trees and shrubs are dotted haphazardly around the space.

There's a low buzzing sound coming from somewhere and I look round to discover that Malcolm has turned the oven on to preheat. He's placed the plastic bags on the countertop with the groceries still inside. He's fetched slippers from somewhere and he sits at the table with his legs crossed and I can't see completely from where I'm standing but I think he's attempting the crossword in the paper.

I have no idea what to say or do. I get the impression he

wants me to unpack and make myself at home, but I don't feel right.

'Excuse me,' I say, my voice catching like a lump in my throat. 'What exactly is happening here?'

He puts down his pen and looks up at me, as if he's the confused one.

'Dinner,' he says, with a firm nod.

'Yes. I know. But...' I search my brain for a way to make this all less strange, but I'm standing in odd socks in a man I scarcely know's kitchen on Christmas Day with a petrol station-bought turkey on the countertop. I think we have long passed weird, so I decide to just spit it out.

'You don't expect me to cook alone, do you?'

He's expressionless as he looks at me. The deep lines around his eyes and mouth don't so much as budge.

'I mean, you're going to help, right?'

'I wasn't planning to.'

My eyes widen. 'Oh, really.'

'I'm not a good cook.'

I jam my hands onto my hips. 'That sounds like an excuse to me.'

He smiles and the lines in his face deepen. 'I'm not. I'm not at all. I can just about make beans on toast.'

I think of the smell of burnt toast that seems to have lessened now and I believe him.

'Okay. We'll start with basics,' I say, making my way to the countertop to begin unpacking.

'You're going to teach me?' he scoffs.

I pull out potatoes and carrots first. 'You can start with these. Where do you keep your peeler?'

'Don't you think I'm a little old to learn how to cook now?'

'No. I do not,' I say, pulling out the rest of the ingredients for dinner from the bags. 'You're never too old to learn something new.'

I expect him to grumble and find an excuse to get back to his crossword. And If he does, I won't argue. It's his house after all. He's paid for dinner and given me and Ellie a warm house to enjoy a good meal in. But he rolls up his sleeves with a force of determination that is both unnecessarily intense and wholly admirable.

We stuff the turkey, boil the ham, peel potatoes and carrots and chat effortlessly. I tell Malcolm about Declan and he says, 'What a prick.' I drop a carrot on my toe with shock and Malcolm says, 'Don't waste good vegetables on the prick.'

He tells me about his wife who passed twenty years ago and his voice cracks every time he says her name. 'My Alison was a beauty. My Alison was an amazing cook. My Alison had the best taste in décor. My Alison was the love of my life. She was the only one who could keep the peace between me and my daughter.'

I try asking him about what happened. How they ended up not speaking. 'You must miss her,' I say. 'Almost as much as you miss your wife.'

Malcolm doesn't reply. He bends down and opens a low cupboard. I worry when it takes him a long time to stand back up. But slowly he pulls himself upright and turns round to display a bottle of wine.

'I hope you like red,' he says.

I smile.

He fetches two ginormous glasses that I'm almost certain are gin goblets and not wine glasses. He struggles a little with the cork, but finally it pops and he pours generously into both glasses. We join Ellie in the sitting room with our wine as we wait for the turkey and ham to cook. Ellie sings along with the songs at the top of her lungs and Malcolm says, 'You really need to get that child some singing lessons.'

The movie ends and another begins straight away.

'*Frozen*,' Ellie shrieks with delight when the opening credits to her favourite movie begin to play. She spins around and sings and I have to warn her countless times not to twirl into the fire. Malcolm spends a lot of the movie with his hands over his ears and his face scrunched.

'Ellie, shh. Not so loud,' I say, draining my glass and feeling the wine go to my head.

I look at Malcolm to find his glass is barely touched. Instead, his head is flopped onto the back of the couch, his mouth is open and a raspy snore rattles his chest. Ellie soon tires of spinning and comes to sit beside me on the couch. Within minutes, there is a small child asleep on one side of me and an elderly man asleep on the other and it feels exactly as I imagine Christmas should. I sit contently for quite some time before the sound of the front door opening startles me and I hurry into the hall.

Shayne clutches his chest and jumps back when he sees me.
'Bea. Wow. Hello?'

His surprise is natural and reasonable and yet it still rattles me and I find myself stumbling over words.

'I, eh, your grandad invited me. And Ellie. Ellie is here. She's asleep. He's asleep too. Your grandad, I mean. Asleep on the couch. We had some wine. Well, I had wine. He didn't really drink his. And I'm cooking dinner. It's in the oven right now, and, eh...' I pause and catch my breath as if I'm coming up from under water. 'And so, yeah, I'm cooking.'

He nods as if anything I just said makes sense and doesn't raise a million questions.

'It's nice to see you again. I didn't think I would.'

'No. Yeah. Yes. No.' I shake my head and try again. 'I didn't think so either. But then I bumped into your grandad—'

'At the hospital again, was he?' Shayne asks.

I know it's a rhetorical question but I find myself answering nonetheless.

'Yeah. On the bench again.'

Shayne sighs and I can sense his sadness that his mother and his grandfather don't speak. I wonder if I should bring it up, but I squash the thought quickly, knowing it's the wine talking.

'He wasn't wearing a hat again,' I settle on saying instead.

Shayne laughs and I know it's come out like a small child telling tales. Ellie does it all the time. *So-and-so took my toy car. And they wouldn't let me be the leader. And they did a wee-wee on the floor.*

'Is there any more wine?' he asks.

I nod. 'In the kitchen.'

'Another glass?' he asks.

'Sure,' I say, too quickly, and he laughs again.

'Let's leave them to sleep for a while.' He tilts his head towards the kitchen. 'Anything you need help with? I am a mean carrot-peeler.'

'Like your grandad,' I say, but the joke is lost on Shayne as he looks at me confused.

'Nothing. Never mind. Carrots all done. But there's a crossword in there that we could tackle while we wait for the turkey to finish?'

Shayne snorts. 'A crossword.'

'Yeah,' I say, suddenly serious. 'Don't people do stuff like that at Christmas?'

'I didn't know a Christmas crossword was a thing.'

I feel a heat creep into my cheeks. 'No. I mean, it's Christmas. People take the time to do the stuff they normally don't. Like, they sit down and drink wine and watch a kids' movie even though they hate the songs. And they do the crossword while they wait for the turkey. And they just talk, you know.'

'Yeah,' he says, smiling brightly. 'People should talk at Christmas.'

Despite the wine making my head fuzzy, I wonder if he's referring to his mother and his grandfather.

'I'm sorry. I didn't mean…' I trail off before finding a better approach. 'I'm just happy to be here. I didn't really have Christmas growing up.'

'You didn't.'

I shake my head. I don't want to get into a *woe is me my childhood sucked* conversation so I simply say, 'That was a long time ago. It's different now. I have Ellie.'

A huge smile unzips across his face and he says, 'Christmas must be great with a kiddo. So exciting.'

I swallow hard. Suddenly I think talking about my shitty childhood would be a lot easier than lying about my currently shitty adulthood.

'Do you smell burning?' I say, abruptly. I don't smell anything but I'm desperate to change the subject.

Shayne sniffs the air. 'Nope. No burning. But something smells A-mazing.'

He's right. The air smells delicious as scents of browning turkey waft from the kitchen and beckon us.

'Let's leave those two sleeping beauties to it,' he suggests.

'*Sleeping Beauty*,' I echo, much too loudly for the small space of the hall. 'That's on next.'

'Well, I'm afraid you're going to miss it. We have a dinner finish cooking.'

'We?'

'Well, clearly Grandad is no help, and I'm not going to leave you to do all the work alone.'

'You can cook?' I say, delighted.

'Nope,' he admits, oddly proudly. 'But that's never stopped me before.'

I belly-laugh. It makes the wine inside me swirl but I don't stop.

'You're a lot like your grandfather, you know.'

'Yeah.' He smiles, taking it the way I meant it. As a compliment. 'I think I am.'

TWENTY-FIVE

Dinner is spectacular. The turkey is moist. The stuffing is herby and crunchy. The carrots and potatoes are cooked to perfection. The ham is mostly still raw in the middle, so we set that aside and decide who needs ham when you have turkey anyway. Malcolm finishes his wine and Shayne pours me another giant glass. There isn't any left for him and I apologise and plead with him to take my glass.

'I didn't back-wash, I promise, hic,' I say.

He shakes his head and says, 'I'm not a big red fan. More a white guy.'

'That's a big fat lie,' Malcolm says, and Ellie says, 'You shouldn't talk with your mouth full, Malco.'

Everyone laughs.

Mid-meal, Shayne runs out to his car to fetch a box of Christmas crackers. Ellie pulls every single one, taking it in turns to pull with me, Malcolm and Shayne. At one stage she has seven paper hats, in the colours of the rainbow, on her head at once.

'You didn't have to come, you know,' Malcolm says out of

nowhere. 'I manage just fine on my own three hundred and sixty-four days a year. Christmas is no different.'

Shayne ignores Malcolm's grumbles and pulls the final cracker with Ellie. The snap is loud. Dramatically so, but I'm grateful for the sound that cuts through the suddenly tense air.

'So, why are you here?' Malcolm goes on. 'I can take care of myself. I keep telling you, Shayne.'

'I know.'

'I bet your father had plenty to say when you upped and left.'

Shayne places the final hat on Ellie's head. 'Pink is your colour,' he says, deflecting. Ellie smiles and, thankfully, the tension seems to wash over her.

'I bet his new wife loved that.' Malcolm drags it back, and I can't understand where this sudden anger is coming from.

'They're married fourteen years, Grandad. She's hardly his new wife.'

'She's a gold-digger.' Malcolm huffs. 'That's what she is.'

Shayne sighs and I get the feeling they've had this conversation before.

'She's every bit as bad as that blond girl you're hooked up with. She's not with you for your looks or charming personality, I'll tell you that.'

Something flashes across Shayne's face but it's gone before I can make out what it is. Hurt, or anger. Maybe a little bit of both.

There is nothing wrong with Shayne's appearance; in fact, I'm surprised I didn't notice his good looks before now – not Hollywood handsome, with chiselled jaw and big muscles, but his blue eyes are the colour of the sea after a storm and his brown hair is giving nineties boy-band chic. He's not particularly tall or short, and his go-to look seems to be jeans and a hoodie. And, although I don't know much about him besides, he works in tech and has a Dublin–New York twangy accent, he seems to be a pretty decent guy.

'Lisa and I split up,' Shayne says. And I realise the look on his face was heartbreak. Heartbreak he's buried so deep that it only shows for a split second when his guard drops. I get it.

Malcolm's lips round into an O shape. 'Well, I can't say I'm disappointed.'

'You could say that, actually, Grandad. You know, just to make me feel better.'

'But it wouldn't be true. I never liked that girl. I said it, didn't I? Right from the start. And now you've wasted years on her and look where it got you.' Malcolm glances around his kitchen as if Shayne's being here is some sort of failing.

Shayne pushes his plate away from him as if the sight of food is turning his stomach. 'Maybe, for once, you could try to keep your thoughts to yourself?'

'Don't tell me what to do in my own home.' Malcolm raises his voice and Ellie jumps. She hurries over to me and tucks her head against my arm.

There is still food on all our plates, but I wonder if Ellie and I should leave. I hate to pull her away from a good meal and a warm house, but I don't think it's appropriate for us to be here right now.

'We should go,' I say, draping my arm over Ellie to tuck her closer to me.

'No. Don't,' Malcolm and Shayne say together, so in time it almost sounds like one voice.

'Stay, please?' Shayne adds.

I look at Malcolm. It's his house and I really think the invite to continue on should come from him. I watch him take a measured breath as he looks back at me. But he doesn't say another word, and I suspect he won't. His knitted brows and sad eyes tell me he doesn't want an empty house. Today of all days.

'*Sleeping Beauty* is starting soon,' I say. 'Maybe we could all watch it together?'

A sense of calm follows and it's as if Disney can fix anything. I bite my tongue before I break into a chorus of 'Once Upon a Dream'. Damn wine!

We finish our food, but not until we've all helped ourself to seconds. Malcolm announces the turkey was a bit dry as he piles a couple more slices onto his plate. Ellie runs around the table, full of too much chocolate cake and shop-brand cola.

Malcolm holds up his glass and says, 'It's much better value than the real stuff. And who can taste the difference?'

'Everyone,' Shayne retorts.

And I wonder if this is their thing. Malcolm says one thing and Shayne argues the other, and vice versa. Not in a mean or judgemental way. It's more of a habit. A tic. Something neither of them are even aware of.

'Where's your Christmas tree?' Ellie asks, bringing the chatter in the room to a sudden stop. 'We have a big giant Christmas tree.'

'Oh, do you?' Malcolm says.

'Yep. Huge.'

My heart races. Ellie and I most certainly do not have a Christmas tree. I retrieved the tinsel from her Christmas jumper and draped it over the floor polisher. It didn't add quite the festive feel to the storage room that I was hoping for, but Ellie seemed pleased. I can only assume right now that she's talking about the tree at crèche. Or the one in the hospital lobby.

'It smells nice too but if you gets too close its prickles getcha.' She rubs her nose with both her hands and I realise she's referring to the giving tree outside St Stephen's Green Park.

'There's cards on the tree and if you're alls by yourself, you can take one for your chin-ney. We don't gots a chin-ney. But Santa came nee-way. Didn't he, Mammy?'

'Whoa,' I say, almost winded by Ellie's rambling confession. 'Yes. Yes he did. Cos you were such a good girl.'

Shayne breathes in, and I sense he's overly invested in every word Ellie is sharing.

'We're missing *Sleeping Beauty*.' I say, trying to redirect the focus.

'Hang on.' Shayne raises a finger in the air. 'Tell me more, Ellie.'

He looks at me as if to say, *Let's hear her out*, and I have no escape. I can only hope Ellie doesn't dob us and our storage room living in.

'I like trees,' Ellie says, bouncing on the spot, and suddenly that four-year-old concentration span that drives me crazy when we're running late and getting dressed for crèche is a mammoth task becomes my favourite thing.

'Well then, we need a tree,' Shayne says, rolling with the director's cut.

'I haven't had a tree in twenty years,' Malcolm says.

'Since Grandma and Mam left, I know,' Shayne says. 'But maybe....' He takes a breath. 'For this little lady.' He looks at Ellie.

Malcolm's eyes glisten and I want to hug him. Again, damn wine.

'Absolutely,' he says. 'Yes indeed. We need a tree.' He looks at Shayne. 'Go on, then. You know where the axe is.'

Shayne looks back at him, perplexed.

'You loved the shed as a kid,' Malcolm tells him. 'And there's a garden full of trees out there. Take your pick.'

Shayne stands up from the table and bends in the middle to come down to Ellie's height. 'Will you help me?'

Ellie throws her arms in the air and Shayne opens the kitchen door that leads into the snowy and overgrown garden.

Malcolm shouts at them to close the door as an icy wind slices in. They're scarcely out of earshot when Malcolm turns to me and with a charming and slightly cheeky grin says, 'Did you hear that, Busy Bea, my grandson is single. But you'd want to be quick, he's a fine catch.'

I choke on air.

TWENTY-SIX

It's not long before Shayne and Ellie return with a tree that Shayne can just about manage to carry tucked under his arm.

'What's that?' Malcolm asks, slowly getting to his feet.

Shayne sets the tree down between them. It's tall and narrow, coming up past his shoulders.

'That's one funny-looking Christmas tree.' Malcolm rolls his eyes.

'I did my best,' Shayne says. 'It's so snowy outside I couldn't see a thing. And this was green and tall. It does the job.'

'If you say so.'

'I do.' Shayne nods. 'And besides, Ellie likes it.'

'I like it, I like it,' Ellie says, clapping her hands.

Water is staring to pool on the tiles where the last of the snow melts from the branches.

'Don't slip, Grandad,' Shayne says, as he picks the tree up once more. 'You either, Ellie, be careful.'

I smile at his consideration for both the elderly and the very young. He takes the tree into the sitting room, where *Sleeping Beauty* is playing on the television. Malcolm fetches the coal. He struggles with the weight of the half-full bucket and I hurry to help. We place it in the corner and Shayne pops the tree in. It's tricky to get it to stay standing in the bucket and we have to move the coals around at the base like little weights locking it in place. We wash our hands and return to admire our handiwork.

'It's crooked.' Malcolm tuts.

'It's fine,' Shayne says.

'It's the bestest,' Ellie chirps.

'Do we have any decorations?' I ask.

Malcolm shakes his head. 'This was stupid. It's just a regular garden tree in a bucket.'

Shayne raises his hand. 'Hang on,' he says, then disappears.

He returns moments later with a roll of toilet paper, the paper hats and the remains of crackers that are already cracked.

'We just need a little colour,' he says, the American in his accent sounding thicker and excited.

Ellie takes the hats and hangs each one carefully on a branch. Then she takes the hats from her head and adds those too. However, I'm unsurprised when she keeps the yellow one for her head. Next, Shayne shows her how to roll the cracker halves into colourful balls, which attempt to unroll almost as soon as they let go. They pop them on various branches like paper baubles. Lastly, Shayne and Ellie wind toilet paper round and round the tree.

'Just like tinsel,' Shayne says.

Malcolm folds his arms. 'Nothing like tinsel. I hope the neighbours don't see this thing.'

Ellie leaves her decorating spot and takes the old man's hand as she guides him closer. 'Do you like it, Malco?' she asks.

His brittle exterior melts like butter as he holds her hand and a huge smile takes over his whole face. 'I think it's wonderful.'

When I spent Christmases in foster care, sitting at the tables of people I barely knew and watching them interact effortlessly, I always wondered what it would be like to be a part of a family.

What it would be like to be inside the bubble, rather than on the outside staring in through the shimmering surface. Right now, watching Malcolm hold Ellie's hand the way a loving grandfather might and telling her the world's quite possibly ugliest abomination of a wannabe Christmas tree is wonderful, is the nearest I have ever felt to being inside the bubble.

After, Shayne opens a box of Cadbury Roses and we all sit down to catch the last of *Sleeping Beauty*. It's perfectly mundane and by far the best Christmas in years. It's dark outside when the movie ends, and Malcolm is napping again.

I stand up to stretch my legs and say, 'We should probably get going.'

'Nooooo,' Ellie grumbles with chocolate-rimmed lips. 'I don't wanna go.'

'You're more than welcome to stay,' Shayne says, sounding as deflated as Ellie about the prospect of the day coming to an end. 'I could open more wine. Grandad has a cupboard full. There's some gin there too if you'd rather—'

'No, no, God no,' I say, quickly. The thought of sneaking back into the storage room tipsy fills me with dread.

'Okay, at least let me drop you home, yeah?'

My dread cranks up a notch to complete panic. Shayne can't drop us back to the hospital. What would I even say? 'Oh, I love cleaning vomit so much, I even pop in hoping for some Christmas puke'?

'Ah, that's a really nice offer but I couldn't put you out,' I say.

His smile is warm and lights up the whole room. 'It's no trouble. It's not as if I'm missing tantalising conversation here.'

We both glance at Malcolm sleeping soundly on the couch once more.

'You've had wine.' I try again to put him off.

He shakes his head. 'Didn't actually. White guy, remember?'

I remember, but I find myself wishing he liked red wine and can't drive.

'I think this little one needs a walk,' I say, tilting my head towards Ellie, who is curled like a seashell on the couch next to Malcolm. She looks cosy and ready to join him in the land of nod. It breaks my heart to drag her out in the cold.

Shayne squints as he looks at Ellie and I can tell he thinks I'm crazy, but he doesn't criticise or contradict my parenting.

My eyes narrow. Ellie falls asleep. I want to stay.

'It's pitch-dark out there.' Shayne points towards the window, where tall streetlamps are doing a stellar job of painting the snowy landscape with a golden glue and it's really quite beautiful, as if a Christmas card has come to life outside the window. 'And freezing and there isn't a soul out there. I can't let you guys walk alone.'

'We'll be fine,' I say, thinking of the short walk round the corner to the hospital.

'Really, Bea, please. I just don't feel right letting you trek across the city alone.'

I remember Shayne thinks we have to walk back to my old apartment, and the thought of walking all the way back across the city after he leaves us sends panic down my spine. But I have no choice. I cannot let anyone find out where Ellie and I really sleep. Not even Shayne or Malcolm. If anyone reported how dire things are for us the authorities would take Ellie away. I can't lose her. A walk across the snowy city is a small price to pay to keep our secret safe.

'You know what,' I say, staring at the dark sky outside. 'If you're still offering, a lift would be great.'

'I'll get my keys.'

Shayne goes outside to start the car and I turn the TV volume down and cover Malcolm with a blanket. I find a pen on the coffee table and fetch the petrol-station Christmas card from behind the toaster. Inside reads *Merry Christmas and Happy*

New Year in a dark bold font. I simply add, *with love from Bea and Ellie xx* and leave it and the pen on the coffee table.

Then I scoop Ellie into my arms, noting how much she's grown and how heavy she's getting. I slip my wellies back on and follow Shayne to a sporty silver car that doesn't seem at all ready for the challenge of navigating the slippery roads. Thankfully he doesn't bring up the lack of car seat again, but nonetheless guilt sits in my gut like a weight and it's so heavy it feels as if it wants to pull me to the ground. Maybe Ellie would be better off if they did take her away. At least she's have a car seat to keep her travel safe. And a cosy warm bed. And meals like today all the time. And Disney movies on TV. I push the thoughts aside quickly, remembering that, although I had all of these things when I was in foster care, it didn't fill the void where a loving family should be. Ellie has me. I love her more than air. We can figure the rest out.

Shayne drives carefully and I begin to think we'd have been faster on foot. And yet, all too soon my old apartment block comes into view. It looks very different today, with the shops underneath closed up for the occasion. There's no sandwich board outside the coffee shop. No buckets of multicoloured flowers in water outside the florist. No chatter of customers stopping by. Shutters are down and everyone is at home with their families. It's exactly as it should be. Except for the final shutter that I know belongs to a small lashes and brows start-up business. The snow is cleared in a small area directly in front of the door and there is something bright and glossy on the ground. I strain my eyes for a better view and jolt when the glossy blue something moves and I realise it's a sleeping bag. When Shayne parks the car next to the kerb, I can see a head of salt-and-pepper hair with a dark green beanie on top poking out. I balk and clutch my chest.

'What is it? What's wrong?' Shayne asks.

'Someone's there.' I point.

'Oh shit. Yeah.'

Shayne hops out of the car and hurries towards the sleeping bag and I open the back door and lift Ellie into my arms. I hold her tight, as if my warm embrace can keep us safe from our own homelessness.

'Hey, buddy,' I hear Shayne say as he crouches next to the sleeping bag. 'Buddy, can you hear me? Are you okay?'

I edge closer. Scared. I'm not afraid of the poor unfortunate man sleeping on the ground, but seeing him cold and lonely, taking shelter in an icy doorway, terrifies me. A painful reminder that it could so easily be me. I lost myself today in Disney cartoons and delicious turkey, and it was marvellous. But already, it is over. Shayne will leave us here, in a place I pretend to live, and I will have to drag an exhausted child across an empty city to hide in a closet. The thought of it bends me in the middle and I almost let it break me. But I pull myself upright and roll my shoulders back. *No!* Ellie and I just have to hide for a little longer, long enough to save a month's rent and find a new, real flatshare. I can do this. I have to. Ellie needs cartoons and good food every day and I am going to do everything I possibly can to make sure she gets it.

'Buddy,' Shayne calls out again, and the fear in his voice cuts through the icy air and demands my attention.

'Is he okay?' I call back, disturbing Ellie. She lifts her head off my shoulder and yawns.

'Home,' she says, sleepily, and my heart pinches.

'Is he okay?' I repeat, louder this time.

I see Shayne shake his head before I hear him say, 'He's breathing, but I can't wake him. He's like ice.'

I walk over, my feet crunching in the thick snow.

'It must be minus something out here,' Shayne goes on as he looks up at the cloudy sky that might spit heavy snow at any moment. 'We can't leave him here. He won't make it through the night. Especially not if it gets any colder.'

I nod. 'We should call an ambulance?'

Shayne shakes his head. 'We need to get him warm right now. I say we get him into the car and drive to the hospital.'

I balk for a moment. I think about a journey across the city with a dying man and my four-year-old in the back of the car.

'What if he's dangerous?'

Shayne looks at me seriously. 'I think this poor man is a little too busy struggling to survive, to have time to hurt anyone.'

I nod. I hate myself for going there. I can only imagine what people would say about me if they knew. They'd blame drugs. Or booze. Or maybe a gambling habit.

'Get him into the car,' I say.

I put Ellie down so I can help Shayne lift the man. We manage to get him onto his feet and he drops in and out of consciousness.

'What's your name?' Shayne asks.

It takes six attempts and baby steps across the footpath but finally we get him into the car and learn his name is John and he's been homeless eleven months.

Eleven months. The thought of still living in the storage room in almost a year's time consumes me and quickly I remind myself of my savings that are going to get Ellie and me out of this mess. In eleven months our lives will be back on track. In eleven months we will be okay. We have to be.

I sit in the back seat with Ellie and John. Shayne starts the engine, but before we drive off he twists round in his seat to look at me.

'You okay?'

'Yeah. Just worried about John,' I say, which isn't a complete lie.

'Yeah.' Shayne swallows, turning back round. 'Homelessness is so sad. But we're going to get him help.'

TWENTY-SEVEN

I tried to visit John on St Stephen's Day. But the fact that I didn't know his second name, whether or not he'd been admitted and if so to what ward made finding him as difficult as searching for a needle in a haystack. Ellie and I spent the day wandering the city instead. I hoped the cinema would be open so we could kill a couple of hours, but it wasn't. I was torn between being glad to save the price of the tickets and add it to a flat deposit and flustered, cold and bored as we dotted in and out of shops we couldn't possibly buy anything from.

Today, two days after Christmas, I am glad to get back to a routine. I drop Ellie to crèche. And Órlaith is back on reception at the hospital. Her face lights up with the challenge of finding John Doe.

'I always wanted to be a detective,' she tells me. 'Like your one in *Murder, She Wrote*.'

'Wasn't she a writer?' I ask, almost certain.

'No. No,' Órlaith says, with conviction. 'Definitely a detective. Anyway, leave it with me. I'll find the homeless guy.'

The homeless guy. The words are like a knife to my gut.

'John,' I say. 'His name is John.'

She dismisses me with a wave of her hand. 'Yeah. Yeah, I know. John Doe. That's actually funny, isn't it?'

My face hopefully says that it is not funny at all, but since I'm asking her for a favour here I don't pull her up on it.

'I'll pop back at lunchtime, yeah?' I say.

'Cool. I should have found something out by then.'

A queue is forming behind me and I step aside. I'm about to go back upstairs and see if there is any rice pudding left over after patients' lunch, but the double doors part and I spot Malcolm on the bench under the oak tree. I hurry out.

I'm not quite halfway across the car park when he points at my feet and shakes his head. I'm wearing my work shoes. My wellingtons are in the storage room, where they will stay hidden behind a bucket until it is time to change into them and pick Ellie up.

'I know, I know,' I say, hurrying towards him and looking down at my feet. 'But I'm just popping out quickly to say—'

'Well, you shouldn't hurry anywhere in those. Take your time. What's the rush?'

'I'm on my lunch break, I have to get back. But I just wanted to thank you for Christmas.'

'Why?'

My nose scrunches. 'Sorry?'

'Why are you thanking me?'

He's serious as always, but I'm not sure how to answer. Most people just accept the platitude and move on. But Malcolm is asking for an actual breakdown of my gratitude.

'Dinner was delicious,' I begin. 'I haven't seen Ellie eat so much in such a long time. She was so full I'm surprised she didn't have a tummy ache.'

'You cooked. Not me,' he says, without blinking.

'Well yes, but in your kitchen.'

'So, thank me for my kitchen, then.'

'Oh, erm, okay. Thank you for your kitchen, I suppose.'

He nods, satisfied. 'You're welcome. Thank you for your card.'

'Oh, you liked it?' I smile, feeling warm inside.

His brow furrows. 'I didn't say that. I said thank you.'

'Oh.' I try not to smirk at how pedantically Malcolm chooses and uses words. 'You are also welcome, then.'

He looks at the empty space beside him on the bench and I suspect he's waiting for me to sit down.

'Is Shayne with you?' I ask, cutting myself off as I reach the last syllable, expecting Malcolm to tell me his grandson isn't his keeper or some such retort.

I'm surprised when he points across the cleared and salted car park at a sporty silver car I instantly recognise. I smile when I see Shayne sitting behind the wheel. I wave and he waves back.

'Isn't he going to sit beside you?' I find the words tumbling out of my mouth.

Malcolm folds his arms. 'I didn't ask him to come here. And I did not ask him to sit beside me.'

'He followed you?'

'It appears my grandson has trouble letting me out of his sight. Ridiculous, since he's leaving to go back to New York in a few days.'

'He's leaving?'

'That's what I said.'

I am disappointed for Malcolm. His gruff exterior doesn't hide his loneliness from me. I can see it as clearly as if he is made of glass. I glance at my watch; I have fifteen minutes of my break remaining. I'm hungry, but I would rather spend the time with Malcolm. I sit beside him, shivering without a coat.

'You're shaking the bench,' he grumbles.

My teeth chatter. 'Sorry.'

Malcolm stands up and unbuckles his chequered coat. My mouth gapes when he tries to pass it to me.

'Oh, no, I can't take that. You'll freeze.'

I didn't notice Shayne get out of his car and I jump when I feel him tap my shoulder. 'Everything okay?' he asks.

'She's cold,' Malcolm says. 'But she won't take my coat.'

Shayne runs a hand through his hair in a way that suggests he might have a headache. 'It's okay, Bea. You can take it if you need it. Grandad is going inside anyway, and I have the car here to pick him up when he's done.'

'Oh, your daughter,' I say, feeling excited that he has finally decided to talk to her. 'If you give me her name, I can find out which ward she works on, if that helps?'

Malcolm looks at me, confused.

'My friend Órlaith on reception can look her up on the computer.'

Malcolm takes a deep breath. 'I've changed my mind. I want to go home.'

'But, Grandad, your appointment,' Shayne says, and I can sense his frustration or worry.

'Are you seeing a doctor today?' I ask, gently. 'I can help with that too, point you in the right direction. It's a big hospital. Sometimes people struggle with finding which department is where. I spend a lot of my day giving people directions, actually.'

Malcolm stares at me with glistening eyes, and I'm concerned that he's afraid a doctor might give him bad news today.

'Take me home, Shayne,' he says with a cough.

Shayne shakes his head. 'Grandad, you really need to see this doctor. You need to find out what's going on. What if you're really sick?'

'What if I'm dying, you mean.'

'Jesus, Grandad.' Shayne steps back, horrified by the idea.

Malcolm begins to shiver and I drape his coat over his shoulders. He's too invested in his argument with his grandson to notice or to shake it off.

'We're all dying,' Malcolm goes on. 'Some of us just sooner than others.'

'Can we please just go see what the doctor has to say?' Shayne pleads.

'I don't need a doctor to tell me I'm old. My knees have been telling me that for twenty years already.'

Shayne folds his arms and sighs. 'If you cancel now, it could take weeks to get another appointment. Months maybe.'

I can tell Shayne is stressing out. But it's obvious that the more he tries to command Malcolm the further he will dig his heels in. I glance at Malcolm's chequered coat and, although it's a long shot, I have an idea.

'Do you like chess?' I ask.

Malcolm taps his chest. 'Me?'

I nod.

'I played once upon a time,' he says.

Shayne seems surprised by this revelation.

'My Alison and I liked the game. But that was a long time ago. I don't play any more. It's not a one-player game.'

'I didn't know you and Grandma liked chess,' Shayne admits.

'I wasn't always an old codger.' Malcolm chuckles. 'I had hobbies, once upon a time, you know.'

Getting off topic, I steer the conversation back. 'I could use a good chess player.'

Malcolm looks at me, unconvinced, and I can see the words *take me home* written on his face.

'You see there's this patient, Mrs Morgan, a lovely woman,' I begin, and I can tell I'm losing him. I speed up. 'Anyway, she is a great chess player. Too great. No one can beat her.' There's a twinkle in his eyes and I can see a slight spark of interest emerge. 'I'd love if she could play someone on her level, you know, like a real challenge.'

'A worthy adversary,' he says.

'Yes. Exactly.'

He taps his chest again. 'And you think that someone is me?'

'I hope so.'

'And this has nothing to do with getting me inside for my appointment.'

'Oh, it has everything to do with getting you inside for your appointment,' I confess. 'But it's also about Mrs Morgan and chess.'

'I'm old, Busy Bea, I didn't think I was senile, but for the life of me I can't see how chess and seeing my doctor are related.'

'Well, there needs to be a prize to make it worth your while, right?'

He cocks his head in a way that says, *This just got interesting.*

'If you win, Shayne has to back off about any and all medical appointments.'

His eyes twinkle, intrigued.

'But if you lose—'

'I won't lose.'

'If you do... then you go see this doctor. See what they have to say.'

Malcolm inhales sharply. My teeth chatter harder than ever and Shayne says, 'Sounds like a fair deal. What do you say, Grandad?'

Malcolm slides his arms into the sleeves of his coat and rolls his shoulders to settle it into place. 'Fine. Let's play.'

TWENTY-EIGHT

It takes me ages to find the chessboard, and I'm worried that Malcolm will lose patience and leave. But I needn't have been concerned. When I finally find the games, under a stack of papers in the nurses' station, and return to the ward, I find Malcolm sitting in a plastic chair by Mrs Morgan's bed and they are deep in conversation about politics. I hate to interrupt them, but I am anxious to get the game played before Malcolm's appointment time.

'Okay,' I say, balancing the board and all the pieces on the edge of Mrs Morgan's bed. 'When you're ready, players, make your move.'

The game begins and soon the level of concentration consumes the room. I prop Mrs Brennan up with several pillows so she can watch from her bed, and some patients from the other wards trickle in to observe masters at work.

Soon, there is a semicircle of patients around Malcolm and Mrs Morgan. It's the most excitement we've had on the ward in months. Shayne and I fall to the back of the small crowd.

'Thank you,' he whispers.

'Don't thank me yet,' I say. 'He might win.'

'That's okay,' Shayne says, 'I've already spoken with the doctor. I have his prescription here.' He pats his pocket. 'I'll pick it up in the pharmacy downstairs on our way home.'

My heart soars, relieved that, however the game goes, Malcolm is going to get his medicine.

'I haven't seen him smile like this in a long time,' Shayne says, his voice cracking.

'I knew they'd hit it off,' I say, quietly confident that Malcolm has made a new friend in Mrs Morgan. And possibly Mrs Brennan too, who shouts sporadically, 'Finish her,' with as much vigour as if we were locked in a real-life battle of *Mortal Kombat* instead of one of the most reserved board games you can get.

'Did you hear anything about our friend John?' Shayne asks.

'Not yet. But my friend on reception is looking into it.'

Shayne shoves his hands into his pockets and rocks on the spot, rolling from his heels to his tiptoes and back again.

'Poor guy,' he says. 'It's just so sad. We've a huge homelessness problem in New York. But I didn't realise it was almost as bad here.'

'Yeah,' I say, swallowing hard. 'It's definitely a problem in Dublin.'

'I wish there was more we could do, you know. To help. I donate to some charities back home, but it feels like a cop-out. Imagine if we could sit down with these people and really ask them what they need. Maybe get them set up with a job, or a skill. Something to get them back on their feet.'

'Maybe they have skills,' I say, and it comes out snappy. 'Or jobs already. I doubt it's all that black and white.'

'Yeah. Yeah, you're right,' he says, picking up on my tone. 'I just feel sorry for them.'

'Well, don't. Your pity isn't going to help them. Shit like that just makes it worse.'

His eyes widen. 'Bea, I'm sorry. I didn't mean—'

'It's fine. It's fine,' I say, quickly. My cheeks sting and I'm embarrassed that I snapped.

'You okay?'

I clear my throat. 'Yeah. Fine. But can we talk about something else please?'

He looks at me with concern and I can tell he's thinking I've overreacted and he's wondering why. I die a little inside.

'Woo-hoo.' Malcolm's voice cuts through the air, and I've never been more thankful to hear anyone. 'I won, I won.'

Shayne looks at me, pats his pocket once again and winks. 'Thank you for this.' He gestures towards Mrs Morgan's bed, where Malcolm is shaking her hand and thanking her for a great game as if they've just played Wimbledon. 'I haven't seen Grandad this happy in years. Honestly, I can't tell you how much it means to me.'

My insides flutter. It means a lot to me to see Malcolm happy too.

'He can come back, you know. Any time. Visit his new friends. I think they'd all like that.'

Shayne smiles. 'Yeah. I think that would be great.'

'And maybe, if he comes here again, he might speak to his daughter.'

Shayne sighs. 'Yeah. Maybe.'

He doesn't sound convinced and it saddens me.

'Could you talk to her?' I ask. 'Maybe if she knows he's trying to reach out—'

Shayne's face changes, like dark cloud suddenly settling in on a spring day.

I raise my hands as if I'm surrendering, 'I'm sorry. Forget I said anything.'

His eyes glisten as he says, 'It's just—'

'Please, it's okay.' I cut him off. 'You don't owe me an explanation. I shouldn't have said anything.'

'Join us for dinner,' he blurts.

'What?'

'Tonight. Please? This has been really great for Grandad and maybe we could talk about my mom over dinner. He opens up to you more than he ever does with me.'

'That's him opening up?' I giggle, and hope Shayne picks up on my joke.

Thankfully he laughs too.

'So, you'll come? I booked the Silly Hen on Camden Street. I have no idea if it's good, but the Tripadvisor reviews are great so...'

He trails off, no doubt seeing the look on my face.

'It's really good,' I say, which I realise makes it sound like I've actually been there myself and not just heard the doctors and nurses here rave about the great food. I can only imagine what a place like that costs, with its urban minimalist décor and Moët sign in the window.

'I'd love to, but I have Ellie,' I say, giving him the first excuse that comes into my head.

'Bring her.' He shrugs. 'I'm sure they have a kids' menu.'

I make a face that confirms a place like that definitely does not serve nuggets and chips.

'Okay. We'll book somewhere else. Where does Ellie like?'

My budget can just about stretch as far as McDonald's, but it means dipping into my flat deposit savings and I just can't, not when anyone could discover us in the storage room any day.

'It's a lovely offer, thank you. But I have plans this evening.'

I watch Shayne deflate like someone letting the air out of a balloon. He can tell I'm lying and I hate myself for it. I wish he knew how much I'd love to join them. But I can't possibly tell him that, without explaining that I'm just too broke.

'Okay. No problem. Maybe another time.'

The generic phrase makes me sad. We both know, that more often than not, *maybe another time* means *never another time*.

'Well, like I said,' he says, as he begins to walk away. 'This was great, but I better get Grandad home.'

'You'll come back though, right? You'll bring him back tomorrow?'

Shayne nods. 'Sure.'

TWENTY-NINE

Despite Órlaith's best Angela Lansbury impersonation, she doesn't find out much about John. She knows he was discharged after twenty-four hours and someone organised for him to go to a charity-run homeless shelter. She doesn't know if he actually made it there, or how long he can stay. I'm filled with sadness to think John may end up on the streets again. And if he does, in this weather the outcome won't be as good next time.

I find that the first person I want to tell is Shayne, but I don't have his number, and calling round to Malcolm's house to deliver something that may be bad news or may be just plain gossip doesn't feel right. I try to keep busy, which is easy with every bed on every ward full, and cross my fingers that Shayne brings Malcolm back today.

Thankfully, just after lunchtime I hear the familiar gruff voice and someone saying, 'No, Grandad, I can't ask them for an armchair.'

On the ward, I find Malcolm sitting next to Mrs Morgan's bed again. He's shifting in the plastic chair and complaining. 'This thing is as hard as a rock. I better not get haemorrhoids, I tell ya.'

'Grandad!'

'The beds aren't much better,' Mrs Brennan croaks across the ward.

'Oh, stop complaining,' Mrs Morgan grouses back. 'Settle down, Malcolm. Rest your bones.'

'Or sit here,' Mrs Brennan says, pointing to the chair beside her bed. 'It's softer. Better for the... you know... the situation.'

The chair beside Mrs Brennan's bed is identical in size, shape, colour and texture. In fact, I'm willing to guess every chair in the hospital is the same, solid bluey-grey plastic.

Malcolm picks up the chair beside Mrs Morgan's bed and attempts to carry it across the ward. He makes it halfway before he needs to set it down to catch his breath. Shayne hurries over to help.

'Where do you want it, Grandad?' he asks.

Malcolm points to Mrs Brennan's bed and then returns to Mrs Morgan's bed and extends his hand. She looks at him, and I can almost see time rewind in her eyes. As if she's a young woman, being asked by a handsome young man to dance.

'Will you join me?' he asks.

She smiles and take his hand. He helps her into her fluffy maroon slippers, and holds her dressing gown open so she can slip her arms in. Then they walk over hand in hand and sit down on the waiting seats beside Mrs Brennan's bed.

'Do either of you ladies play poker?' Malcolm asks.

'Grandad,' Shayne says, in the same tone I use on the very rare occasions when I pull Ellie up on naughty behaviour.

'Chess was fun, but I think we should play a real game now,' Malcolm goes on, with a cheeky wink. 'What do you say?'

'I don't know how to play poker,' Mrs Morgan confesses.

'Me neither, I'm afraid,' Mrs Brennan adds.

'Not to worry. It's nothing I can't teach you,' Malcolm says, shoving his hand into his pocket and pulling out a deck of cards.

Shayne's face is a picture as he looks on open-mouthed.

'Is this all right?' he asks me, as if I have the authority to approve anything around here.

'So long as it's not strip poker we should be fine,' I whisper.

It takes a few rounds, but soon the ladies pick up the rules. I leave them to it, dipping my head back in every so often between floor-washing and bathroom-cleaning. Shayne sits in the corner with a laptop across his knees. He's wearing thick-rimmed burgundy glasses that I've never seen on him before and his face is a picture of concentration. I can only assume he has the luxury of working from home and I find myself hoping it means he's staying in Ireland a little longer. At first I think it pleases me because he'll be here for Malcolm, but I quickly realise it makes me happy for me too. I'd miss him if he left. Butterflies flutter in my tummy at the thought of missing him and I'm glad when my phone dings and distracts me from exploring the feeling more. I glance around, making sure Elaine is nowhere in sight, before I slip my phone out of my pocket and find a message from Cora.

> Hey. Well I survived Christmas and a million hints from my mam about making her a grandmother. Ugh!! Anyway, I'm home and I'd LOVE to catch up. You free later? I could pop around to your new place 😊 You still need to send me your address BTW xx

I start to type a reply but anything I say feels false and lie-like. I slip my phone back into my pocket and promise myself I'll call Cora later. I can't wait to hear all about her family Christmas.

The ward gets busy, just like yesterday, as curiosity brings other patients to join in the game. Someone takes out their wallet and soon there are notes and coins on the side of Mrs Brennan's bed like a scene from *Casino Royale*, except instead of tuxedos and evening dresses everyone is in pyjamas and slippers. After a couple of hours, exhaustion creeps in and patients retreat to their respective wards and rooms once again.

'Thanks for coming,' I say, as Shayne helps Malcolm tidy up.

Mrs Morgan is back in bed, and Mrs Brennan is asleep, snoring softly, with a rosy hue in her cheeks. She's been ghostly pale since before Christmas. I know a game of poker isn't a miracle cure for her failing health, but it makes me happy to see a hint of colour on her face, even if it means nothing more than that she had a fun couple of hours with new friends.

'How about dinner tonight?' Shayne says.

His question catches me off guard.

'Or do you have plans again?'

'I... I...'

I'm not sure what to say. Anything I say this time will most definitely be an obvious excuse, and I'd hate for him to think I don't want to join him for dinner when the truth is that, if things were different, I'd love nothing more.

'Ellie likes McDonald's, right? Or is she more of a Burger King kid?'

'Ew, Burger King.' I make a face.

'Okay, that's settled then. McDonald's it is.'

'You don't have to do this,' I say. 'I'm sure McDonald's isn't exactly your cup of tea.'

'It can't be worse than that place Shayne made us go last night,' Malcolm joins in, shoving the last of the cards back into a small cardboard box with a picture of an eagle on the front.

'Fine dining,' Shayne says.

'Oh.'

'If I wanted to eat flowers on my dinner, I'd take a bite out of the garden,' Malcolm goes on, shaking his head.

'So, you see, McDonald's is perfect,' Shayne says.

'Oh.'

I add up the cost of a Big Mac and a Happy Meal in my

head and hope that splashing out will make me seem a bit more normal. I'll have to make sure it's just this once though, I can't set my flat deposit back again.

'Okay. Sounds good,' I say.

Shayne's eyes twinkle and I notice, how incredibly blue they are today. Like the sky after rainclouds clear away.

'I'll pick you up. Will we say seven?'

My breath catches as I think of him pulling up outside my old apartment and waiting for Ellie and me to walk through the doors.

'I... I have to collect Ellie from crèche. And traffic can be bad. I'll meet you there. How about McDonald's on Grafton Street at seven instead?'

'Okay, cool,' he says, obviously thinking nothing of my change of plan. 'Perfect.'

Butterflies return to my stomach and spend the rest of the day there. It's the first time in weeks that I have actually looked forward to something, and it's such a refreshing feeling that if I think about it too hard I get teary. It's only a burger with some friends, but it's a big deal. Huge.

THIRTY

I wish I had something nicer to wear. My straight-leg blue jeans have a stain on the left thigh that I've tried to hand-scrub in the bathroom sink at work, but it's stubborn and needs a spin cycle. I wear them regardless, and match them with a woolly cream jumper that I think is Cora's and has got mixed in with my stuff. I've lost so much weight that everything is too big, sitting on me as if I am a coat hanger, but Ellie smiles at me as she sits on an upturned yellow mop bucket and says, 'You're the prettiest mammy in the world.'

I kiss her head and tell her she looks like a princess. She's wearing pink leggings with 'Frozen' written down the side and a matching pink jumper with a glitter Elsa on the front. Her clothes fit her just fine, and I'm so grateful that the crèche provides her with three healthy meals a day. I only have to worry about feeding her at the weekend. Or this one-off McDonald's.

We wrap up in our coats and hats and gloves, and sneak out of the storage room. We've become extremely good at getting in and out undetected. Ellie thinks it's a fun game.

'First one to make a sound loses,' I remind her every time, and then we pretend to zip our lips with our fingers.

I peek into the hall, and when I'm sure no one is coming we make a dash for it.

'I win, I win,' she says, as soon as we reach the stairs and it's safe to be seen.

'Yes you do, chickpea. You're sooooo good at this game. And remember, sometimes you fall asleep at Mammy's work cos I'm so busy. We still live in our lovely apartment, don't we?'

'Busy Bea,' Ellie chirps, echoing Malcolm.

'Yes, yes. I'm a busy bee.'

My gut clenches every time I fill Ellie's head with the same lie. But I cannot risk her telling anyone that we are living at the hospital now. And besides, it's only temporary. Soon we'll have a new flat and she can tell all her friends, and nosey Alannah, about that.

Outside, the snow is melting and the ground is slushy and wet. I left my wellies in the storage room, and I know Malcolm will have something to say about it. Just thinking about it makes me smile. Ellie holds my hand and skips contently by my side as we walk. She tells me about the Lego tower she built.

'And I shared all my blocks.'

'Good girl.'

'And then, and then, and then...'

Ellie talks nonstop the whole way across the city. And we blend in effortlessly with the other people out and about braving the cold. We are just a mother and her happy child, strolling carefree. No one would ever look at us and think we have no home to go back to. And I am grateful for that, at least.

McDonald's is crazy busy. Everyone has finally had their fill of turkey and ham and is desperate for the familiarity of fast food. Ellie and I lap the place a couple of times searching for Malcolm and Shayne. Thankfully, Malcolm's chequered coat and colourful scarf stand out, and on our second trip upstairs I spot him and Shayne seated in the corner. Shayne raises his arm and waves and Ellie lets out a shriek of delight as she lets go of my clammy hand and races towards them.

'Malco, Malco, Malco,' she calls out, wrapping herself round the old man.

'Careful, Ellie,' I call back, worried she might hurt him.

But Malcolm belly-laughs and I know he's fine. He sits her on his knee and asks her what she would like.

Ellie sings her order off the top of her head. I join them at the perfect-size-for-four table and my bum has barely touched the plastic bench seat when Shayne stands up and asks, 'And you, Bea. What can I get you?'

'Oh, no, honestly. Ellie and I can get our own.' It comes out slightly offended, which it's not, but I think subconsciously I want to stress how much I *can* do this. *It's just a McDonald's*, my mind plays on repeat.

'It's just a McDonald's,' Shayne says, and I'm frazzled for a second, as if he's reading my thoughts. But his tone is completely different to mine. Careful and kind. 'Let me get this, please. I'm the one who dragged you both here in this weather, after all.'

I take a measured breath and smile. I know this is what friends do. They buy each other a meal every so often. And under normal circumstances I'd happily accept the kind gesture and next time would be on me. But I can't afford those kinds of indiscretions any more. What if his order is a large meal, or he wants a coffee I haven't budgeted for? My mind is racing and I realise Shayne is staring, waiting for me to speak and make some sort of sense.

'I'm not actually hungry,' I say, and his face falls. 'I grabbed something in the canteen earlier.' My stomach rumbles right at that very moment and betrays me.

'I'm hungry,' Ellie says, and reminds Shayne about her chicken nugget Happy Meal request.

I know Ellie won't finish her nuggets or chips. It was spaghetti Bolognese day in the crèche, her favourite; she can't have much room left.

Shayne nods and goes to order.

'You look hungry to me,' Malcolm says as I take off my coat, the restaurant suddenly feeling stuffy. 'You're skin and bone.'

Thankfully I don't have to change the subject – Ellie does it for me when she breaks into song. Something about a blackbird and a chicken, although I'm not sure she has the lyrics quite right.

Malcolm bounces her on his knee and when we get to the chorus for the fourth time he joins in. A group of teenagers at a table nearby turn and giggle. When Malcolm notices them, he sings a little louder.

Shayne returns with a tray full of food. Everyone takes theirs, then lastly he places a McFlurry and a coffee in front of me.

'I hope you're not too full for dessert,' he says, a little unsure.

My insides fizz with excitement. Both because I'm famished and can't wait to tuck into cold ice cream and warm coffee, and also because it's kind and thoughtful and I'm not used to anyone thinking about me. Not even Declan before all of this.

I have to look away for a moment and repeat the silent mantra in my head, *Don't cry, don't cry, don't cry.*

There is more singing, although Shayne stops and blushes when he notices the teenagers pointing. There is conversation.

'I won five quid,' Malcolm says, proudly referring to the earlier game of poker.

Shayne rolls his eyes. 'Grandad.'

Malcolm chuckles heartily. 'I gave it back. That Mrs Morgan is a terrible poker player. She should stick to the chess.'

Ellie falls asleep on my shoulder and Shayne offers to drive us home, but I make an excuse about Cora picking us up.

'Maybe we could do this again before I leave?' he asks as we walk down the stairs. Someone has spilled Coke on the bottom few steps. Without a word, Shayne links Malcolm and holds him close.

'You're still leaving?' I say, my heart heavy with sudden sadness.

'Have lots to sort out back home.'

My heart feels heavy hearing him refer to New York as home. I've only known him a short time, but he has become such a large part of my life. Of mine and Ellie's lives. It's hard to believe he doesn't belong here.

'Oh... I thought you could work remotely.'

'I can.' He runs his free hand through his already messy hair. 'But my apartment and my ex... you know the way.'

'I really do,' I say, all too quickly.

'So is that a yes? We can do this again soon?'

We reach the bottom step and Malcolm wriggles free from Shayne's grip like a stubborn child. Shayne turns his attention to me. His huge blue eyes bore into me, pleadingly.

Tonight was wonderful. It was mundane, sticky, noisy, a little smelly and so, so normal. I wish it didn't have to end. I wish he didn't have to go. I push the sadness deep down.

'Okay,' I say, quickly, deciding that I can totally budget to buy him a coffee in exchange for another wonderful evening.

'Okay,' he says, and I *think* he might be almost as excited as me. 'Can I give you my number? You know, so we can text and not have to meet on a park bench.'

'I like the bench,' I say, truthfully. 'But yeah. Your number would be good.'

THIRTY-ONE

I spend most of my day at work looking out for Malcolm and Shayne, but they don't visit. As disappointed as I am, I can tell Mrs Morgan and Mrs Brennan are more so.

'He's just afraid I'll beat him this time,' Mrs Morgan says.

'In your dreams,' Mrs Brennan retorts with a humph.

I wonder what they might be up to. I hope they're using Shayne's final days to spend some quality time together.

It's Elaine's first day back after Christmas and she has a face like thunder. I work up the courage to say, 'Are you okay?' And wait for her to tell me to mind my own business.

But, instead, she looks at me with teary eyes and says, 'My father is sick.'

'Oh,' I say, surprised she shared something so personal, and didn't follow it with a direct order of what floor to wash next, or bed to change, or shower tray to scrub. 'I'm sorry to hear that. Is it serious?'

'I don't know.' She shrugs as if she's afraid to find out. Her eyes are glossing over and if she blinks, I think tears might spill.

'Didn't he tell you?' I say, fully aware that I am prying now and expecting her to snap at any moment.

'No.'

'Doesn't he want to talk about it?'

Her face pinches, and I think she is weighing up whether to tell me more or not. There's a few seconds of us standing side by side in awkward silence where I wonder if it would be okay to walk away and get back to work, until she finally says, 'We don't speak. We haven't spoken in years.'

'Oh,' I say again, now more invested than ever.

Surely not, I think, looking at Elaine's sweet heart-shaped face. Her silver bob sits blow-dry perfect below her ears every day, rarely with a strand out of place. Her steely blue eyes hide behind thick-rimmed lilac glasses as if time has faded their brightness. Malcolm has a round head, no hair and remarkably good vision for a man his age – he was doing the crossword without glasses, and that print is tiny. But Shayne wears glasses, I saw when he was using his laptop.

'He sent me this,' Elaine goes on, producing a Christmas card from behind her back. There is a picture of a front door with large wreath on the front.

'That's nice,' I say, cringing as I search my brain for better words.

'I haven't seen him in over a decade and he sends me this. And sends it here. To the hospital. Órlaith said he handed it in on Christmas Day, can you believe it? There was a temp on reception and Órlaith only found out about it today.'

'Better late than never, eh?' I plead with my brain to stop blurting out the first thing it comes up with, but Elaine makes me nervous. She always has, but much more so since I've been living in the storage room on *her* ward.

'What the hell am I supposed to do with this?' she says, and I think it's more than a generic phrase, I think she's actually asking me for advice. *Me?*

'Talk,' I say.

She snorts. 'God, if only it were that simple.'

'It can be.'

'Oh, Bea,' she says, a slender tear finally escaping her eye to trickle down her cheek. 'You've no idea how complicated my life is.'

'Nobody has any idea of how complicated anybody's life is,' I say firmly.

She straightens up and I hear her back crack and I know this conversation is over.

'We should get back to work,' she says, pressing her foot on the pedal of the giant bin in the hall and tossing the card in.

'Yeah. Work.'

'Take a look at the window in St John's ward, please. There's something sticky on the ledge. Needs a good scrub.'

'Scrub window ledge.' I nod. 'Sure. No problem.'

She walks away, but then stops abruptly to turn her head over her shoulder.

'Oh and you won't—'

'Tell anyone about this,' I finish for her. 'No, of course not.'

Another tear falls and she catches it on the top of her finger as she mouths, 'Thank you.'

I wait until she is long gone before I press my foot on the pedal of the bin and duck my head in. It smells of yoghurt and rotting apples and I gag before I retrieve the card. The bin lid snaps shut with a loud clank and I hurry into the patients' bathroom. Safe behind a stall door, I sit on the loo and open the card.

My dearest Elaine,

This is not easy to write, but I am running out of time and I cannot bear to go without telling you I love you. Since I don't have a current address for you, I've been stopping by your workplace in the hope of bumping into you. But the truth is, I don't even know if you work here any more. And yet, I can't seem to stay away. What an old fool I am. I hope this reaches you. And I hope some day you can forgive me. I love you and I never stopped.

Dad x

My heart aches. I suspect delivering this card is why Malcolm was at the hospital on Christmas morning. Trying to repair the broken bonds with his daughter is what has brought Malcolm and Shayne into my life. I have to help. I have to help Malcolm and Elaine heal. I just have no idea how.

The rest of the day passes in a blur. It's almost impossible to get the sticky gunk off the window ledge. I get it eventually, but the time eats into my day and the rest of my workload piles up. I am almost a full hour late to pick Ellie up. Alannah is behind the reception desk with a face like she's been sucking lemons.

'Tough day?' she asks.

'Yes.' I nod, feeling a bead of perspiration trickling from my underarm to my inner elbow.

'I hear ya,' she says, pressing her fingers against her temples for effect. 'But at least it's nearly the new year. Any nice plans for New Year's Eve?'

'No babysitter,' I say, quickly.

'Ah. Pity. I'm going into town with a few of the girls from here. There's a black-tie thing on in the Westbury. Should be a bit of craic. Just nice to have a chance to dress up, you know yourself.'

I nod as if I know. But I have never set foot inside the Westbury in my life. I doubt I could afford a glass of water in the place, never mind an actual ball. I give myself a moment to imagine it and I decide it must be as close as you can get to being a real-life Disney princess for a night.

'So that'll be fifty euro, please,' Alannah says, holding out her hand for the late fee.

My mouth gapes. 'What? No. You said twenty-five an hour.'

'Or part thereof.' She looks at her watch. 'It's an hour and four minutes, so...'

I scoff. 'Four minutes. You're joking, right?'

She clicks her tongue against her teeth. 'Sorry. 'Fraid not. I'd love to let it slide, but the other parents... you know... wouldn't be fair. Has to be the same rules for everyone.'

'I'm not asking for special treatment.'

'I know. I know,' she says in a way that implies asking for special treatment is exactly what I'm doing. 'But if the other parents find out, there'll be complaints.' She presses her temples again. 'So I really can't—'

'But we've been standing here talking for at least five minutes. I wasn't more than an hour late.'

'But Ellie is still inside, so technically...'

'This is ridiculous,' I snap.

Alannah shoves the card machine at me and stares blankly. The screen requests €50 and my chest constricts as I tap my card. I could cry that my coffee-with-Shayne budget has just gone on Alannah's big mouth. I can't stand her, I decide. If she wasn't running one of the cheapest crèches in Dublin, I'd tell her to her face or punch her. I probably wouldn't actually punch her, but just thinking about it makes me smile.

She takes the card machine back with smug satisfaction and says, 'I'll get Ellie for you now.'

Ellie comes skipping into reception. I notice the yellow paint on her cheek and in her hair before I notice the painting she's proudly carrying. She shoves the paper towards me.

'Oh, what's this?' I say, looking down at a page full of stick people, a yellow sun and some green splodges that I think might represent the grass.

'This one might need a bath tonight?' Alannah laughs, pointing at her hair.

'We don't gots a bath at Mammy's work,' Ellie says.

'No, no, I mean at home, dear,' Alannah says, laughing harder.

'Ha.' I choke. 'Kids. What will they say next?'

'But we don't got one, Mammy,' Ellie says, confused.

'So tell me, who is this?' I ask quickly, distracting her.

'Me and you.' She points to some very large-of-head stick people, one tall and one short. 'And Shayne and Malco,' she says, pointing to the remaining figures.

'Family day today,' Alannah says warmly. 'The kids were painting their mammies and daddies, brothers, sisters and grandparents. Isn't it just adorable.'

'Yes. Lovely.' I swallow.

'We're going to paint our houses tomorrow,' Alannah continues.

My heart pounds, and it's as if I can hear the swish-wallop of my blood racing in my veins, like a storm at sea. A headache grips me and I'm desperate for fresh air.

'Come on, Ellie.' I gather all her stuff from her basket and bundle it under my arm, not taking the time to put it on her before I grab her hand and hurry outside.

'Byeeeee,' Alannah calls after us.

My chest is so tight it's hard to breathe. I inhale deeply through my nose, but it's as if the air gets stuck before making it to my lungs. I try again. And again. Faster and faster.

'Mammy?' Ellie says, sounding distressed. 'Mammy?'

I try to comfort her. To tell her everything will be all right, but I can't draw my breath. I can't breathe or see or hear. Suddenly everything is black.

Oh God, Ellie!

THIRTY-TWO

I open my eyes and everything is white! It's not an exaggeration to say that for a moment I panic that I'm dead.

'Ellie,' I croak out before I realise that the whiteness above me is a hospital ceiling, complete with fluorescent light and the odd greyish stain that has formed over time. I try to sit up but something pinches the soft part inside my elbow. I look down to find a drip running into my arm.

'Ellie?' I call out again. 'Where's my daughter? Hello? Hello?'

A young woman in the bed across the ward sits up and says, 'Oh. You're awake.'

'Have you seen my daughter? She's four. Blond curly hair and—'

'The nurse has her.'

Relief washes over me, and suddenly I am light-headed again. I throw the sheet back and swing my legs over the edge of the bed. I'm in a hospital gown that opens at the back to reveal my underwear. I reach behind me and grab it, then I clutch the drip stand in my other hand and start walking.

'Are you sure you should be up?' the woman in the bed across the ward asks.

'I have to find my daughter.'

'Really, you don't look well. I'm sure if you just call the nurse...'

I ignore the concerned young woman and keep going.

'Bea,' Elaine says, coming into view on the corridor. She cups her face with her hands upon seeing me. 'I was just coming to check on you.'

'Where's Ellie?'

Elaine lowers her hands and although her eyes are narrow and full of concern she is smiling. 'She's fine. She's downstairs with Órlaith.'

The relief is intense and it's followed by my legs attempting to crumple from under me.

'Okay, okay,' Elaine says, hurrying to help me. She tucks her hip next to mine and drapes my arm round her shoulder. 'Back to bed, young lady.'

Elaine tucks me into bed the way I've watched her settle in the elderly patients upstairs for years. I'm warm and cosy and tired. A type of tiredness that I've never felt before. It's as if my bones are hollow and have no strength. My head is heavy against the soft, fluffed pillow and I am desperate for sleep. Maybe I could catch a few minutes if Ellie is content downstairs with Órlaith. I forgot how good an actual bed feels. Not a friend's two-seater couch where my legs don't fit, or a storage room floor crammed between buckets and mops, but a real bed. With a spongy mattress, and soft blankets and feathery pillows. A place to stretch out flat and drift off. It's glorious, really.

'Ellie,' I say, again, my eyes closing.

I feel a hand on my shoulder and a whisper of 'Shh, rest now.'

I jolt upright, startled and once again forgetting where I am.

'Ellie,' I call out, my throat dry and raspy. 'How long was I asleep?' I'm not sure who I'm asking. The woman in the bed across from me maybe, but when my vision starts to focus I can see she is sleeping.

Elaine is back and she's smiling still, but it's tense and I can tell something I don't want to hear is coming. I recognise her expression, a wiry smile and pinched brow. It's usually followed by a request to clean up vomit or unblock a toilet.

But her tone is soft and caring as she walks towards my bed and says, 'Ah, you're awake.'

'Ellie,' I croak out.

'Still fine. She's just fine. Órlaith had to go home, so she's been hanging out with me upstairs.'

I'm not sure what time it is, but I know Elaine's shift would have been over long ago.

'Thank you,' I try to say, but sound fails to come out as my emotions take over.

'We've had a great time. She was telling me all about her fun day in crèche.'

I hold my breath, waiting for Elaine to go on. I can sense something huge coming and I am terrified Ellie told her we've been sleeping in the storage room. I think I'm going to be sick.

'But I'm afraid I really do need to get home,' Elaine goes on. 'My cats have been in all day, and—'

'Yes. Yes of course,' I say, feeling awful that I've held her up so long already. I sit up, ready to stand.

Elaine scoffs. 'What are you doing?'

I stare at her blankly, not entirely sure what she's asking when the answer is obvious.

'You can't go home, Bea,' she says.

'But Ellie,' I say.

Elaine sighs and shakes her head. 'We need to get to the bottom of what happened to you.'

'I... I... I'm just tired.'

'When was the last time you ate?' she asks, becoming serious. 'The doctors are worried your BMI isn't where it should be, and I've never seen you in the canteen.'

I open my mouth but no sound comes out.

'Are you eating properly, Bea? I know there's all sorts of pressure on young women to be stick thin these days, but—'

'I'm just tired,' I snap, firmly shutting this conversation down, and Elaine knows it.

'Okay. But you need to stay. I tried calling the number we have for your boyfriend but I got a disconnect message, said the number wasn't in use.'

'He changed his phone,' I blurt.

'Ah. That makes sense. Well, if you give me his new number, I'll call him.'

'He's flying.'

'Oh.' Her eyes narrow.

'He's a pilot.'

'Yes. Yes, I heard.'

'So he's away a lot.'

Her eyes narrow even more until they appear barely open.

'Is there someone else I can call for you, then?'

'Yeah, of course,' I say, trying to sound casual, but the tiredness and stress makes it come out squeaky and strained. 'I'll call my friend. Cora.'

Elaine nods. 'Okay, great. I can stay for another hour or so, give your friend time to get here and take Ellie.'

I nod. My clothes are folded on the bedside chair and Elaine fetches my phone from the pocket of my jeans.

She extends her hand, but before she passes it over, she pauses and says, 'You would tell me if there was anything wrong, Bea, wouldn't you? I know we're not exactly close, but if I can help in some way...'

'Everything is fine. Like I said, I'm just—'

'Tired,' Elaine finishes for me.

'Yeah. Tired.'

Elaine smiles and says, 'Okay, well, I'll go get Ellie. She's been asking to see you, and I'm sure you could both use a hug.'

The thought of Ellie's chubby arms round my neck fills me with joy as I watch Elaine walk away. I call Cora's number but it goes to voicemail. I try again and again.

'Hi, this is Cora. I can't answer right now, but if you leave a message, I'll call back.'

'Cora, it's Bea... erm, I'm sorry I haven't been in touch—' My voice breaks and I take a deep breath before I go on. 'But, eh, I'm in the hospital, like, I'm the patient, I mean. It's nothing serious. I just fainted, I think. But, eh, I hate to ask, but, erm, do you think you could take Ellie tonight? I'm sorry, I just...' I trail off, realising tears are trickling down my cheeks and I'm sure she can hear it in my voice. I take a deep breath and try again. 'Anyway, so if you could give me a call back, that would be great. Thanks.'

I lower the phone as a squeal of 'Mammy' rings in the air and a head of golden curls bounces towards me.

'Easy now, easy,' Elaine calls after Ellie, who has no intention of taking it easy.

She clambers onto my bed with a degree of difficulty and I take her hand and pull her close. When both her knees are on the bed, she nuzzles her head into the crook of my neck and I take a deep breath, drinking her in.

'Hey you,' I say.

'I gots a lollipop,' she tells me. 'And fizzy juice.'

'I hope that's okay,' Elaine says, standing back.

I smile, grateful.

'Did you get hold of your friend?' Elaine asks.

I shake my head.

Elaine's face falls. 'Oh. Oh dear.'

'She's probably working. She's a radiographer so the night shift, maybe?'

'Here?' Elaine points to the ground but I know she's asking if Cora works at St Helen's.

'No.' I sigh. 'A private hospital, outside town.'

'Oh. Oh dear,' she says again.

'It's okay. I'm feeling much better anyway so—'

'Bea.' Elaine shuts me down, sounding both irritated and frustrated. 'You need to stay for observation, that's just how it is. I can't let you back to work like this. What if you pass out on the ward? You need to see the doctors in the morning and get the all-clear.'

'But Ellie—'

'I'll take her,' Elaine says.

I choke on air. I couldn't possibly take Elaine up on her offer to watch Ellie, for a variety of reasons. Ellie doesn't know Elaine, and I'm sure spending the night in a stranger's house would be distressing for her. But more so because, as soon as Ellie does get comfortable, Elaine will start asking questions, which will inevitably lead to Ellie spilling the beans.

My heart races.

'Oh, Elaine, that's so kind but—'

'No buts, Bea. You're staying.'

Every inch of me wants to fight Elaine on this, but it's not as if I can get up and go home. And even if I could, Elaine won't let me back to work until I have the all-clear.

Defeated, I try one last approach.

'Just let me make one more call?' I say.

'Sure.'

I press call with shaky fingers and hold the phone to my ear. The answer comes after a single ring.

'Hello.'

'Hi. It's Bea. I need a favour.'

'Oh.'

'I'm at the hospital. They want me to stay the night. Could you take Ellie, please? I wouldn't ask but it's just—'

'I'm on the way.'

I lower the phone and Elaine looks at me with a gentle but measured expression that asks, *well?*

'He's coming,' I say, holding Ellie tight and feeling beyond grateful for Shayne.

THIRTY-THREE

Ellie falls asleep in the crook of my arm while we wait for Shayne. It's not a long wait, but it's still enough time for my mind to race. I run over a potential conversation when he arrives. I should probably start with an apology. *I'm sorry for calling out of the blue, I know you didn't give me your number so I could turn you into my emergency contact.* I cringe, just thinking about it. *I owe you so much more than a coffee. I don't have anyone else. I am almost thirty years old and the only constant in my life is my four-year-old.*

I must drift off to sleep again, because my eyes shoot open to raised voices on the corridor.

'I've been home for a few weeks,' I recognise Shayne's voice saying.

'Does your father know you're in the country?' Elaine asks, and her tone is laced with hurt.

'Yes. I've been to visit him.'

'And that bitch?'

'If you mean his wife, then yes, I've seen her too.'

'Oh, I'm sure you have.'

'Mam, stop.'

My intake of breath is so sharp it disturbs Ellie, who tosses and turns before snuggling back to sleep. I already knew Shayne was Elaine's son. Somewhere in the back of my mind, when I suspected that Malcolm was her father, I did the family tree maths. But hearing him call her Mam still shocks me.

'They're in there,' Elaine says, and I can only assume she is talking about Ellie and me.

I hold my breath as I hear the squeaky sound of footsteps approach on the highly polished hospital floor. Shayne peeks his head round the door slowly, as if he might be disturbing me.

I feel lighter and more awake as soon as I see him.

'Oh, Bea.'

'I'm okay.'

My throat is dry and my voice is scratchy and I don't sound particularly okay at all, and the look on his face says he doesn't believe me.

'What happened?'

I blush. 'Not sure.'

His face pinches. I am sure, of course. I know I had a panic attack. Or, at least that's what Google says.

'I'm so glad you called,' he adds, and I know he means that. I am so glad I called too. Suddenly all the thoughts and worries that were in my head before he arrived fade away. I don't feel the need to apologise or explain. I can say nothing at all and I know that's okay. Trouble is, I wish I could tell him. I ache to tell Shayne every damn detail of the last couple of weeks. I so desperately want to tell someone how hard it's been. I want to tell someone I'm scared and lonely and stressed on a level that I didn't even know it was possible to be. I want to let it all spill out, because maybe just maybe then it will stop eating me up from the inside out. And the only person I could possibly imagine telling is Shayne. And that scares me.

'What are they saying?' Shayne asks, looking around the dimly lit ward, and I know he's talking about the doctors.

'Nothing, really. They just want me to stay for twenty-four hours for observation. I don't think it's necessary, really, but you know what Elaine is like—'

I cut myself off quickly, remembering their relationship.

'Oh, I know,' he says dryly. 'So, tell me, what kind of bedtime story do we need here?'

I stroke Ellie's hair. 'Princesses. She loves all the Disney princess, but I think we might have gone past story time.'

Shayne nods, and I can literally see him making a mental note.

'I really do appreciate this,' I say, suddenly serious. 'I know taking my kid wasn't what you signed up for when you gave me your number but...'

'I'm happy to help.'

'I know, I know, but—'

'It's just a little babysitting. I've got this, I promise. I will Disney Princess the crap out of this.'

'You're already my knight in shining armour,' I say, and then I cringe instantly once those horrendously corny words slip out. 'That sounded much funnier in my head. I swear.'

Shayne snorts and laughs. 'Oh God. That's the best you can do? Blame the drugs.'

'I don't think they've given me anything,' I confess.

He laughs harder. 'Erm, maybe blame them anyway.'

He gets closer, squeezing himself between the edge of my bed and the plastic chair where my clothes are folded, and I only realise now that my bra is sitting on top of the pile like a lacy beige cupcake. My face glows with embarrassment.

Between telling him that he's my medieval hero and inadvertently flashing my underwear, I wish a giant hole would open and suck my hospital bed into it. *Maybe they did give me drugs after all.*

He scoops Ellie into his arms and she purrs like a little kitten as she cuddles into him without fully waking.

'Thank you,' I whisper.

'No, thank you.'

My eyes narrow.

'For trusting me with her. I won't let you down,' he says, and my heart flutters and I have to bite my lip so I don't say the shining knight thing again.

Elaine comes onto the ward. She's changed out of her uniform into beige trousers and a cream linen blouse that compliments her silver bob. I had no idea she was quite so elegant outside of work.

'It's getting late. We need to think of the other patients,' she says, and we all glance around the ward.

There are six beds. Three facing three. And only two are occupied. The woman in the bed opposite me has been sleeping soundly for the last hour or so.

'If you have everything you need, Shayne, I'd appreciate if you were on your way.'

Elaine speaks to Shayne with the same tone and mannerism she uses when speaking to patients' families. It's professional and caring, but it's certainly not how I would expect a mother to interact with her son.

'Sure,' Shayne says, and the atmosphere chills me to the bone.

'Get some rest, Bea,' Elaine says, turning to walk away.

'You could come with us?' Shayne calls after her.

She snaps back round as if he has said something dreadful. Her face is pinched and full of revulsion.

'Will *he* be there?' she grumbles, and she sounds so like Malcolm.

'Yes. Obviously. It is Grandad's house.'

Elaine rolls her eyes and it's obvious she doesn't appreciate his sarcasm.

'He wants to see you,' Shayne says. 'He doesn't have much time.'

My heart aches and I hope Elaine won't waste what little time is left. But she straightens her back and says, 'He knows where to find me.'

'Mam, please?' Shayne begs.

Elaine raises her hand, signalling the end of the conversation. 'That child needs bed,' she says.

Shayne rubs Ellie's back, the way a loving father might, the way Declan used to, and it pains me to think that Ellie won't have that in her life any more. With Declan gone, and Shayne going back to New York, and Malcolm... I can't even bring myself to think about Malcolm leaving. But soon, Ellie won't have any male role models in her life. And I will be lonelier than ever.

'I'll see you tomorrow, Bea,' Shayne says.

He bends and kisses my head and immediately apologises. 'I'm sorry, I'm so sorry. I don't know why I did that.'

Elaine looks on, open-mouthed.

Familiar butterflies swirl in my stomach as I replay the feel of his lips on my skin.

'I... I...' A redness creeps across his nose and spreads into his cheeks. 'I better get going.' He rubs some more circles round Ellie's back, protectively. 'I'll take good care of her.'

I smile. I know he will. I don't tell him that in doing so he's also taking good care of me. I don't say it, because I think we both already know it. And the butterflies turn into full birds, flapping their wings furiously as my belly flips with feelings I'm not sure I've ever had before. Not even for Declan.

THIRTY-FOUR

I sleep better than I have in weeks. I'm woken every couple of hours for observations – blood pressure, medications, that sort of thing – but I barely open my eyes and I fall straight back to sleep after. When morning finally comes round and the clink and clatter of teacups on trolleys wakes me, I ache for just a few more minutes' sleep.

'Breakfast,' Tonya, the catering lady, chirps as she pushes her rattly trolley onto the ward. The smell of warm toast and melted butter makes my mouth water.

'Bea!' she says. 'What are you doing here?'

'Dizzy spell.' I blush.

'Working too hard,' she puffs out. 'This place will have us all run ragged.'

I pull myself to sit up and stuff the pillow behind my back. 'I'm going home today,' I say.

Tonya slides the portable table waiting at the end of my bed over my knees and sets a tray down on top. Tea, toast, cornflakes and apple juice await. I cannot wait to tuck in.

'Ah, I bet you'll be glad to get home. There's nothing like climbing into your own bed after a hospital stay, eh?'

Home. Own bed.

Tonya's words are a like a punch to the gut. 'Um,' I just about manage to say.

She shifts her attention to the woman in the bed opposite.

'Morning, sleepyhead,' she says, waking her.

'Not hungry,' the woman mumbles, turning over and pulling the blanket over her head.

'Okay, no worries. I'll just leave it here for you.'

She doesn't reply, and I think she's gone straight back to sleep. Tonya places a tray, identical to the one she gave me, on the table at the end of her bed.

'So much food gets wasted around here.' She sighs. 'I don't know why they have us serve breakfast so early. No one is hungry.'

I. Am. Starving. It takes every ounce of willpower I possess to wait until Tonya leaves before I tuck into the breakfast feast before me. And then every remaining ounce not to hop out of bed and savage everything on the tray across from me too.

The doctor and a team of medical students come round after breakfast. Their youthful faces and unsure dispositions remind me so much of Cora's and my time in college. We were in different departments but we'd meet on our break and keep score of how many patients we'd diagnosed correctly and how many we'd got embarrassingly wrong.

'Anaemia,' one of the students says.

'Iron looks fine to me,' the doctor replies, looking at the file he has picked up from the end of my bed. I don't remember anyone taking bloods. And I momentarily panic about how long I was out of it. How long I left Ellie unsupervised. My chest tightens, and I'm glad I'm not attached to any sort of monitor right now or the alarm might start going off.

'Eating disorder,' another student, who is painfully thin herself, suggests.

'Hmm.' The doctor gives this one greater consideration. 'BMI low, but not dangerously.'

'Drug use?' comes another suggestion from a student in the back.

'Excuse me?' I snap. 'I'm right here, you know. I can hear you.'

'Again, bloods clear,' the doctor says.

'You tested me for drugs?' I am furious. And embarrassed. And furious again. 'I work here,' I say, as if anyone who works in a hospital could never fall victim to drug use. 'And I have a young child. I do NOT take drugs. Jesus.'

'No. No one is saying you do,' the doctor says, softly and finally looking at me. 'This is just a teaching exercise.'

'Okay, well, I think we've learned enough now. I would like to go home.' I swallow hard and correct myself. 'To leave. I would like to leave now. Thank you.'

The doctor turns towards his students and he must mouth something, because they all turn and leave together like a collective of doves, flocking towards the door.

'Bea, your labs are all fine. You're a perfectly healthy young woman,' he says, turning towards me again. 'But I am thinking your stress levels are unusually high. Is there anything worrying you? Pressure at work? Or at home perhaps?'

I scoff. He cocks his head.

'I'm a single parent to a four-year-old. Some days are hard.'

'Okay.' He nods, getting it. 'I'll write you off sick for a week. I think resting up at home will do you the world of good.'

A tear escapes, but I catch it and flick it away before he notices.

'Is someone coming to pick you up?' he asks. 'Best not to drive for a few days.'

I don't bother to tell him I don't have a car. I simply nod. 'My friend will be here soon.'

'Okay. Good. And remember what I said. Plenty of rest. Okay?'

'Not sure how easy that will be with a four-year-old to entertain but I'll do my best,' I say.

He smiles, as if I'm making a joke. Maybe I am.

He leaves and I pull the curtain round my bed and get dressed. It feels good to escape the breezy hospital gown and I'm thinking about sneaking down to the storage room to fetch my toothbrush when Tonya returns to clear up.

'Waste,' she says, dumping the tray full of food from the woman's bed into a black bin bag. 'Pure bloody waste.'

My stomach knots watching good food get thrown away, and I wonder how much waste there is throughout the hospital every day. My eyes follow Tonya and her rattly trolley towards the ward doors, where I find Shayne standing with his hip leaning against the frame. I wonder how long he's been there and I wait for Ellie to come bounding in. I can't wait to hug her and hear all about her sleepover.

'I didn't know if it was okay to come in,' he says, straightening up but remaining standing on the spot.

'Where's Ellie?'

'She's with my grandfather.'

My lips round into an O shape and Shayne quickly jumps in with, 'I hope that's okay. Ellie wanted to stay a little longer. She's had breakfast and they're watching a movie. *Beauty and the Beast.*'

'Ellie loves that one,' I say.

'I thought maybe we could get that coffee we talked about?' he says.

My face must tell him that I'm not sure because he races in again with, 'Unless you're not feeling up to it. I mean, you are just getting out of hospital, so if it's better we can pick Ellie up and I can drop you straight home.'

'No!' I gasp, much too loudly.

The woman in the bed opposite stirs at last, rubs her eyes and sits up. 'Did someone take my breakfast?'

'Yeah. A while ago. Maybe if you call them, they'll make you some toast,' I suggest.

She nods, and presses the bell on her bed frame. When I draw my attention back to Shayne, I notice he has taken a step back and I can see confusion or worry on his face.

'Is everything okay, Bea? If you're worried about Ellie, we can go straight there.'

I'm not worried about Ellie. I can tell how fond of her Malcolm is and, as she's never had a grandparent in her life, I know Ellie is enjoying every moment spent with him too.

'Coffee would be great,' I say. 'They only serve tea here. I mean, who wants tea first thing in the morning.'

'I love tea,' the woman chimes in. 'Do you think they'd bring some tea too?'

'You could ask,' I say.

'Service is terrible here,' she grumbles.

'It's not a hotel,' I say, irked. 'You missed breakfast, but I'm sure Tonya will oblige and get you something.'

'Speaking of hotels,' Shayne says, and I can see he's switching from one leg to the other as if he feels awkward. 'I wasn't sure if you'd need these.' He reaches into his back pocket and produces a sealed plastic bag, with a foldable toothbrush and micro toothpaste. 'I'm not trying to say you've bad breath or anything...' He runs his hand through his hair. 'But I'm guessing you don't have any of your stuff with you?'

I recognise the travel-size plastic bag. They sell them downstairs in the tuck shop for silly expensive and I always wondered who would actually buy them. Now I know it's nice Irish American guys.

'Thank you. I feel disgusting.'

I take the bag and hurry towards the bathroom. I'm halfway down the corridor when I realise I'm sneaking and trying not to get caught. I laugh at myself, before I slow my pace and make my way to the patients' bathroom as an actual patient. For the next few minutes at least.

My phone rings as I'm drying my hands.

'Hello,' I say.

'Bea, Jesus, are you okay? I'm so sorry I missed your call.' Cora's voice is a mix of the familiar exhaustion we shared in college after a long shift, and panic. 'I was on the night shift. Is everything okay?'

I think of Ellie watching movies in Malcolm's sitting room. I think of the tiny toothpaste Shayne bought me. I push the thoughts of the pokey storage room and our closet life aside and, truthfully, I say, 'I'm okay. Sorry I scared you.'

'Tell me what you need? I can stop by your apartment and pick stuff up for you. Will one of your flatmates be home?'

My guts twist with the usual guilt that leading Cora to believe my life is wholly different than it is brings.

'I'm okay,' I say again, with more conviction this time. 'I just fainted is all, and I was worried about Ellie. But everything is okay now. I really am sorry for calling and being so dramatic.'

Cora inhales sharply, in a way that hints that she doesn't believe me.

'Look, honestly, I'm fine. Just tired and need some sleep. I'm sure you do too after the night shift.'

'I'm wide awake,' she says, and I instinctively groan and cover it quickly with a cough. 'I'd love to pop by for an hour or two,' she goes on. 'Check out your new place and cuddle Ellie for a while. I'll bring soup and some bread from the bakery round the corner from my place. You still love sourdough, right?'

My mouth waters thinking about it. What a lovely way to spend a morning. Warm soup and crusty bread in a cosy flat. Too bad it's only a dream.

'Cora, I'm knackered. I'm sorry. Ellie's in crèche and I'm going to crawl into bed for a while. I hope you understand.'

'Course, course,' she says, and I can imagine her animated body language as she tries to hide her disappointment.

'But we'll catch up soon,' I say. I promise myself that we will. Maybe a walk in the park, or a stroll by the Liffey. Something that doesn't cost a penny.

'Sure,' Cora says, and something about her tone feels off. As if there is something she's not saying. I can't get off the phone fast enough.

'Bye,' I say.

'Bye.'

I return to the ward with fresh breath, and feel lighter just seeing Shayne sitting on the edge of my hospital bed, waiting.

'Let's get you out of here,' he says, hopping up.

Tonya is setting a fresh tray down on the woman's table.

'You going home, Bea?' she asks, with a smile that tells me she's happy I've been discharged.

'I'll be in work tomorrow,' I say.

'Didn't you get a doctor's letter, surely you need some time off?'

'Nah, I'm all good,' I lie. 'See you tomorrow.'

THIRTY-FIVE

I can feel Shayne's eyes on me the whole way as we make the long walk from the ward, through the hospital and out to the car park. He helps me into the car and I buckle up.

'Ready?' he asks, but I know there's another question in there and it's making me nervous.

'Where are we going?' I ask.

'No idea,' Shayne says. 'I haven't been in Dublin in eight years, so I don't really know anywhere.'

'Wow. I didn't realise it was that long. But your grandad and your mam have been to visit you in New York though, right?'

The women in work like to talk. And bragging about foreign travel is the order of most days.

'Oh, we're just back from the Maldives, lovely this time of year.'

'Really? We prefer the Caribbean ourselves.'

'Oh, no, ladies. Europe is so much easier to get to. You just have to try the Amalfi coast. Oh, the wine. Oh, the food. I'll need to diet for a month.'

If Elaine had taken a trip to New York in recent years, I'm sure she'd have mentioned it to at least one colleague, who would have mentioned it to someone else, and the gossip would have inevitably spread like wildfire as usual. Then again, I've never heard Elaine share much. I didn't know she had a son before now either.

I realise I've zoned out and am staring out the car window. We haven't started moving yet and I'm not sure if Shayne has asked me a question or not.

'What did you say?' I try, hoping he's said something.

'I was just saying I don't know Dublin, so maybe you could suggest somewhere? Is that little place under your apartment good?'

'Oh, that place,' I say, surprised he noticed it when we were busy helping John. 'Nah, not great. Coffee is bitter.'

'Oh. Pity.'

'Why don't you Google somewhere,' I suggest, trying to shove the focus as far away from my old apartment as possible. 'Be nice to try somewhere I haven't been before either.'

He pulls out his phone and taps on it for a while before saying, 'Mr Bean's.'

'Sure.'

He laughs, and turns his phone round so I can see that the logo of the coffee shop proudly sports a picture of Rowan Atkinson in a brown suit, with a cream shirt and a red tie.

'Ha ha, Mr Beans,' I say, 'Like coffee beans. We *have* to try there.'

He reads on and says, 'Um, it says the best coffee in the mountains.'

'The mountains?'

'It says it's in the Dublin Mountains. Oh, probably a bit far.' His face falls.

The Dublin Mountains are about a half an hour away by car. Perfectly far away from my old life, and I feel lighter just thinking about the view of the city from up there.

'If your grandad is okay to watch Ellie for a bit longer, I don't see why we can't try it.'

'Okay, cool. Mr Bean's here we come.'

Shayne starts the car and we drive. The snow is almost completely melted now and city life has reverted to normal. I wish it was that easy for me and Ellie. I wish all our trouble could melt away too.

'You should try to sleep for a while,' Shayne suggests as we leave the city behind, and I realise I've been quiet for ages.

'I'm okay,' I say, truthfully.

I can't remember the last time I felt this rested.

Shayne doesn't seem convinced and I sense him taking his eyes off the road every so often to check on me, and I can feel a question brewing under the surface.

When I can't take it any longer, I blurt, 'What? What is it?'

He takes a deep breath that noticeably puffs out his chest, and I feel the fine hairs on the back of my neck stand on end. Declan used to inhale like that right before he said something I didn't want to hear. Right before he brought my life crashing down like pieces raining from a broken Lego tower.

All sort runs through my head. *He's going to tell me he knows and he has to report me to the authorities. Or tell Elaine, at least.* Suddenly I'm sweating and I need air. I roll the window down a little and an icy breeze whips in, but it doesn't help.

'Just say it,' I snap.

'Okay.' He exhales. 'But don't take this the wrong way.'

'Oh, just say it, just say it,' I pant, shoving my face closer to the wind, gasping for air.

The countryside is coming into view as we make our way onto the steep, winding roads that hug the mountainside. Tall, leafless trees line both side of the road, their branches interlinked and shivering in the breeze, like old friends supporting each other.

'Just say it,' I say again, exasperated.

There's another sharp intake of breath, and this time he blurts, 'I don't think you should go back to work tomorrow.'

'What?'

'I don't think you're ready. I'm sorry, but look at you. You seem so... so...'

Homeless! I want to scream.

'Look, this isn't my place. I get that. We don't know each other all that well. But I'm worried about you.'

'You're worried about me?' I echo in a barely audible whisper.

'Yeah. It's weird, I know. But I just feel...' He trails off and I should probably say something but I am lost for words.

A feeling I can't quite put my finger on swirls inside me. I think it might be a memory, from when my parents were still alive. A memory from when people truly worried about my wellbeing and said or did things that I might not like, but they did it for my own good. Like enforcing a curfew on dark evenings, or forbidding chocolate before dinner. It's been so long since anyone has worried about me that way that I had all but forgotten the feeling. I know what it's like to have people care. My foster parents cared for me. They fed me and clothed me and did their best to make me feel welcome in their home. But they didn't worry about me. They didn't worry that I never felt like I belonged or that getting paid to have me in their life made me feel like a bag of groceries or a new skirt. My feelings didn't keep them awake at night. Cora cares about me too. Deeply. She wants me to be happy and she thinks that, without Declan, some day I will be. Be she doesn't worry about me, because she doesn't have any idea that she needs to. I hid the dark parts of my life from her so well, she has no idea that it's so dark now I can barely see any more. But somehow, despite my best efforts to keep hiding in the shadows, Shayne sees through the darkness, as if he can pull the shutters open and my heart is lying bare for him to explore. I don't understand what is happening, or why it is this way with him. But the absolute last thing I am going to do is take his worry and concern the wrong way.

'We could help, you know,' he says. 'With Ellie. Grandad and I could watch her while you get a few days' rest.'

'Thank you. But you've already been great. Malcolm is sick, the last thing he needs is a giddy four-year-old—'

'Ellie is everything he needs. When I left this morning I'm not sure either of them heard me say goodbye because they were laughing so hard. Do you know the last time I heard my grandfather laugh?'

I shake my head.

'Neither do I.'

My heart splits with a mix of gloom and hope. I am saddened to think of Malcolm without laughter in his life for so long, but I am filled with joy that Ellie, my little Ellie, can bring him happiness.

There's a sudden gap in the trees and a car park appears as if out of thin air. The dark grey gravel is loose and crunches under the car tyres like milk pouring over Rice Krispies as we turn in. We're the only car there, and I suspect the cold snap has kept people at home. Shayne parks in a spot overlooking the city. Houses and fields stretch out below us like a giant game of Monopoly. He leaves the engine running and unbuckles his seat belt to lean forward for a better view.

'It's so green,' he says. 'I miss that in New York.'

The sky is grey and thick cloud hangs low. I know if we were to step outside the icy wind would pinch our cheeks, and yet there is something so inviting out there. Something so indisputably lush and endearing about the landscape below. *Home.* Even without a house of my own, I am looking out at my home.

'He doesn't have much time,' Shayne says, his voice cracking.

I swallow and I'm glad he's not looking at me because I think I might cry if he does. 'Yeah. I heard you tell Elaine.'

'It's terminal.'

'How long?' I ask, and I want to shovel the words back into my mouth as soon as they spill out. 'I'm sorry. You don't have to say... that was insensitive.'

He shrugs. 'It's okay. I wish I knew.'

'Oh.'

'He won't ask the doctors.'

'Maybe it's better that way. I mean, do any of us really know how long we have anyway?'

He turns towards me and his glassy eyes hurt my soul.

'He's talking about going to some festival at the beach tomorrow,' Shayne says.

'The Kite Flyers festival in Malahide.' I nod knowingly. 'Looks great, I saw it on Instagram.'

'Yeah. That's the one. He barely has the energy to pull up his socks and he wants to go fly a kite.'

'Then we'll pull his socks up for him.'

Shayne rubs his eyes before he brings them to meet mine.

'I think you might be right; I need some time off work.' I swallow the enormous wedge of panic that admitting that out loud and the financial setback that will come along with it stirs. 'But I don't need to sit around feeling sorry for myself. I need to go kite-flying.'

He laughs. 'Are you serious?'

'Very. And it will be so good for Ellie too.'

His face glows, and although it's freezing outside I feel warm and fuzzy inside.

'Do you still want that coffee?' he asks

I glance out the window at the small log cabin, nestled at the edge of the car park under some tall trees. The door is firmly shut, and there is a *CLOS* sign hanging crookedly on the front. The *ED* has clearly worn off over winter.

I laugh. 'I don't think we're getting coffee.'

'I'm sorry,' he says. 'This was a terrible idea.'

I shake my head. 'This was a great idea.'

'Driving miles to a closed coffee shop in the middle of nowhere was a great idea?'

'Yes! Because now, we're going kite-flying.'

He smiles, and my insides flutter. 'Yes, we are.'

THIRTY-SIX

I almost miss Cora's call. My phone is on silent and I've also turned off the vibrate function. The buzz, buzz, buzz of a phone vibrating on the ground is too risky when your life is that of a storage closet stowaway.

'Hello,' I whisper, placing the phone to my ear.

'Hey. Just checking in. How are you feeling?'

'Much better, thanks.' I lower my voice even more.

'Where are you? I can barely hear you.'

'Ellie's asleep,' I say, truthfully.

'Ah, okay. Up for a visitor yet? I'm off tomorrow.'

'Erm...'

'It's just a catch-up, Bea. I haven't seen you in ages. I promise not to tire you out.'

It's getting harder and harder to keep avoiding her. And each time I fob her off hurts my soul a little bit more.

'I miss Ellie too,' she says, scratching at my heart.

Ellie is tucked up in a mound of blankets on the storage room floor, sleeping with a huge smile on her face. She was exhausted after a fun day with Malcolm. They walked in the park. Fed some ducks. Got some ice cream in December. Got some brain freeze, which they both complained about for a solid thirty minutes. Watched a movie. Ate popcorn and jellies for lunch. Ordered pizza. With pineapple. Ellie loved it. Shayne said it was a crime. Malcolm taught Ellie to jive even though she stood on his toes countless times. Shayne wanted to drop us home, as usual.

'I would really rather you stay with him,' I said, and I didn't feel guilty about using Malcolm's health as a cover, because I truthfully don't want him to be alone.

'But—' Shayne tried to protest.

'Please. Just take care of him.'

Shayne nodded. 'I'll see you tomorrow for some kiting?'

'Yes you will.'

'And I don't suppose there's any point offering to come pick you up?'

'Nope. We'll meet you there.'

'Okay.'

'Okay.'

There was a moment at the front door where we were so close that if either of us leaned forward, our lips might have touched. And there was a moment at the front door where I really, really wanted that to happen. But, instead, Shayne said, 'Good night.' And Ellie and I started walking.

'Why didn't you call Finton?' Cora says, and I wonder if she's been talking all this time while I zoned out.

'Hmm?'

'Last night. He's back from his sister's in Mayo. He'd have picked you up. Brought you and Ellie to ours.'

'I don't have his number.'

'Oh. God, really?'

'Nope.'

'Jesus, Bea.' I can hear her embarrassment. 'Hang on, I'll give it to you right now. In case there's ever another emergency. Have you got a pen?'

I do not have a pen. But even if I did, I'm not going to write down Finton's number. Or punch it into my phone, or whatever else Cora is about to suggest. But, even if I had Finton's number, I would never call him.

I don't answer her and when I leave a long pause, I think we are both thinking similarly.

'Who watched Ellie?' Cora asks, her voice almost as low as mine. 'Surely she didn't stay in the hospital with you?'

I want to scream that Ellie is in the hospital with me right now. But, of course, I bite my tongue. I can literally hear the alarm bells chiming in Cora's head. My story has more holes than my work tights. I should probably regret calling her in blind panic last night. Setting her sniffer instincts off, like a dog after a bone. But I don't. I miss confiding in my best friend. Part of me wishes I could tell her everything. But another part, a greater, more guarded part, knows I will have to settle for telling her some.

'I called Shayne,' I whisper at last.

'Who?'

I take a breath. 'My boss's son.'

'Oh wow,' she says, and I can almost hear her eyes widen and a wicked smirk creep across her face. 'Beatrice Alright, you cheeky devil, the boss's son.' She laughs. 'I like it.'

'It's not like that,' I say quickly. 'I'm friends with his grandad.'

'You're what?'

'Long story, but I met this old man who needed some help, and then I met Shayne and turns out they're Elaine's father and son. But they don't speak.'

'Wait? Who doesn't speak? The old man? Is he a patient?'

'No. No. Not like he can't speak. He can. A lot, and he can be pretty sarcastic actually.'

'Riiiight. But you're friends with him and his sarcasm.'

'Yes.'

'And the son? Are you friends with him too?'

'The grandson,' I correct. 'Malcolm's grandson. Elaine's son.'

'Okay, gotcha. So who doesn't speak?' she asks, excitedly invested. I imagine her lying on her couch with her feet up, enjoying hearing all about the new people in my life. I haven't had new people to gossip about like this sense our college days and a warm wave of nostalgia washes over me.

'Elaine and Malcolm. Something must have happened years ago, and they haven't spoken since.'

'Oh, that's sad,' she says. 'And the son?'

'He's home from New York, bad breakup, so he's taking care of Malcolm.'

'So he's single,' she chirps.

'Cora!'

'What? It's just an observation. Is he hot?'

'Cora,' I scold again, my voice finally above a whisper.

'Ha ha, so he is.'

'It's not like that.'

She continues to giggle. 'You said that already.'

'Did I?'

'Yes. Which means it *is totally* like that. Oh my God, Bea. You like the hot grandson.'

I do. I really, really do.

'He's going back to New York soon,' I say.

'Well, then you need to hurry up. Does he know you like him?'

'Declan and I just broke up,' I say. 'I'm not looking to date anyone right now. Shayne is just a friend. That's all.'

'Um.' I hear Cora purse her lips and I can tell she doesn't believe me. Of course she doesn't. I am a terrible liar. But the truth is nothing can happen between Shayne and me, and not just because he's leaving the country soon. Even if he stayed in Ireland, I can't date the guy. I'm already running out of excuses every time he offers to drop me home. I can tell he suspects something isn't quite right. I cannot risk anyone, even Shayne or Malcolm, finding out the truth.

'Cora, will you keep it down,' I hear Finton's voice in the distance. 'I've work at six a.m.'

It's Cora's turn to whisper as she says, 'I gotta go. But text Shayne. Even if it's just a simple good night. Let him know you're thinking about him before you fall sleep. What's the harm in that?'

'Yeah. Maybe. Na'night,' I say.

'Night.'

The line goes dead and I lower the phone and hold it against my chest for a while, thinking. Maybe I could send Shayne a text. I could thank him again for his help with Ellie and for picking me up. I could tell him I'm excited about kite-flying tomorrow. But I said all of those things already and, besides, it's late. He's probably already asleep. I finally work up the courage to take Cora's advice and send a simple 'good night,' but when I turn my phone round, I see that a message has already come in.

> Bea. I miss you. Can we talk? Dec x

I almost drop my phone. It's a new number, and no doubt a new phone. I hum and haw for a long time before I save it to my contacts and type out a reply with shaking fingers.

> What is there to talk about?

There's a moment after I press send and before his next message arrives where I want him to apologise. I want him to say he made a terrible mistake and he loves us. I want him to want us. My screen lights up and I read his next message.

> Everything.
>
> Ellie. Me. You.
>
> Us.
>
> I miss you so much.
>
> I never should have left.

I lower the phone and stare at the ground, replaying his words over in my mind. I wait for relief. Or happiness. Or that warm feeling that comes with kind words from a loved one. But I feel nothing. Not a single thing. It doesn't make me feel better to know he's thinking about us. I doesn't fill me with happiness to know he regrets leaving us, the way I fantasised that it would. That first night on Cora's couch, I lay awake for hours just willing him to text and say something so very like what he's finally said now. Lying there, staring at Cora's ceiling, I would have taken him back in a heartbeat. I would have swept over everything and hidden it under the carpet for the rest of my life. But now, sitting cramped in a smelly storage room, it's all so different. I am numb and cold and Declan's insincere words slide past me as if I am made of ice. I bring my gaze back to my phone and type again.

> It's late

His reply is instant.

> Can we talk tomorrow?

Another message chases it.

> Please? I love you.

I scoff and Ellie stirs. I hold my breath, hoping she won't

wake. Thankfully, she settles back into a deep sleep. I watch her for a moment, consumed with love. I love every inch of her. Her button nose, her rosy cheeks, the subtle dimple in her chin. I would give my life for her if I had to. And right now, I think that's exactly what I would be doing to if I agreed to talk to Declan. He doesn't love me. I know that much now. I'm starting to suspect he never did. But he is Ellie's father. And, while it's hard to believe after the way he's acted, I want to think he loves her. Maybe he wants to come back into her life. I have to at least find out. My heart hurts, and, much as I don't want to, I send another message.

> Okay.

Great!

Where are you staying?

I can come meet you?

How does 10 a.m. sound?

'Are you kidding me?' I say aloud, as if I am expecting a response from the universe.

> I am busy in the morning.
>
> Meet me at 6 p.m.
>
> The coffee shop under the apartment.

My heart aches as I type the word *apartment*. A place where the three of us once seemed to fit so well, like jigsaw pieces designed to slot together. Our jigsaw is broken now. Missing a piece and bent out of shape. Even with all three pieces united again, I don't think they will slot back together any more.

Okay. No problem. 6 p.m. is good. I can't wait.
Dec x

I try to sleep but when I close my eyes it feels as if the ground beneath me is spinning. I think about Malcolm and Shayne and kites and how excited I was for a day with people who are the nearest to a family I have ever known. But they are not my family. I don't have family. But Ellie does. And I have to prioritise that. I have to let Declan back in. Even if it breaks my heart.

THIRTY-SEVEN

The snow has completely melted. Even the slushy brown stuff that seemed determined to gather at the sides of the roads, or under the sill of shop windows, is finally gone, and the city is once again full of traffic and people. But, if possible, the clear blue sky allows the last few days of December to feel even colder than ever. I wrap Ellie up well for the weather and she moans that her scarf is too scratchy and her hat is too itchy, but she never tries to take them off. We follow the footpath along by the Liffey and down the quays, leaving the city behind us. It's another kilometre or so before the gates of the Phoenix Park come into view, but Ellie never once complains about tired legs. Instead, her mouth gapes and she says, 'Wow,' as she points at the stone pillars at the park entrance. Huge, fresh green wreaths hang in the centre of each pillar, adorned with red and gold bows, like a perfect Christmas postcard. I tell Ellie to stand next to one of the pillars and I pull my phone out of her pocket and take her picture. She's adorable, wrapped in winter woollies and with a warm and innocent smile lighting up her beautiful face. I make the photo my home and lock screen wallpaper and shove my phone back into my pocket. Then I take her hand and we walk again.

Shayne and Malcolm are waiting by the bike hire area. Malcolm is hatless as ever, with a large kite tucked under each arm. One pink. One blue. Shayne also has two kites, albeit both smaller. Ellie squeals with delight when she sees them.

'Malco. Malco,' she calls out, wriggling her fingers free from my grip. She hurries up the path towards them.

'Don't fall,' I call after her, but she picks up speed and launches herself at Malcolm.

He and the kites almost topple over, but Shayne steadies him, dropping both his kites in the process.

I run to get them.

'Ellie,' I scold, both angry and embarrassed. 'You have to be careful. You could have hurt Malcolm.'

Ellie's eyes tear up and Malcolm looks at me, frustratedly.

'She's just excited,' he says.

'But if you fell—'

'Then I'd be down instead of up,' he says, with a comical jig as if he has all the energy in the world.

Shayne and I look at each other, noting how tired the movement makes him. And Ellie laughs and copies him. Bouncing on the spot with one foot hopping in front of the other. At four years old she doesn't see the barrier of age. It's both endearing and stressful.

'I'm sorry,' I mouth to Shayne.

He makes a face that says, *Don't worry about it*. And I try not to.

'Well, are we flying kites or are we wasting a good morning standing around?' Malcolm asks, taking the pink kite from under his arm and passing it to Ellie.

Ellie jigs on the spot again, this time with dance moves of her own creation, and stretches grabby hands out.

'Unicorns,' she says, observing the pattern of several flying unicorns and cupcakes and rainbows dotted sporadically all over the kite.

'Wow, are you sure it's big enough, Grandad?' Shayne laughs when Ellie takes the kite that is at least one and a half times as tall as she is.

'They didn't have bigger,' Malcolm says, seriously.

'I'm afraid ours are much smaller,' Shayne says, still laughing as he passes me a perfectly regular-sized plain green kite.

'Thank you,' I say, taking it.

Ellie's face doesn't approve. 'Yours doesn't gots unicorns, Mammy.' But her scowl is quickly wiped from her face when Malcolm's huge blue kite whooshes into the air.

'Look, look, look.' She points, barely able to contain her excitement, and then she cheers and laughs.

Malcolm's kite flies high as he holds the string tightly. The wind is strong and the kite zigzags left and right, with its tail thrashing like a serpent. Shayne's kite is next up. Its small stature is emphasised next to Malcolm's beastly kite. Ellie and I try hard to launch hers but there seems to be a knack to it that neither of us can quite get. Shayne helps and soon there are neon pink unicorns dancing in the sky. My kite falls flat on its face a few times before I finally manage to get it airborne and, when all four kites swirl overhead, brightening the sky with their vibrant colours, Ellie exclaims, 'This is the best day ever.'

My heart soars, because I think she might just be right.

The wind picks up and I have to help Ellie keep hold of her kite. Shayne assists Malcolm, who is wholly unimpressed.

'I can do it. I can do it,' he protests like a cranky toddler with an inflated sense of their own capabilities.

But despite his grumbles he leans into Shayne every so often and I can tell that deep down Malcolm is grateful for his grandson's support. And once in a while, I catch him look at

Shayne in a way that says he is grateful for his grandson in all ways.

When our arms are tired and our stomachs are rumbling, Shayne suggests we let the kites down and grab some food. Ellie grumbles and starts sulking until Shayne mentions hot chocolate and marshmallows, and then she is the first to start walking.

Some deer dart past and, when Ellie's face lights up, Malcolm says, 'This is where they come for a rest after Christmas. They are tired after flying all round the world with Santa.'

'I hope this place is still here,' Shayne says, as we begin walking towards the zoo area of the park. 'You remember it, don't you, Grandad? We used to come here every Sunday with Mam when I was little.'

There's a flash of something in Malcolm's eyes. Nostalgia and joy. But it's fleeting. He shakes his head and says, 'Don't remember.'

Shayne sighs and I feel for him. I cup his ear and whisper, 'He remembers.'

Shayne smiles. I pull away from him and raise my voice for everyone to hear. 'I think I know the place. I used to go there with my parents. Before they passed.'

There's a sharp intake of breath. Malcolm or Shayne's, it's gone too quickly to know whose.

'It's okay,' I say. 'It was a long time ago.'

'I'm sorry,' Shayne says. 'I had no idea.'

'Really. It's okay. I don't usually talk about them.' My voice cracks on the last word and I'm not sure why. I don't talk about my parents. I guess because I've never really had anyone to talk about them to. I told Declan, of course, and he said all the right generic things. And then we never really talked about it again.

'Hey,' Shayne says, stopping walking. 'You okay?'

'Yeah. Course.'

He doesn't believe me and he sidesteps closer to me.

'C'mere,' he says, draping an arm over my shoulder the way friends do.

Cora has thrown an arm over my shoulder many times, but it's never felt quite like this. There's something about my hip nestled against Shayne's and his warm breath brushing over the top of my head that makes my knees want to buckle. There's a sudden heat. As if December has melted away and it's a summer's day and I'm skipping carefree through a meadow of flowers. I allow myself to fall into the daydream for a moment. Fall and fall and fall. And then I hit the ground with a bang as I remember Declan. The father of my child. The man I have to sit face to face with in a few hours and try not to gouge his eyes out for my daughter's sake.

'I'm starving,' I say, breaking away from Shayne to pick up the pace.

'Erm, Bea,' he says, catching up with me.

He looks back over his shoulder at Malcolm.

I cringe. *Shit! How could I forget?*

'Sorry,' I blurt, my cheeks heating up with embarrassment. 'Hot chocolate overexcitement.'

Shayne edges closer to me. 'You sure you're okay?'

'Yeah,' I squeak, standing poker straight. 'Course.'

There is a wedge between us for the rest of the day. I know, because I put it there. My heart is full of Shayne and Malcolm, but my head is full of Declan and Ellie. Shayne stops asking me if I'm okay after about the tenth time when it because obvious that I am not, but I don't want to talk about it. Malcolm, however, doesn't pick up on the obvious and says things like, 'Cat got your tongue, Busy Bea?' or, 'Bees don't buzz in winter, I suppose.' Or my favourite: 'Beatrice Alright, can't fly a kite for shite.' Ellie recited that one on repeat for at least a half an hour. She threw in some dancing and some clapping too.

'Lovely, thank you, Malcolm. You know there'll be war if she goes into crèche still singing that.'

Malcolm belly-laughs. 'Any why shouldn't she? How is she ever going to improve her singing if she doesn't practise?'

I can't argue with that.

When the weather drops another couple of degrees, Shayne says, 'I better get you home, Grandad.'

Unsurprisingly, Malcolm protests. 'I'm perfectly fine.'

His teeth chatter and his voice wobbles and Ellie copies him, chopping her top and bottom teeth together quickly.

'Well, I'm not,' I say, truthfully. 'I can't feel my toes.'

Malcolm looks down at my feet and a sweet smile lights up his face when he spots my bright red wellies.

'They're my favourites,' I tell him.

He places his hand to his chest and his smile widens more.

'Right,' he says. 'Let's call it a day. Busy Bea's feet hurt.'

Shayne flags a taxi and I have to tell him sternly to take it first. 'You need to get him home. Ellie and I will get the next one.'

Shayne reluctantly agrees and helps Malcolm into the taxi.

'I'll call you,' he says, before he hops in after his grandfather and closes the door.

I wait until the taxi is out of view before I take Ellie's hand and walk towards the bus stop.

'I love Malco,' she muses, skipping beside me. 'And Shayne too.'

The turn of phrase gives me pause. Because somewhere deep inside I think she might mean it. I think my little girl is building a relationship with Malcolm and Shayne, and I wonder what her father will have to say about that. I guess we'll find out soon enough, I think, as our old bus pulls up and we hop on.

THIRTY-EIGHT

Ellie doesn't seem to recognise the apartment block above the coffee shop, or, if she does, she doesn't refer to it as home. She's more concerned with which cookie to choose as we both follow our noses towards the scent of coffee and sugar wafting from the open door.

I glance at my watch. It's six oh five p.m. We're five minutes late. The café closes at seven p.m., giving us less than an hour to talk. But as I glance around the funky café with its minimalist industrial décor, I can't spot Declan. Ellie and I approach the counter and she presses her nose against the glass display table, eying up the limited selection of cookies remaining at this hour of the day.

'Eeny, meeny, miny, moe.' Her brow furrows as she concentrates.

The teenage girl with pink hair and a handful of facial piercings behind the counter tells Ellie, 'The chocolate chip ones are the best.'

The chocolate chip ones are almost as big as Ellie's head and twice the price of all the others. Ellie tugs my arm.

'Can I have a chocolate chip one please?'

I wince, but decide I'll eat whatever Ellie can't finish. I order an apple juice too and take out my phone to pay. Then a voice behind me says, 'What? No coffee?'

'Daddy.' Ellie's face lights up.

Declan opens his arms and she throws herself into his grip and he lifts her off the ground.

'Trying to cut down on my caffeine,' I say.

He makes a face and I hate that he can always tell when I'm lying.

'You look great,' he says, as if I've changed massively in the couple of weeks since he last saw me.

I don't return the compliment.

'I'll get this,' he says, as if buying a cookie and juice for his own daughter is some sort of grand gesture. 'Are you sure I can't tempt you with something, Bea?'

Much as I would absolutely love a coffee, I shake my head. I refuse to give him the satisfaction of buying anything for me.

'Just these,' he points towards the cookie and juice, 'and an Americano please?'

He taps his phone and the girl tells us to take a seat and she'll bring them down to us. Ellie chooses some high stools inside the window so she can people-watch.

'Will she be all right up there?' he asks me as I lift her up and push her in so she can reach the narrow, bench-style table against the window.

I snort. 'She's always fine sitting here,' I tell him.

Another lie. Ellie has never sat here before in her life. I try to push away the irritation that now, suddenly, he is concerned for his daughter's wellbeing after she's spent nights sleeping on a storage room floor. I try to keep a lid on my feelings, reminding myself that he can't possibly know we're sleeping at the hospital.

Declan and I sit on stools either side of Ellie and the barista sets our order down.

'Enjoy,' she says, walking away.

Declan takes a sip of coffee, and I can tell by his face that it's much too hot and he's burned the roof of his mouth. I allow myself to smirk for a moment before wiping it off my face.

'How was Christmas?' he asks, turning to help Ellie poke the small plastic straw into the carton of juice.

'So good,' I say. 'We spent it with friends.'

'Ah, how is Cora?' he asks, a little juice spilling over the edge of the straw as he pokes it in.

'She's fine. She was with her parents for Christmas.'

'Oh, lovely. So you were in Wexford for the big day. I bet Ellie enjoyed that.'

'No,' I say, firmly. 'Cora was in Wexford. Like I said, Ellie and I spent the day with friends. Here in Dublin.'

He looks confused and I enjoy it.

'We goed to Malco's house,' Ellie says, with a mouthful of cookie.

'Malco?' Declan asks.

'Yes, Malcolm and Shayne. You don't know them,' I go on. 'But they kindly hosted Christmas and it was wonderful. The best Christmas Ellie and I have ever had, hands down.'

Declan tries his coffee again, and when he finds it's still too hot he pushes it away and sighs. 'I'm so sorry, Bea. I never should have put you in that position... spending Christmas with strangers.'

My gut clenches as if I've just been punched. I spent many, many Christmases with strangers growing up. That's not what this was. It's not what it felt like. Christmas with Malcolm and Shayne was wonderful. It was fun and welcoming and special. I want to tell him, but I know no matter what I say it will sound like a petty retaliation.

There is some silence, before I take a deep breath and ask, 'Why are you here?'

Declan rubs his face with his hands, then lowers them and

clasps them on his lap, as if he's not quite sure where to put them.

'I fucked up, Bea.'

Ellie almost drops her cookie and a look of horror sets on her face. 'Oh, Daddy, that's a bad word. Bad words are naughty.'

'You're right, Ellie, I'm sorry,' he tells her.

She accepts his apology, smiles and returns to munching on her giant cookie. Declan leans back, so Ellie is no longer blocking his view of me. I lean slightly so my gaze can meet his. I want to look him in the eye for this conversation.

'Do you really mean that?' I ask.

He draws a cross on his chest with his fingertip.

'And your wife? Does she know you're here? Telling me this?'

'She does. It's over. I told her it's you I want. You and Ellie.'

I narrow my eyes. I don't believe him. I not sure I even want to. Just a few weeks ago, he told me she was his priority. Now it's me and Ellie. Something has changed his perspective, but I'm not sure it's us.

'So yummy,' Ellie says, dragging the sleeve of her coat across her mouth to dry up the chocolatey mess.

'That's good, chickpea,' he says. 'Eat up.'

'So what are you saying here, Declan?' I ask.

His eyes burn into mine until I feel the heat of them, as if they are scorching my soul. I want to look away and avoid getting singed, but I don't let myself.

'Can we rewind? Go back to the way everything was.'

The inside of my head is pounding and my brain is screaming, 'No! No! NO!' But I look at Ellie, swinging her legs back and forth, sitting carefree between her parents, and I know I have to hear him out.

'I spoke to the landlord,' he goes on, before casually trying his coffee for a third time. 'The fecker upped the rent cos there was so much interest, but it's worth it. He can't put a price on being back home with you and Ellie.'

Anger explodes inside me, like fiery lava. Ellie and I have been sleeping on a cold floor all this time and our old home was vacant? I close my eyes, but open them again quickly when I find everything spinning. My brain pulses and I wish I could clamp my hand over my mouth to make holding a huge scream inside easier.

'What do you say, Bea. Can we give it another go?'

My fists clench and shake as I force them to stay by my sides. I take some deep breaths to try to make the pounding inside my head stop.

'Bea?' he says.

Ellie drinks her juice and there's a loud slurping sound as she guzzles the last few sips. My eyes water, watching her. She's full of happiness as she enjoys her sugary treats. It's just a cookie and some juice, but I will most likely be unable to afford either once I start paying rent somewhere. I'm not even sure what groceries I will be able to afford. Declan is offering us our old life back. A warm, safe home, and healthy food in the fridge. Ellie needs that. She deserves it. As much as I would love to hop off this stool, gather her into my arms and walk out the door, I can't.

'Yeah, okay, maybe we could give it another go,' I say, and the words taste like bitter coffee in my mouth.

'That's my girl,' Declan says. 'I'll get all the paperwork sorted. We'll be home before you know it.'

Home, I repeat silently in my head. Ellie will have a home again. It will all be worth it. It has to be.

THIRTY-NINE

'Are you fucking mad?' Cora asks me when I call her to tell her about Declan.

'He was a mess, Cora. You should have seen him. At one stage I thought he was going to cry.' I lie, hoping she'll believe that Declan is really broken without us. Maybe I can even convince myself.

She grunts, disapprovingly. 'So, that's it? You're really taking him back.'

I hold the phone away for a moment so she doesn't hear the deep, steadying breath I take before I say, 'Yes! I am.'

'Oh, Bea. There's nothing I can say, is there?'

'To make me change my mind?' I ask. 'No. Nothing.'

'Just think about what he did. How much he hurt you. He lived a double life, for goodness' sake. You can't trust him. How can you still love him after all that? I'm sorry, Bea, I just can't get my head around this.'

I know I can't trust him. And I don't want to love him. I'm certainly not in love with him any more. But we have a history. He was a huge part of my life, the biggest part, for a long time. I can't just wave a magic wand and wipe away the memories.

'He's the father of my child,' I say.

'And he treated that child just as badly as he treated you. Oh, Bea, please. Please don't let him back in. He doesn't deserve you. Either of you.'

I wonder how this conversation would go if Cora could see me now. I'm sitting, cross-legged, on the storage room floor. My left leg has gone numb, and when I stretch it out pins and needles shoot all the way into my arse. I don't flinch. I'm used to some part of my body going numb in the cramped space. It's usually my legs, but sometimes I wake up with a dead arm or shoulder too. Of course, Cora doesn't know any of that. She thinks I'm calling her from Ellie's and my cosy room in our new lovely flatshare. I googled a picture of a generic box room online after our last call and sent it to her.

'Oh, nice. Small, but nice,' she replied, ever supportive.

Thankfully, it's been easier to fob her off about visiting since I told her about Malcolm and Shayne. She's so excited I'm spending my free time with them, she hasn't mentioned my nonexistent new flat in days.

'What about his other kids?' she asks. 'You know, the nearly grown-ups who you didn't even know existed.'

There is so much anger in Cora's tone. I know the majority of it is directed towards Declan. But I think there is a small part aimed at me too. She's furious I'm being so stupid. She's worried I'm forgiving a man who literally turned my life upside down just weeks ago. A man who lied to me, who betrayed me, who abandoned me. A man who let me fall head over heels in love with him, all the while knowing his heart was never mine to take. A bad man. A man I am about to give my life to once again because I have to.

I open my mouth to tell Cora I love him. I think they are the words she needs to hear to help her understand. But no matter how hard I try, I cannot push them out.

'He's Ellie's dad,' I find myself repeating, because it's the only truth I can share in this whole, horrible mess. I don't want to lie to my best friend. But I don't want to tell her anything more, either.

'Does Ellie know she has brothers?' Cora continues.

'I haven't told her yet,' I admit. 'They live in London. I don't know how this will all work.'

'Jesus, Bea. Don't you think you should find all this stuff out before you agree to move back in with the guy? Like now that you know about his kids, will they be in your life? And Ellie's? And what about the ex-wife? That's a whole other shitshow to contend with.'

My head is thumping as Cora goes on and on. Bashing Declan. I stop listening. My attention has turned to Ellie, who is coughing in her sleep. I hold the phone between my ear and shoulder and try to turn her on her side.

'And another thing,' I just about hear Cora say before vomit spews from Ellie's mouth and she wakes, sweating and crying.

'I gotta go,' I say. 'Ellie's sick.'

I drop my phone onto the ground and pull Ellie close to me. She's still half asleep, and crying fitfully as vomit sticks to her hair and clothes. I retch as the acidic smell is amplified in the tiny room with no window. I peel off Ellie's jammies and wrap her in the blankets that have thankfully avoided the line of fire. Then I set about cleaning up, and sneaking Ellie into the bathroom for a wash. It's monotonous and my eyes burn with tiredness. Ellie is sick a couple more times during the night and we repeat the process. When the morning finally rolls around, Ellie has stopped throwing up but she's as green as the curtains on the day ward. If I send her to crèche like this, Alannah will call me within the first ten minutes and force me to keep her home for three days. I do the only thing I can think of and call Shayne.

'Hello.'

'Hi. It's Bea. I'm so sorry to call so early. Did I wake you?'

'No. No. It's okay.' I can hear from his groggy voice that I have most definitely woken him.

'Oh God, sorry.'

'Bea. Stop apologising,' he says, waking more. 'What's wrong?'

'It's Ellie. She's sick.'

'Oh.' He immediately sounds worried and I can hear that he's sat up, probably in bed.

'It's okay. It's okay,' I hurry to reassure him. 'It's nothing serious. She puked a few times last night.'

'Oh.'

'Yeah. Must have picked something up. Thing is, I can't send her to crèche and—'

'You have work.'

I wince, realising that both times I have called him since he gave me his number have been to ask for a favour.

'I do.'

'Say no more,' he says. 'Grandad and I are going on a boat ride today.'

'Oh, okay. No worries. Forget I asked. Enjoy the ride.'

'No. Wait. It's one of those drive around the city on a truck-boat things that drive into the Liffey when you're done. And apparently, we all wear Viking hats and channel our inner Celt or something. I dunno. It was Grandad's idea.'

'Sounds great.'

'It does, doesn't it?' I hear him smile. 'So would Ellie be okay with that? She's not afraid of the water or anything, is she?'

'Oh no, I couldn't impose. You've a whole day planned.'

'A whole day that would be so much better with Ellie there. Unless, of course, you can blow off work and come too?'

My stomach flips. I would love nothing more than to spend the day driving around the city in a Viking boat truck thing like a tourist. But Elaine would hit the roof if I asked for time off with such short notice. And besides, I need the money.

'I'd love to, but...'

He sighs. 'It's okay. I get it. Just thought I'd ask.'

I smile even though he can't see me.

'What time will I pick Ellie up? Will I swing by your place before work?'

'No!'

'Erm...'

'I mean, I'm already on my way to work. Left early.'

He doesn't say anything but I swear I can almost hear the cogs in his brain trying to make sense of why I would go to work early after being up all night with a sick child. I decide it's best to brush over it.

'Could you pick her up at the hospital? Closer to you anyway so hopefully less hassle?'

'Who's that?' I hear Malcolm's raspy voice in the background.

'Bea,' Shayne calls back. 'Ellie is going to come with us today.'

'Good. Good.'

'How about I meet you in reception in thirty minutes?' Shayne asks.

'Perfect.' My insides relax. 'Thank you so much.'

Ellie manages to eat a banana and polish off some juice that I saved from last night's supper on the wards. Her colour is much brighter now, too. And by the time we are walking downstairs to reception she is her perky self.

Shayne is waiting by the front desk. His eyes brighten as soon as he sees us. Malcolm is standing next to him too; he looks more hunched than usual, and a pang of concern punches me in the gut. He looks even more unwell than Ellie did earlier. Maybe a day boating isn't such a good idea after all. I try to catch a word with Shayne but Elle is talking nonstop.

'No hat,' I cut in, at last, pointing to his head.

'You're wasting your breath,' Shayne says, 'we already had this argument before we left the house.'

'Silly Malcolm,' Ellie says. 'Jack Frost will bite you and you'll get sick.'

'And you were sick last night, chickpea,' I remind her. 'So you must wear your hat today, okay?'

Ellie shakes her head. 'No. Scratchy.'

'I know, I know, but it keeps you warm and keeps Jack Frost away,' I say, popping her woolly pink hat with its small bobble on her head.

She pulls it off immediately and throws it on the ground.

'Ellie,' I say sternly, as I fetch it and put it back on.

It comes off again and she stomps her foot. Malcolm stretches his arm out to Shayne and opens his hand. Shayne looks on, confused for a moment, before he says, 'Oh. Getcha,' and reaches into his pocket for a blue-and-green knitted hat that he passes to his grandfather.

'It's not as nice as yours,' Malcolm tells Ellie. 'It doesn't have a bobble.'

'Is it scratchy too?' she asks, making a face.

'It's a little bit scratchy, but it's warm.'

Malcolm pops the stripy hat on his head, and I can tell he's instantly irritated and itchy. I try not to laugh. Ellie smiles brightly and puts her hat on her head too.

'Attagirl,' Malcolm says, taking her hand. 'You ready?'

'I ready.'

'Thank you,' I mouth to Malcolm.

He winks.

Shayne's smiling as he turns to me and whispers, 'It's a miracle.'

FORTY
NEW YEAR'S EVE

Ellie hasn't stopped talking about the Viking boat thing in three whole days. *And then Shayne said this. And Malcolm did that. And then we saw this. And then we saw that.* Sometimes she rambles on so quickly and intensely that she runs out of air and has to pause to take a deep breath as if she's a whoopee cushion refiling before bursting again.

Ellie hasn't stopped talking. And at the same time, I haven't heard a word from Shayne since. He offered to drop her back to my apartment after pizza, but I made up some lame excuse that I can't even remember now and asked him to bring her to the hospital again. I was cleaning the men's bathrooms when he arrived, and Órlaith on reception watched her until my shift finished. I texted him straight after.

> Thank you so much. Ellie had the best day. You're a life-saver. Tell Malcolm I said hi.

I added a kiss and took it back out several times before I hit send. His reply was instant.

> Any time. We had the best day too. Grandad says hi. Shayne x

I've read his message countless times since. *Grandad says hi. Shayne. Kiss.* Kiss! He typed a kiss. I run my finger over it again and again and try not to read too much into it. It's just a sign-off, I tell myself. Nothing more. I've sent a couple of messages since. One thanking him and Malcolm again for looking after Ellie. Another to tell him that Ellie is now obsessed with Vikings. And a final message to ask how Malcolm's itchy head is and enquire if he will be wearing hats all the time outdoors from now on. Shayne hasn't read a single one.

On New Year's Eve, I send one more.

> Hi. I have the day off. I was wondering if you're free?

I follow it quickly with another.

> And your grandad too, of course.

My heart sinks when a long time passes and no reply follows. I resign myself to a day wandering around the city with Ellie, killing time until we can go to bed again, long before the clock strikes twelve. Everywhere is busy. People are drunk by early afternoon, and they are overflowing from bars and restaurants and spilling onto the streets, full of 'Auld Lang Syne' and booze and excited to ring in a new year. We try visiting the ducks in St Stephen's Green Park, but there's a guy taking a wee at the edge of the water, weaving from side to side, with a can of Guinness in his hand. I take Ellie tightly by the hand and we move on to visit the Disney store on Grafton Street. Ellie is overjoyed as we walk through the door and straight to the dress-up section. A teenage staff member with a full face of airbrushed-perfect make-up and long, styled hair approaches and sweetly says, 'We're closing.'

My mouth rounds. 'Oh.'

'Sorry,' she says. 'Closing early, so we can go out.' She points to the couple of guys, around the same age, standing behind the counter. 'But if there's anything you want, I can check it out for you now.'

'Oh no, that's okay.'

'You sure, it's no trouble.'

I glance at the price tag of the blue-and-gold Cinderella dress Ellie is hugging and my eyes water.

'Sorry, chickpea. Time to go.'

Ellie begins to cry, and clutches the dress tightly.

'We have to go,' I repeat, as I prise the dress out of her small hands. Ellie wails loudly, a full tantrum erupting. The staff look on, unimpressed.

'Please, Ellie,' I plead with her, close to breaking point, as if she will take pity on me and instantly snap out of her tantrum. 'Please stop.'

I place the dress back on the rack, and lift Ellie into my arms. She bucks against me and I can't make it outside quick enough.

'Byeeeeee,' the girl behind the counter chirps as we walk away.

Outside, the shutters of all the shops are coming down and Ellie becomes distracted by a guy with a guitar busking. He's really very good as he sings one of my favourite Coldplay songs. I glance at my watch. It's four p.m. I had forgotten everywhere closes early on New Year's Eve. Town seems to be divided into people with kids, who are heading home with a takeaway of choice tucked under their arm as they push a buggy or hold hands with a toddler, preparing for a night in front of the TV, and childless people, dolled up in their finest. Women are mostly dressed in sequins and sparkle from head to toe like the glitter baubles on the giving tree outside St Stephen's Green Park. The guys shimmer less, but are equally energetic. There's something in the air. I can't quite put my finger on it. It's like happiness mixed with nostalgia mixed with vodka. Or something like that. A collective sense of joy as one year comes to a close and another begins. A sense that all the shite that happened this year will magically vamoose at midnight, as if the stuffed fairy godmother toy in the Disney store will spring to life at midnight and wave her wand, and a new year and a fresh start will sprinkle all of us like glitter raining from the clouds. I give it until ten past before someone throws up on the corner of Grafton Street, someone else steps in it and everyone realises that it's just the same shit, different year.

'C'mon, Ellie,' I say, as a group of cackling girls about my age zigzag towards us in short skirts and chunky heels. 'We should go.'

But I don't go. I seem to be stuck to the spot, unable to take my eyes off them. They seem so carefree and youth sits brightly in their faces, even under layers of make-up. They stop at a small gelato bar that despite the minus-three temperature is busy, with a queue snaking out the doorway. They don't notice me as they line up outside, shivering in fashionable but totally unsuitable for the weather clothes. I suspect I look years older than them. I feel older. My bones ache as if I've broken each one at some point or another and my eyes are heavy and I have to battle with each blink to keep them open.

'Mammy.' I hear Ellie's little voice cut into my thoughts. 'Mammy. Maaaaammmm.'

'Yes. Yes,' I say, widening my sleepy eyes to look at her. 'You okay?'

'Can we get ice cream?'

'Um.'

I really don't want to refuse such a simple request. And with Declan back soon, I guess there will be money again for things like ice cream and cinema trips. It will all be better, I tell myself. It has to be. That's why I'm taking him back, after all. I'm doing it for Ellie.

'Pleeeeease,' Ellie tries again and I realise I haven't given her an answer.

I nod. 'Sure. Let's get ice cream.'

I take a deep breath, that's so cold it seems to shock my lungs, and I lead us to join the queue.

One of the girls, in a tiny miniskirt and platform Converse, notices us.

'Oh my God, your little sister is so cute!' she says, smiling at Ellie as if she's a pixie or a fairy or some other sort of magical creature. 'And you guys look so alike. Don't they look like literal twins?' She nudges the ribs of her friend, who turns and says, 'Totally.'

The first girl keeps going, her speech a little slurry from booze but not so bad I can't make out what she's saying. 'I nearly got stuck babysitting tonight. I've four younger brothers. But I told my parents no way, you know. I have a life too, yeah? You're making me feel guilty now.' She follows with a giggle and hiccup.

'Your sister is the best,' she tells Ellie as if she knows me. 'You're so lucky.'

Ellie giggles and points at me. 'She's my mammy.'

'Oh fuck, shit.' The girl stumbles back. Then she laughs hard. As if I'm the funniest thing she's ever seen. 'So sorry. I totally thought you were like our age.' She wiggles her finger in the air and I think she is trying to draw a circle around her and her friends. 'I guess I'm more drunk than I thought. Hic.'

'I guess so,' I say, but I am smiling. My bones may ache from sleeping on a hospital floor and there may be bags under my eyes that would put a Tesco bag for life to shame. And I may spend the majority of my days with the elderly and convalescent. But to a stranger, I'm just a girl, and I like that.

I buy Ellie a strawberry ice cream, and I even splash out and get a pistachio one for myself. I plan to sit in the park for a while, but the gate is locked and Ellie is too tired to keep walking. When rain starts out of nowhere we take cover in the doorway of a closed shop. Soon, puddles are forming on the street and I suspect the best thing we can do now is settle in for a long night back at the hospital.

FORTY-ONE

Ellie and I join Mrs Brennan and Mrs Morgan on the ward for a game of cards. Mrs Brennan's son Vincy and his wife, Rachel, have come to visit, and join the game. We're about halfway through a second round when Vincy reaches into a paper bag next to the bedside locker and produces a bottle of prosecco.

'That's not allowed,' Mrs Morgan says quickly with a wagging finger.

'Well, if you don't want any,' he says, hiding the bottle behind his back.

'That's not what I said!'

He chuckles. I should say something. I should back Mrs Morgan up and reiterate that alcohol is strictly prohibited for patients. But it's New Year's Eve, and who knows if it will be Mrs Brennan's last.

'I'd love a glass if there's one on offer,' I say, boldly.

Vincy has come prepared, with a screw-cap so there's no faffing about with a corkscrew, and no loud pop. But it's nonetheless exciting when he twists the lid off and some fizz spills over the top.

'Hang on,' I say, with a finger in the air. I dash to the water cooler on the corridor and fetch several plastic cups. A cheery grin lights up Mrs Brennan's whole face when I return with cups in hand.

Vincy pours a small splash of prosecco into each cup and I pass them round. I give Mrs Brennan the fullest cup, and pass Mrs Morgan an almost equally overflowing one.

'Here's to the new year,' Vincy says, raising his cup.

'To the new year,' everyone echoes, and with all our cups in the air we tap them together. There's no clink as the flimsy plastic connects, but it's a still a joy.

'You're a good boy,' Mrs Brennan says, sipping from the clear plastic cup with her pinkie extended. 'The best thing to ever happen to me, you are. And when I'm gone—'

'Stop it, Mam. Don't talk like that,' Vincy says, cutting his mother off. 'You'll be fine. You'll see.'

'The kid is right,' Mrs Morgan says, smiling at Vincy as if he is Ellie's age and not a middle-aged man. 'You're not going anywhere. Not until you learn to stop cheating. Now, are we playing cards or what?'

A heated game of poker ensues, and, while none of use lose ourselves quite enough to forget where we are, the prosecco is delicious, the company is fun and it's altogether a lovely New Year's Eve indeed. We play for as long as Mrs Brennan and Mrs Morgan can keep their eyes open, but what feels all too soon the elderly patients are flagging and Vincy announces it's time to go.

He kisses his mother on the cheek and promises to come back soon.

'Thank you for tonight,' he says, taking my hand and shaking it. 'Mam talks about you all the time. You and your grandfather. The man who taught her to play poker.'

'Oh, he's not...' I begin to explain my relationship with Malcolm and quickly realise I'm not sure I can. I could say he's my friend. Which would certainly be true, but it doesn't seem to fit as quite the right explanation. In the short time I've known him I've grown to care about him in a way I'm not sure I've experienced before. I never met my grandparents; both sets were gone before I was born. But caring for Malcolm these past weeks is how I imagine it must feel to have a grandfather. Someone to fall asleep on the couch with on Christmas day as an overplayed Disney classic hums in the background. Someone to cook dinner for, or fly a kite with or fear that they'll catch cold in the snow without a hat. Someone to worry about. Someone who the thought of them being ill fills you with dread.

I clear my throat and start over. 'I'll tell Malcolm your mam says hello.'

'And happy new year,' Vincy adds.

I nod. 'Happy new year.'

All the visitors seem to leave in one swarm, and soon the wards are churchlike-silent. Ellie has fallen asleep, curled into a small ball on the plastic chair near Mrs Brennan's bed. I scoop her into my arms, tuck her close to me and breathe her in.

'Good night,' I whisper, although Mrs Brennan and Mrs Morgan are sleeping as soundly as Ellie and don't hear me.

In the storage room, I tuck Ellie into the makeshift bed on the floor and cover her with blankets. The prosecco is pressing on my bladder and I've got to pee. I wait until Ellie turns on her side and sucks her thumb, soundly asleep, before I leave the room and close the door behind me.

I hurry in the loo, and I'm washing my hands when I hear faint crying. I cock my head towards the door, struggling to make it out over the sound of the water running. The water stops and my heart drops as I hear it clearly. Ellie!

I race out of the bathroom and down the corridor, but I'm too late. Ellie is in the hall. Her eyes are red and her shoulders are heaving as she cries hysterically. But worse than my distressed little girl is the woman standing beside her, holding her hand. Elaine!

'You leaved me,' Ellie cries, her voice breaking after each word.

My heart is beating furiously and inside my head is loud as I hear the swish-wallop of my blood racing through my veins. I paste on a smile, and try to ignore how my insides shake as I walk towards them.

'I was just in the bathroom,' I tell Ellie, and it comes out wobbly and high-pitched. I reach out an open hand and add, 'C'mon on now, time to go.'

'Heading home, are you?' Elaine asks, cocking her head towards the double doors at the end of the corridor that lead out to the main part of the hospital.

'Mm-hmm.' I can just about manage to push sound out.

'Because Ellie tells me she woke up and you were gone.'

'Oh, yes, she fell asleep while we were visiting Mrs Brennan and Mrs Morgan.'

'Mammy drinked protecco, but I'm not allowed any,' Ellie says, wriggling free from Elaine's grasp so she can jam her hands on her hips.

'Oh really?' Elaine asks, intrigued. 'And is this while you were sleeping in the closet?'

Ellie giggles. 'Noooo, silly. I goed to bed after.'

'I... I...' I choke. I am choking on air. I swallow hard and try again. 'I can explain.'

Elaine raises an eyebrow with a face that tells me she'd love to hear me try.

'Sometimes, Ellie naps in the closet. If I have to work late, and crèche is closed. I know it's not ideal.'

'Naps?' Elaine says.

'Mm-hmm.'

'For an hour or two,' Elaine goes on.

'Mm-hmm.'

'Right,' she says, turning towards the storage room to open the door.

I grab Ellie by the hand and follow quickly.

'Ouch,' Ellie protests, but I don't let go. 'Mammy, you're squishing me.'

I loosen my grip as the door swings open and Elaine takes in the view of blankets on the floor, Tesco bags of our stuff poking out there and there. Ellie's colouring book and pencils on a shelf. Our toothbrushes in a plastic cup, and some clothes that I hand-washed in the bathroom sink earlier hanging to dry over the handle of the floor polisher.

Elaine's hands cup her face and her shoulders round as she says, 'Oh, Bea.'

I have no words as I stare inside the small, dimly lit space where it is obvious Ellie and I have been sleeping. Have been living. Tears trickle down my cheeks, but I am not crying. I am too panicked to cry.

'Oh, Bea,' Elaine repeats. 'How long?'

I let go of Ellie's hand to drag my hands around my face. Lies spin through my head at lightning speed. *It's not what you think. I'm just storing some stuff there. We stay over to get ahead of traffic. I was bagging up clothes for charity.* But anything I can think of sounds stupid and ridiculous and doesn't hide the blatantly obvious.

'How long?' Elaine repeats, gently.

Tears are falling fast and heavy now. They fall off my chin and splash onto the collar of my top. 'A couple of weeks or thereabouts.'

'Jesus, Bea.'

'Ellie's dad left and I couldn't afford rent on my own.'

'Had you nowhere else?'

I shake my head.

'A friend.'

'We tried, but her boyfriend...' I trail off.

'Right, yes, okay. And Ellie's dad, does he know what's happened? Where is he now?'

I rub my eyes and gather myself. 'He's back. We're back together,' I say, the words hurting as I push them out. I hate Declan for putting me and Ellie in this position. But I hate him even more, right now, for leaving me with no choice but to take him back. 'Ellie and I are going home. He's sorting the flat literally as we speak. Please don't fire me.'

'Christ, Bea. Your job is the least of your worries right now.'

'Please,' I beg.

'Okay, okay,' she says, quickly. 'Calm down. I'm not going to fire you. Your job is safe. I just want to make sure you're safe too. Is Daniel at the flat?'

'Declan,' I correct. 'Um. Not exactly. Not yet. But he's sorting it.'

'Do you have somewhere to go tonight, Bea? You cannot stay here.'

'I... I...'

Oh God, why can't I speak. And I just peed but I feel as if I need the loo again. My whole body is struggling to function. Ellie is spinning on the spot, humming a Christmas song to herself, oblivious to our lives falling apart. Thank God.

'Yes,' I say, at last. 'I'll call him. I'll call Declan. He'll come get us.'

Elaine nods and I can tell she wonders, if it's that simple, what we were ever doing in the closet in the first place. If only she knew.

My hands are trembling as I take my phone out of my pocket and I almost drop it a couple of times before I manage to press the call button. It rings for a while before an answer comes.

'Hello?'

I jolt when a female voice answers and my instinct is to hang up, but Elaine is staring at me. I have to keep it together.

'Hello,' I reply. 'Is this Declan's phone?'

'Yeah,' she says, and I hear that she's chewing gum.

'Who's this?' I ask.

'Eh, who are you?' she says, becoming guarded.

'I... eh... I'm Bea.'

'Right. Hi, Bea. Declan is in the shower at the moment, do you want me to give him a message?'

'The shower?'

'Yes. Are you all right?' she asks.

'How do you know Declan?' I ask.

'Excuse me?'

'You answered his phone, and you said he's in the shower. I'm wondering how you know him; it seems—'

'I'm his girlfriend,' she snaps, clearly irritated. 'He doesn't mind me answering his phone.'

I find that hard to believe, but that's the least of my concerns right now. Declan has a girlfriend. A bloody girlfriend. Jesus. One of how many, I wonder. There could be tonnes of us.

'But I'm his girlfriend,' I say.

I almost feel guilty when I hear her gasp. She is clearly as naive as I once was. Falling under Declan's spell.

'Who did you say you are?' she says, and it sounds like she swallows her gum.

I hang up.

Elaine is watching me with inquisitive eyes. 'Is he coming?'

I regret the prosecco as acid works its way up the back of my throat and I feel as if I might be sick.

'Just one more call,' I say.

Elaine folds her arms. Ellie dances on the spot. I call Shayne. It rings out. *Oh God!* I try again. Nothing. On the third failed attempt Elaine loses patience.

'Do you have somewhere to go?' she asks.

For a moment I consider whether Ellie and I could sleep outside, maybe under a tree or in a doorway, but I shake the idea off as dangerous almost instantly. I wonder if we could check into a hotel, but I only have the budget for a night or two and what would we do then? Finally, when my gut clenches as if a fist is burrowing into it, I look Elaine in the eyes and shake my head.

She exhales sharply, and her face fills with sadness. 'The shelters will almost definitely be full by now,' she says, looking at her watch. 'But I know someone at St Clement's. They owe me a few favours.'

My guts tighten more, until it makes me bend in the middle. 'No, please. They'll take Ellie. They'll put her into care.'

'Oh, Bea.'

'Please,' I beg. 'Please. I can't lose her. She's all I have in the world.'

Elaine sighs. 'They have family rooms. Not many, but some. No one is going to take Ellie away, okay?'

My heart races. I want to believe her, but I'm not sure I do. I decide that, if they try, I will call Declan again. Girlfriends or not, I will call him. I never want Ellie to feel as lonely as I once did. If she can't be with me, then at least she has her father.

Ellie spins into the wall, bangs her head and begins to cry. I pick her up and hold her close, comforting her, and her small, warm body comforts me back.

Elaine lowers her mobile from her ear and says, 'Right. They have space.'

Finally, I cry. Raspy heaves spill out of me and, even when it startles Ellie, I can't stop.

'It will be all right,' Elaine tells me. 'We'll get you back on your feet.' Then she turns her attention towards the storage room and adds. 'Let's get you packed up, eh?'

FORTY-TWO

Elaine escorts us downstairs. She insisted on helping us with our bags, and now a Tesco plastic bag of teddies dangles from her hand. Her other arm is linked round mine, vise-like, and she keeps repeating, 'It will be all right, Bea. It will.' As if hearing her trying to convince herself she is doing the right thing somehow helps me or Ellie in any way. Ellie, thankfully, is sleeping in my arms. Her chest is pressed against mine and her head is resting on my shoulder. I can feel her warm, gentle breath on my neck as her legs flop beside my hips with each step forward. I'm struggling to keep hold of her and the other bag, but Elaine clearly has no intention of letting me go.

A taxi is waiting outside the main hospital doors. And the driver takes the plastic bags that encapsulates Ellie and my entire lives, and places them into the boot.

'Straight to St Clement's, please,' Elaine says commandingly, as if Ellie and I are planning to make a run for it at the first red traffic light. Where she thinks a homeless woman and four-year-old child plan to go is beyond me.

'It's a tenner extra for the kid's seat,' the driver says, opening the door, and I can see a grubby, backless *Toy Story* booster seat that is suitable for a child older than Ellie.

'Yes, yes, that's fine,' Elaine says, passing him some cash. 'This should cover it.'

'Grand,' he says, and then he turns his attention to me and his eyes ask if I'm getting in.

'You'll be all right, Bea,' Elaine says once more. 'They're expecting you. Millicent who runs the charity is a lovely woman. We had her father with us for end-of-life care a few years back. Very sad. Before you joined us, I think. Anyway, Millicent is looking forward to meeting you. She'll be at reception when you arrive. And everything will—'

'Be all right,' I finish for her, unable to bear hearing her say it again.

There's a flash of something on her face. Sadness, or pity, I think. I'm too exhausted to try to make it out.

'Yes. Yes, it will.'

'Come on, Ellie,' I whisper as I bend into the car and secure her in the *Toy Story* seat. 'Shh, shh, it's okay.'

Ellie doesn't wake fully and when I climb in beside her I guide her head to rest on my shoulder. I take some deep, measured breaths and try to slow my racing pulse. But it doesn't help. My heart is beating furiously, as if it might vibrate through my chest wall and kill me. If it wasn't for Ellie, I'm not so sure death would be such a bad thing. My heart beats even faster, scared of the dark places my mind is going, and I try hard to get a grip.

'You all right back there?' the driver asks, sitting in behind the wheel.

'Yes.' I manage a meek mumble.

'Don't worry. That bastard will never touch you again,' he says, and I'm not sure what Elaine told him. Maybe he thinks Declan hit us. If only he knew that what Declan has done to us is just as soul-destroying. With a confident nod as he starts the engine, 'Let's get you to safety,' he adds, as if he should be wearing his underwear outside his trousers, the way all good superheroes do.

I can only imagine the strings Elaine had to pull to get me and Ellie into St Clement's. A respected charity for the homeless, it used to be a foodbank, but as homelessness in the city worsened the charity expanded and now they have several rooms for the needy. People I used to feel pity for. People we have become.

The drive is across town is short without traffic, and in less than ten minutes the driver announces, 'We're here, love. Safe and sound.'

We come to a stop outside an old, whitewashed building that appears to have once been a large church, or a convent perhaps. There are still stained glass windows and some crosses etched into the walls.

As Elaine promised, Millicent is waiting for us. We don't have to go as far as reception to find her; she greets us at the car door as soon as the driver hops out and opens it for us.

'Hello, Beatrice,' she says, with a kind smile, 'and this must be Ellie.' She extends her hand and Ellie shakes it.

Millicent is a small, round woman with huge eyes and rosy cheeks.

'I know this is scary,' she says, taking the plastic bags from the driver. 'But everyone here wants to help, and you can stay as long as you need to, okay?'

Past words, I just about manage a single nod.

Millicent shows us around, with a bag in each hand. And I wonder what the etiquette is. Should I take my bags, or leave her to look after them like a host? My face stings with the not-knowingness of it all. Millicent is saying something about cooking rules, and a reading group. I'm not taking any of it in. I spot a table tennis table somewhere, and a kettle and some teabags. I think I spy a toaster and a fridge too. There's bathrooms and showers. And there's a smell that reminds me of the hospital – like boiled veg masked with bleach.

'This time of year is pretty busy, unfortunately. The cold weather makes sleeping rough dangerous,' she says, leading us up some stairs with a threadbare-in-patches maroon carpet. 'We only have a foldaway bed, but maybe you could share for tonight. We can make better arrangements in a couple of days when all the staff are back to work after the holidays. There'll be some admin stuff, but we'll worry about that then. Let's just get you settled for now.'

After weeks sleeping crouched in the corner, sharing any sort of bed with Ellie sounds like a dream. Millicent leads us into an upstairs dormitory. It smells much more pleasant up here. Like apple shampoo, or summer potpourri. In spite of the lovely smell, the dorm also reminds me of the hospital, with its six beds. Three on each side, with their headboards spaced evenly against the wall behind them.

'This is yours,' Millicent says, pointing to a narrow bed shoved into a free space near a small wardrobe. She leaves the bags down on a leather armchair that looks as if a small animal has chewed the armrest. 'Sheets are clean, don't worry. Springs aren't great though. Sorry about that.'

'Thank you,' I mouth, but no sound comes out.

She places her hand on my shoulder and squeezes gently.

'This is a lot, I know,' she says. 'But don't be scared. You're safe now.'

I wonder what Elaine told her about my situation. It's clear Millicent thinks I'm hiding from someone. Perhaps, I am.

'I'll leave you to get settled,' she says, pulling her hand away, and when she lets me go I suddenly feel cold. 'But if you need anything, I'm working all night. You'll usually find me near the coffee machine. Or playing table tennis, if I can muster up a partner.'

'Thank you,' I try again, and this time a meek sound like a mouse is trapped in my throat comes out.

Millicent leaves and I don't have time to say a word to Ellie before she climbs into the waiting bed and tucks the covers under her chin. I had forgotten how small she looks in an actual bed. My eyes sting and I want nothing more than to climb in beside her and sleep until this whole nightmare ends. But as I slip off my runners, my phone vibrates in my pocket. I pull it out, praying it's Shayne returning my call, but instead I find Cora's name on the screen. My finger hovers over the accept button but I let it ring out. I can't pretend to be okay. Not right now. But it has stopped for less than a second when it starts again. *Go away. Please, please go away*, I beg silently in my head. When it almost rings out for a third time is when I begin to worry that something might be wrong. Cora never calls persistently like this. Not even that time in college when she thought she had the world's worst hangover but it turned out to be appendicitis and she needed emergency surgery. I pick up.

'Hello,' I say, and it comes out as if I'm breathless.

'Bea,' she says, sounding equally short of air.

'What's wrong?' I ask.

'It's Finton. We broke up.'

I inhale, not sure what to say. Finton is an asshole. I haven't recently come to this conclusion, and it's not because he didn't want a small child sleeping on his couch indefinitely. That's not what he signed up for, I get that. I don't like him because of how he treats Cora. Always demanding so much of her time and her headspace, as if he deserves all of her and she shouldn't waste space on anyone else. He always has something negative to say about everyone. Cora's mam is too loud apparently, and her dad too quiet. Her friends and colleagues too passive-aggressive. I don't know what he says about me behind my back. I don't care. But I care that for years Cora has carried the weight of hiding it. And yet, as I hear her try to squash gentle sobbing, I am broken-hearted for her, because losing someone who is the biggest part of your life is shit, asshole or not. I should know.

'Can I come around to yours?' she asks. 'I can't be here.'

'Oh.' I swallow, flopping onto the bed next to Ellie. It groans under my weight and reminds me of the camping trips my parents took me on when I was a kid. I try to pretend Ellie and I are on an adventure just like the ones of my childhood but, as I glance around the dorm, filled with other women equally broken and lost, my imagination is not that good and it's hard to pretend that this room is anything but an endurance test for us all right now.

'Bea?' Cora whispers, requesting my attention again. 'You still there?'

'Yeah. Sorry. Just shocked. I dunno what to say, Cor. This is massively shit. I'm sorry.'

'Yeah. Thanks. We can talk about it at your place, eh? What's your address again? My brain is a mess and I can't remember for shit.'

My mind races. I would love nothing more than to open my front door and wrap my arms round my best friend and give her the hug she so badly needs. The hug we both need. But I don't have a front door. And no matter how hard I try, I cannot think of an excuse for the situation. I can't lie to her any more. Not now, when she needs me.

'I'm not at home right now,' I say.

Cora chokes back a muffled cough. 'Oh. Erm. Okay. No worries. Later then? I should probably go for a walk anyway, I'm a mess.'

'Cora.' I take a deep breath.

'Um.'

'I need to tell you something.'

'Okay.'

She sounds confused, and I can't blame her. Why would I

pick this exact moment to tell her something important? I wish I didn't have to.

'I won't be at home later, either,' I say.

'Oh.'

'Yeah. That's what I need to tell you. It's my situation. It's eh, well, it's complicated.'

'Oh.'

I realise I am phrasing this in the worst possible way.

'I just—'

'Will you shut the fuck up,' someone shouts from across the dorm. Ellie wakes with a jolt and grabs my arm, wide-eyed and trembling. I pull her close to me.

'What was that?' Cora asks.

'I gotta go.' I hang up, panicking as a tall woman with bleached-blond hair and fiery eyes charges towards me.

'You think you're the only one with problems?' she continues to shout, even though she's right next to me and Ellie now.

Ellie screams and I can feel her racing heart through her little chest.

'You're killin' me buzz,' she says. Close up I can see her eyes are glassy and her pupils are dilated.

I wonder if she can see me. Or Ellie. Or if we are a blur.

'Please,' I say, placing my finger over my lips. 'You're scaring my daughter.'

'Oh, you're scaring my kid,' she mimics.

Ellie starts to cry. 'I want to go home,' she sobs as she ducks behind me, hiding as best she can.

The woman presses her hands over her ears as if the noise hurts. The noise outside her head, or the noise inside. I'm not sure. But I've been there. I know what it's like when your mind is so busy that the sound of a pin dropping is enough to slice your brain in half.

'Are you okay?' I ask.

She lowers her hands and there is a moment where I think she will apologise, or open up maybe, but without warning her hands are in my hair and she's tugging me off the bed. Ellie tries to keep hold of me and I reach for her, but I'm dragged away.

I scream.

'Let my mammy go,' Ellie cries, standing on the bed like a tiny solider trying to help.

The woman tugs harder and I feel bits of my hair pull away from my scalp as I struggle against her. My arms flap and my shoulders buck as I try to shake her off.

'Stop it. Stop it,' Ellie screeches.

I feel the woman's grip on me slacken for a moment and my heart races faster than ever; I'm afraid that when she lets go of me she'll hurt Ellie. I take a deep breath and jam my elbow into the woman's ribs with as much force as I possibly can. A guttural grunt bursts out of her. Ellie yelps again. But my efforts seem to strengthen the woman's resolve and she slips an arm round my neck, pressing on my windpipe. I will Ellie to run for help, but she's frozen in place, scared and screaming.

Suddenly, I recognise a man racing towards us. John! From the street.

'Let her go,' he bellows.

The tugging stops and I can straighten my head.

'Ah you're no fun, John,' the woman complains, rolling her eyes. 'I was only fucking with her. I do it to all the newbies. You should see your face.' She chuckles, pointing at me. 'Bloody hilarious. Like you're going to piss your pants. I wouldn't have hurt ya, you know.

I rub my neck where she has very much hurt me, and then I race to Ellie and hold her tight.

'You all right?' John asks.

He looks the same, yet different. He's wearing a clean flannel shirt and jeans and he's had a haircut and a shave. He looks well rested too, just like any regular man. Equating him with the homeless man at death's door that Shayne and I took to the hospital is almost impossible.

'Don't mind her.' He points towards the woman. 'She's harmless, really.'

I glare at her. It hurts to breathe and I am certain my neck is already starting to bruise.

'Come on. Let's get you a cuppa or something.'

The last thing I want right now is tea, but I need to get Ellie out of this room. I need to get her to safety. I need to let John help.

John leads us towards a small kitchenette and fills a kettle with some water.

'There's bikkies in the fridge,' he tells Ellie.

'It's okay,' I tell her when she has trouble letting me go. 'You can take some.'

Ellie clings to my leg and shakes her head. John makes two cups of tea and places them on a small round table that wobbles when you press on it. We sit, and I take Ellie on my knee.

'I'm so glad you're okay,' I tell him as I wrap my hands round the cup and savour the warmth against my skin. 'I tried to find you at the hospital but they said you'd gone to a shelter.' I look around as if to say, *here*.

'You checked on me,' he says.

'I work at the hospital. Or at least, I think I still do. I need to talk to my boss.'

He cocks his head.

'She found out we've been sleeping in the storage closet at work.'

He snorts. 'Oh fuck.'

'Yes. Exactly.'

'She's not happy,' he adds.

'No. But she's rarely happy.'

John and I chat for a while. He tells me he was married once, and has two adult kids. 'About your age,' he says, with a sigh. 'Haven't seen 'em since they were kiddos though. The wife couldn't take me gambling any more and booted me out. Can't say I blame her. Managed on me own for a while but the gambling got worse and worse and I lost everything in the end. Don't even know where the wife and kids are living these days. Hard to believe, isn't it?'

'It's easier to believe than you might think.'

Finally, Ellie feels brave enough to slide off my lap, and I relax ever so slightly as I watch her nervously tiptoe towards the fridge.

'It's okay, chickpea,' I encourage her.

Her face lights up when she pulls a packet of Rich Tea biscuits from the fridge and bites into one. I'm finally smiling when I feel John's hand on mine. I stop smiling instantly and flinch, and am about to pull away when his lips press against mine and I feel his tongue poke into my mouth. My gag reflex kicks in and I jump back, knocking over my chair. It hits the ground with a bang.

'What?! No,' I say, embarrassed and uncomfortable. Outraged and confused.

Ellie watches me, open-mouthed, a chewed-up biscuit in her mouth.

'Sorry, what I mean is, I'm not looking for anything like this.' I point to him and then to me. 'I'm not interested.'

'Hmm, yeah, that's not exactly how it works around here,' he says, dryly.

'Sorry?'

'God, stop apologising.'

'Sorry,' I say, again. I'm not actually apologising. I'm just so shocked it seems to be the only word slipping out of me right now.

'Look, I'll keep big Lizzie off your back, but I won't do it for nothing, you know,' he says, with a wink that makes my blood run cold.

'You want me to kiss you?'

He snorts. It's loud and ugly and I make a face, repulsed.

'I'll need a bit more than a kiss, love.'

Jesus.

'Or' — he scrunches his face — 'I'll let big Lizzie know you'd be happy to be friends with her, if you know what I mean.'

Suddenly I'm glad John doesn't know where his wife and kids live. For their sakes.

'Okay,' I say, calmly, as if my insides aren't shaking. 'I get it. Let me get my little girl settled and I'll come find you.'

He shakes his head. 'I'll wait here.'

'Okay,' I say, again a nervous wobble creeping into my voice. 'I'll find you here, then.'

'Don't be long. Or I'll come find you instead,' he says with a wink.

I take Ellie by the hand and walk away. As soon as we turn the corner, I scoop her into my arms and run. I run through the corridor, past the table tennis table, where thankfully Millicent hasn't found a partner, past an unmanned reception desk and out onto the street. I keep running until the shelter is out of view, and I run some more until my legs burn and my knees feel as if they are going to give way. Then I hail a taxi.

'Greenway Road, please,' I say, climbing in and preparing to spend whatever it costs to get the hell out of here.

FORTY-THREE

Ellie cries the whole journey. I try to comfort her, but my thoughts are scrambled and I'm not sure I'm even making any sense.

'I love you. I love you so much,' I tell her in a gentle whisper as if my love is all I can offer her, and I know she needs so much more.

'Is she all right?' the driver asks, glancing back at us in the rear-view mirror.

'I'm not sure.'

He sets his eyes back on the road and I can tell he wasn't expecting an honest answer.

The journey feels painfully long despite no traffic. I pay the driver and I scarcely give a thought to how much the fare depletes my savings. I'd have paid every penny I have to get Ellie and me out of there.

'Whatever is wrong, love...' he says, as I open the door. 'She'll be fine. Kids are resilient.'

'Yeah,' I say, wishing it was that simple.

I stand statue-still on the footpath, holding Ellie's hand as I watch him drive away, then I take a deep breath and turn round to face Malcolm's house.

The curtains are drawn, but there don't seem to be any lights on inside. Nonetheless, I walk through the gate. Loose stone crackles under Ellie and me with each step, and I crane my neck towards the house, hoping to hear the sound of TV or radio. But the house is silent and still. I slide the porch door back and ring the bell. Moonlight shines on the wellies waiting inside the porch and a couple of tennis rackets have fallen face first on the ground. I wait for an answer but the house stays sleeping.

'I'm cold,' Ellie grumbles, pulling her hand out of mine so she can wrap her arms round herself to keep warm. We left the shelter in such a panic, neither of us have coats.

I ring the bell again, deflating more by the second. Nothing. I try again. Silence. I pull my phone out and call Shayne. Finally, I hear a noise. Shayne's ringtone coming from an upstairs window.

'Hello,' I call out.

'Hello,' Ellie echoes.

'Hello. Shayne,' I try again, louder.

'Shayne,' Ellie says, louder too.

I begin shouting and waving my arms as I continue to let my phone ring. 'Hello! Hello! Is anyone home?'

My voice is scratchy and breaks. I clear my throat and try again.

'Shayne. Malcolm. Anyone! It's Bea and Ellie. Please let us in.'

The curtain twitches and I hold my breath. Finally, Shayne's face peeks through the gap.

'Hey. Hey. Oh my God, hi.' I wave, relief flooding my senses, and I'm instantly light-headed.

'Bea,' he mouths.

I nod. The window opens and this time when he says my

name I hear something in his voice. He's not happy to see me. I take a step back, realising how strange this must be for him. It's late, on one of the biggest nights of the year, and I have turned up on his grandfather's doorstep screaming like a banshee and begging to be let in. He must think I'm absolutely mad. And right now, I can't argue that I'm not.

'What is it? What's wrong?' he says.

'Everything,' I say. The honesty slips out of me so quickly that it doesn't have time to shock me.

'Hang on. I'm coming down.'

I hear heavy footsteps race down the stairs and the door opens quickly. He's wearing a grey tracksuit and the colour washes him out, or else he's unwell, because his face is worryingly pale.

My staring must make him uncomfortable, because he runs his hand over his hair and says, 'I wasn't expecting anyone.'

'I know. I'm sorry.'

He doesn't say another word, just steps aside, and I know it's okay for Ellie and me to come in. He closes the door behind us and when the heat of the house surrounds me I realise how very cold it was outside after all.

'Can I watch telly?' Ellie asks, and makes her way towards the sitting room without waiting for Shayne's answer.

'I'm sorry, she—'

'What's wrong?' he says, cutting across me.

I swallow hard. 'I didn't mean to disturb you. I just...' I push my shoulders back and steady myself. 'You weren't replying to any of my messages.'

'You came all the way across town to tell me to text you?'

I shake my head and tears swell in my eyes, I try not to blink.

'I was giving you some space. I don't want to mess things up for you with Ellie's dad.'

I wipe my eyes, suddenly not teary any more. 'What?'

'Ellie told Grandad that her dad is back in the picture.'
'She said that?'
'Well actually, I think it was something about cookies. Grandad just read between the lines.'

Thoughts swirl inside my head like a mini tornado. I can't seem to grab hold of a single one.

'This timing is awful but I have to tell you,' Shayne says, glancing over his shoulder towards the stairs, and I think he might be expecting Malcolm to join us at any moment and there's something he wants to get out first.

Even if I could find my voice, I wouldn't say anything right now. Because whatever Shayne has to say, I want to hear it.

'Maybe I shouldn't say this. Actually, I definitely shouldn't. But I like you, Bea. I feel things when I'm around you. It's kind of why I didn't go back to New York. I wanted more time with you. And thank God I did, because it gave me more time with Grandad too.'

I open my mouth and still nothing comes out.

'And I know how inappropriate this is. You're trying to fix things with your ex. He's Ellie's dad for God's sake. And here I am dumping all this on you. But don't worry, I'll be gone soon. After—' His voice breaks and he cuts himself off.

The television comes to life in the sitting room and sound carries towards us through the open door. And finally, when I know Ellie can't hear me over the sound of a TV presenter's enthusiastic New Year's Eve hyping, I find words.

'Malcolm is wrong. Declan is not back. He never will be. It's over.'

A wave of emotions plays out on Shayne's face. Surprise. Relief. Concern and finally confusion.

'But Ellie said he was at your apartment.'
'We met at the coffee shop below the apartment.'
'I know the one.' He nods, clearly remembering Christmas and John. *Bloody John.* I came here desperate to tell Shayne

about John, but suddenly I don't want to give men like John or Declan any space in my head.

'It was just a coffee,' I go on.

Shayne tilts his head. 'He didn't stay over?'

I snort. 'He couldn't. We don't live there any more.'

Shayne looks more confused than ever.

'You moved?'

I have to tell Shayne the truth. Not because I've shown up on his grandfather's doorstep in a fit of blind panic. Not because I have nowhere to go. But because I want to. I need to confide in someone and I desperately want that someone to be him. A good man. The type of man my father was. So different from the type of man Ellie's father is. I inhale until my lungs feel as if they might burst and I blurt, 'We're homeless.'

'Sorry?' he says, as if he didn't quite hear me.

'Ellie and me. We're homeless. We have been for a few weeks. Declan left and I can't afford rent. We've been living at the hospital since.'

His hand is in his hair again and his face is all scrunched up. It's so hard to say, but looking at Shayne I think it might also be hard to hear.

'Your mam found us tonight. Well, she found Ellie. In the storage closet. That's where we've been sleeping.'

'Fuck!'

'Yeah. A bit of a shitshow.'

'So what did she do?' His voice is gentle, like summer rain, and I can tell he's fearful of spooking me. But I won't run. Not from him.

'She sent us to a shelter.'

He shakes his head. 'Those places can be—'

'Awful,' I cut in before he has to say more.

'Tough,' he says.

'Yeah!'

'Why didn't you come here?'

I don't tell him I wanted to but he wouldn't answer his phone. I don't want to put that on him. I also keep quiet about John and big Lizzie. Thankfully, nothing happened besides a couple of assholes scaring the crap out of Ellie and me.

'I'm here now,' I say.

He smiles. 'You are.'

Shayne takes my hands in his and it's been such a long time since I've felt the touch of another adult that a warm fuzziness builds inside me. He strokes his thumb over and back across my palms.

'You can stay here,' he says with a confident nod. 'You and Ellie, as long as you need to.'

I smile. He's kind and his thumb is sending pulses down my spine. But he can't invite us in. This is Malcolm's house.

'Shouldn't we ask your grandfather first?' I say, meekly.

I notice for the first time that Shayne's eyes are red and puffy. Redder and puffier than mine. In my own fit of panic, I didn't notice before now. *Shit!*

'Shayne?' I say, gently.

He shakes his head. 'He's at the hospital. I'd just got back when you arrived.'

I cover my mouth with my hand.

'Pneumonia,' Shayne says, a tear trickling out from the corner of his eye. 'It's not looking good.'

My chest tightens and it feels as if someone is twisting a vice round my heart.

'Can I see him?'

'Yes. Of course. He'd like that.'

'Can we go now?'

Shayne rubs his eyes. 'Yes. They said I can visit any time, normal hours don't apply.'

I cover my mouth with my hand, all too familiar with what that means.

Wait for us, Malcolm. Please wait!

FORTY-FOUR

Shayne drives quickly on the icy roads, and under other circumstances I would ask him to slow down. We're parked at the hospital and walking towards the main doors within minutes. The electric doors part upon detecting us and we walk through. I walked out these same doors just hours ago convinced my life was all but over. Now, as I walk back in, I am reminded that life is precious and you must fight for it. I will Malcolm to fight. Fight just a little longer.

Shayne guides us up the stairs and towards a ward I've cleaned many times. It's all so familiar, and yet in this moment, with my brain drowning in a sea of emotion, it's as if I am arriving at St Helen's for the first time ever.

Malcolm's bed is nearest the window. A sky-blue blanket is wrapped round him and his face is as white as the ceiling above him as he lies with his eyes closed. I clutch my chest, startled by how frail he appears.

'Malco,' Ellie squeals with delight as she races towards his bed.

'Carefully, Ellie,' I call out. 'Be gentle.'

She slows and takes her time as she approaches him. I watch her take his hand and his eyes flicker.

'He knows you're here,' Shayne says.

'Would you like to hear a story, Malco?' Ellie asks.

Malcolm's eyes flicker once more and his head bobs ever so slowly up and down.

Ellie uses the bedside chair as a step and climbs onto the high hospital bed. She tucks her hip next to his and begins.

'Once upon a time...'

Shayne's fingers slip between mine and I squeeze back as we watch a four-year-old tell her favourite story to her favourite person.

'Your mam,' I whisper, thinking of Elaine at last.

Shayne shakes his head.

'Does she know he's here?'

Shayne nods.

'But she hasn't come in?'

'I don't think she can bring herself,' Shayne says.

'She's working tonight,' I tell him. 'She's here somewhere.'

Shayne shakes his head again. 'It's too late, Bea. There's too much water under the bridge for them.'

I watch Malcolm's laboured breathing as he listens to Ellie's story with a subtle smile.

'I'll be back,' I say. 'You okay to watch her?' I tilt my head towards the bed.

'Sure,' he says. He's about to say something else, probably to tell me how hopeless it is, or to give up, but I turn on my heel and hurry away.

I find Elaine on the women's ward. She's found the empty bottle of prosecco beside Mrs Brennan's bed. Her face falls somewhere between a disapproving eye-roll and a pleased smirk.

'Good for you, Mrs B,' I hear her whisper.

She tucks the empty bottle under her arm but almost drops it when she turns and sees me.

'Bea. You're back.'

She adjusts the bottle, tucking it firmer.

'Is everything okay? Where's Ellie?'

'She's here,' I say.

Elaine tries to squash a groan but it comes out anyway. She glances at her watch and shakes her head. 'It's late. They lock the door at the shelter by ten. You can't just waltz in and out as you please, I'm afraid there are strict rules about that sort of thing.'

'I know,' I say. 'I'm not going back.'

'Oh, Bea, for goodness' sake,' Elaine huffs, dragging her hand across her forehead. 'Have you any idea of the strings I had to pull to get you in there in the first place and now—'

'I know,' I cut in. 'But it's not somewhere Ellie and I feel safe.'

Elaine rolls her eyes. 'Oh really. It is quite literally a safe house, Bea. Or would you rather a small child continue to sleep next to a mop and some bleach indefinitely? Because let me tell you here and now, that cannot and will not happen.'

'We're going to stay with Shayne and Malcolm,' I say.

The colour drains from Elaine's face.

'Ellie is with them now.'

She raises her hand and closes her eyes as if it pains her to hear another word. But I can't stop. Not when Malcolm has so little time.

'He's here,' I say, tentatively. 'Malcolm. He's a patient.'

I wonder if I should help her to sit down. She looks as if she needs to.

'Do you want to see him?'

Elaine sways, and I cup her elbow and lead her to sit in one of the uncomfortable plastic chairs.

'Are you okay?' I ask, taking the bottle from under her arm

and setting it back on the bedside locker where it started out. 'Do you need some water or something?'

She shakes her head.

'I'm sorry, I didn't mean to give you a shock.'

'I know he's here, Bea.' She sighs. 'Órlaith told me.'

'Oh.'

'So, you can go now.'

I swallow disappointment. But before I walk away I say, 'Room 218, if you change your mi—,'

'Bea. Go!' Elaine snaps, pointing a ridged finger towards the door.

I sigh, bow my head and walk away. On the corridor, bright fluorescent lights hit me. One of the lights is wonky. The bulb flickers sporadically and it makes a buzzing sound as I pass under. I freeze on the spot and listen to the hum. Like a bee in summer working hard to collect nectar from a sunflower. My mind races. A busy bee. Malcolm's nickname for me. The bench in the car park where he sat alone for hours. Snowflakes melting on his bare head as he waited for the courage to step inside. Wellington boots and hand-knit scarves. A chequered coat and a petrol-station Christmas card. Disney movies. Tennis rackets in flower pots and kite-flying. Malcolm may only have been in my life a matter of weeks, but already my head is full of memories and my heart is full of love. I can only imagine what my life would have been like with a grandad like him caring for me.

I turn quickly and my heels make a squeaking sound against the floor that I polished yesterday and I march back towards Elaine.

Her face is in her hands when I find her. She doesn't look up when she sees me, although I know she's aware I'm here.

'Do you know why I spent the last two weeks locked away in a closet?' I say.

She still doesn't look up.

'Because I had nowhere else to go. I don't have a family. I don't have anyone who loves me. There is no one to care if I sleep in a closet, or on the street, or even if I sleep at all. Do you know what I would give to have someone love me the way your father loves you?'

Elaine lowers her hands and when her eyes meet mine I can see they are teary.

'You have no idea what you're talking about,' she says.

'I know he waited outside in the snow for a chance to bump into you.'

Surprise flashes in her eyes.

'And not just once. He sat out there day after day. He was desperate to fix things. And I don't know what's broken between you. It's none of my business. But he's your father and, whatever it is, don't you want to talk it out?'

Elaine sighs. 'We can't talk it out.'

'Sure you can. And with Shayne's help—'

'Bea!' She cuts me off. 'We can't. I don't remember what it is.'

'Oh.'

'Lots of little things. After my mam died, we sort of sparked off each other. One thing after another. One harsh word after another, until one day he said he wished I'd died instead.'

I gasp.

'So, you see...' She shakes her head. 'Not talking is easier than talking, if all you ever say upsets each other.'

'He couldn't have meant what he said.'

Elaine makes a face. 'He missed my mam. And I was hard work. Always so opinionated.'

I smile, meekly, knowing who she inherited that trait from.

'He's sorry,' I tell her. 'He's heartbroken. I think he has been for years.'

'No!' she says with a loud sigh that seems to let all the air out of her and shrink her, and I can tell she is heartbroken too.

'I'd give anything to have a family. And you're throwing yours away,' I say, and once again I turn and walk away.

FORTY-FIVE
ONE WEEK LATER

By mid-January it is as if Christmas never happened. The decorations are taken down and put away for another year. The buzz and excitement of the festive period has been replaced with complaining about the cold weather and counting down the days until spring. Ellie is back in crèche, I am back at work and Malcolm is back at home. There was nothing more the doctors could do for him, and they promised Shayne he would be more comfortable in his own bed. They were right. Shayne brought the television upstairs. It took us hours to figure the wiring out, but finally we got it connected and it sits proudly in the corner of Malcolm's bedroom. He and Ellie watch Disney movies most evenings after crèche. Shayne and I take turns cooking, or we cook together. Malcolm rarely manages more than a bite or two. Ellie and I share a double bed in the spare room. Ellie says it's like sleeping in the garden, with pink-and-lilac floral curtains, a cerise-pink carpet and embossed multi-coloured wallpaper. Shayne says he remembers his grandmother choosing the colour scheme when he was just a child and Malcolm never wanted to change it. I imagine the whole house is the same as when Elaine grew up here.

Elaine and I do not speak at work. She emails my cleaning schedule to me in advance and she turns her back if she meets me on the corridor. The storage room is locked and if I need anything I have to ask the other cleaners, who've been given keys, to fetch it for me.

'What's up Elaine's ass?' I overhear Claudia, one of the senior cleaners, ask, shouting over the sound of the hoover.

'No idea,' Emer, a junior, shouts back. 'Made me redo the men's bathroom yesterday. Like what the hell!'

'She's being a total bitch!' Claudia rolls her eyes.

'Her dad is sick,' I say, and clamp my hand over my mouth as soon as the words come out.

Claudia stomps her foot on the back of the hoover and shuts it off. Her eyes narrow as she glares at me and it's obvious she's unimpressed that I've cut into their conversation. I turn away, and yelp when I almost physically bump into Elaine. I hear the others snigger behind me. Elaine's expression is like thunder. I hope she didn't hear me over the hum of the hoover, but I have a horrible feeling she did.

'Claudia?' Elaine calls out.

'Mm-hmm.'

'Can you clean the men's bathrooms please?'

Claudia's face pinches. 'But Emer did it already.'

'Claudia, now please?' Elaine says.

Claudia nods and unplugs the hoover and begins to wind up the flex.

'Can you help her?' Elaine asks Emer. 'You can leave that there.' She points to the hoover.

Emer's face makes me want to laugh, but I don't, of course. Claudia and Emer don't say a word as they walk away.

Elaine waits until they are out of earshot before she turns towards me. 'You don't have to do that, you know.'

'Sorry?'

'Defend me.'

'Oh. I—'

'Believe me, I've been called worse. Besides, the bathroom was still filthy. Emer's idea of clean and mine are very different.'

'Right, eh, okay. Sorry. I won't say anything again.'

Elaine nods, fetches the hoover and drags it away behind her. She stops and turns her head over her shoulder. 'Go on lunch, Bea.'

I glance at my watch. 'But it's only twelve thirty. I'm not scheduled until one.'

'Take the extra time.'

'Oh.'

I don't question Elaine. I'm not about to turn my nose up at thirty free minutes. I make the snap decision that the extra time will allow me to dash across the city and catch Cora at work. Our texts and calls have been awkward since New Year's Eve and I've been longing for a chance to speak in person. I haven't been able to call round to her flat because my evenings are taken up with Ellie and Malcolm, and I am worried about her.

Outside, the bus arrives bang on time and traffic is light. I'm overjoyed that the friendship gods are on my side. That is until I reach the multistorey, high-tech private hospital where Cora works and she spots me. Hurt, sadness, anger and disappointment all merge on her face to create a sour expression as she juts a hip out and says, 'I can't talk now. I'm working.'

'Please?'

She shakes her head, and without warning I bend in the middle and start to cry.

'Oh, Jesus, Bea.'

Cora rushes to me and envelopes me in a hug.

'Tell me. Talk to me. Please tell me what the fuck has been going on?' she begs.

'Lunch?' I manage to say, dragging my sleeve under my nose, but it doesn't help much. I'm a blubbering, snorty, slightly snotty mess.

'Yeah. Yeah. Course. Come on. My break started ten minutes ago.'

In the canteen, Cora and I grab ham and cheese wraps that despite the fancy minimalist wrapper smell like feet and taste like cardboard. We eat them nonetheless as we lap the grounds, talking and talking. I spill everything. I start with Declan and his new girlfriend or girlfriends. She says a leopard doesn't change its spots. Then I tell her about the closet and she cries and apologises as if it was somehow her fault. I tell her I'm staying with Shayne and Malcolm now, and finally, choking up and barely able to push words out, I say, 'He's dying.'

'Shit. That sucks,' she says.

I cry some more. I cry for Malcolm. I cry for myself and I cry for Ellie. Cora cries too. For the relationship she wanted, but never got, with Finton. Then she takes my phone and rings the landlord at Declan's and my old flat.

'Hello, I'm looking for Declan Stanley,' she says.

There's some mumbling on the other end.

'Oh, I see. I see,' Cora says, her voice a half-octave lower than usual and painfully posh-sounding. 'It's just, I'm a doctor at Clifford Hospital and we've been trying to reach Mr Stanley with some very sensitive medical results.'

More mumbling comes.

'Ah yes, but unfortunately a mobile number really isn't going to help. I will need to post the files. It's very important that he takes them straight to his GP. I'm afraid I really can't say more, but I cannot stress—'

More mumbling.

'Mm-hmm. Mm-hmm. Okay good. Great. Thank you.'

Cora lowers her phone and punches something into her notes. Then she looks at me with bright, giddy eyes and says, 'We've got him. I've got his address in London. Let's see the bastard get out of paying child support now.'

I grab her and I hold her longer and tighter than I ever have before.

'We've got him,' I whisper, getting lost in the moment.

Cora and I both jump when my phone vibrates in my pocket.

'It's Shayne,' I say, instantly panicked that he's calling during work hours.

I can't get the phone to my ear fast enough. 'Hello.'

'Can you come home?'

'I'm on my way.'

FORTY-SIX

Malcolm is waiting by the door. He's still in his pyjamas. The same blue-and-white pinstripe ones he's been wearing for the last couple of days. But over them he has his coat and a custard and maroon scarf I haven't seen before. As usual, he's hatless. But his bare head concerns me less today than usual. I am more worried about the slate grey of his face, or the purple hammocks under his eyes.

'What are you doing?' I say, sounding exactly as I do when I'm about to scold Ellie for bad behaviour.

'Where are your wellies?' he asks, glancing at my feet and then my face.

I'm wearing my work shoes. I left the hospital in such a hurry to get to Cora, I forgot to slip them off.

'It's not snowing any more,' I say.

He tuts. 'Who's this?'

Cora edges out from behind me. 'Hello,' she says, meekly. Cora never sounds meek. She taps her chest. 'I'm Cora. Bea's friend.'

'The one with the shitty boyfriend who wouldn't share a couch?' Malcolm says.

I wince and am about to say something to try to smooth it over, but Cora gets there first. 'Yes, that's me. He's not my boyfriend any more.'

'Good.' Malcolm's nod is firm. 'Are you coming?'

I'm not sure if he's asking Cora or me and I have no idea where we're going.

Shayne comes skidding into the hallway behind Malcolm. His face is flushed as if he's been running and there is a bobble hat sticking out of the pocket of his jeans.

'You're here,' he says.

I nod.

He looks at Cora.

'Oh. Shayne, Cora. Cora, Shayne,' I say.

'Nice to meet you,' Shayne says, and his New York accent sounds a little thicker than usual.

'You too,' Cora says. 'I've heard a lot about you.'

'Cora!' I squeak.

She laughs and Shayne looks mildly worried, but his expression quickly softens and he smiles.

'We need to get you back to bed,' I say, casting a worried eye on Malcolm.

'So I can lie there until I die?' he grumbles.

I gulp. 'No!' I say, although I hate how wobbly it comes out. Because Malcolm is right. Without meaning to, or even thinking about it, that's exactly what I meant. The realisation hurts my heart. I try again. 'I think you need some rest.'

'My arse is numb,' he says, rubbing it as if checking it's still there. 'I'm dying. Bed or not. It won't make much difference in the end.'

I don't know what to say. I look over Malcolm's shoulder at Shayne, but he seems to be as stuck for words as me.

'Whatcha fancy doing, then?' Cora asks.

Malcolm points at her. 'I like you.'

She smiles with her whole face.

'Get the kites. Get the kid. And let's go,' he says. He tries to punch the air but his arm only makes it halfway up before it flops back by his side with exhaustion.

Suddenly there are three other hands in the air. Shayne's. Cora's. And mine.

'You heard the man,' Cora says, taking charge because frankly Shayne and I can't. 'We need Ellie!'

'What about work?' I ask.

Cora swats the air with her hand. 'I haven't had a sick day in five years.' She gives a gentle cough. 'But suddenly...' She coughs again. 'Yup... definitely down with something.'

'Me too,' Shayne says, and I can't believe that for the first time since I met him, I realise he's probably working remotely. Does that mean he could stay? *Even when Malcolm is—* I push the thought aside, knowing it's for another time.

'Get the kites and the kid,' I repeat.

'What about Mam?' Shayne asks, concerned. 'Will she hit the roof if you call in sick or something all of a sudden?'

I remember Elaine's face earlier in the corridor. There was something in her eyes I haven't seen before. I have no idea what it was, I don't know her well enough, I admit. But I actually think she'll understand. She'll know I'm bullshitting, of course. She'll know I'm perfectly healthy. She'll also know who I'm with and why.

'Get the kites, Shayne,' I say, sounding like I'm taking charge despite my slightly shaky insides. 'And Malcolm...' He looks at me like a lost puppy. My heart skips a beat, missing him already. 'Wear a damn hat.' He shakes his head and I laugh. 'Cora. We need to get my kid.'

She confirms with a gummy smile and a firm nod.

'We'll meet you in the park in an hour,' I tell Shayne and Malcolm.

'An hour,' Shayne says, with an urgency that panics me.

We both know every moment counts.

FORTY-SEVEN

'Cora!' Ellie shrieks.

She's overjoyed to see Cora. And I realise that, while I've been missing my best friend, Ellie has been missing the only other adult who has been a constant in her life since birth. I scold myself for a moment for not talking to my little girl about it.

'Hey there, gorgeous,' Cora says, stretching her arms wide and swallowing Ellie up in a giant bear hug. 'You ready to go fly a kite?'

Ellie has no idea what's happening but that doesn't stop her from agreeing to it all and being so full of excitement her eyes bulge.

'Will she be in tomorrow?' Alannah asks, clip-clopping in new, chunky heels around reception.

'No idea.' I shrug.

'Okay, no worries. Just if you could let us know...'

I stare at her blankly.

'Or you can just pop it in the app. Do you have the app?'

'I have the damn app.'

Alannah jerks her head back until she has three chins. 'You

can pay late fees on the app now too, by the way, so it's in everyone's best interest to keep it updated and active.'

'I have it,' I snap.

'Byeee, Ellie,' Alannah says.

Ellie turns her head over her shoulder and blows Alannah a kiss.

'I loved the manager's shoes,' Cora says.

'Meh, I prefer wellies in this weather,' I say with a shrug.

Ellie talks the entire way across town. Cora laps it up like rays of joy she's been missing. They giggle together and Ellie throws her arms round Cora sporadically and without warning and sometimes it looks as if Cora never wants to let go. I hadn't realised how much they'd missed each other. With everything that was going on, I hadn't taken the time to really think about much I missed Cora too. It's been less than three weeks since the three of us were together like this, but so much has happened it feels like months. Or even years. It's so good to be together again.

The park is busier than I was expecting. People are wrapped up warmly for the weather and scrolling carefree, as if the icy wind and thick cloud overhead is a pleasant as a summer's day. Teenagers whizz by on bicycles, laughing the way that age group do. A toddler wails in a buggy, and a flustered young father tries to calm her. An elderly couple shuffle by, hand in hand, their backs curved like commas.

'The paths are salted down this way,' Cora tells them, pointing towards a windy tarmac pathway that leads towards the main car park.

'Thank you, but we're off to feed the deer,' the elderly man tells us as he steps off the footpath and onto long grass.

'They love the scraps,' the woman says, pointing towards the plastic bag she carries. Then they shuffle away slowly.

'Was that a giant bag of lettuce?' Cora says, struggling to hold in a laugh.

'I think so.'

'Is that allowed?' Shayne asks. 'I mean, are you supposed to feed the wild animals?'

I shrug. 'No idea. But I don't see what harm it could do?'

'It's not as if they're stuck for food,' Malcolm says, stretching his arms out to highlight the wide-open grassy space.

'No. But if it makes them feel good.'

'Do you always do that?' he asks.

'Do what?'

'Make excuses for old people just because they're old?'

'What?'

'You're not supposed to feed the deer. They have everything they need right here. They'll probably have the scutters later from eating shrivelled lettuce. Someone will step in it, ruin their shoes and blame the animals. When really it was two busy-bodies with a bag of left-overs that were the problem.'

'Do you think it will make them sick?' I ask.

'Don't know. But I think if it was a thirty-something-year-old couple, like you two' — he points to Shayne and then to me. I blush, and I hope he doesn't notice as he continues to make his point — 'then I think you'd see it differently. You'd wonder what the hell they were thinking.'

Would I? Am I guilty of treating elderly people differently? I didn't think so, but maybe Malcolm is right. Their bodies may be slower but they're not children, and yet sometimes I am guilty of speaking to them as if they are. I'm not quite sure how to rectify it; it's not as if I can chase after the lettuce couple and tell them they're going to give deer diarrhoea from rotten salad. I decide I'll do better with Malcolm instead. I can start by jumping less every time he so much as sneezes.

'Right, c'mon,' I say, 'it's getting windy and we should get some good height with these.'

I point to the bag of kites Shayne has been guarding with his life. We settle ourselves in front of the Wellington monument, where the grass is too short for the deer to enjoy, there are no trees and kites can take flight in the wide, open skies.

Malcolm's kite is first up. The tail flaps furiously and at one point I hold my breath when a large gust of wind almost takes his feet off the ground. I'm about to warn him to be careful when I remind myself that he is a grown man and can think for himself.

Shayne's kite is next up. He chuckles with satisfaction when it soars even higher than Malcolm's.

'Take that, Grandad.'

I reach into the bag and pass Cora a kite.

'Oh, teal,' she says.

'That's green,' Ellie corrects her.

Cora struggles to get her kite up, but she finally gets the knack and soon she is running around the open space like a child. Ellie takes her unicorn kite and follows her. Their laughter carries in the wind and my heart soars almost as high as the kites. Finally, I toss mine in the air and a sharp gust whips it up.

The kites brighten up the cloudy sky like multicoloured sprinkles on a white-frosted cupcake. Cora begins to sing the kite song from the end of *Mary Poppins*, although she seems to only know a couple of lines from the chorus, and sings them on repeat. Ellie joins in. And Shayne. Malcolm doesn't sing, but the smile on his face as his kite zigzags over his head, flapping like a gloriously colourful bird, tells me that inside his heart is full of song.

I take a step back and watch them: my long-term best friend. My daughter. And two men, who just weeks ago were strangers but right now, as we stand in the freezing park but are somehow warm inside, have become such an important part of my life. I want to remember this moment for ever. I lower my kite, with a degree of difficulty as the enthusiastic wind want to keep playing, and I take my phone from my pocket. I snap several shots and check them out. There are some blurry ones, because everyone is moving too much. Some with the backs of heads, or someone missing. But there is one shot where everyone is there and the camera has caught a smile on all of their faces.

I take a deep breath as an idea comes to me, and scroll through my contacts, stopping when I come to Elaine's number. I don't give myself time to think as I type a message and attach the photo.

> Have you seen Mary Poppins? Mr Banks was a shitty dad, but then he flew a kite with his kids. We're in the phoenix park. Next to the wellington monument. It's not too late to fly a kite with your dad. Bea x

Elaine sees the message and she starts typing. But then she stops. She starts again. And stops. The start/stop continues for a while, until finally the stop remains and she doesn't send a reply. I try not to let it deflate me too much as I rejoin the group, but it's harder to laugh now.

'I need to do a wee,' Ellie announces loudly.

'Can you hold it for a little while?'

Ellie shakes her head. I glance at my watch and I'm shocked to discover more than two hours have passed since I texted Elaine. Ellie begins to hop from one foot to the other.

'I bursting,' she says, her face all scrunched up, and I can tell she's concentrating hard to hold it.

'Okay, okay,' I say, lowering my kite and helping her to lower hers. 'We'll be back in a minute,' I tell Shayne. He makes a face that asks if everything is okay. 'Needs a wee,' I explain.

He nods.

'C'mon, chickpea. Let's find a loo.'

'They're over there,' a familiar voice behind me says, and

my eyes bulge when I turn round and find Elaine standing behind me. 'I don't have a kite,' she goes on.

'Oh.' I swallow my shock. 'You can take mine.'

I bend down and pass her my colourful kite.

She doesn't say a word. Shayne seems lost for words also until he finally says, 'You know, I could use the restroom too.'

Cora seems to catch on quickly. 'Me too. I'm bursting.'

Malcolm and Elaine don't seem to notice us leave. They stand facing each other, their kites by their sides like pistols, as if they are going to turn back to back, take ten paces, turn and shoot. Uncertainty swirls inside me as we gain distance on them. I squash it quickly, reminding myself that Elaine is Malcolm's daughter. Nothing is going to happen to him because we take our eyes off him for a few minutes and leave them to talk.

'I can't believe it,' Shayne says as we walk. 'I wonder how she knew we were here.'

'Didn't she used to go kite-flying with Malcolm when she was a kid?'

Shayne's eyes fill with tears and I feel awful. I thought I was resurfacing a happy memory.

'Yeah,' he says, sniffling.

'Are you okay?' I ask. 'I'm sorry. I didn't mean to upset you.'

'Mam's here. They're talking. Thank you,' he says, a teary crackle breaking up his voice.

'All I did was send a photo,' I say.

'And it was everything.'

FORTY-EIGHT

For the next six days, Malcolm, Shayne, Ellie, Elaine and I fly a kite in the park every single day. Elaine insisted we both take the week off work.

'Claudia and Emer can handle things,' she said, although I knew by the look on her face that she doubts very much that they can, but she also doesn't think it is important any more.

There are other activities too. A horse-drawn carriage around St. Stephen's Green. Malcolm makes the driver stop halfway round.

'It stinks,' he says. 'I'm getting off.'

He's right, the horse is particularly potent, and although at one point I think Shayne might have to carry Malcolm home, the short walk back is delightful.

Ellie has loved sleeping in a bed again, although I have loved it less. Who knew a four-year-old could kick like a horse in their sleep? Elaine spends a lot of time in the kitchen; making soup Malcolm barely manages more than a mouthful of.

'He's not eating any of it,' Shayne said once after a bath of potato and leek that the rest of us enjoyed immensely.

'I don't think it matters,' I said, as I watched her lovingly add salt and pepper to a boiling pot while humming 'Let's Go Fly a Kite'.

On day seven, Ellie wakes before me and grabs her kite. She races into Malcolm's room before I have a chance to catch her.

'Ready?' she chirps, far too bubbly for an hour of the morning that hasn't seen the sun rise yet.

I race in after her.

'Sorry, I'm sorry,' I say. 'It's early. Go back to—'

A shiver runs the length of my spine when I hear Malcolm's laboured breathing, like a rusty hinge swinging. His face is chalky and the edges of his lips are tinged a bluish-green as if he's cold. The heating woke me briefly earlier when it came on and air rattled through the pipes; despite the January cold outside, the house is toasty.

'Get Shayne,' I say, with a raspy voice crack.

Ellie takes a step back, narrowing her eyes, and her little face looks concerned.

'It's okay, chickpea,' I whisper, taking care not to spook her. 'I just need Shayne now. Can you wake him please?'

'Okay, Mammy,' she chirps, instantly appeased.

I take Malcolm's hand in mine. It's clammy and cold at the same time. 'Hang on, Malcolm,' I whisper. 'Please, please wait?'

I hear the pitter-patter of Ellie's feet across the landing. The creak of Shayne's bedroom door. Some mumbles, and then the hurried thud of Shayne's feet charging towards us. The door swings open, crashing against the wall.

'Is he—?'

'Shh.' I place my finger to my lips. 'I don't think there's much time.'

'My mam,' Shayne says. 'We have to call her.'

Although there is much urgency in Shayne's voice, he seems to find it hard to edge closer. I try to encourage him with a smile as I feel the trickle of tears down my cheek. When he finally reaches the edge of the bed, I swap my hand out for his. He's instantly lost in his emotion and he doesn't notice me scoop Ellie into my arms and take her downstairs. I flick on the TV, not paying much attention to which cartoon comes on. I think about telling her that I'm going to go make breakfast, but I don't trust myself to speak without crying. Instead, I kiss the top of her head and back out of the room while she is distracted by the upbeat antics on screen.

I call Elaine's mobile from the hall. It rings a single time.

'Bea?' she says, and I can tell she already knows.

'It's time.'

There's a sharp intake of breath, and I suspect it's the sound of her heart breaking. 'I'm on the way.'

I turn and hurry back upstairs, but I stop on the middle step and sit down. I don't belong in Malcolm's room. His family do. My heart aches but I know my place is downstairs with Ellie. I return to the sitting room and climb onto the couch beside her, tucking my legs under my bum as if it's a mundane Saturday morning back in our old apartment watching cartoons before we tucked into sugary breakfast cereal. The ads are on and Ellie is on her feet dancing to a brightly coloured screen trying to convince her that a talking stuffed blue elephant is exactly what she needs in her life.

There's a knock on the front door, gentle at first, and I almost don't hear it over the TV, but it quickly turns to pounding and by the time I reach the hallway it sounds as if Elaine is trying to break the door down.

'Bea? It's me. Elaine. Shayne?'

'Coming,' I call out.

She doesn't seem to hear me in her panic as she goes on. 'Shayne, it's Mam. Shayne. Are you there?'

I hurry and open the door. Elaine's eyes are red and puffy and her usually perfect silver bob is bristly with odd strands standing up at free will. I can tell she hasn't taken the time to brush it. She's wearing a long grey raincoat that isn't warm enough for the weather. I can see her pink and cream striped pyjamas underneath. And finally I notice engine-red wellington boots on her feet. I smile as I step aside and wait for her to come in. She doesn't budge. I'm not sure what to do. It feels odd to invite my boss into her father's home, and it's certainly not my place, but Elaine seems stuck. I have to say something.

'He's upstairs,' I finally mumble.

She seems to snap out of her daze and her red-rimmed eyes focus and meet mine.

'Shayne is with him.'

'Is he...?' She swallows hard. 'Am I...? She gulps again. 'Is it too late?'

I don't know the answer to her question. But Malcolm has waited years for Elaine, and I hope with all my heart he can wait a few minutes more.

'Go,' I say, choking back tears.

She takes my hands in hers and squeezes gently. Then she kicks off her wellies, with a degree of difficulty as she's slightly unsteady on her feet. She climbs the stairs slowly, her feet not making a sound as they touch each step. I wish she would hurry, but I know she can't. Each step is hard for her. Hard to leave the past behind, and even harder to face the future awaiting at the top of the stairs.

Ellie and I watch cartoons for a long time. An hour, maybe two. I'm staring into space, not watching anything on screen, when I finally hear footsteps on the stairs. I hurry into the hallway and see Shayne and Elaine making their way down the stairs together. Shayne's arm is draped over his mother's shoulder and she is sobbing, softly. I don't know if mother and son are speaking, but they are embracing and I know they both so badly need each other right now. I don't need Shayne to look at me and shake his head to know Malcolm is gone. I feel it in my gut. But when Shayne's sad eyes burn into mine, my knees wobble and I have to concentrate hard to keep them firmly straight so I don't crumple. I must be a pillar now. For them. I search my brain for something to say.

'Can I get you anything? A tea. A coffee?' I ask. I instantly want to shovel the useless words back into my mouth as soon as they tumble out. What good is a warm beverage now?

Elaine smiles. 'Tea would be good, thank you, Bea.'

'Cof...' Shayne chokes up.

'Coffee,' I say for him.

I lead them into the kitchen where just a few weeks ago I spent my best Christmas ever with Malcolm. My stomach clenches, and sadness and heartbreak swirl inside me. I thought my heart broke when Declan left, but I see now that was a bruising. This. Right here, right now, sharing in the Hammingtons' grief. This is true heartbreak and my God does it hurt.

Shayne and Elaine sit at the kitchen table. They talk about funeral arrangements. Songs he might like. How he should wear his favourite coat.

'He loved the outdoors,' Elaine says.

'Yes. He could sit outside for hours. Even in the rain,' Shayne adds.

'And never wear a bloody hat.' Elaine laughs and cries at the same time.

I set about making tea. Smiling to myself that Malcolm wore a hat for Ellie. I press the memory into my brain, making sure I keep it for ever.

I place a cup of tea in front of Elaine and a cup of coffee in front of Shayne. They both thank me but they don't reach for their cups. I don't think they'll drink them. I leave them talking in the kitchen and I fetch Ellie. We tiptoe upstairs to the guest room and get dressed. We pass by Malcolm's bedroom door. It's slightly ajar, but I can't bring myself to look inside. Instead, I press my hand against the timber, and succumb to the powerful wave of emotion that washes over me.

'Thank you,' I whisper. 'Sweet dreams.'

I scoop Ellie into my arms and carry her downstairs. We pull on our shoes and leave. I'm trying to find words to explain to Ellie that Malcolm is gone when I hear my name being called behind me. I turn round and find Shayne hurrying towards us.

'Where are you going?' he asks.

'I just want to give you and your mam some space. You have a lot to talk about.'

'You're coming back though, right? You're still staying here?'

I'm not sure it's appropriate to stay in Malcolm's house any more. It's a time for family. But Ellie and I have nowhere else to go. I wince.

'Is that okay?' I ask.

'Yes. Yes of course.' Shayne reaches into his pocket and pulls out a small white envelope and passes it to me.

I tap my chest before I take it. 'For me?'

'He wanted me to wait until after...' Shayne clears his throat, trying to cough away his tears. It doesn't help. He tries again. 'He wanted me to wait until he was gone to give you this.'

I take it with shaking hands.

'Are you coming back inside?' Shayne asks.

I scrunch my face. 'I'm going to take Ellie to crèche today, I think she needs to be around other kids for a little while.'

'And you?' he says, with round eyes that despite how much he's suffered today are still full of concern for me.

'I'm going to walk for a while. Maybe check in on things at work, so your mam doesn't have to.'

He nods. 'I'll see you later though, yeah?'

'Yeah.'

Shayne walks slowly away, and Ellie speaks for the first time in a while. I hadn't noticed her being usually quiet but it seems all I can think about now.

'I go to crèche today,' she says, 'I see Nita and my friends.'

'Yes, chickpea. Would you like that?'

She smiles and nods. I will tell Ellie about Malcolm. Of

course I will. But not right now. Right now, I want to drop her off with Alannah and her friends and I want to be alone in the park where we happily flew kites and I want to read Malcolm's letter.

It rains as I reach the park. I find a bench, next to some deer who seem unfazed by the large cold drops as they graze in the long grass. I sit down and take off my hat so I can feel the wind and the rain in my hair. It's cold, but I don't put my hat back on. I slide the envelope out of my pocket and I begin reading the words written in pristine handwriting.

Dear Busy Bea,

So I'm dead, eh? Well, that took longer than expected. My knees have been dead for the last ten years, just took the rest of me a while to catch up.

I've outstayed my time, but I did it for my Alison. I had to put things right with our Elaine before I left or Alison would chew the ear off me on the other side.

I can't wait to see her. She'll be so pleased that I fixed things. Yes, yes, I know technically it was you, but I'm dead, let me take the credit for this, eh?

I'm not very good with words – never have been. I should have thanked you in person, but I thought writing them down would be the next best thing. Thank you for sitting beside me on the park bench. Thank you for sharing one last Christmas with me. Thank you for making my grandson smile. It's been a while and I'd forgotten how damn handsome he is. The spitting image of his grandfather! Mostly, thank you for being you. I'm usually quite good at pushing people away, but you stuck. I'm glad you're like honey, Busy Bea.

I've set a few bob aside for you. And some for Ellie too. Before you say anything, yes, you can take it. In fact you must, or I'll be highly insulted and I'll be forced to come back and haunt you, which frankly sounds like a chore I could do without.

Use the money to go back to college, Busy Bea, the world needs doctors like you. People who care past the aches and pains of the body and get right down to the soul.

Take care of that precious little girl of yours. But don't make her wear a hat. Let her get the wind in her hair.

And for the love of God kiss my grandson. One of you has to make the first move. Don't bring me back to the haunting thing again.

With all my heart, Beatrice Alright,

Malcolm x

I lower the paper and turn my face to the rain. The drip-drop against my skin soothes me as I finally allow myself to cry.

FORTY-NINE
ONE MONTH LATER

'You're going to love this place,' Cora tells me as we get off the bus and walk down a narrow road of Weetabix-coloured apartments.

'I hope so, those last two places were shocking.'

'Ah, they weren't that bad.'

'There was a pee-stained mattress in the back garden of the last place?' I say.

Cora laughs. 'Yeah, but the mattress on the bed was fine.'

The estate agent meets us at the door and, as soon as he opens it and we step inside, Cora and I know we're home.

The look on Shayne's face when I told him I was moving out of Malcolm's house hurt my heart. 'I thought we were good together,' he said, visibly wounded.

'We're great together,' I said, kissing him quickly to reassure him. 'But we've been dating for four weeks. It's a little soon to be living together, don't you think?'

I could have elaborated, but I didn't need to. Shayne understood. He knows that Declan leaving ripped my life out from under me. He knows the position it put me in. And I cannot let that ever happen again. I need to stand on my own two feet. I need to know that if this amazing, wonderful, special thing with Shayne doesn't work out, Ellie and I will be okay. Of course I hope it does. I hope Shayne and I are in this for the long haul; but if not, I need to be sure I won't end up sleeping in a hospital closet ever again. Besides, Cora's and my college years were cut short when I met Declan and moved in with him on a whim. A do-over is something we're both excited about. But I'm not nearly as excited about it as I am about starting university in autumn. Trinity College were amazing and have agreed to let me pick up where I left off. In less than three years I will be a qualified doctor. Well, if I pass my exams of course. I've kept my job at the hospital in the meantime, and Elaine jokes that if college doesn't work out she'll save some bed pans for me to empty.

I never once refused to take Malcolm's money. Malcolm was the most cantankerous, grumbling, pass remarkable, impatient, warm, kind, caring, wonderful friend. I will become a doctor because of him. What a gift. Shayne and Elaine were adamant I take the money also.

'Grandad wanted you to have it,' Shayne said. 'It was important to him.'

'You gave me my father back,' Elaine said. 'Nothing can ever repay that.'

'And this is the kitchen,' I hear the estate agent say, bringing me back to the here and now as he guides us around a large open-plan kitchen, with a floor-to-ceiling retractable window that leads into a small but green garden.

'Ellie would love it out there,' Cora says. 'I've never met anyone who loves the outdoors quite as much as she does.'

'I have,' I whisper, conquering an image of sitting on the bench that warms my heart.

'You need to get that kid to wear a hat, Bea,' she says.

'Oh, I think she'll be just fine without one.'

Cora shrugs. Then we look at each other and nod. I shake the estate agent's hand and say, 'We'll take it.'

Cora throws her arms round me so tight she's almost crushing my windpipe. 'Welcome home, Bea Alright!'

A LETTER FROM THE AUTHOR

Huge thanks for reading *The Secret Life of Beatrice Alright*, and I hope you loved Bea's journey. If you want to join other readers in hearing all about my new releases and bonus content, you can sign up for my newsletter.

www.stormpublishing.co/brooke-harris

If you enjoyed this book and could spare a few moments to leave a review, that would be hugely appreciated. Even a short review can make all the difference in encouraging a reader to discover my books for the first time. Thank you so much.

When I was a little girl, my parents took me on a road trip around the west of Ireland – think winding roads and lush greenery that stretched on for miles. So, when we hit a large town or village, we often stopped for a bite to eat and a wee (my seven-year-old bladder insisted). At one particular pitstop, in Galway, we had just finished eating when a frazzled, elderly man arrived in the near empty pub. He was looking for his tour group. A bus was supposed to be taking him and his friends to kiss the Blarney Stone. But he'd muddled the time and missed the bus by over an hour. Everyone had left without him. I distinctly remember him telling the barman that he wouldn't have anyone to talk to for a whole month now, until the next trip. My small heart broke for him.

The barman was kind and generous; he gave the man a

shepherd's pie and 7UP on the house, and said if he was ever needing anyone to talk to, the door of the pub was open.

Thirty years have passed, and recently I was back in the same pub with some friends. I sat in a redecorated lounge, heaving with people enjoying live music and good food, but all I could think about was a lonely old man who I truly hope had many days filled with bus trips and friends.

Thanks again for being part of this amazing journey with me and I hope you'll stay in touch – I have so many more stories and ideas to entertain you with!

Brooke

𝕏 x.com/Janelle_Brooke

ACKNOWLEDGEMENTS

As ever, getting a book into readers' hands is a team effort. I am so thankful for the team around me.

My lovely agent, Hannah, for always encouraging me to make people cry with heartbreaking stories.

My fantastic editor, Emily, who makes everything I write better. And the wider team at Storm, thank you for your Trojan work behind the scenes – ever appreciated.

To my friends and family, who continue to listen when I go on and on and on about books. Writing this story has made me more grateful than ever for the special people in my life.

Homelessness and loneliness so often go hand in hand. If you walk the streets of most cites, you will see someone sleeping in a doorway, or begging with a paper cup on a street corner. Thankfully, there are some amazing groups and charities trying their best to help. A Lending Hand are a group I particularly admire. A small organisation of volunteers sharing community donations of food, tents, haircuts, blankets, medicines, etc. to those most in need. The need is great, and their resources are limited, but yet they never give up. https://www.facebook.com/profile.php?id=100064860007943

Finally, thank you, dear reader. I remain ever blown away that people spend their precious time reading my stories. I am so grateful. I truly enjoyed writing Bea and Malcolm's story, even if it broke my heart at times. I hope you enjoyed their journey just as much.

Printed in Great Britain
by Amazon